MEOW-ZA!

HERE'S WHAT PEOPLE ARE SAYING ABOUT MAX MEOW!

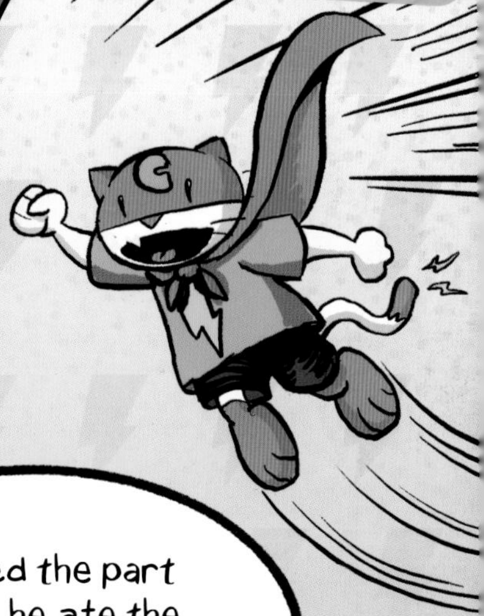

"Max Meow is a riot!"
—Jimmy Gownley, creator of the Amelia Rules! series

"I liked the part where he ate the giant meatball."
—Kevin, 1st grade

"Celebrates friendship, fun, and the fantastic, wrapped up in a ball of adventure readers of any age will pounce on!"
—Jamar Nicholas, creator of the Leon series

"My favorite character was Mindy because she kind of guides Max Meow."
—Santiago, 6th grade

"I give it 5★."
—Cole, 5th grade

"Super laughs on every page!"
—Norm Feuti, creator of the Hello, Hedgehog! series

"A super-fun romp for kids of all ages."
—Meryl Jaffe, PhD, author of *Raising a Reade* *Comics & Graphic No* *Help Your Kids Love*

"It's funny and amazing so ...uld read the book."
...orel, 6th grade

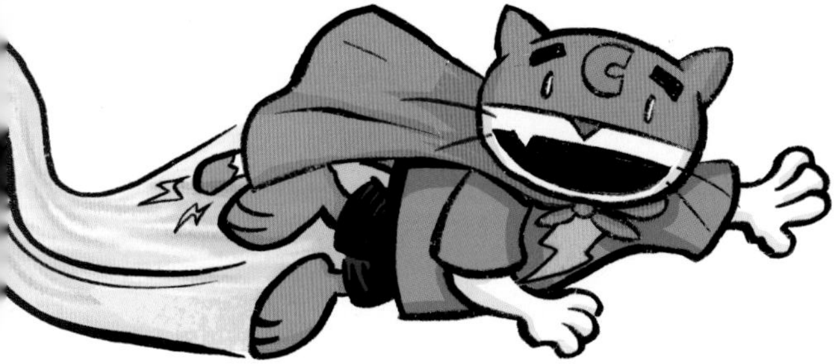

READ ALL OF MAX MEOW'S ADVENTURES!

Max Meow: Cat Crusader

Max Meow: Donuts and Danger

Max Meow: Pugs from Planet X

Max Meow: Taco Time Machine

MAX MEOW!
CAT CRUSADER

JOHN GALLAGHER

RANDOM HOUSE 🏠 NEW YORK

This is a work of fiction. Names, characters, places, and incidents either are the product of the author's imagination or are used fictitiously. Any resemblance to actual persons, living or dead, events, or locales is entirely coincidental.

 Published in the United States by Random House Children's Books, a division of Penguin Random House LLC, New York.

Random House and the colophon are registered trademarks of Penguin Random House LLC.

Visit us on the Web! rhcbooks.com

Educators and librarians, for a variety of teaching tools, visit us at RHTeachersLibrarians.com

Library of Congress Cataloging-in-Publication Data is available upon request.
ISBN 978-0-593-12105-4 (hardcover) — ISBN 978-0-593-12106-1 (lib. bdg.)
ISBN 978-0-593-12107-8 (ebook)

Book design by John Gallagher and April Ward

MANUFACTURED IN CHINA

10 9 8

First Edition

Random House Children's Books supports the First Amendment and celebrates the right to read.

To my family,
Beth, Katie, Jack, and Will—
you're all the coolest cats I know.

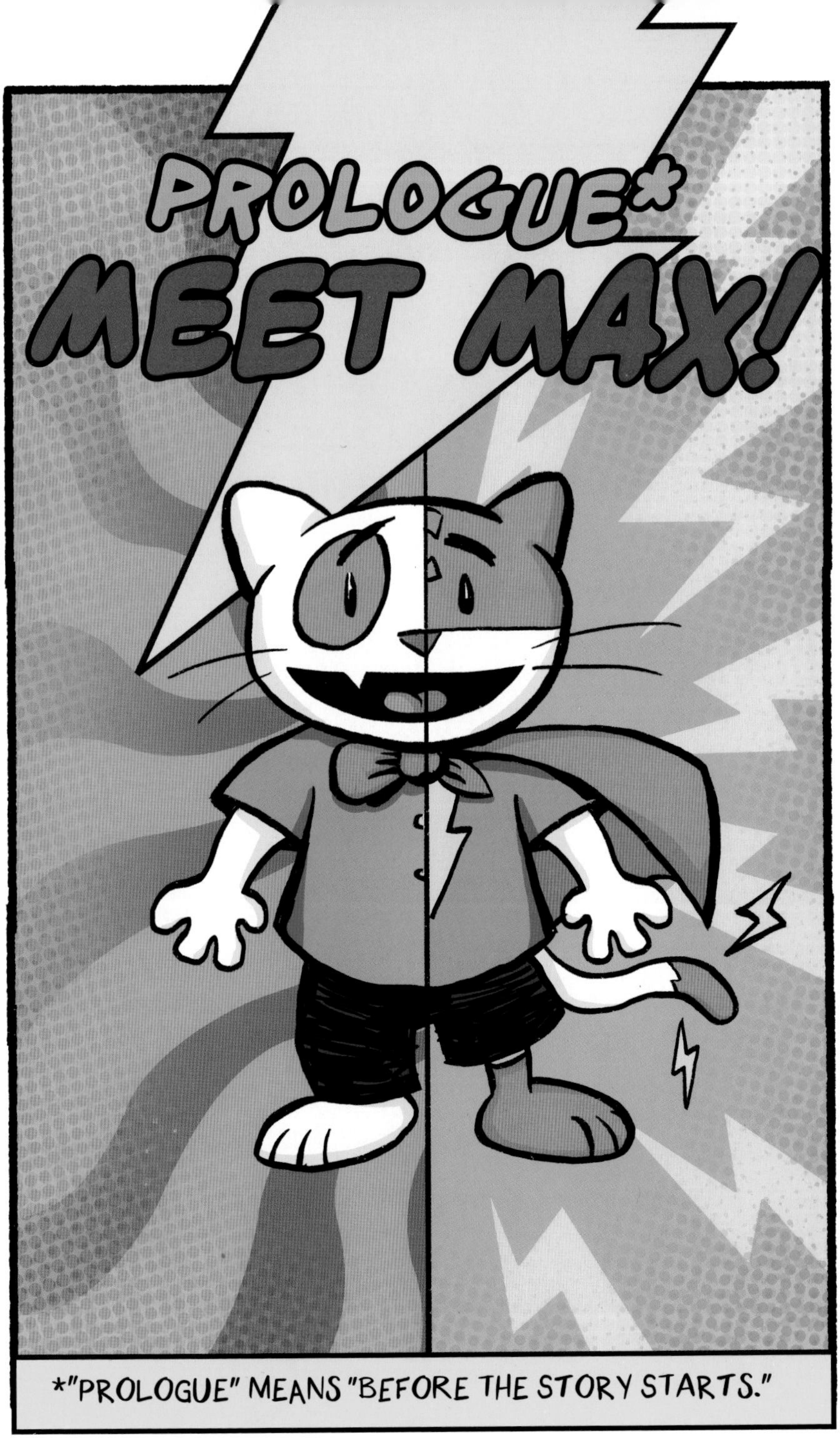
PROLOGUE*
MEET MAX!

*"PROLOGUE" MEANS "BEFORE THE STORY STARTS."

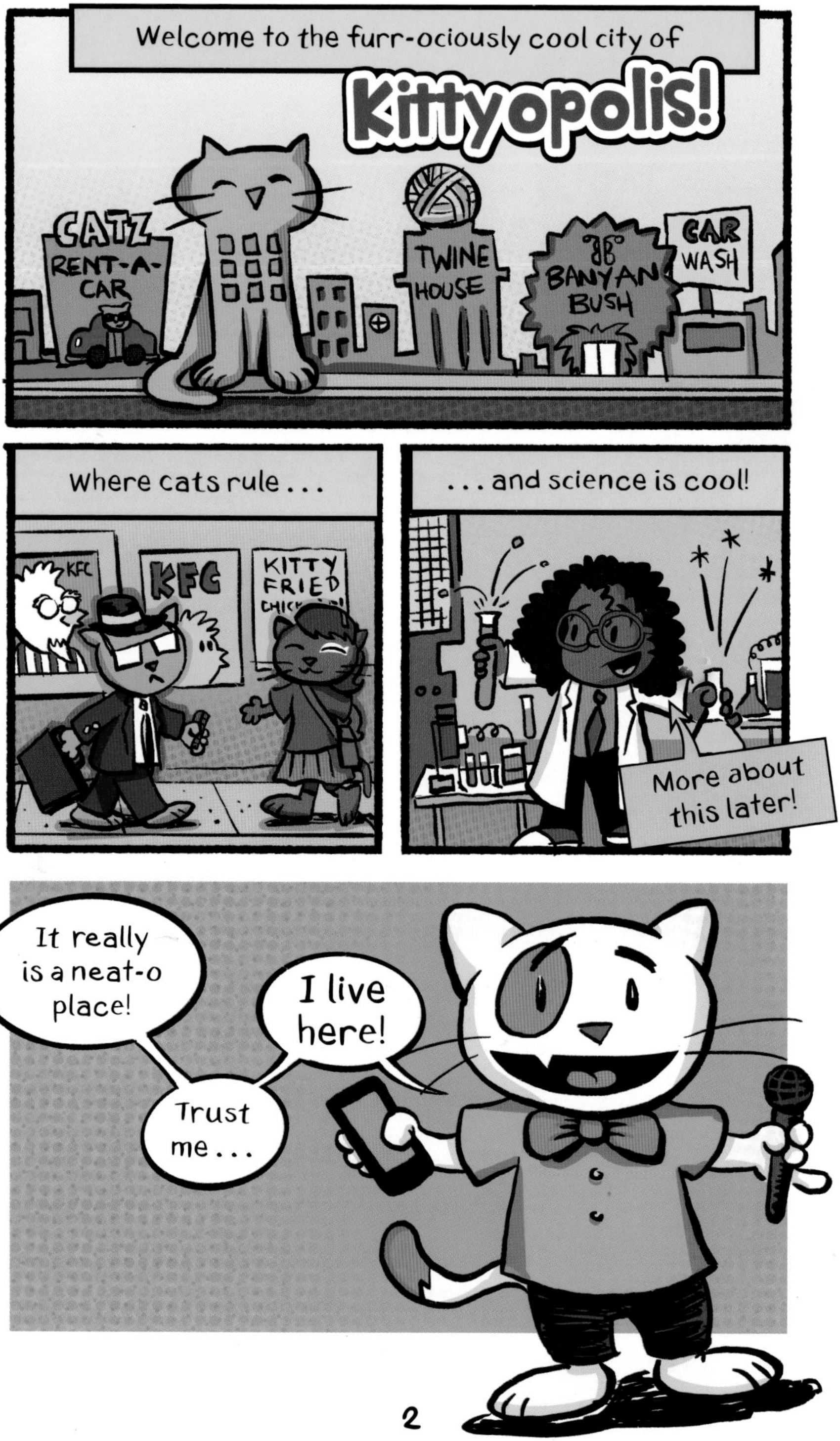
Welcome to the furr-ociously cool city of
Kittyopolis!
CATZ RENT-A-CAR
TWINE HOUSE
BANYAN BUSH
CAR WASH
Where cats rule . . .
KFC
KFC
KITTY FRIED
. . . and science is cool!
More about this later!
It really is a neat-o place!
I live here!
Trust me . . .

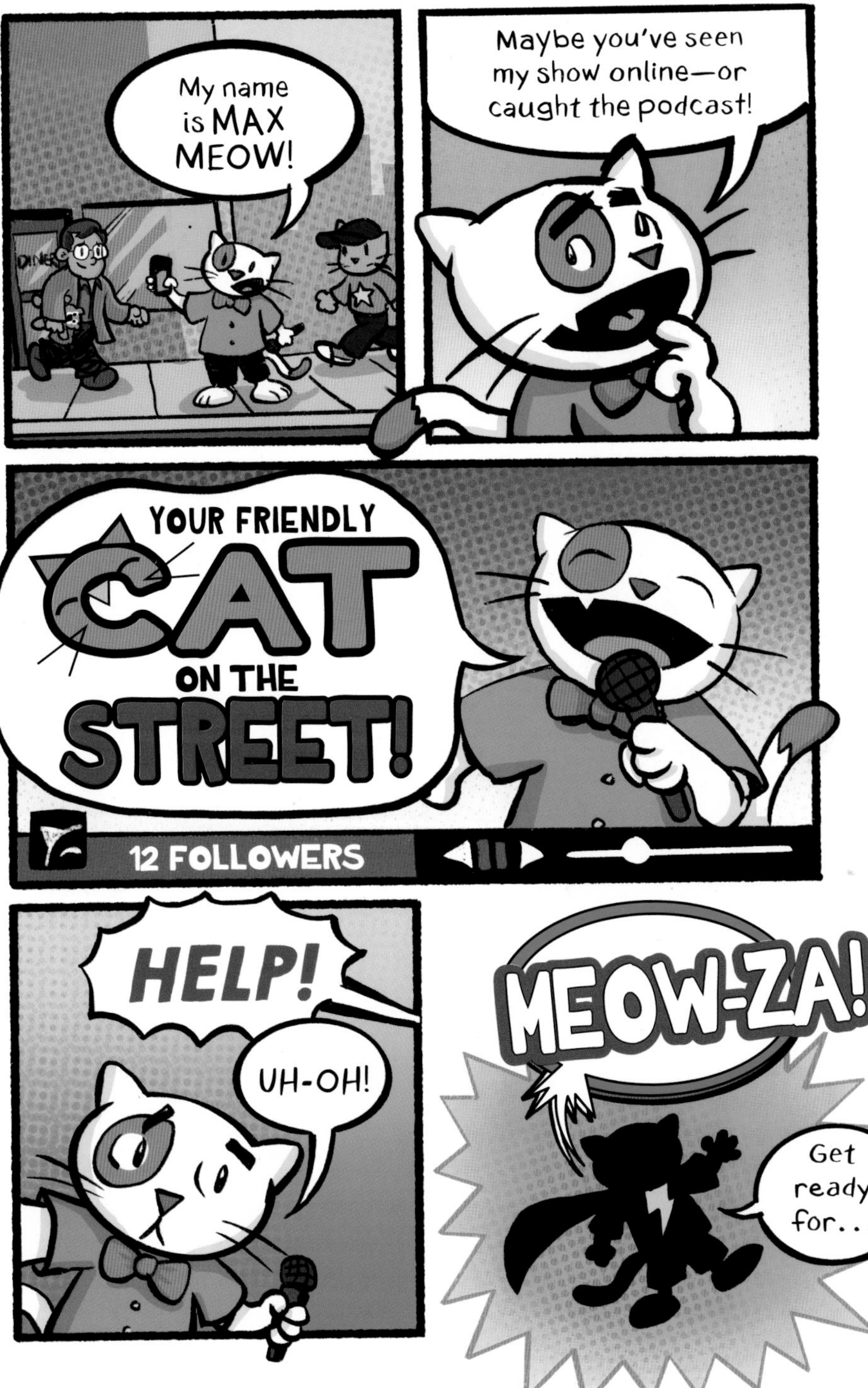
My name is MAX MEOW!
Maybe you've seen my show online—or caught the podcast!
DINER
YOUR FRIENDLY CAT ON THE STREET!
12 FOLLOWERS
HELP!
UH-OH!
MEOW-ZA!
Get ready for...

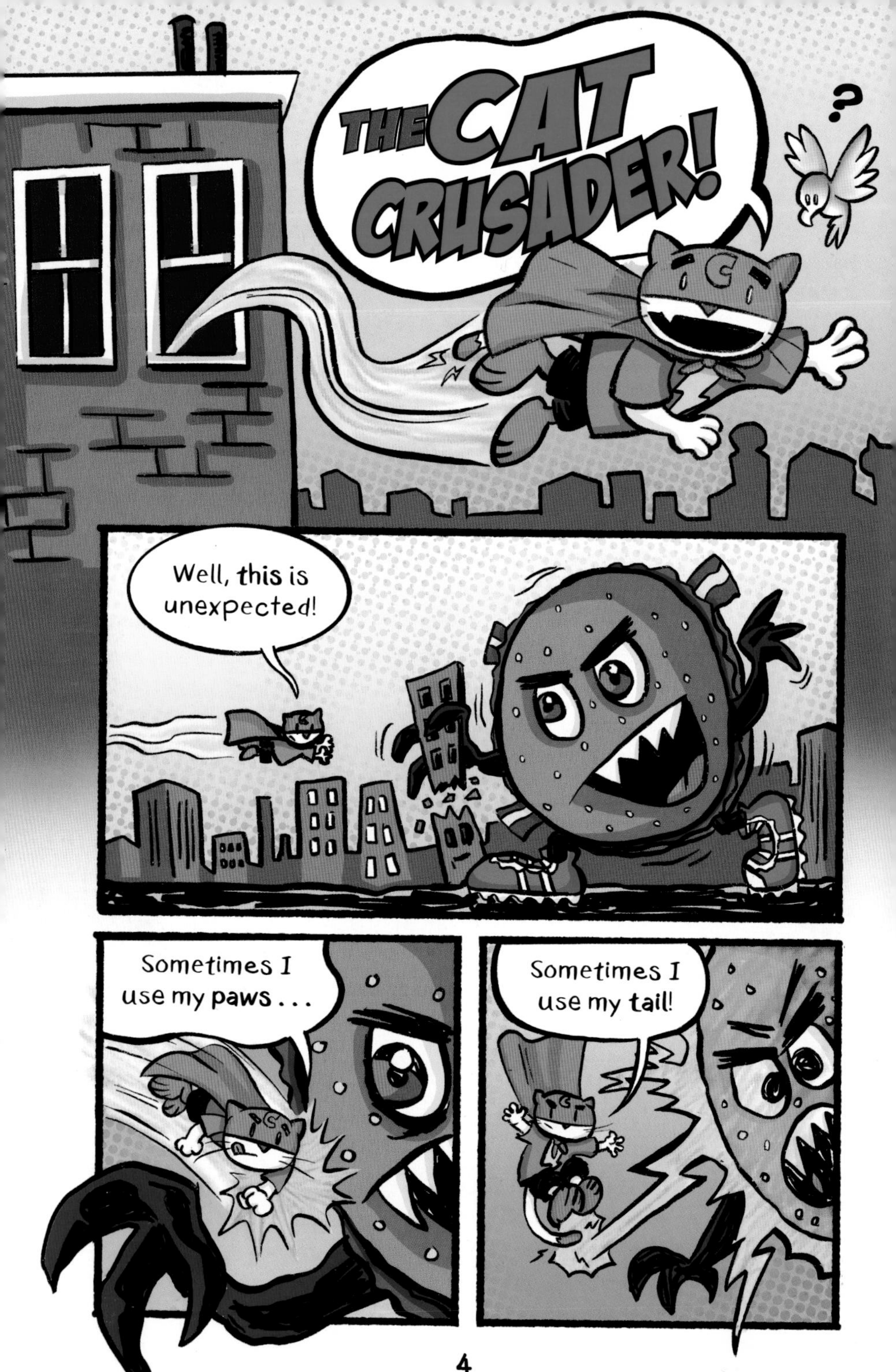
THE CAT CRUSADER!
?
Well, this is unexpected!
Sometimes I use my paws . . .
Sometimes I use my tail!

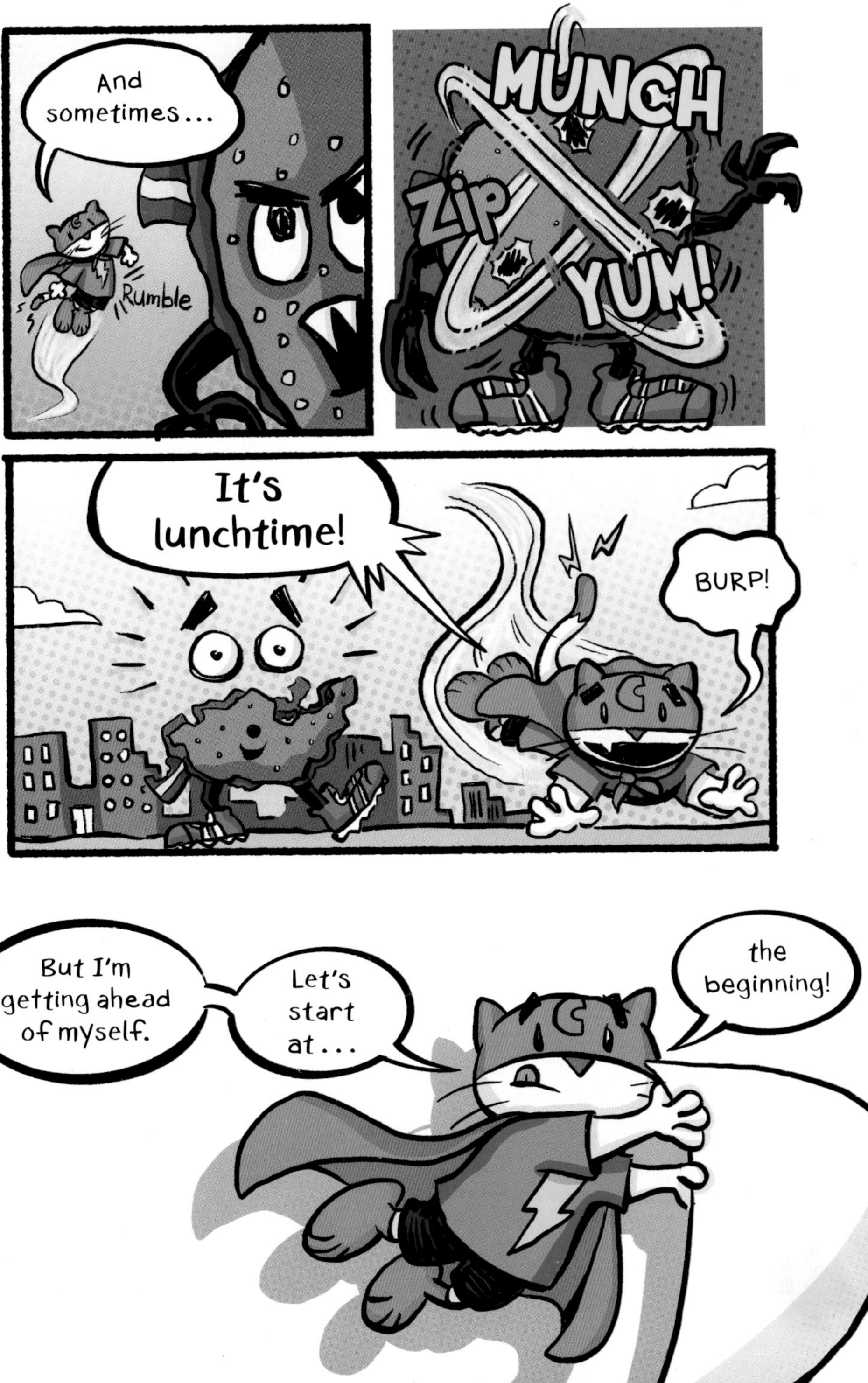
And sometimes...
Rumble
MUNCH
ZIP
YUM!
It's lunchtime!
BURP!
But I'm getting ahead of myself.
Let's start at...
the beginning!

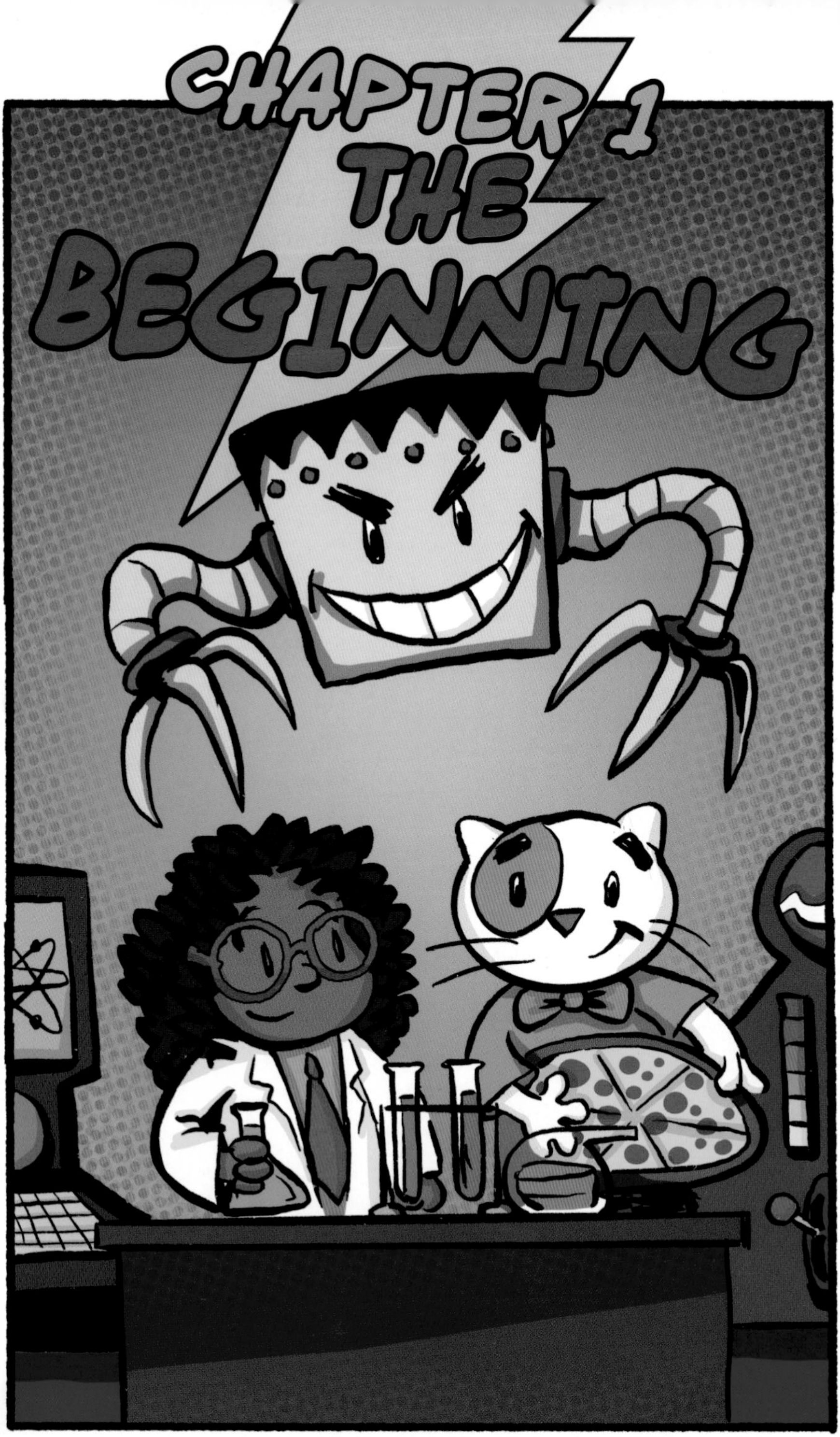
CHAPTER 1
THE
BEGINNING

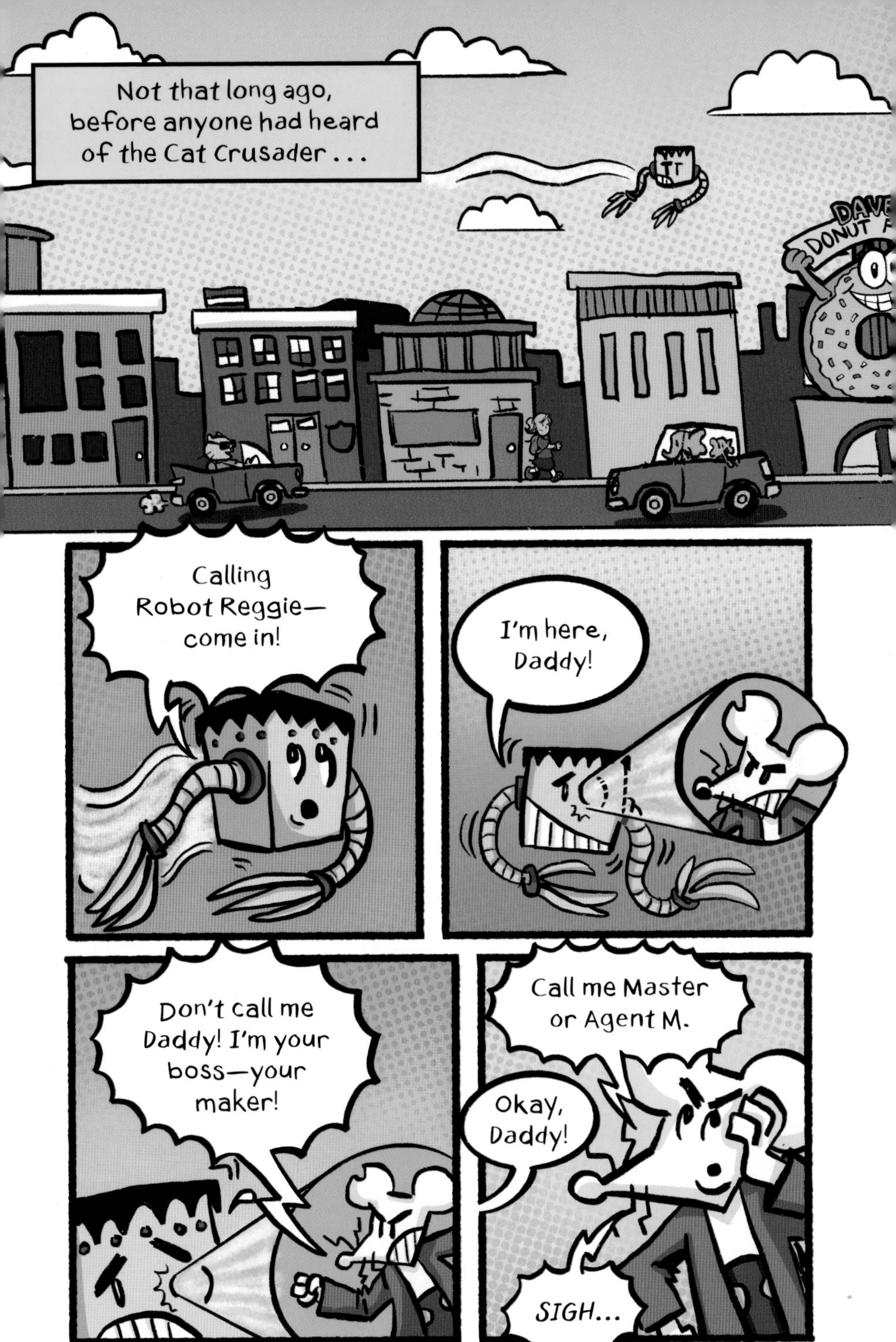
Not that long ago, before anyone had heard of the Cat Crusader . . .
Calling Robot Reggie—come in!
I'm here, Daddy!
Don't call me Daddy! I'm your boss—your maker!
Call me Master or Agent M.
Okay, Daddy!
SIGH...

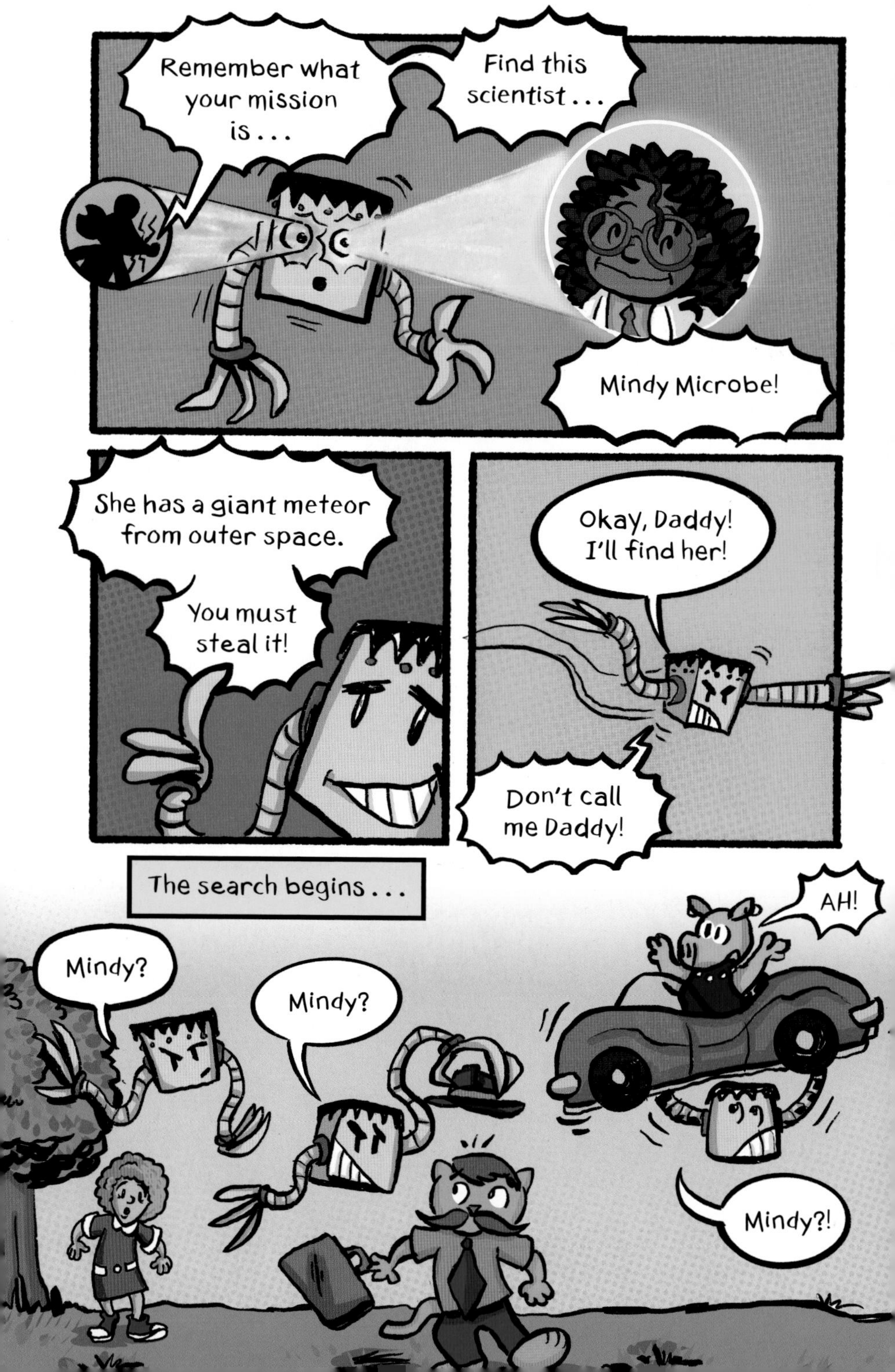

Remember what your mission is . . .
Find this scientist . . .
Mindy Microbe!
She has a giant meteor from outer space.
You must steal it!
Okay, Daddy! I'll find her!
Don't call me Daddy!
The search begins . . .
Mindy?
Mindy?
AH!
Mindy?!

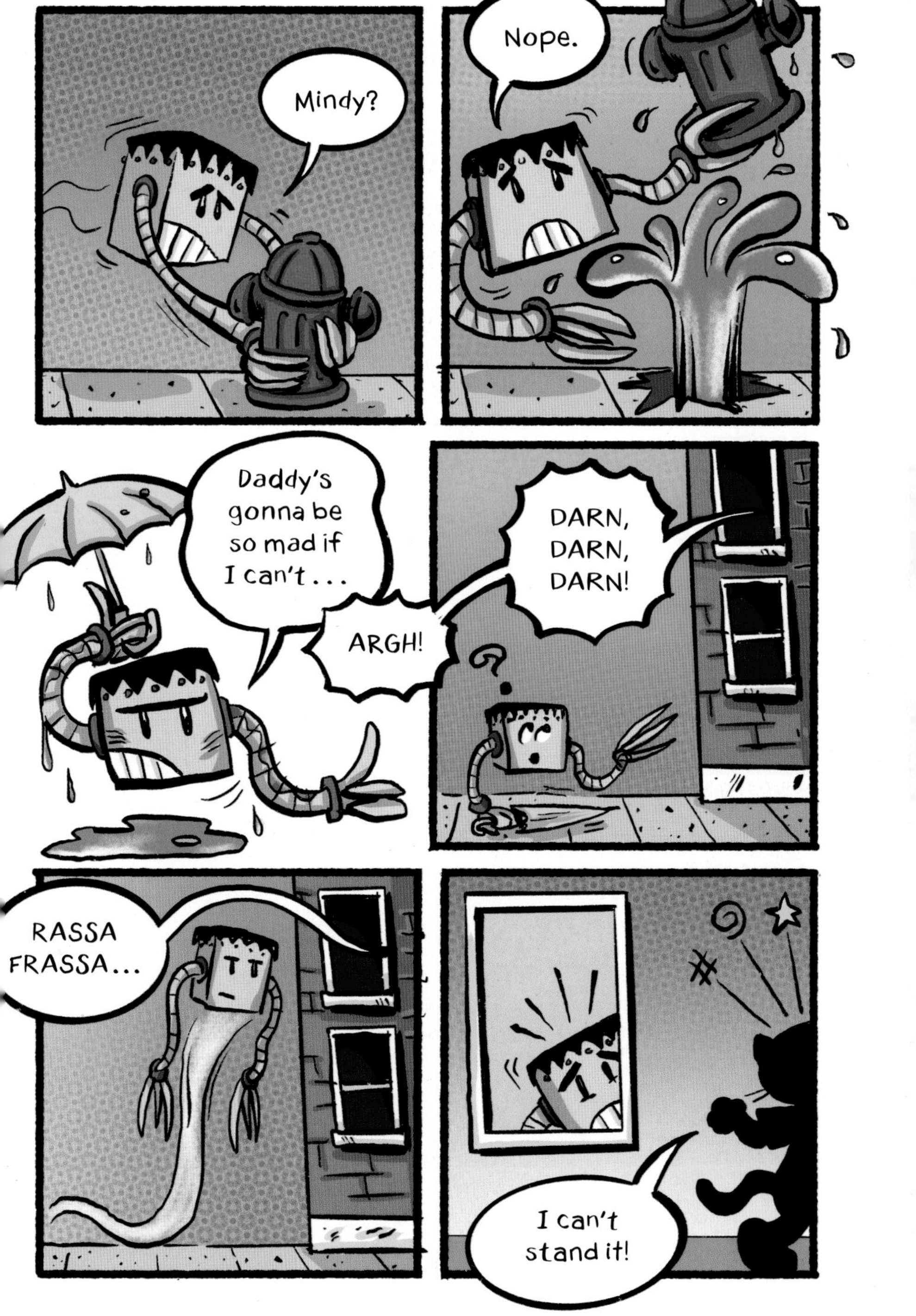
Mindy?
Nope.
Daddy's gonna be so mad if I can't . . .
ARGH!
DARN, DARN, DARN!
RASSA FRASSA...
I can't stand it!

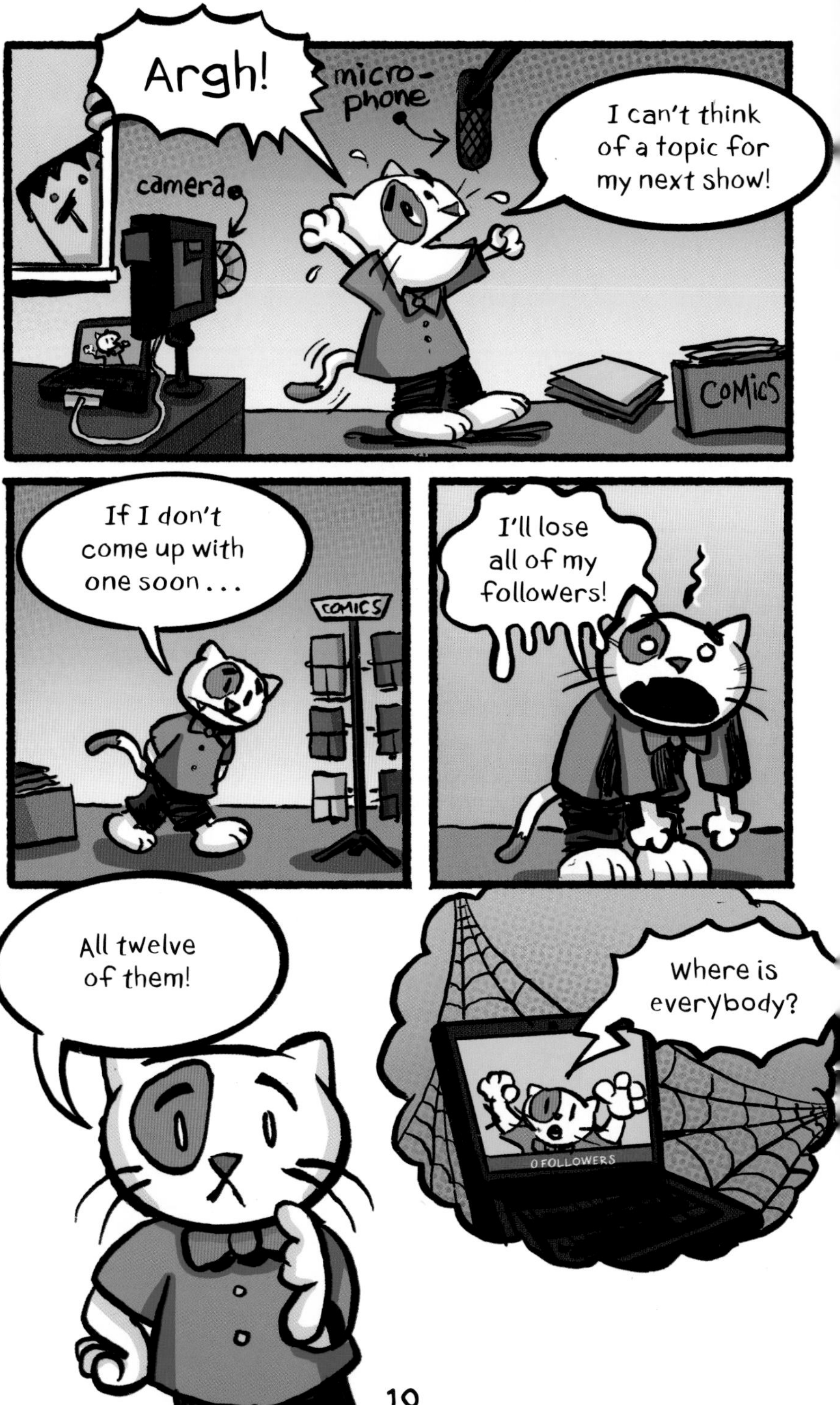
Argh!
micro-phone
camera
I can't think of a topic for my next show!
COMICS
If I don't come up with one soon . . .
COMICS
I'll lose all of my followers!
All twelve of them!
Where is everybody?
0 FOLLOWERS

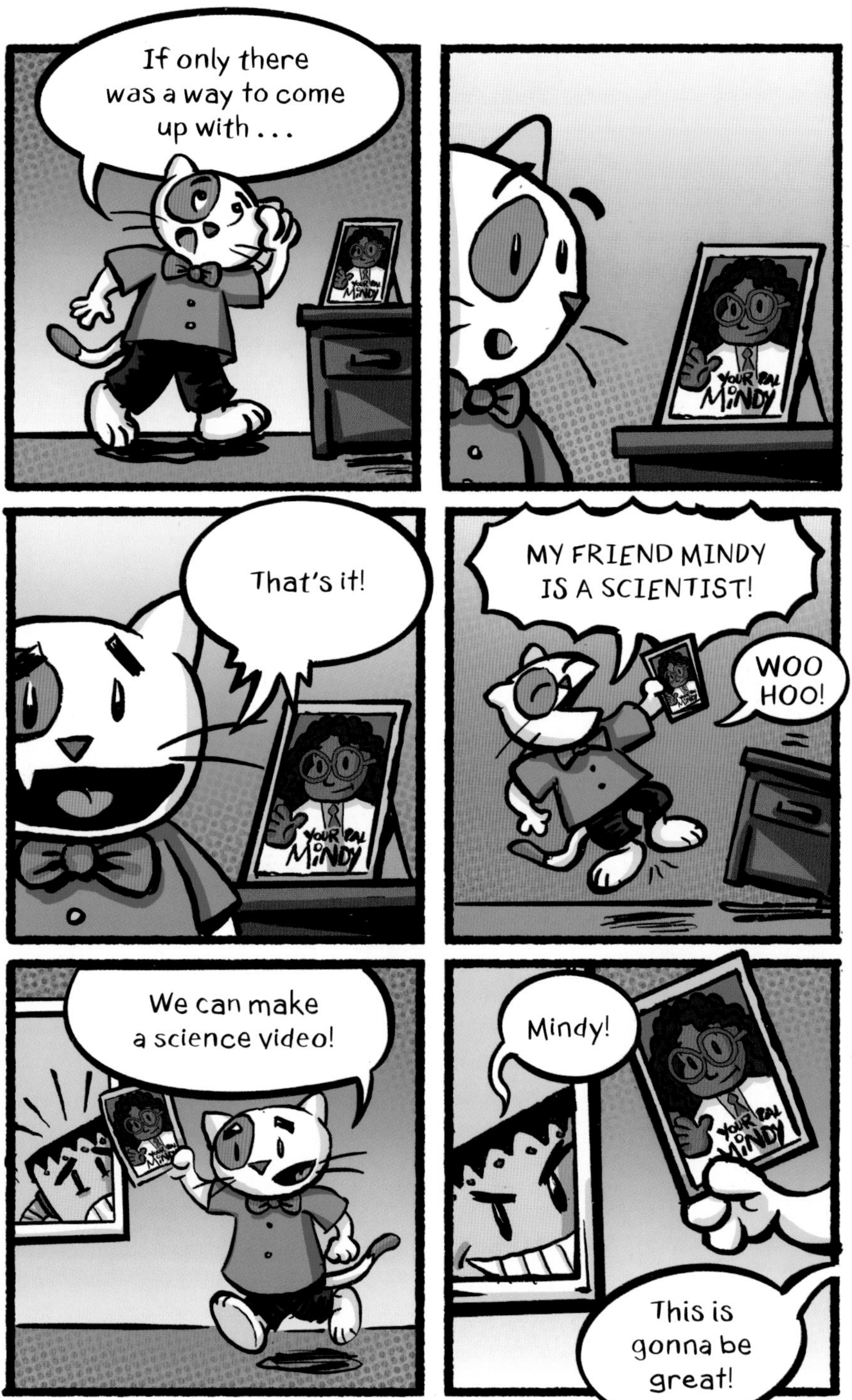
If only there was a way to come up with . . .
YOUR PAL MINDY
That's it!
MY FRIEND MINDY IS A SCIENTIST!
WOO HOO!
We can make a science video!
Mindy!
This is gonna be great!

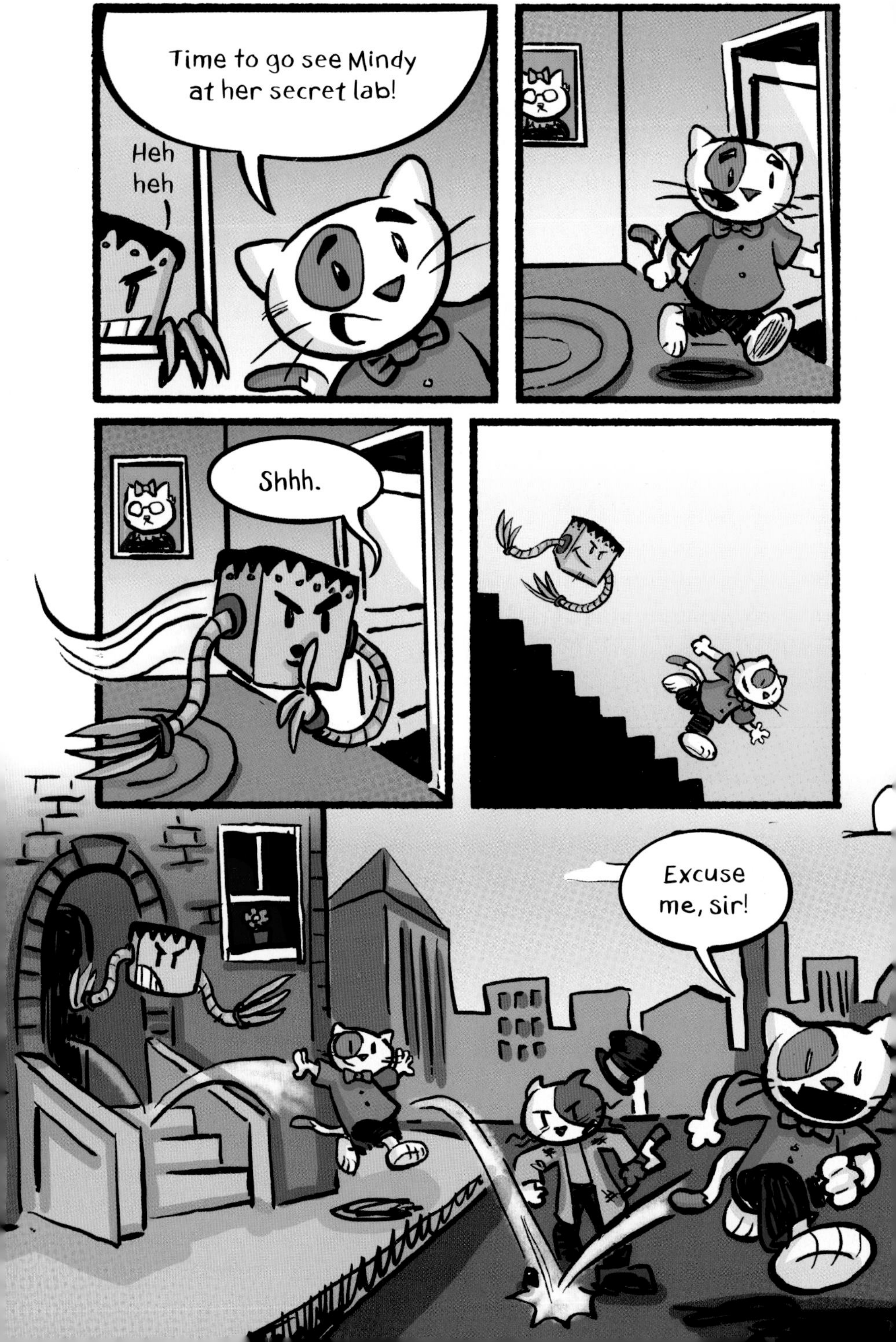
Time to go see Mindy at her secret lab!
Heh heh
Shhh.
Excuse me, sir!

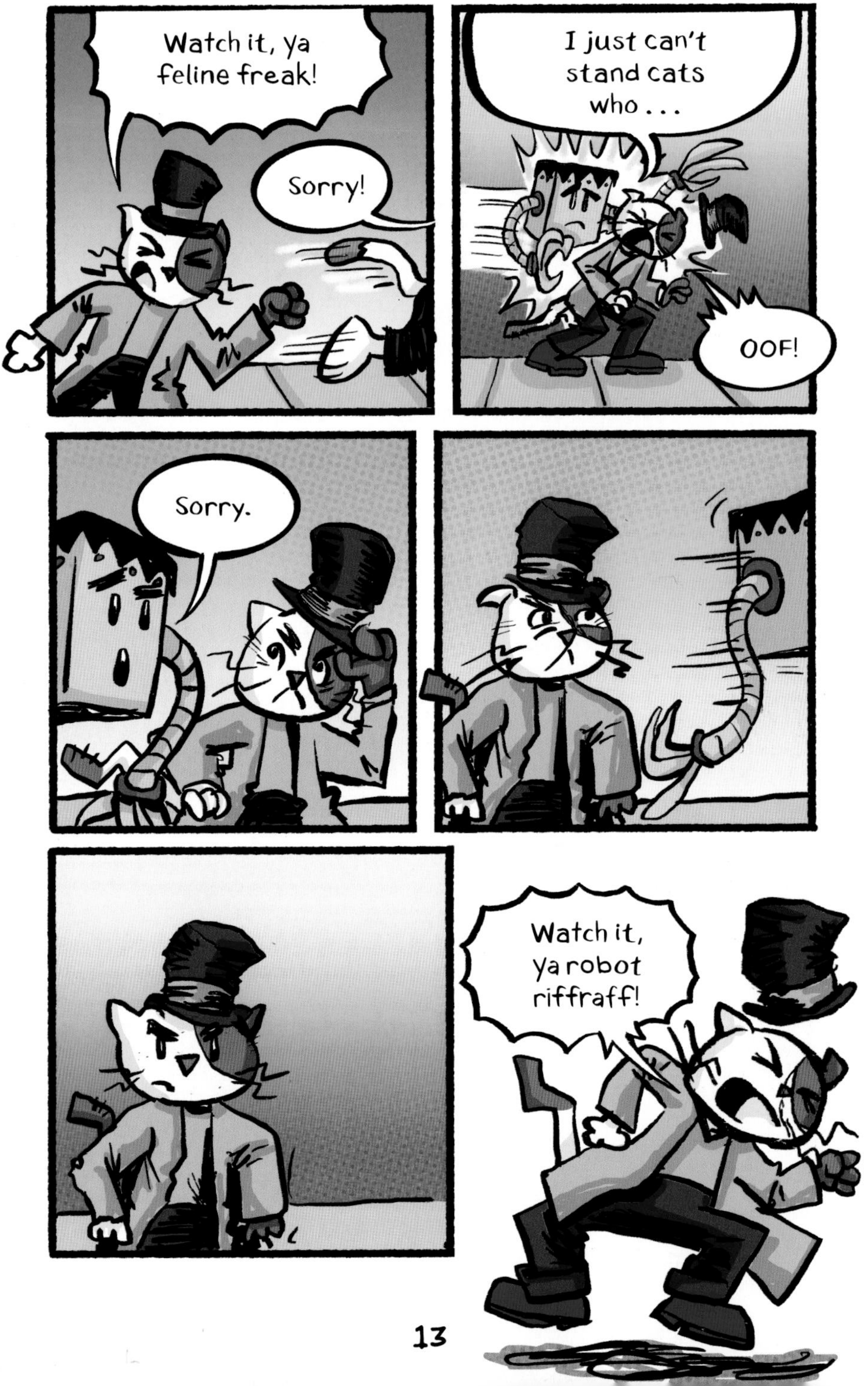

Watch it, ya feline freak!
Sorry!
I just can't stand cats who . . .
OOF!
Sorry.
Watch it, ya robot riffraff!

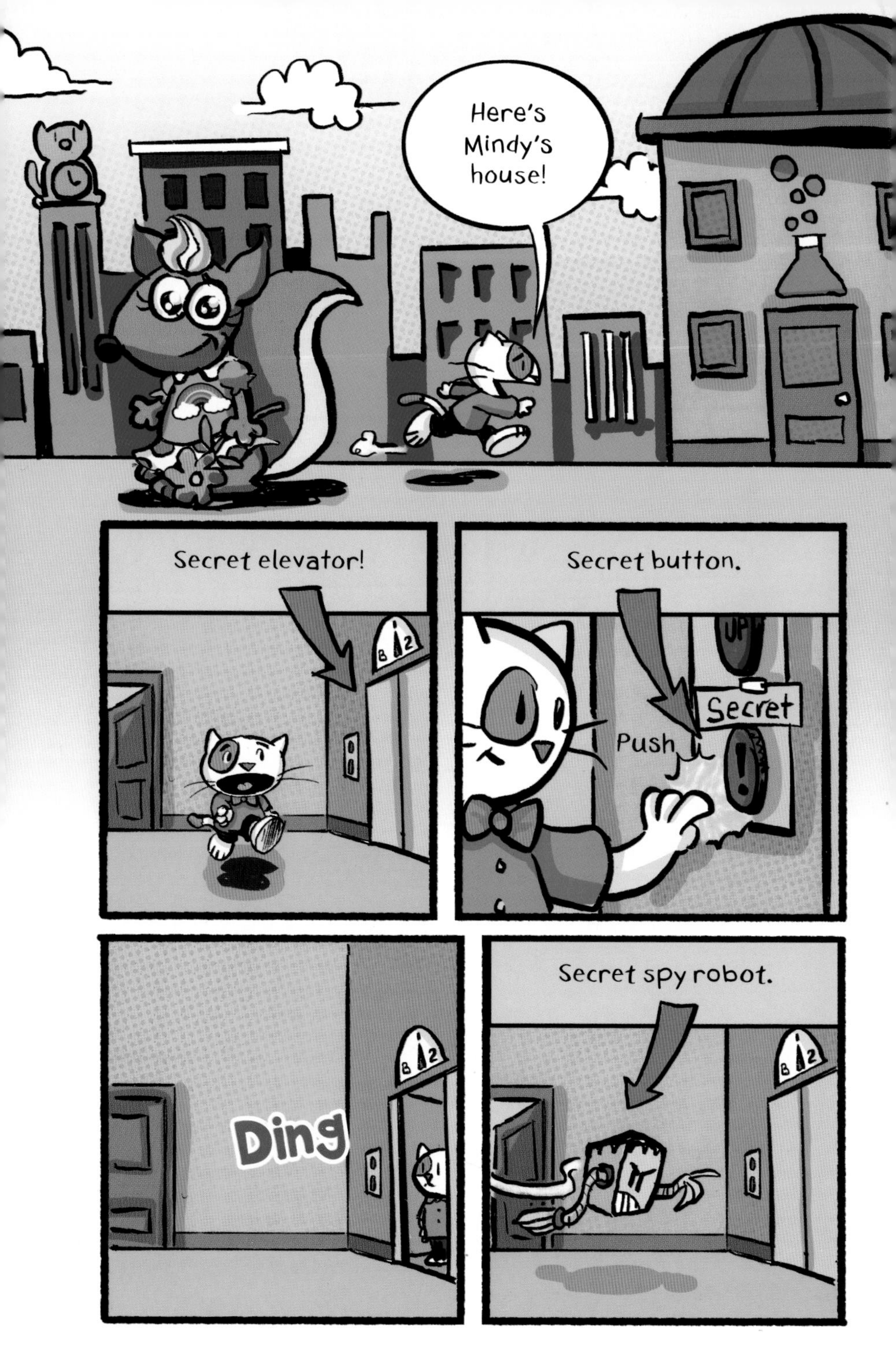
Here's Mindy's house!
Secret elevator!
Secret button.
UP
Secret
Push
Ding
Secret spy robot.

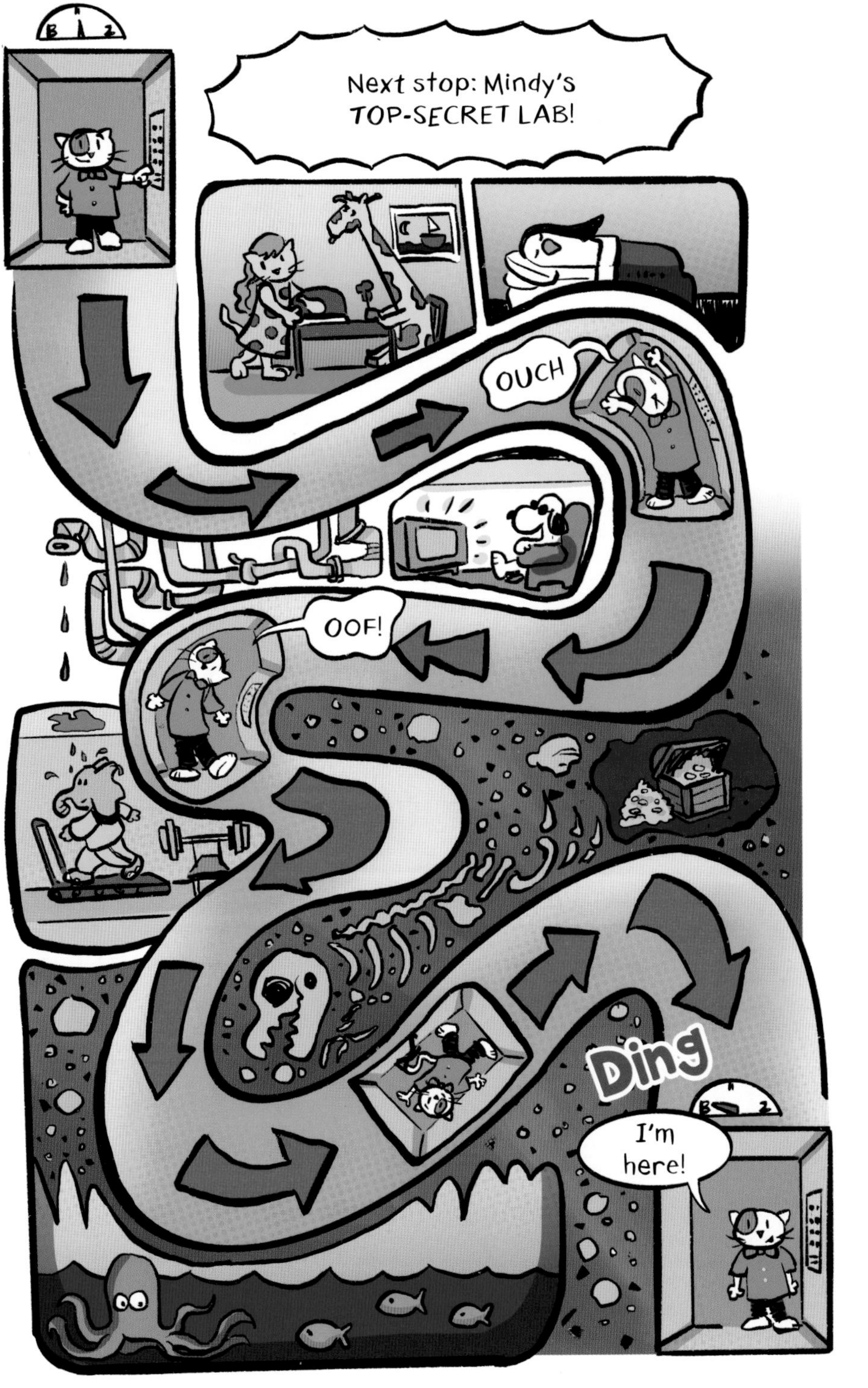
B 1 2
Next stop: Mindy's TOP-SECRET LAB!
OUCH
OOF!
Ding
B 1 2
I'm here!

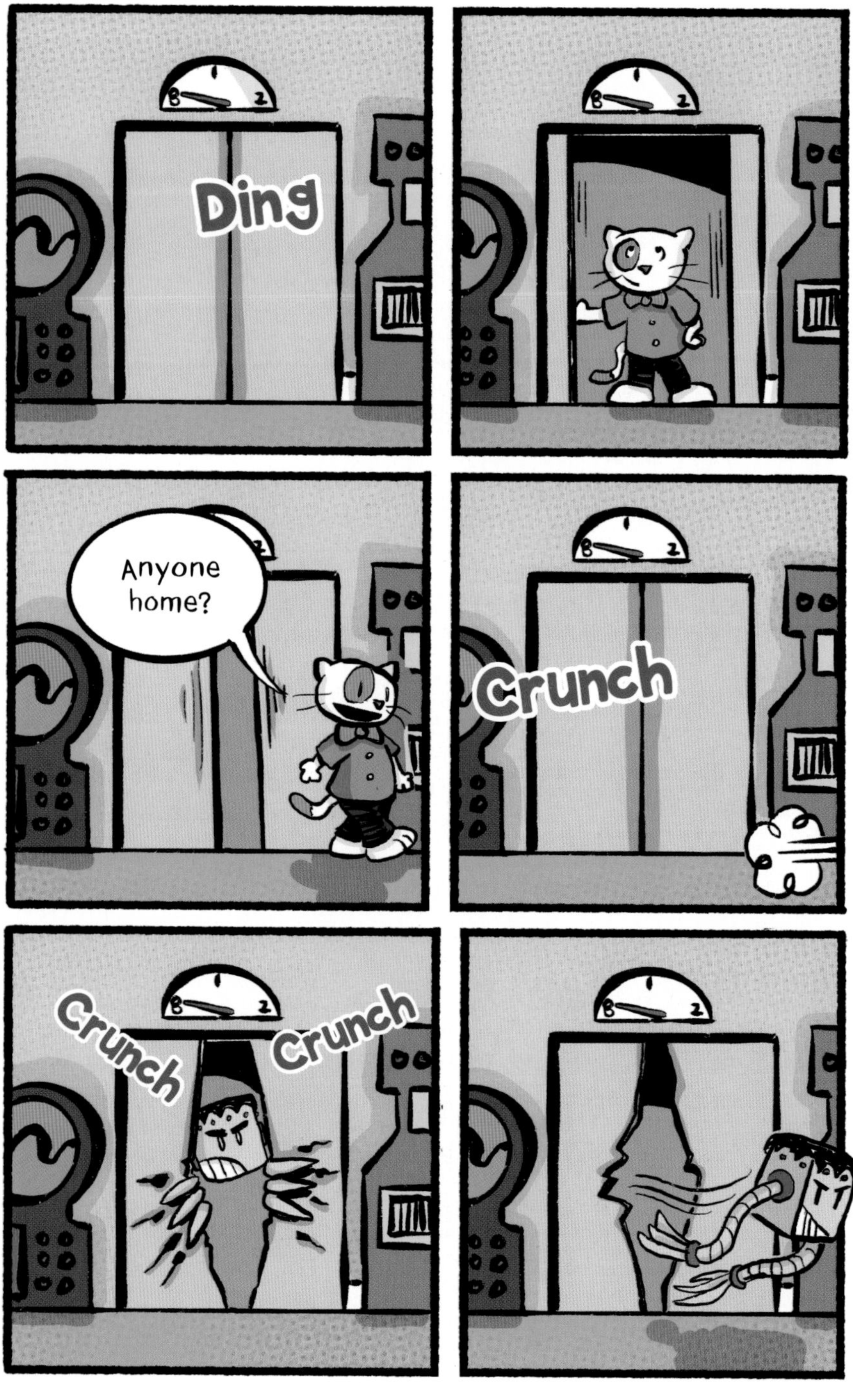
Ding
Anyone home?
Crunch
Crunch
Crunch

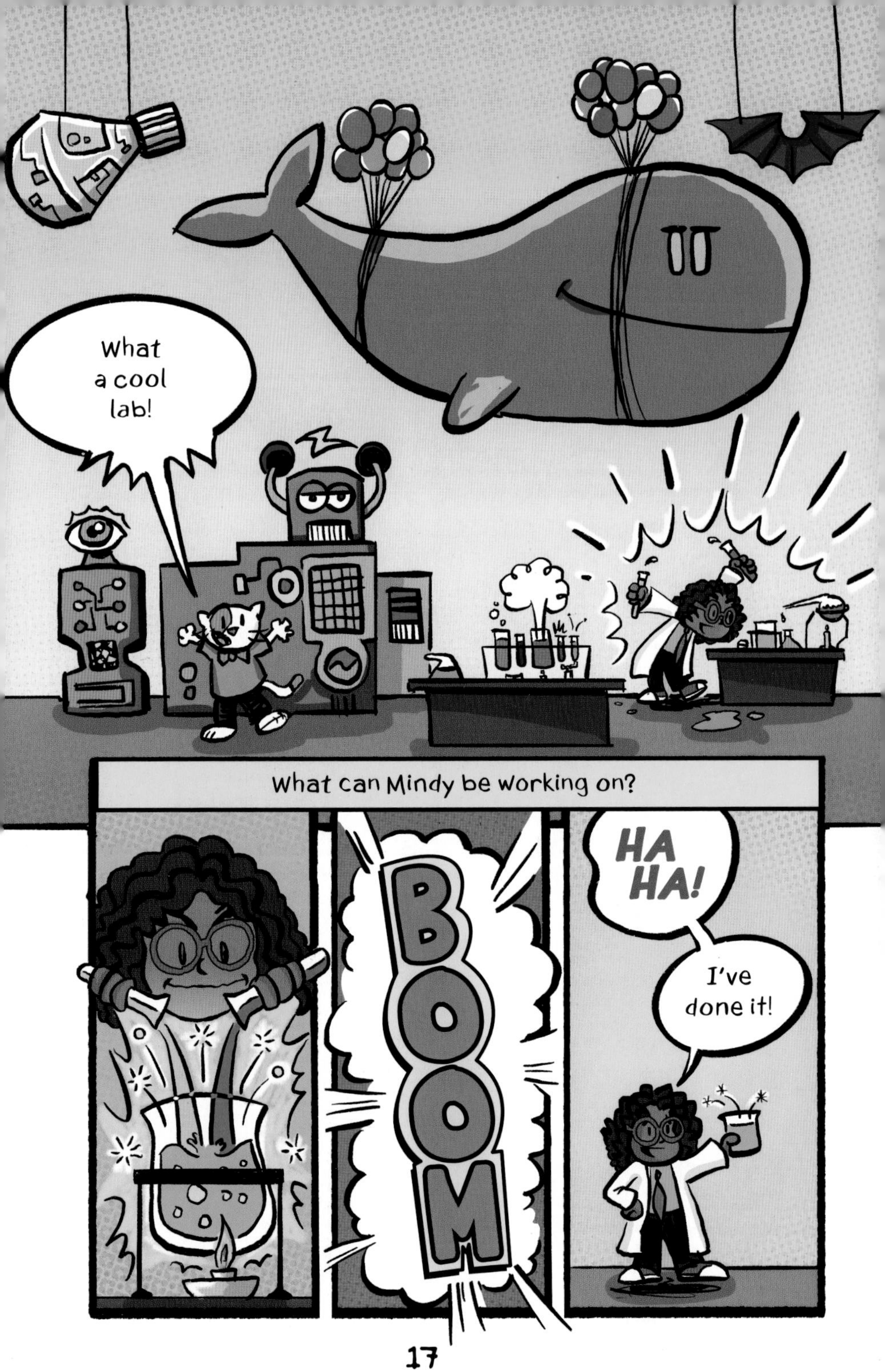
What a cool lab!
What can Mindy be working on?
BOOM
HA HA!
I've done it!

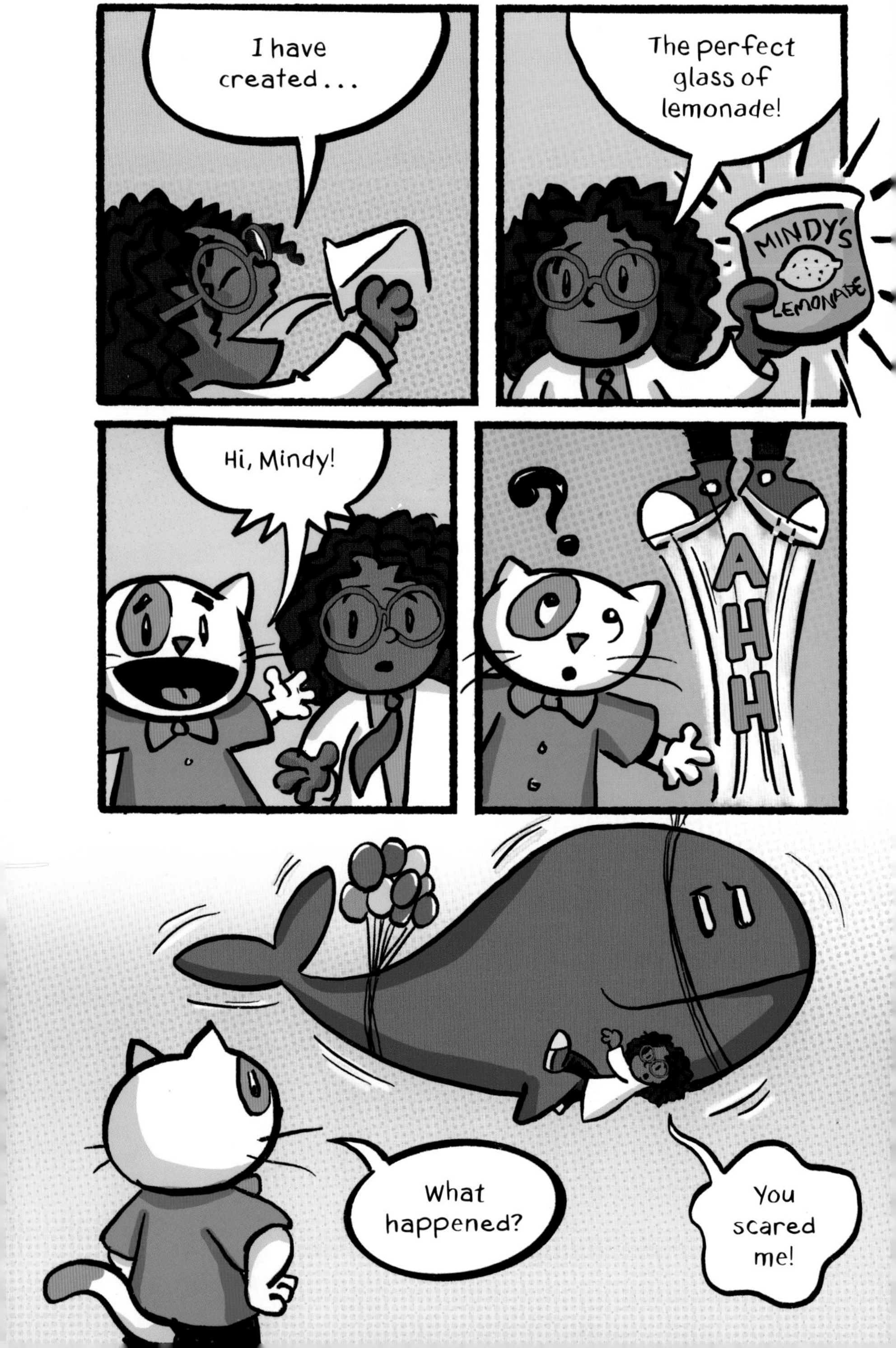
I have created . . .
The perfect glass of lemonade!
MINDY'S LEMONADE
Hi, Mindy!
?
AHHH
What happened?
You scared me!

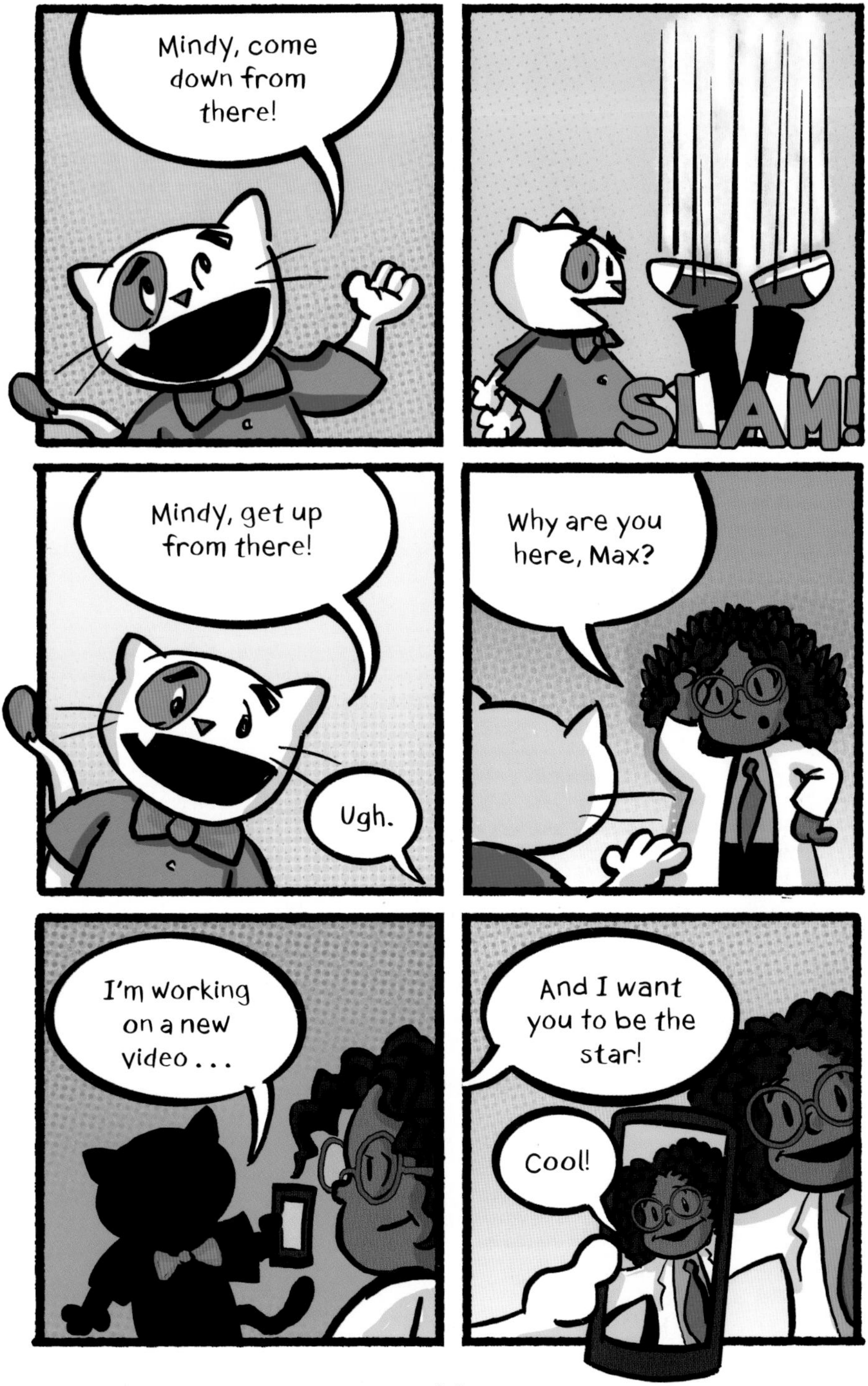
Mindy, come down from there!
SLAM!
Mindy, get up from there!
Ugh.
Why are you here, Max?
I'm working on a new video . . .
And I want you to be the star!
Cool!

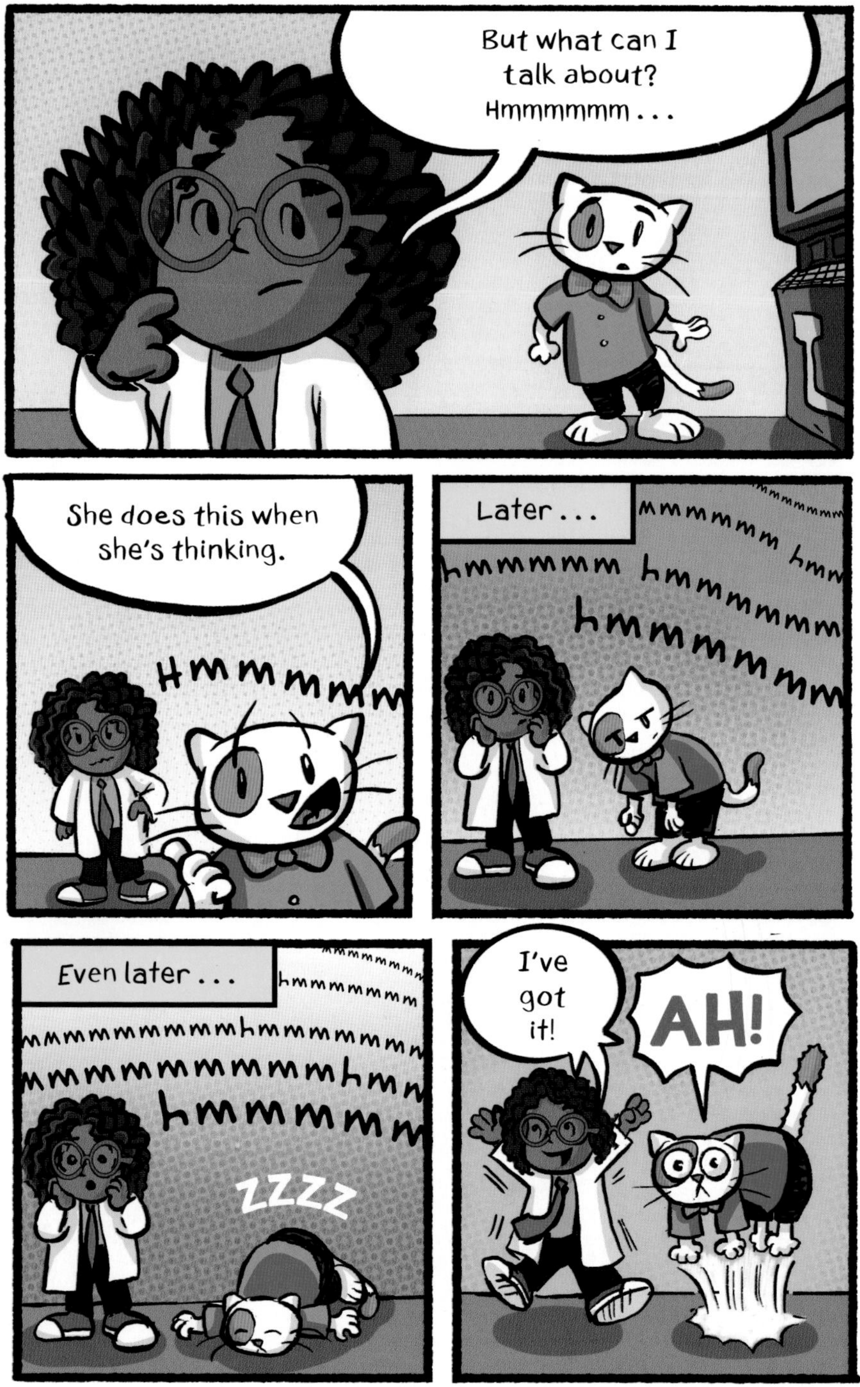
But what can I talk about? Hmmmmmm . . .
She does this when she's thinking.
Hmmmmmm
Later . . .
hmmmmmm
hmmmmmmm
hmmmmmmm
Even later . . .
hmmmmmmm
ZZZZ
I've got it!
AH!

What is it?
A great idea?

YES!

Let's take a tour of my lab!

I'll set up my camera!

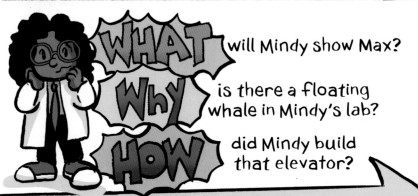

WHAT WHY HOW

will Mindy show Max?

is there a floating whale in Mindy's lab?

did Mindy build that elevator?

Almost NONE of these questions are answered in the next chapter!*

*But PLEASE read it anyway!

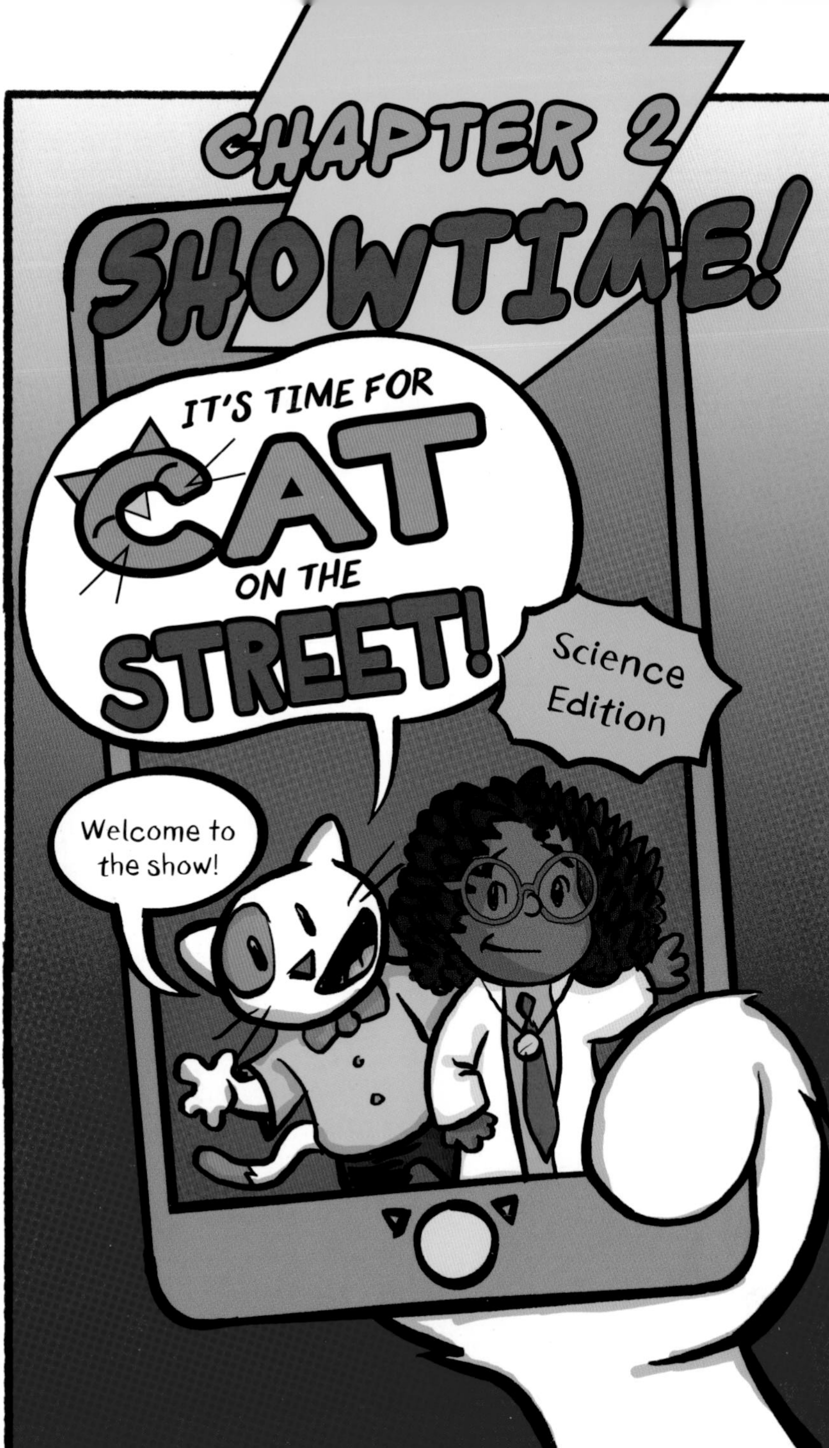
CHAPTER 2
SHOWTIME!
IT'S TIME FOR CAT ON THE STREET!
Science Edition
Welcome to the show!

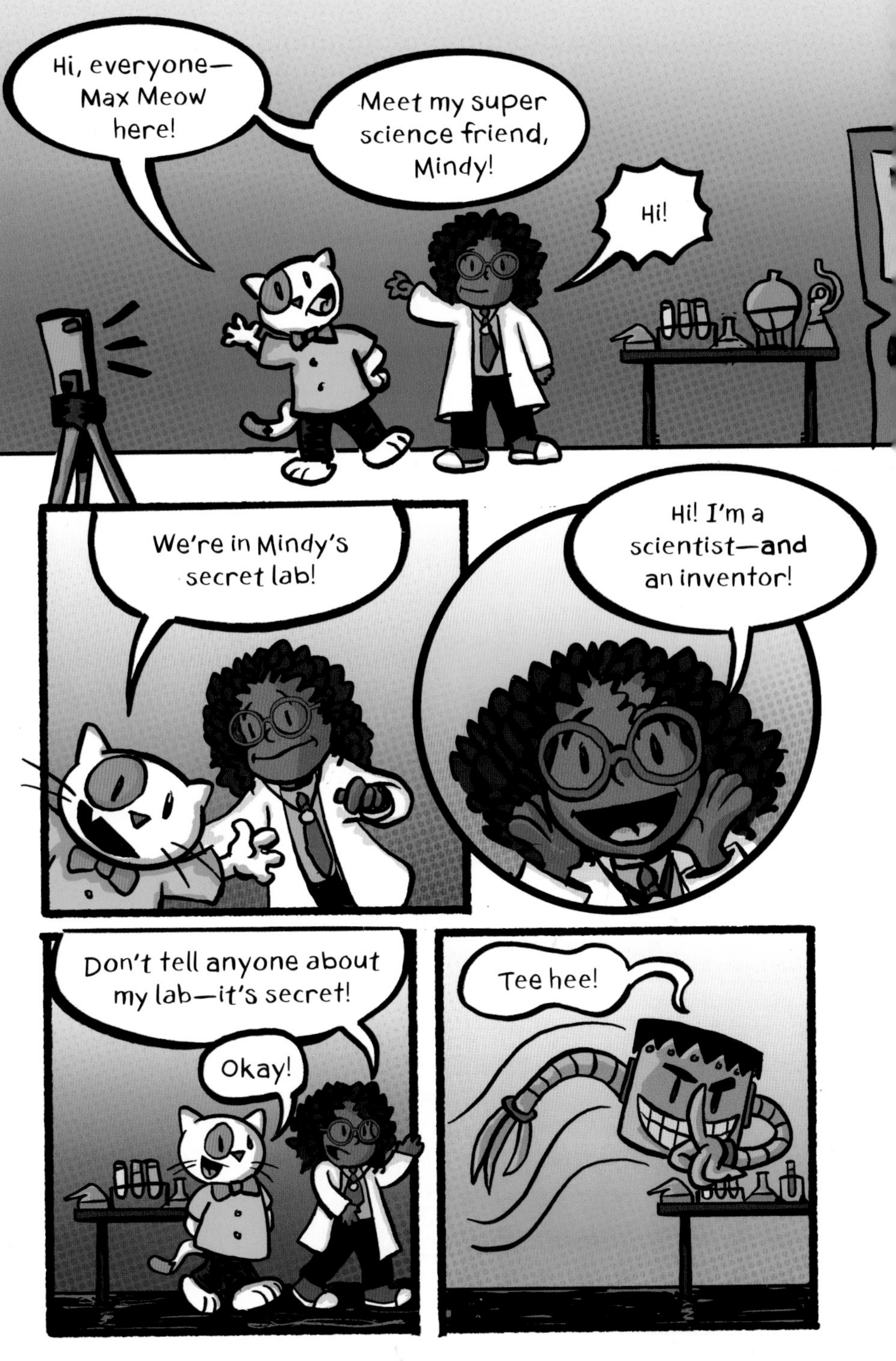
Hi, everyone—Max Meow here!
Meet my super science friend, Mindy!
Hi!
We're in Mindy's secret lab!
Hi! I'm a scientist—**and** an inventor!
Don't tell anyone about my lab—it's secret!
Okay!
Tee hee!

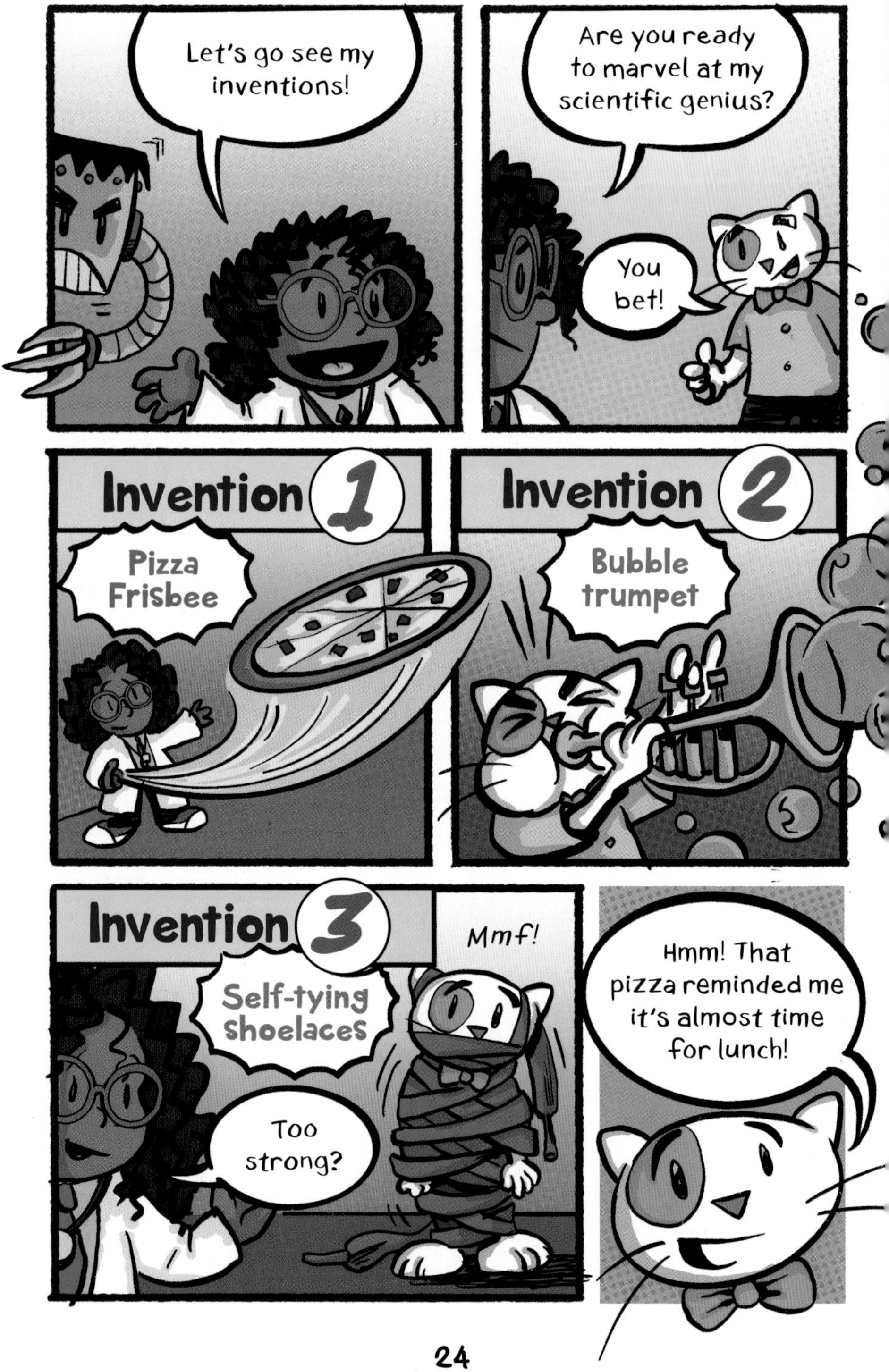
Let's go see my inventions!
Are you ready to marvel at my scientific genius?
You bet!
Invention 1
Pizza Frisbee
Invention 2
Bubble trumpet
Invention 3
Self-tying shoelaces
Mmf!
Too strong?
Hmm! That pizza reminded me it's almost time for lunch!

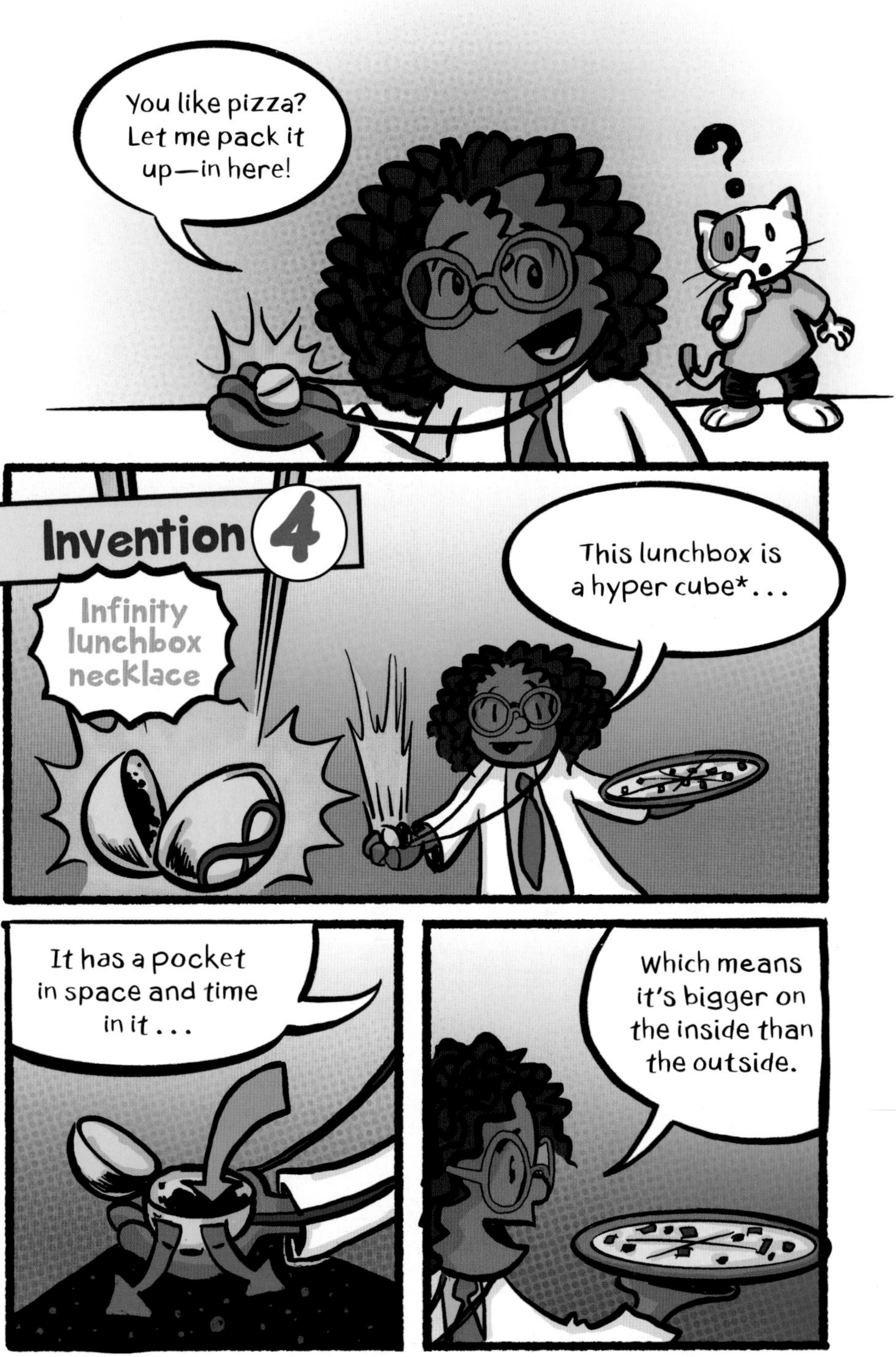
You like pizza? Let me pack it up—in here!
?
Invention 4
Infinity lunchbox necklace
This lunchbox is a hyper cube*...
It has a pocket in space and time in it...
Which means it's bigger on the inside than the outside.

*Also called a tesseract.

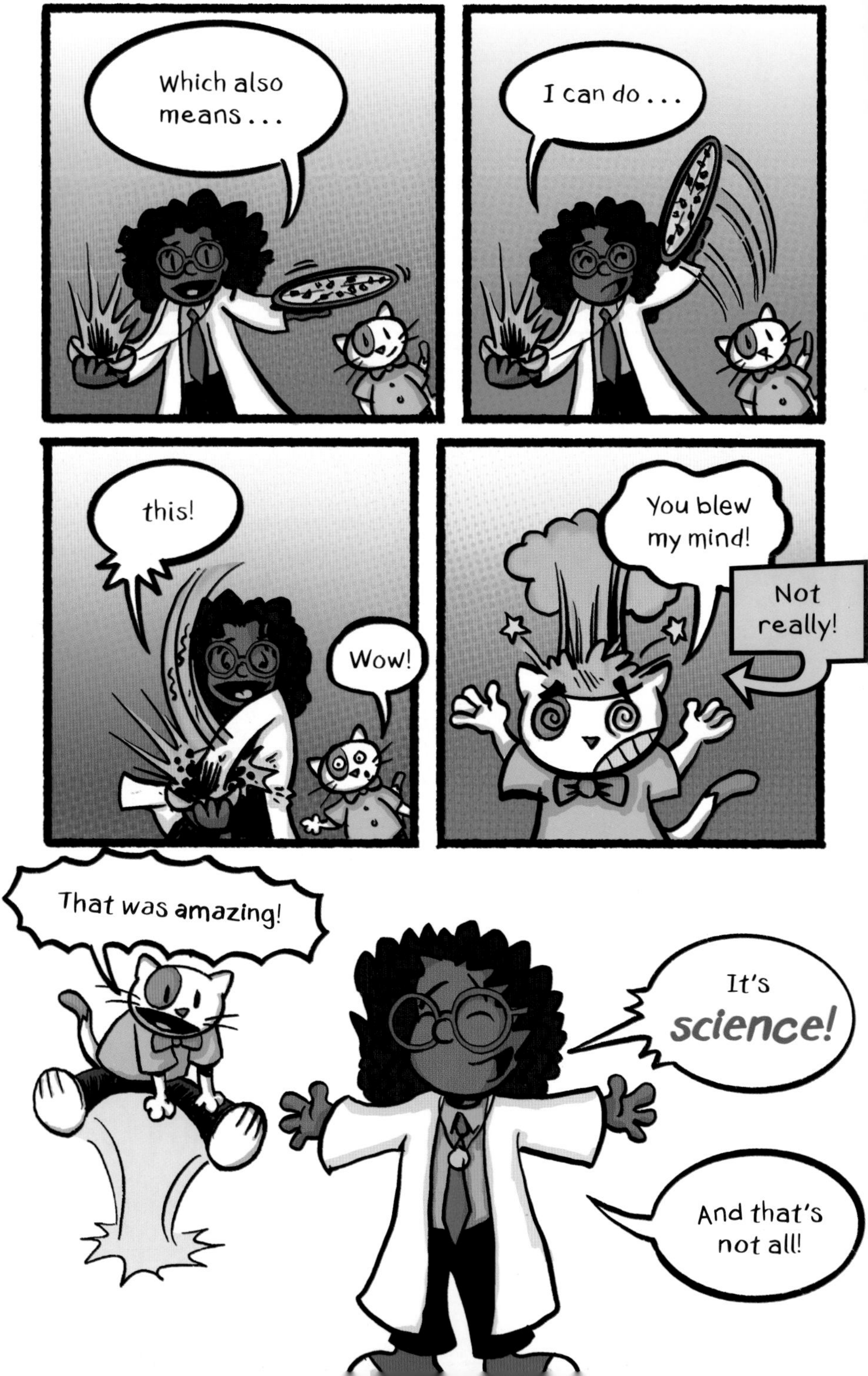

Which also means . . .
I can do . . .
this!
Wow!
You blew my mind!
Not really!
That was amazing!
It's
science!
And that's not all!

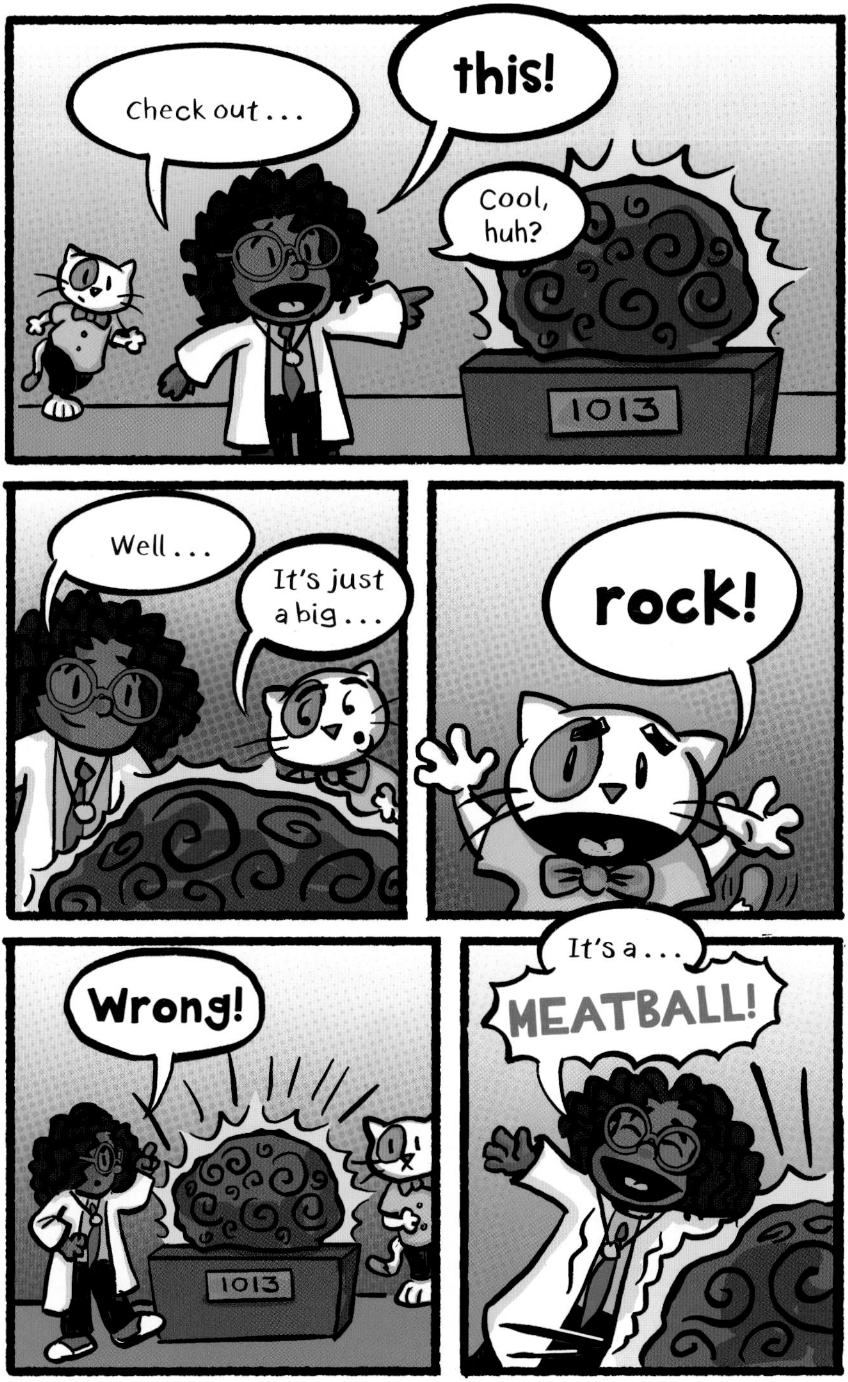
Check out . . .
this!
Cool, huh?
1013
Well . . .
It's just a big . . .
rock!
Wrong!
1013
It's a . . .
MEATBALL!

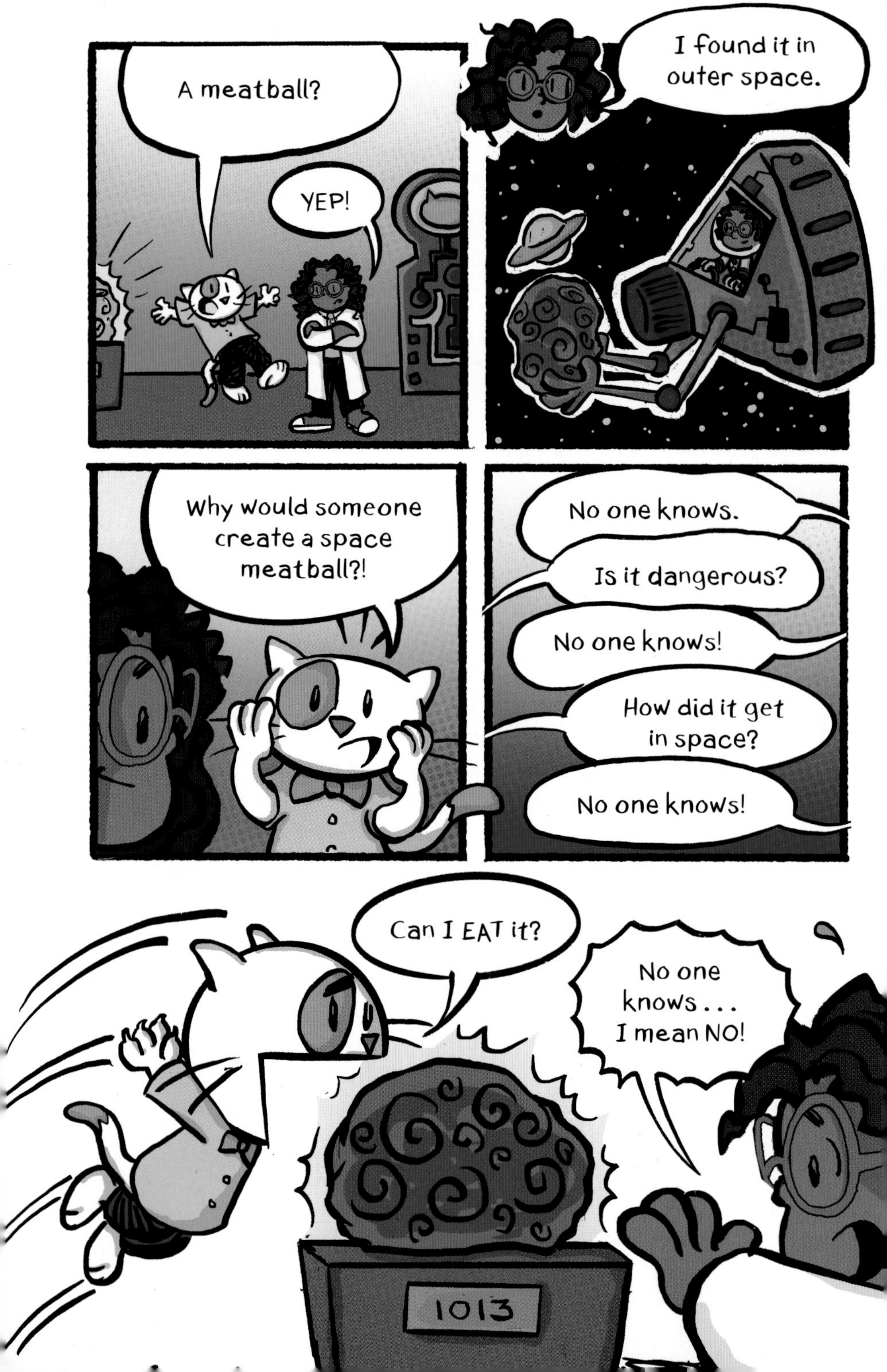
A meatball?
YEP!
I found it in outer space.
Why would someone create a space meatball?!
No one knows.
Is it dangerous?
No one knows!
How did it get in space?
No one knows!
Can I EAT it?
No one knows . . . I mean NO!
1013

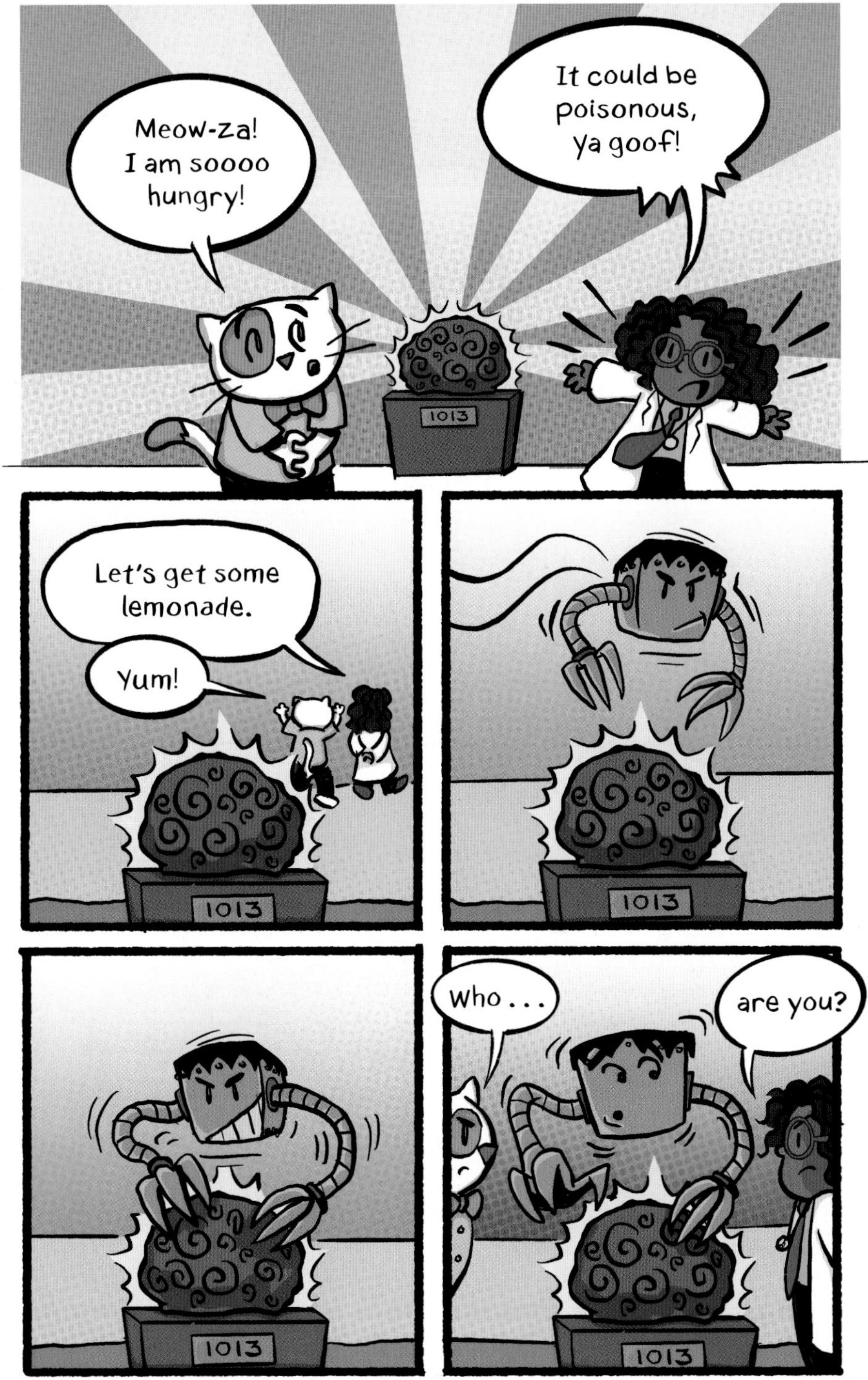
Meow-za! I am soooo hungry!
It could be poisonous, ya goof!
1013
Let's get some lemonade.
Yum!
1013
1013
1013
Who . . .
are you?
1013

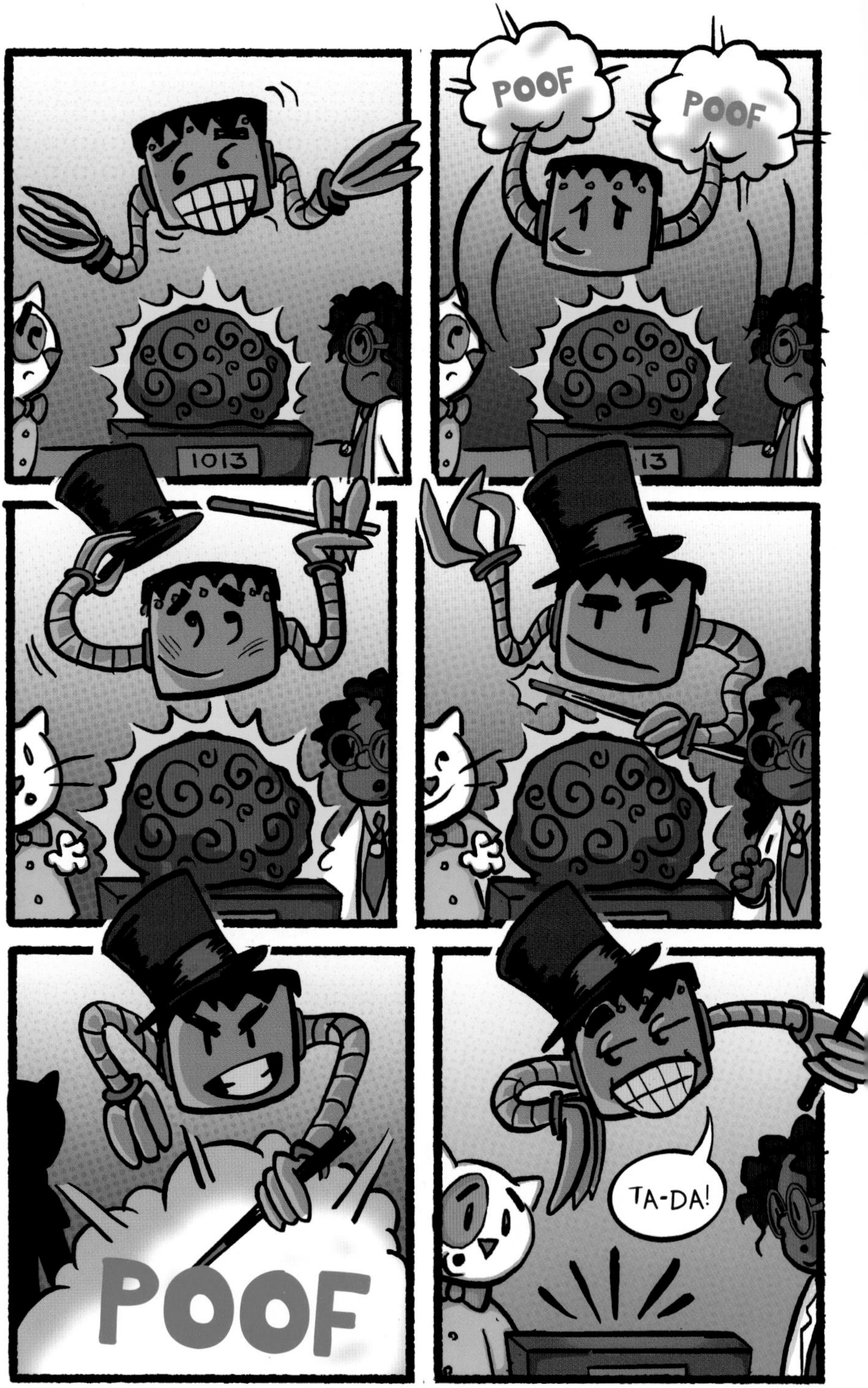
1013
POOF
POOF
13
POOF
TA-DA!

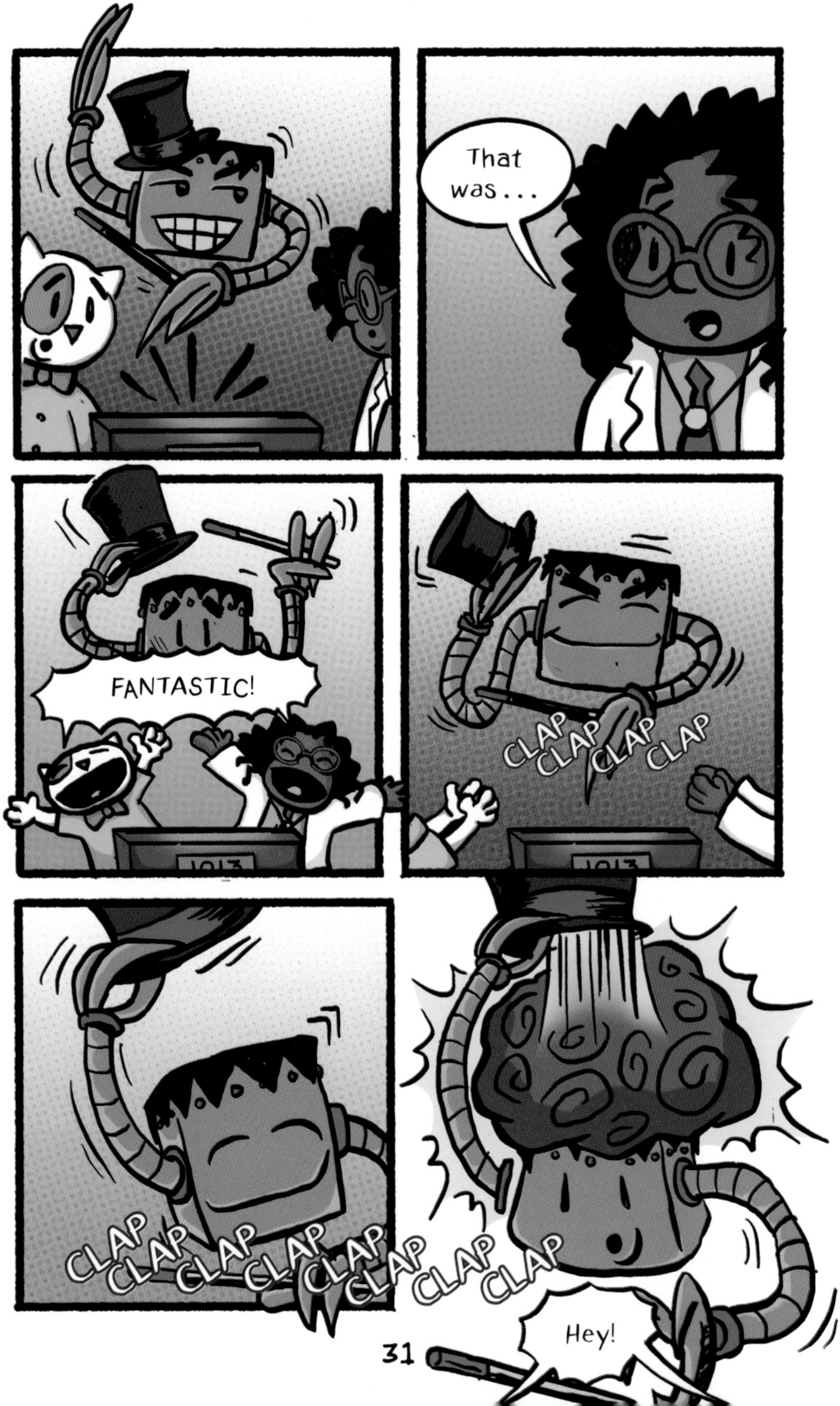
That was...
FANTASTIC!
CLAP CLAP CLAP CLAP
CLAP CLAP CLAP CLAP CLAP CLAP CLAP CLAP
Hey!

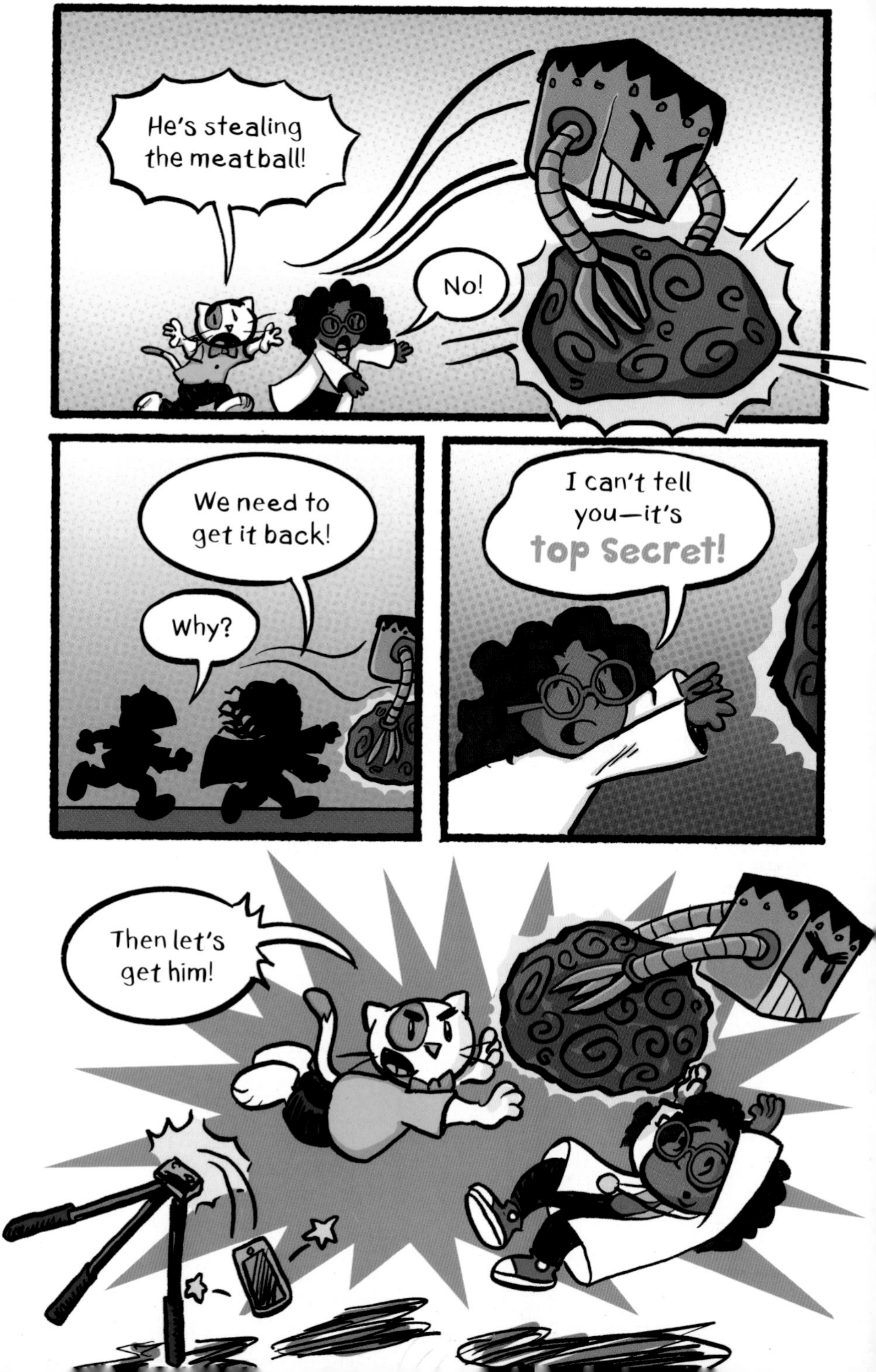
He's stealing the meatball!
No!
We need to get it back!
Why?
I can't tell you—it's top Secret!
Then let's get him!

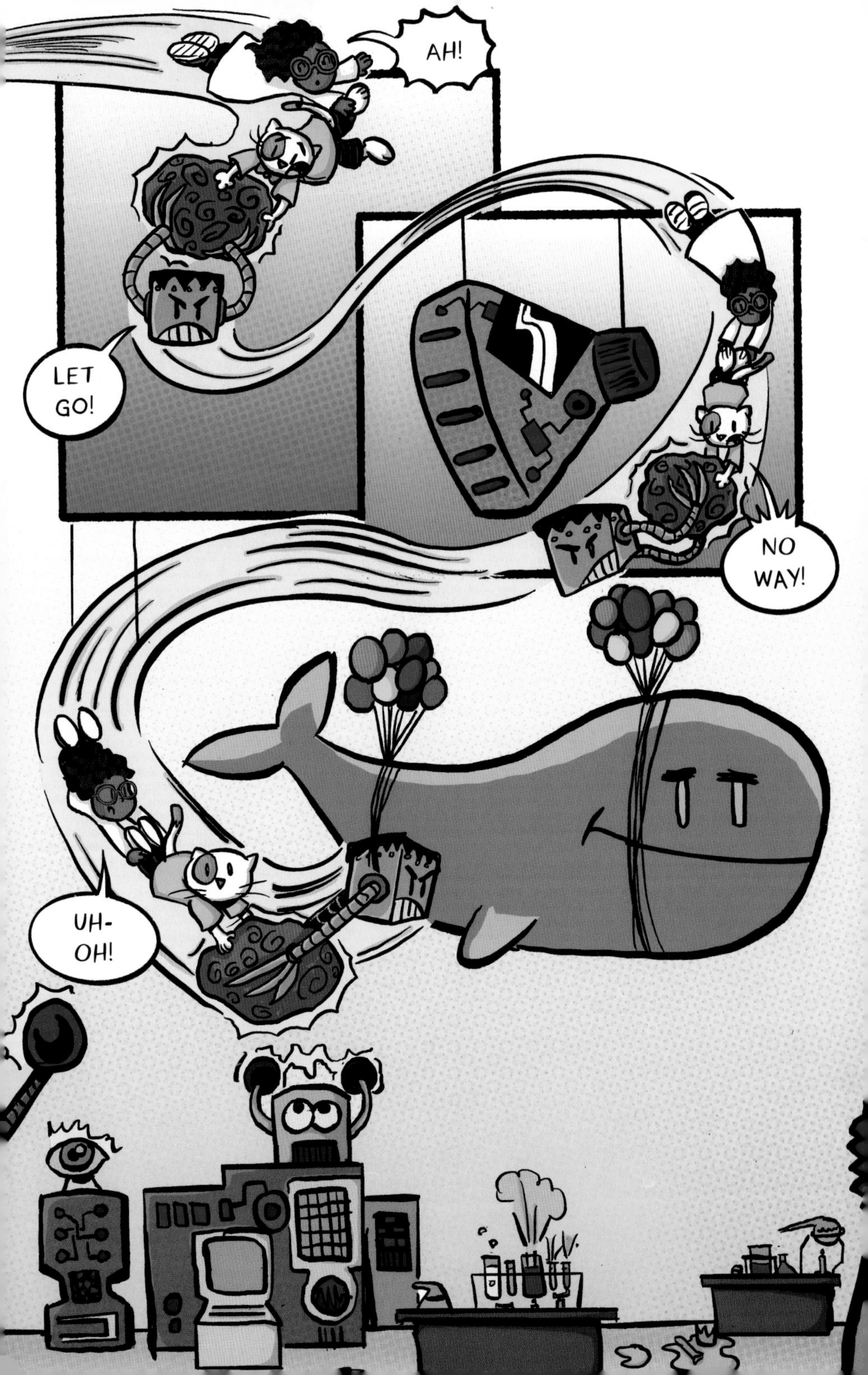
AH!
LET GO!
NO WAY!
UH-OH!

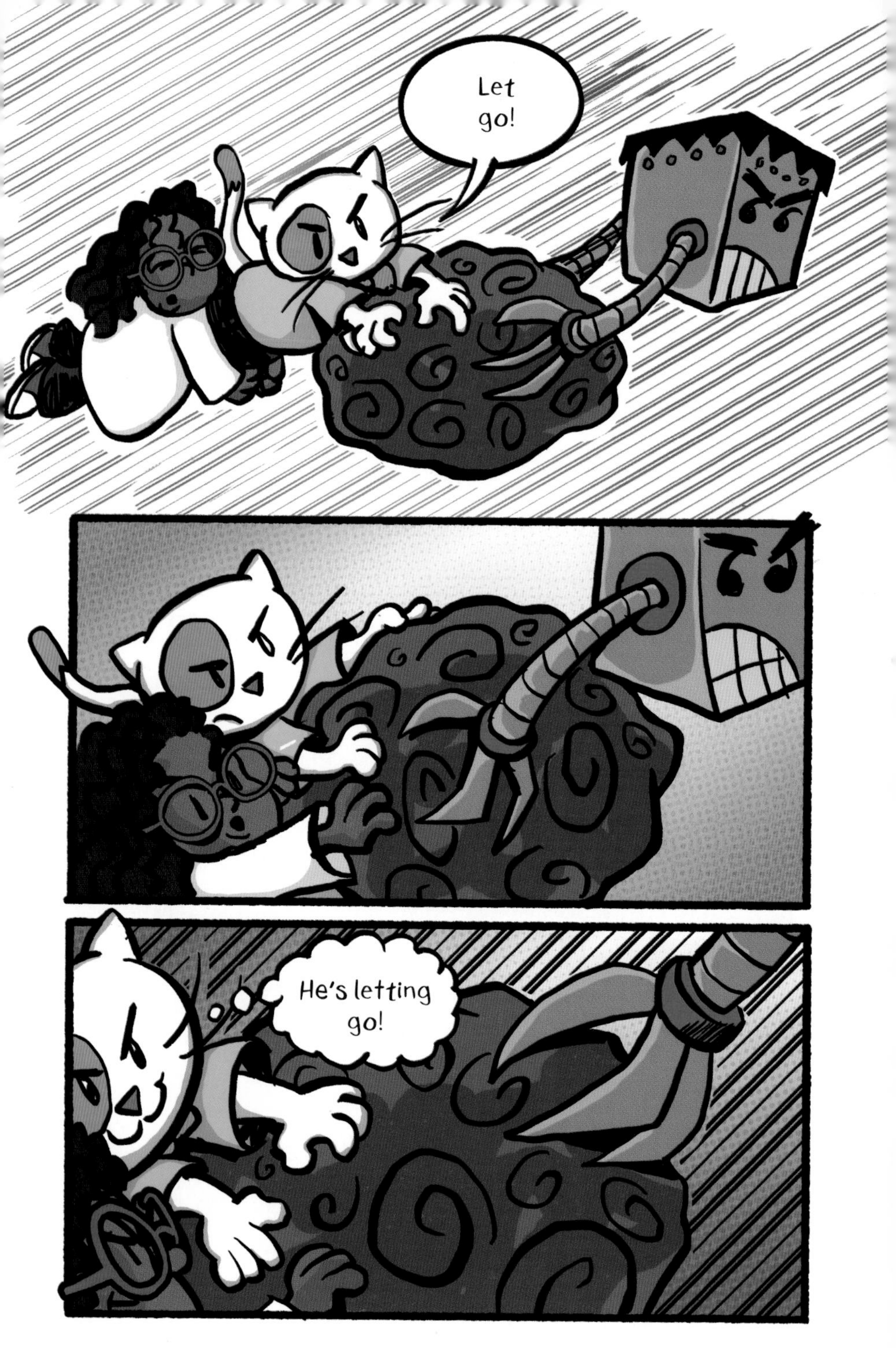
Let go!
He's letting go!

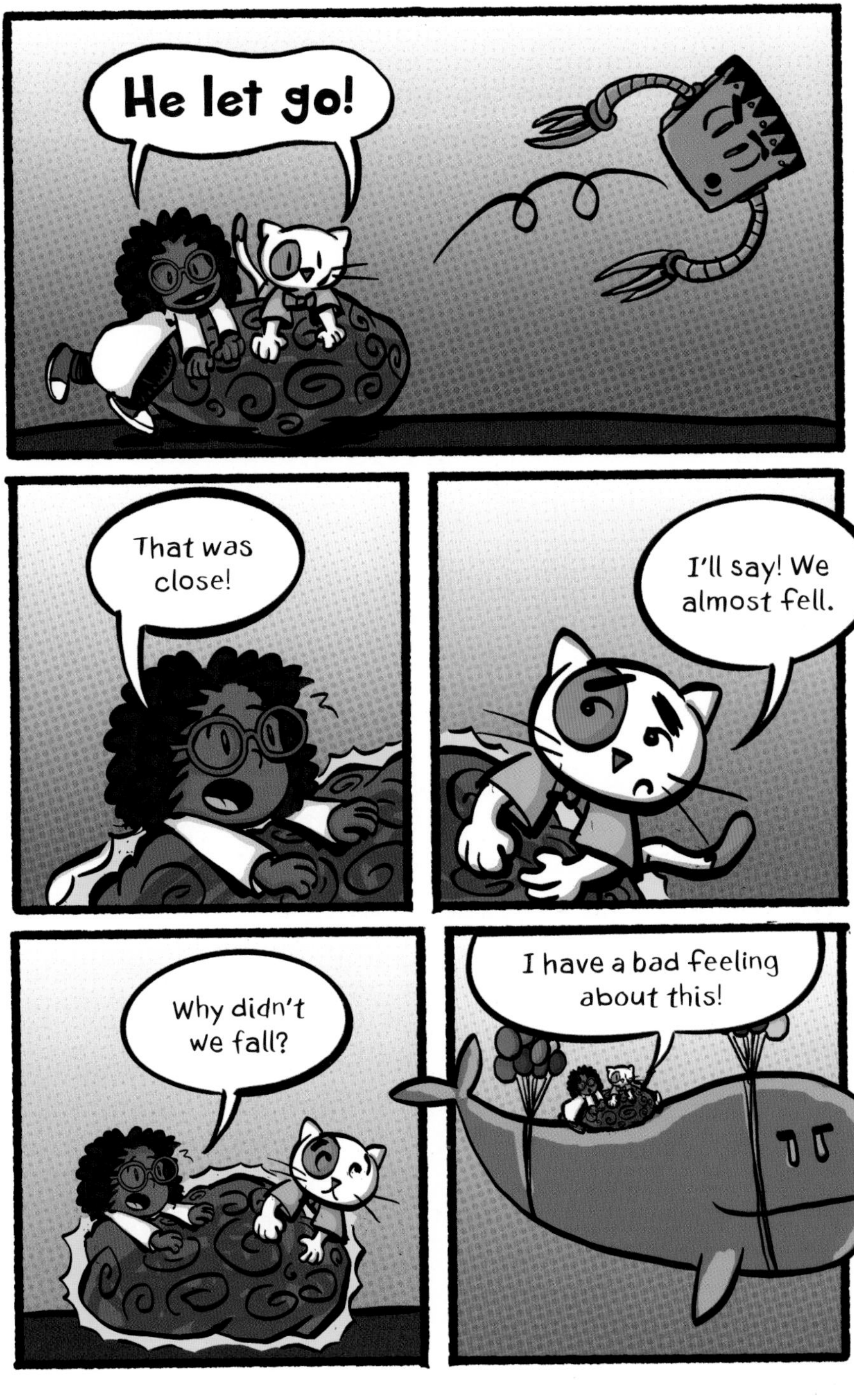
He let go!
That was close!
I'll say! We almost fell.
Why didn't we fall?
I have a bad feeling about this!

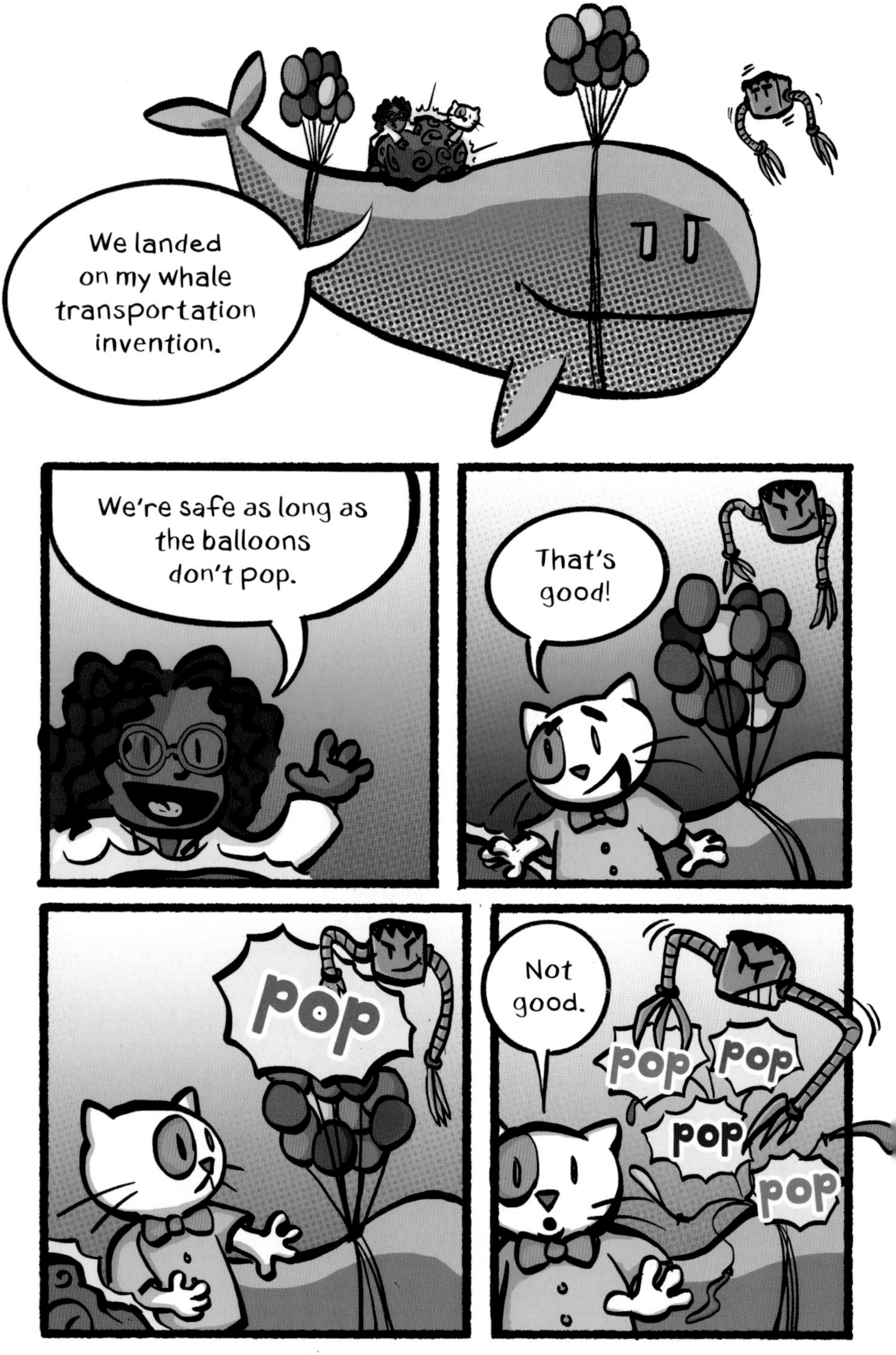
We landed on my whale transportation invention.
We're safe as long as the balloons don't pop.
That's good!
POP
Not good.
POP
POP
POP
POP

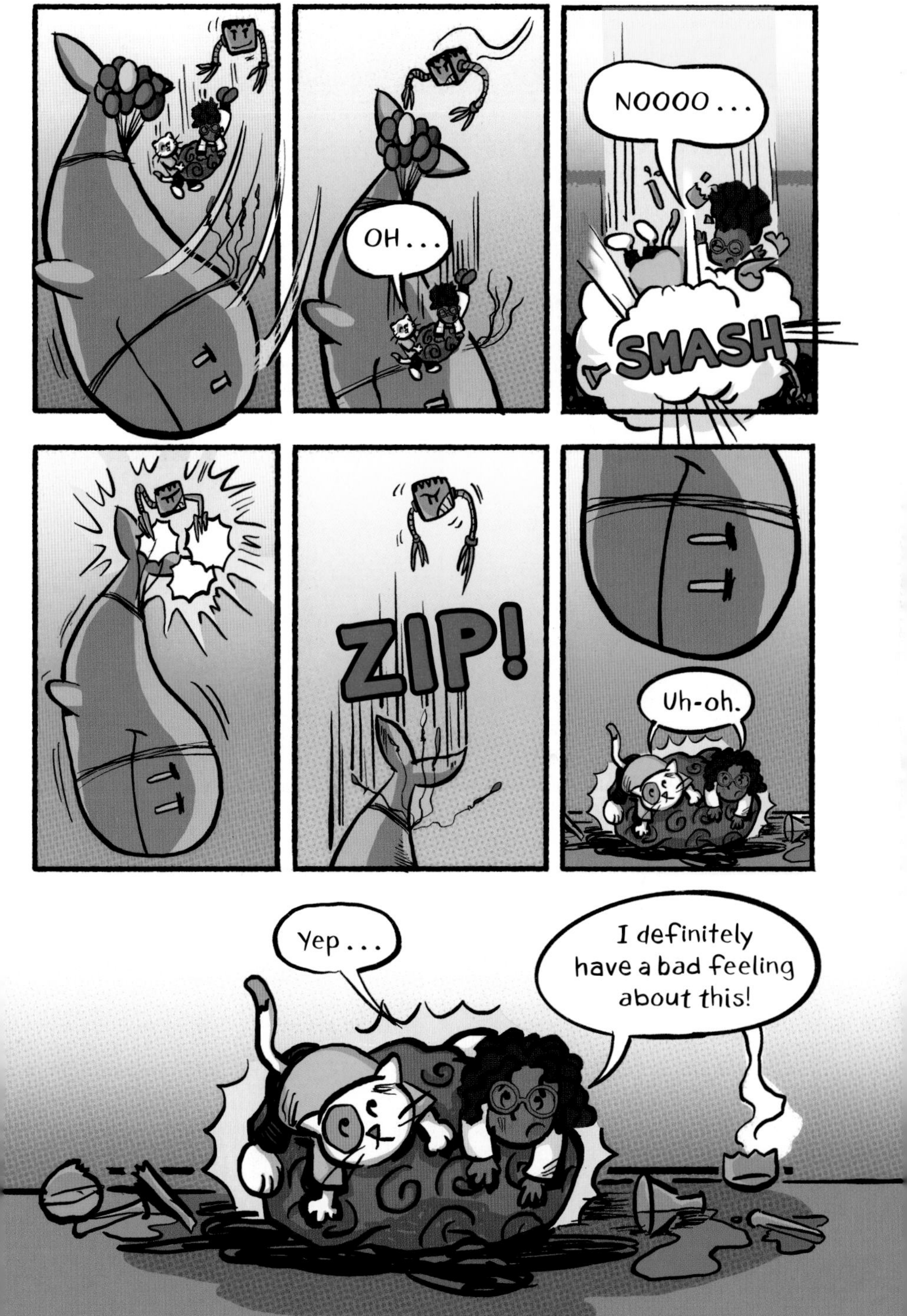
OH . . .
NOOOO . . .
SMASH
ZIP!
Uh-oh.
Yep . . .
I definitely have a bad feeling about this!

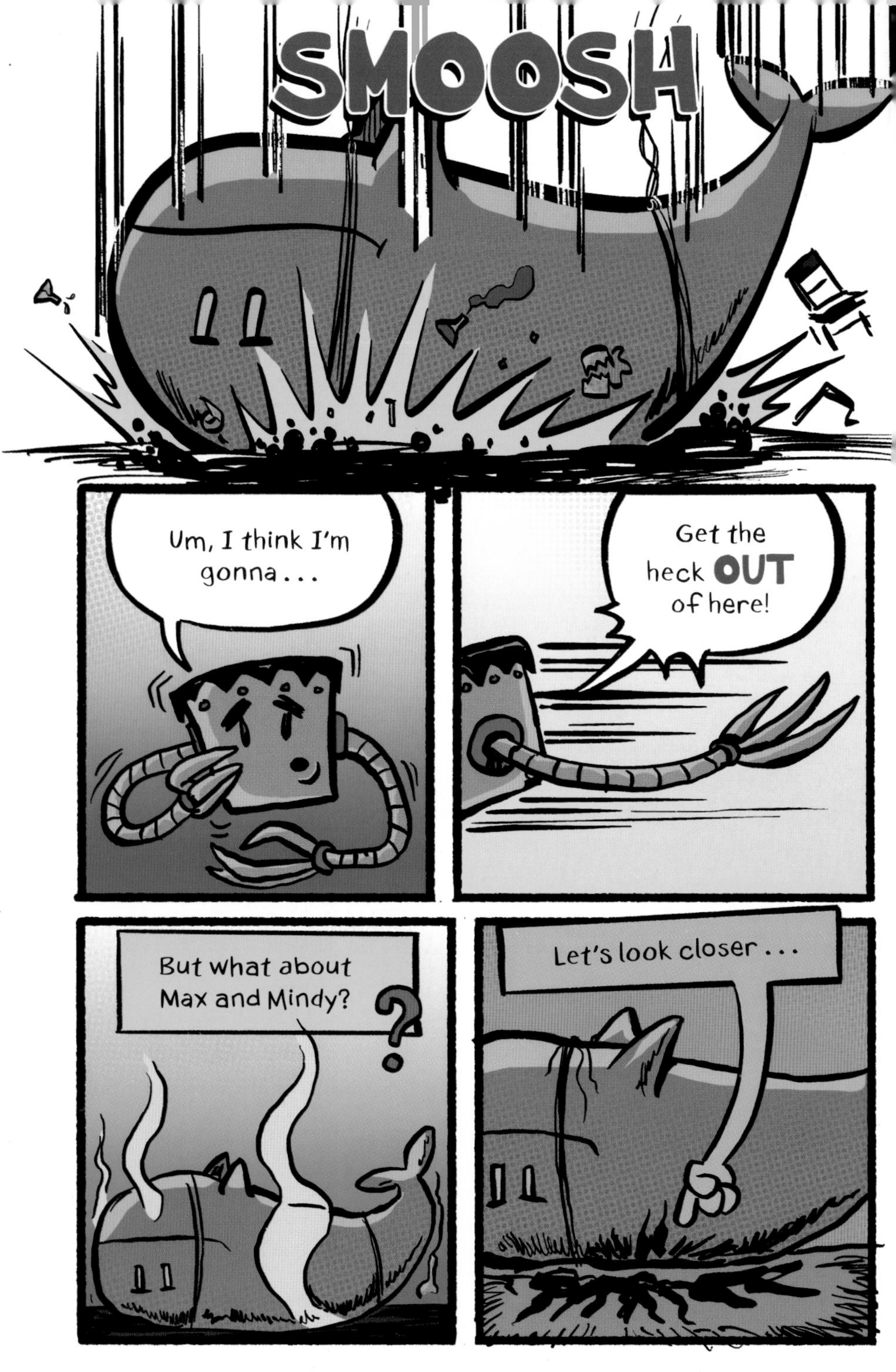
SMOOSH
Um, I think I'm gonna . . .
Get the heck OUT of here!
But what about Max and Mindy?
Let's look closer . . .

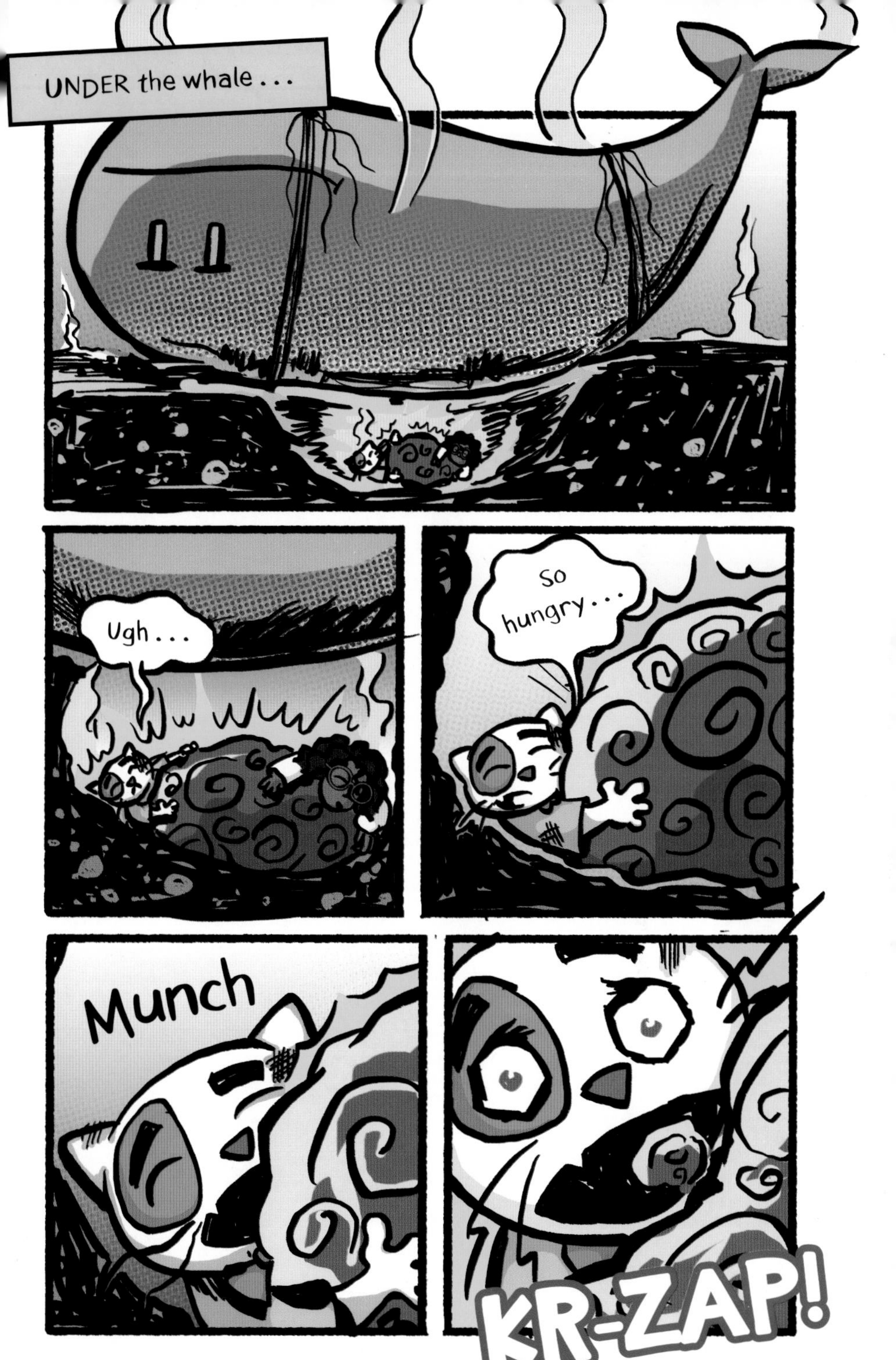
UNDER the whale . . .
Ugh . . .
So hungry . . .
Munch
KR-ZAP!

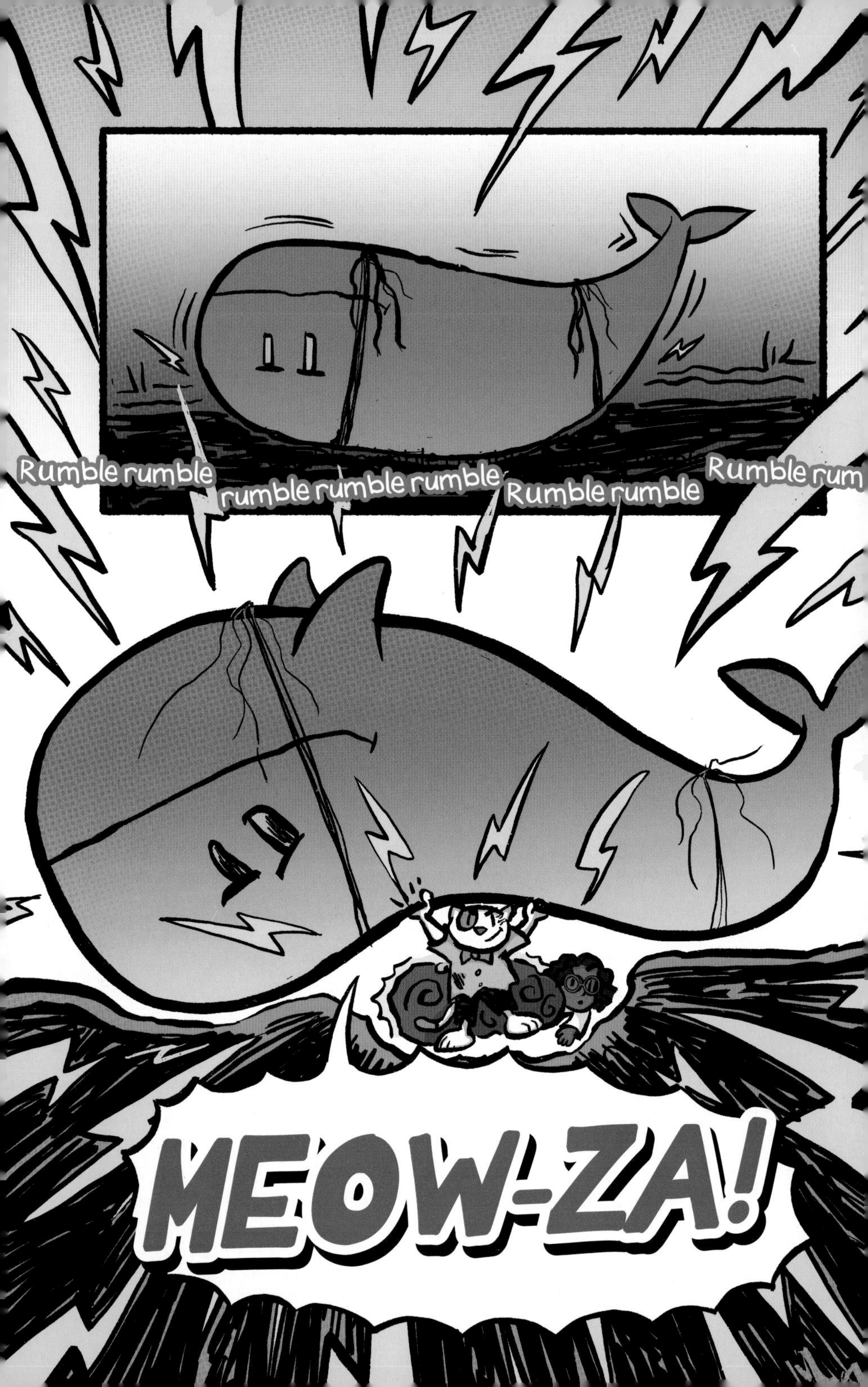
Rumble rumble
rumble rumble rumble
Rumble rumble
Rumble rum
MEOW-ZA!

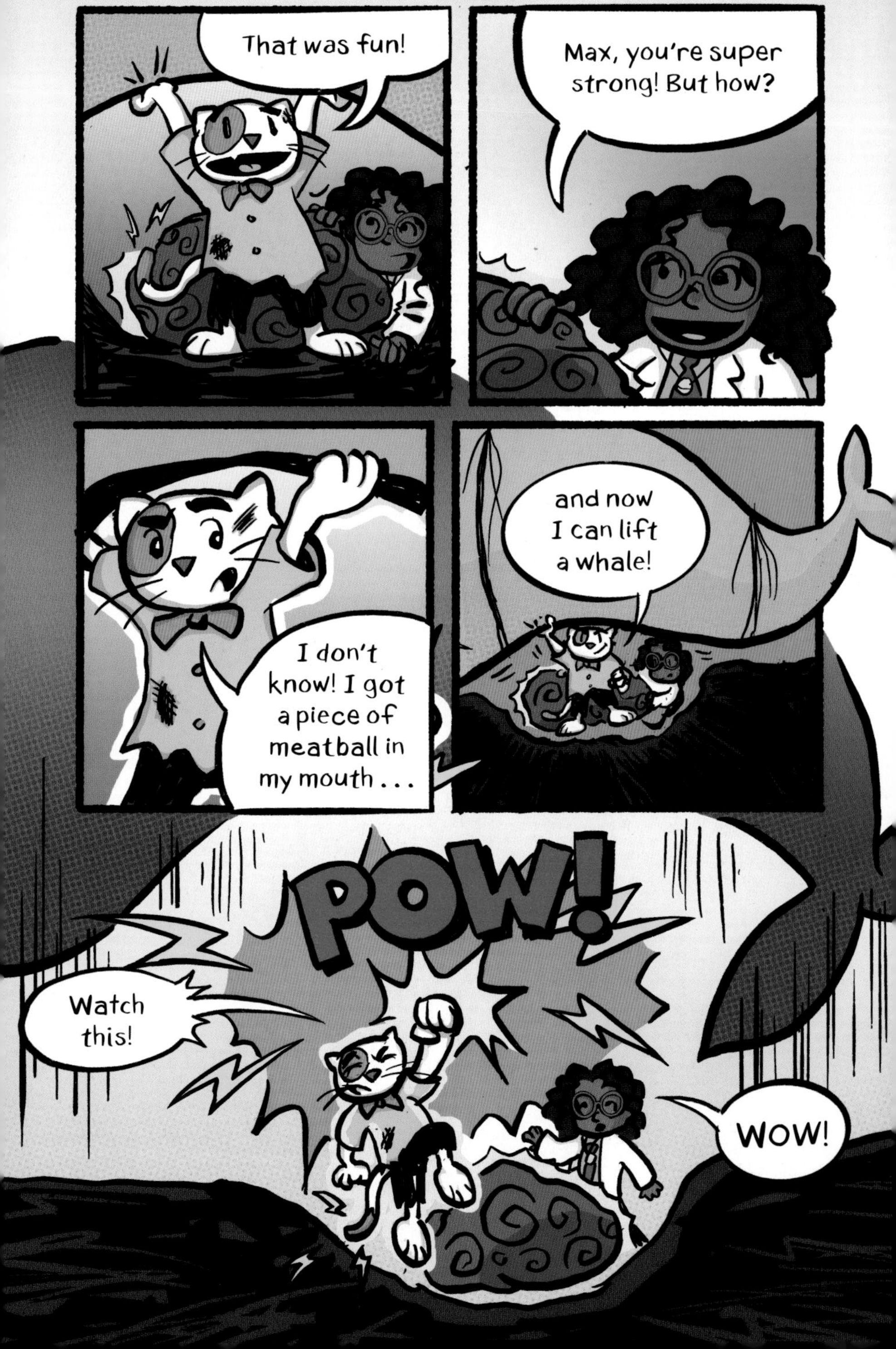
That was fun!
Max, you're super strong! But how?
I don't know! I got a piece of meatball in my mouth . . .
and now I can lift a whale!
POW!
Watch this!
WOW!

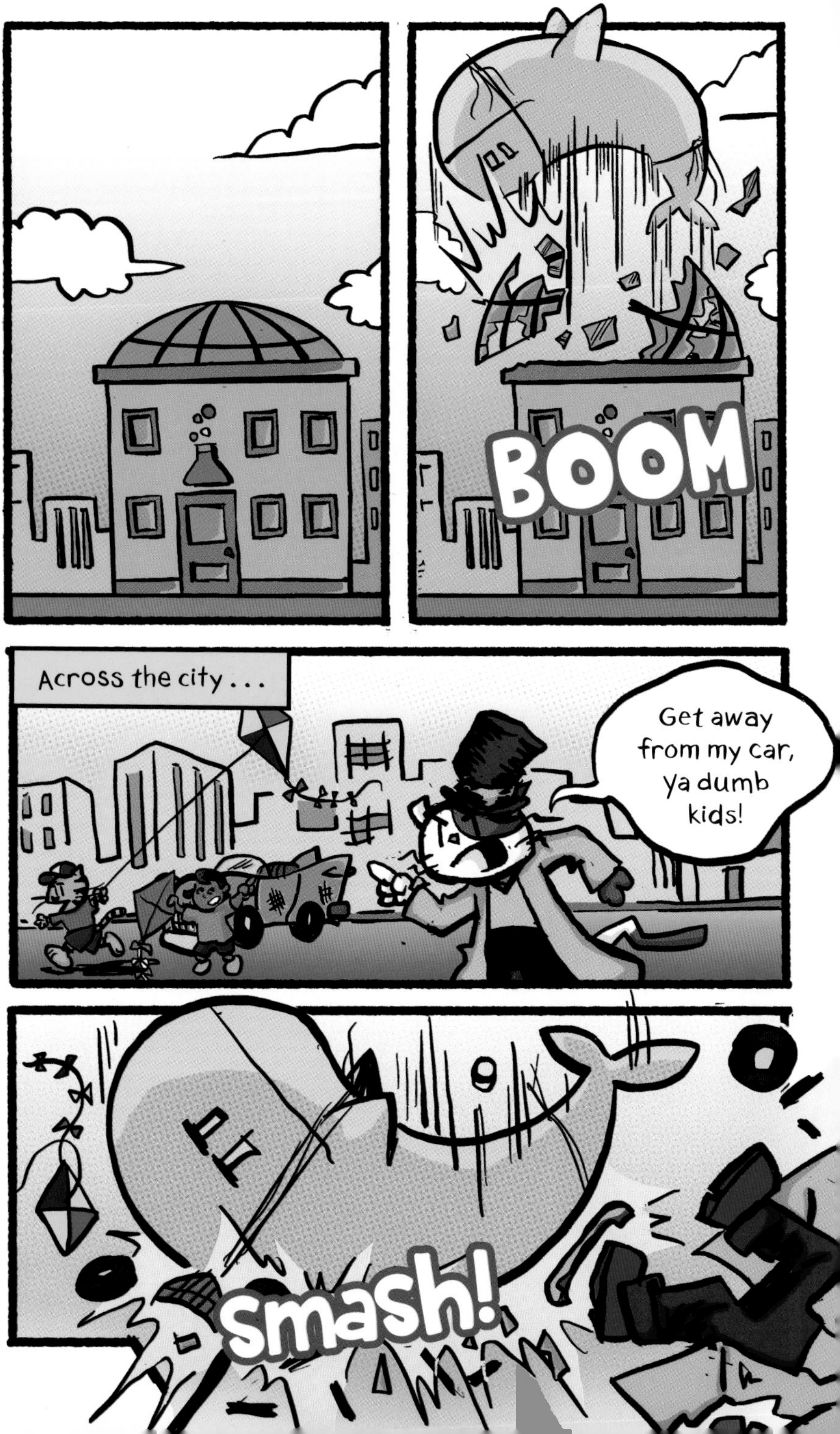
BOOM
Across the city . . .
Get away from my car, ya dumb kids!
smash!

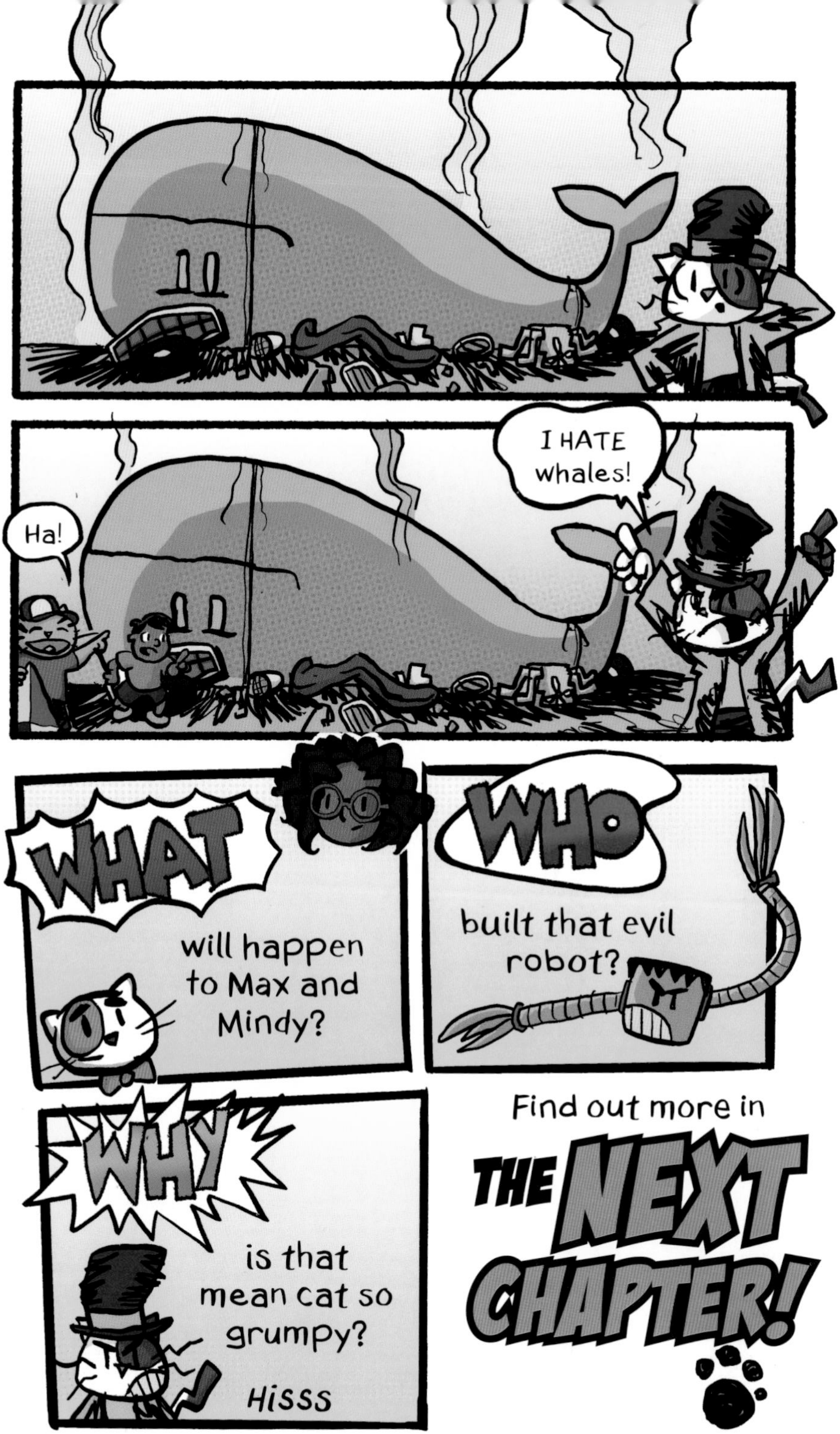
I HATE whales!
Ha!
WHAT
will happen to Max and Mindy?
WHO
built that evil robot?
WHY
is that mean cat so grumpy?
Hisss
Find out more in
THE NEXT CHAPTER!

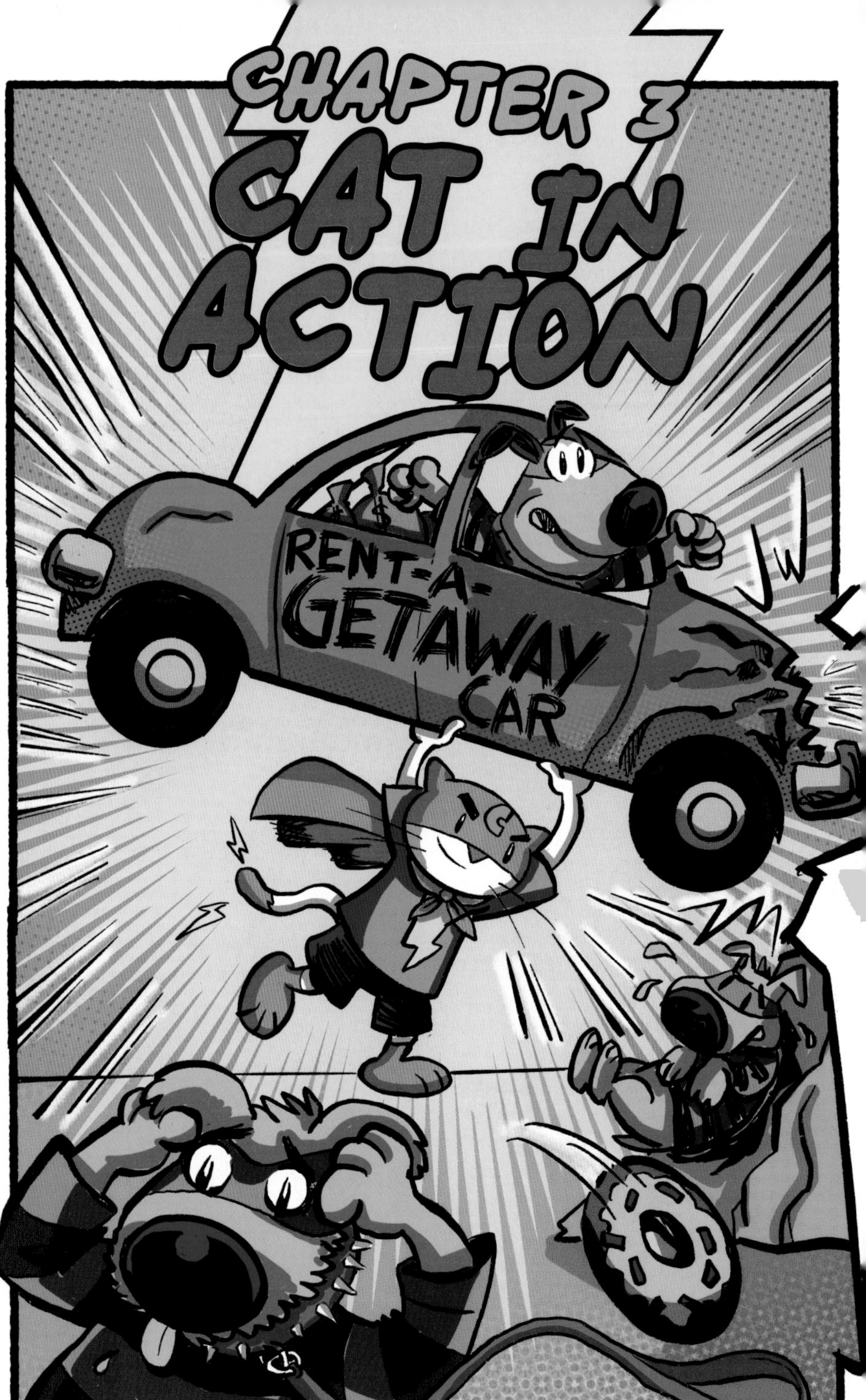
CHAPTER 3
CAT IN ACTION
RENT-A-GETAWAY CAR

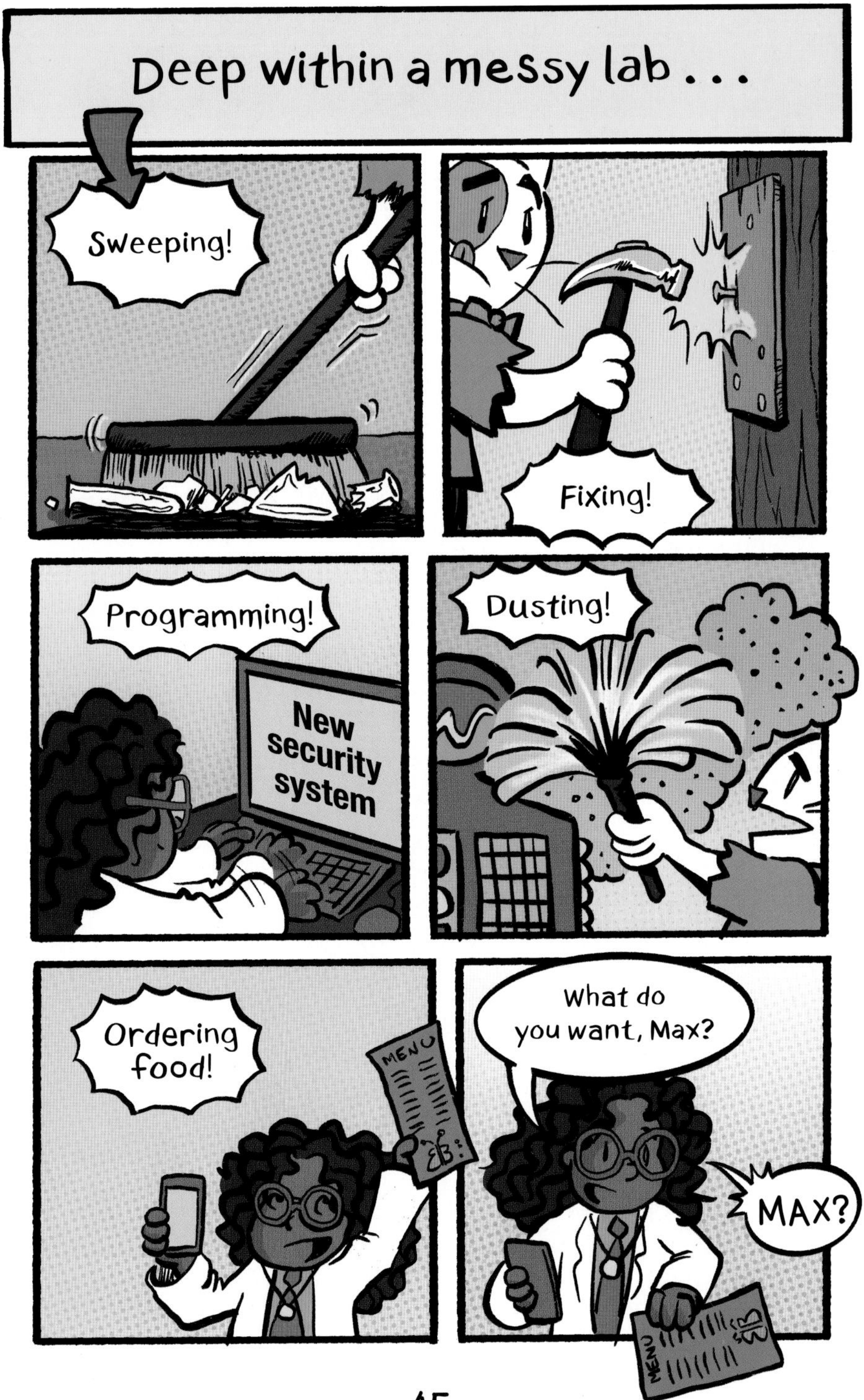
Deep within a messy lab . . .
Sweeping!
Fixing!
Programming!
New security system
Dusting!
Ordering food!
MENU
What do you want, Max?
MAX?
MENU

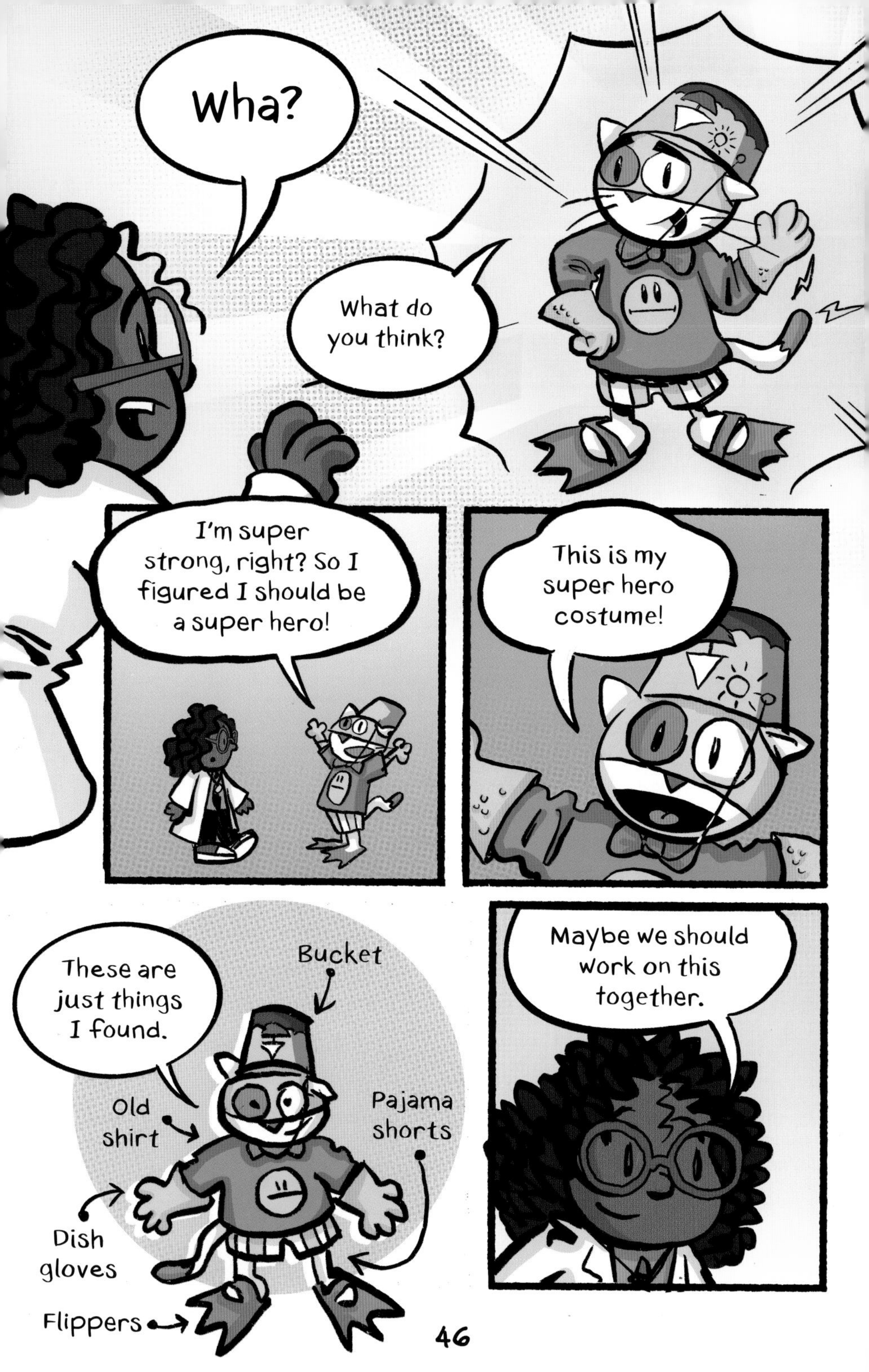
Wha?
What do you think?
I'm super strong, right? So I figured I should be a super hero!
This is my super hero costume!
These are just things I found.
Bucket
Old shirt
Pajama shorts
Dish gloves
Flippers
Maybe we should work on this together.

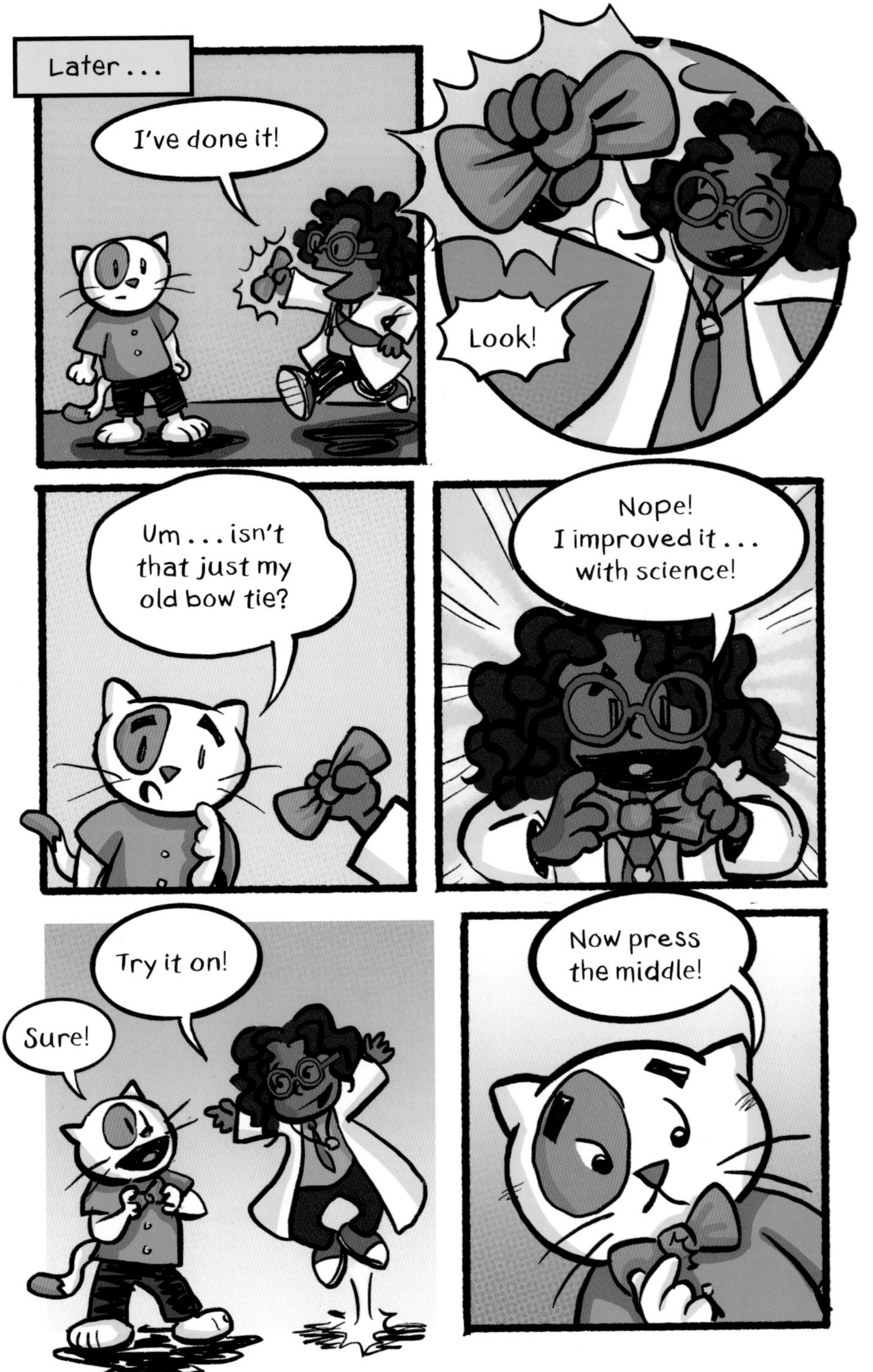
Later . . .
I've done it!
Look!
Um . . . isn't that just my old bow tie?
Nope! I improved it . . . with science!
Try it on!
Sure!
Now press the middle!

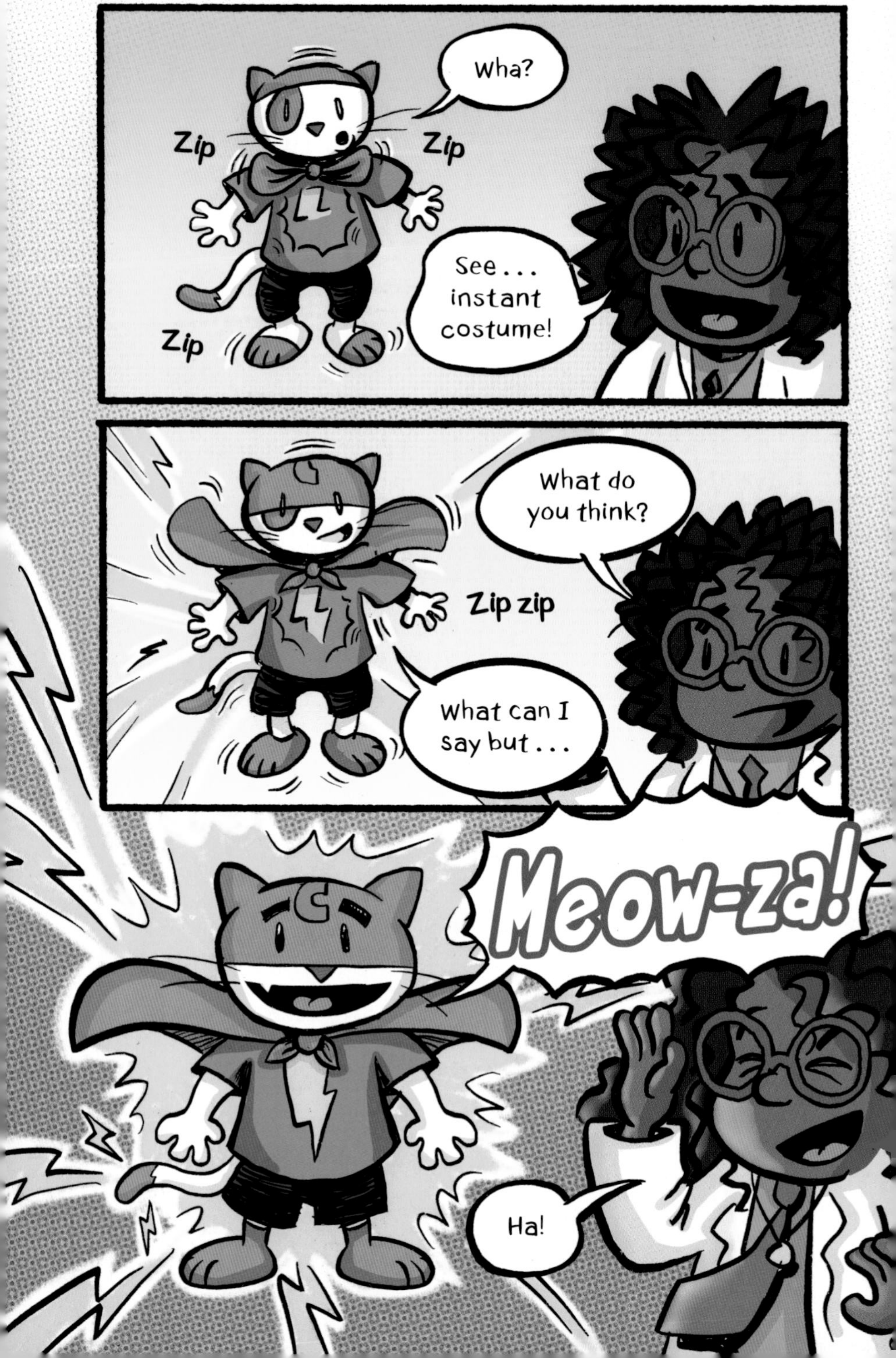
Wha?
Zip
Zip
Zip
See... instant costume!
What do you think?
Zip zip
What can I say but...
Meow-za!
Ha!

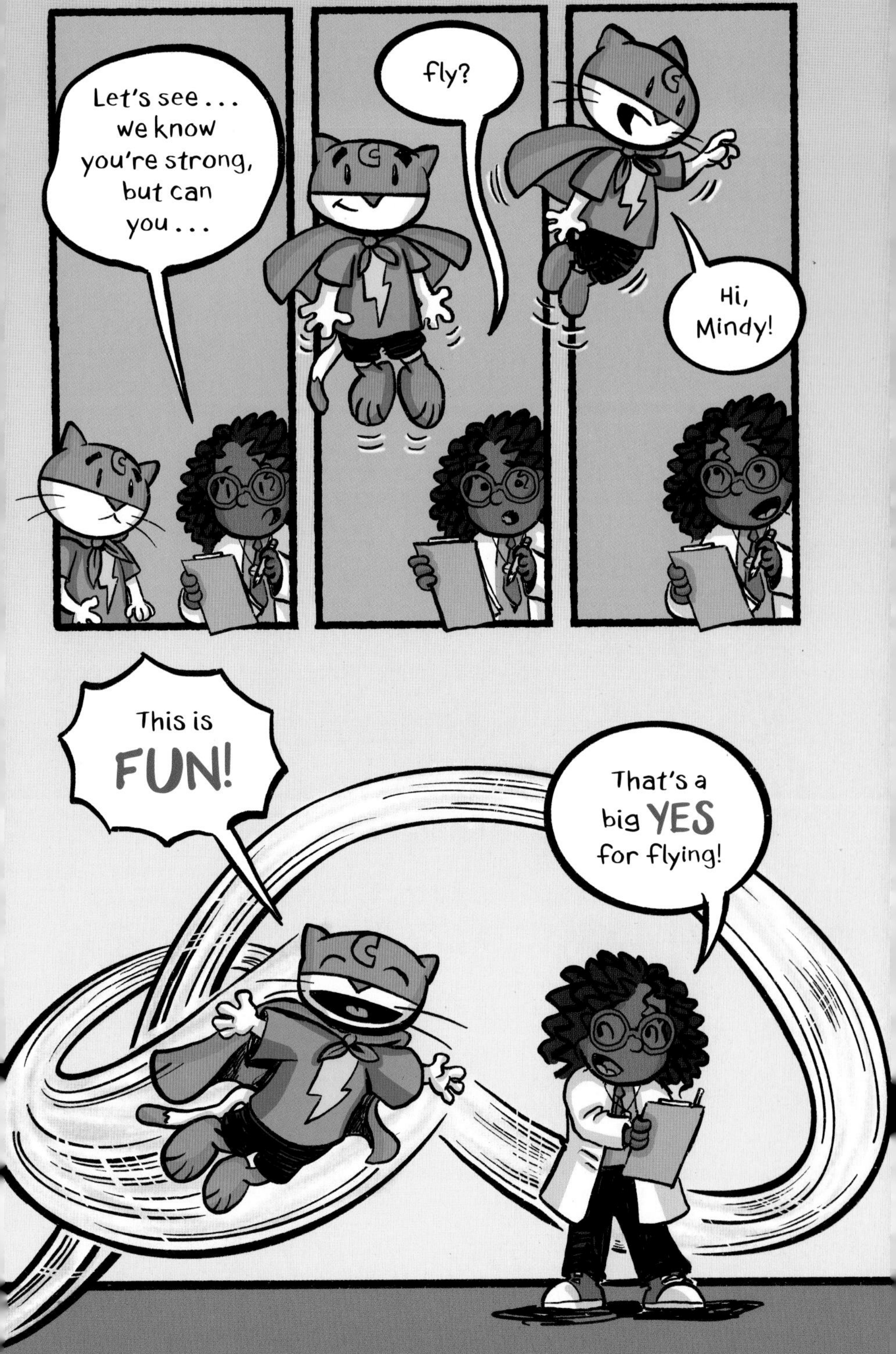
Let's see . . . we know you're strong, but can you . . .
fly?
Hi, Mindy!
This is FUN!
That's a big YES for flying!

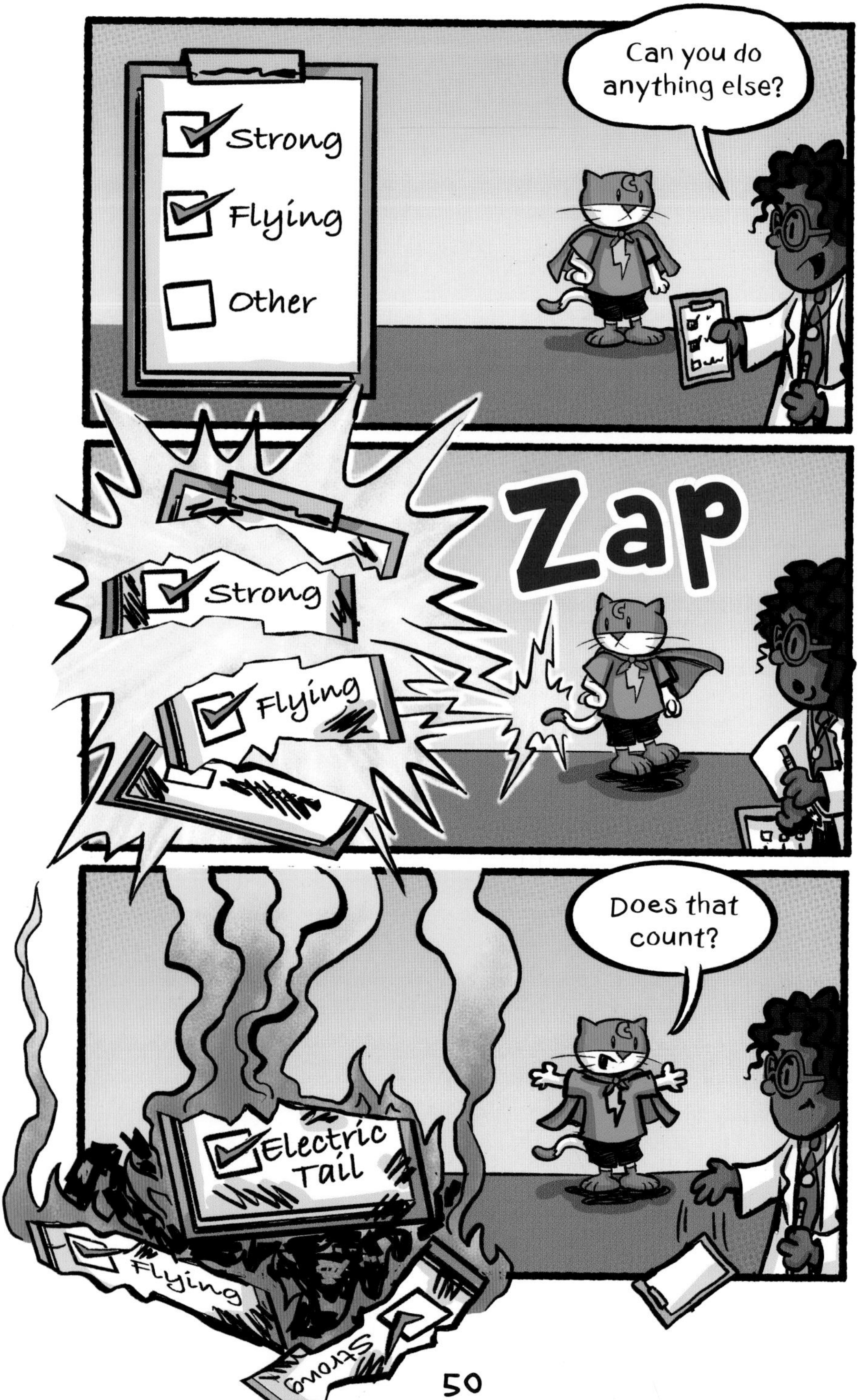
Strong
Flying
Other
Can you do anything else?
Zap
Strong
Flying
Electric Tail
Flying
Strong
Does that count?

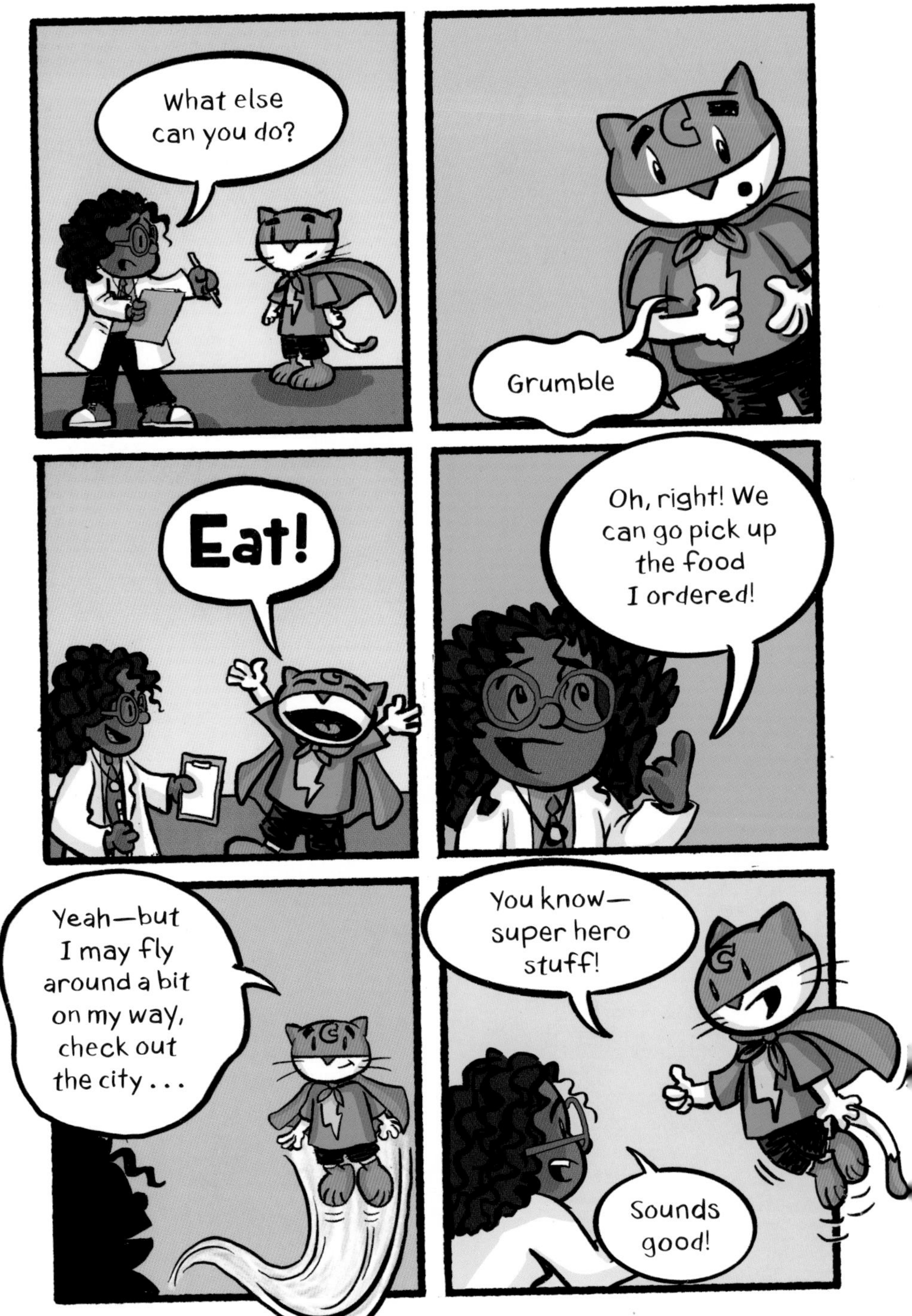
What else can you do?
Grumble
Eat!
Oh, right! We can go pick up the food I ordered!
Yeah—but I may fly around a bit on my way, check out the city . . .
You know—super hero stuff!
Sounds good!

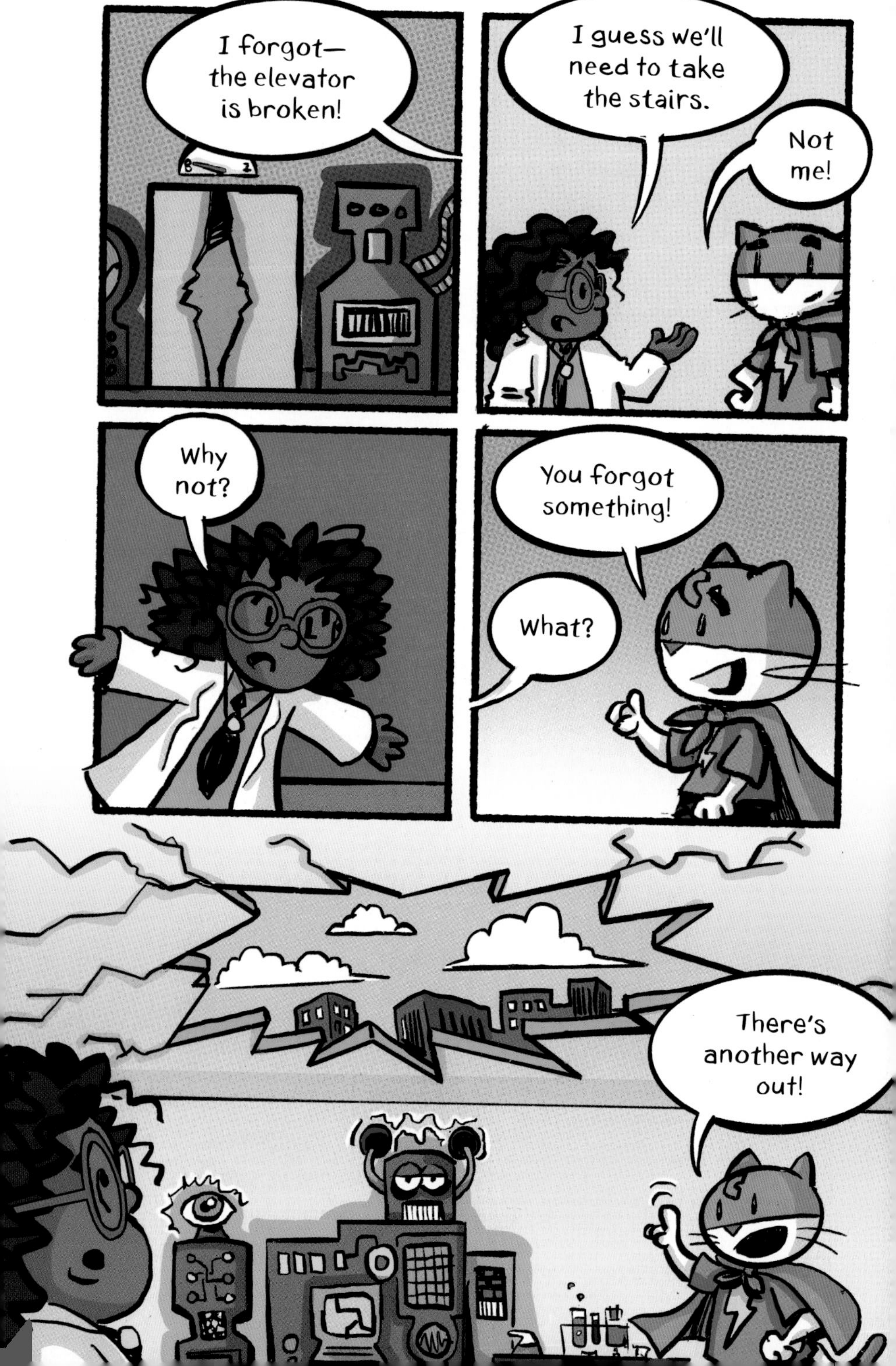
I forgot—
the elevator
is broken!
I guess we'll
need to take
the stairs.
Not
me!
Why
not?
You forgot
something!
What?
There's
another way
out!

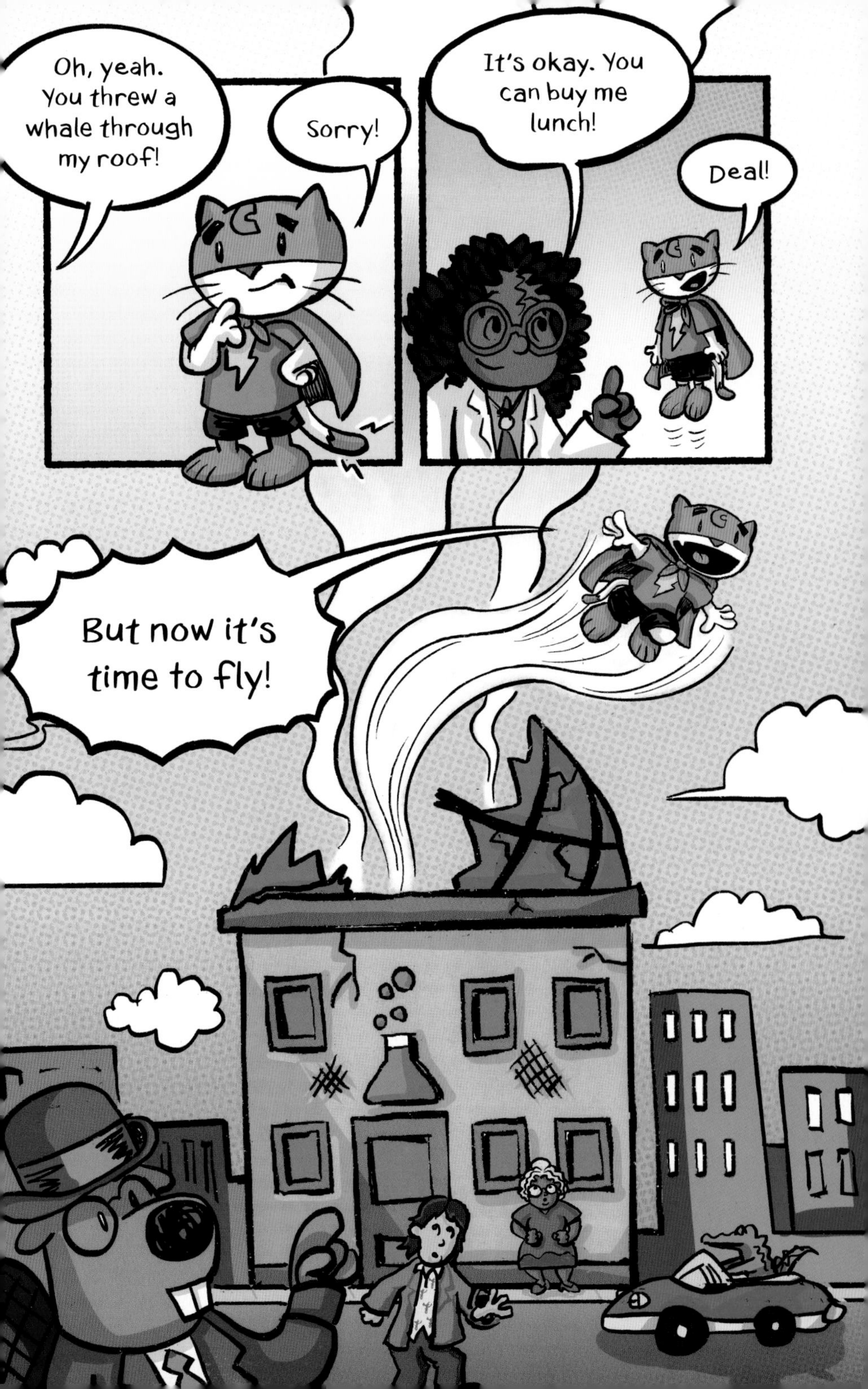
Oh, yeah. You threw a whale through my roof!
Sorry!
It's okay. You can buy me lunch!
Deal!
But now it's time to fly!

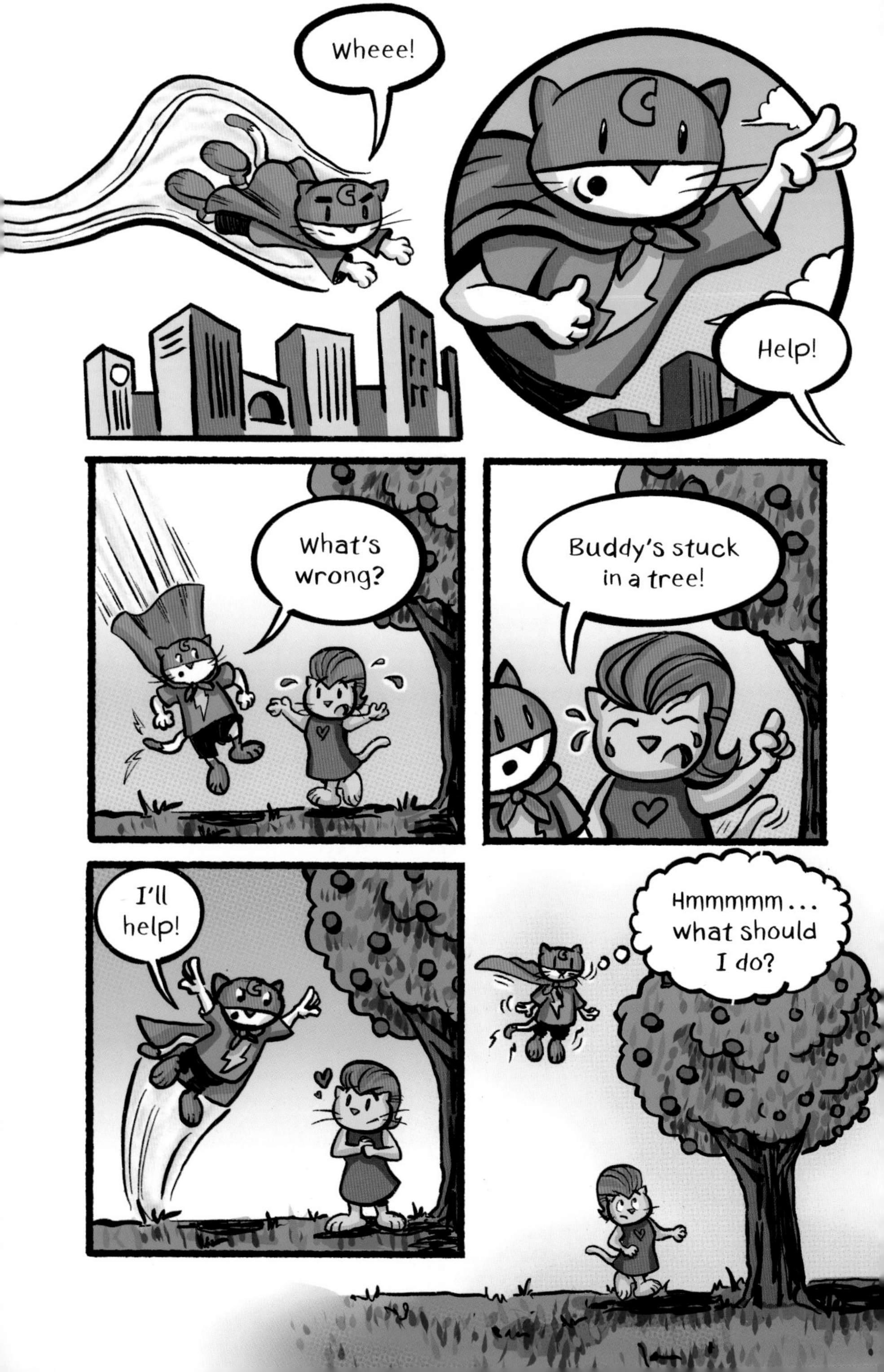
Wheee!
Help!
What's wrong?
Buddy's stuck in a tree!
I'll help!
Hmmmmm... what should I do?

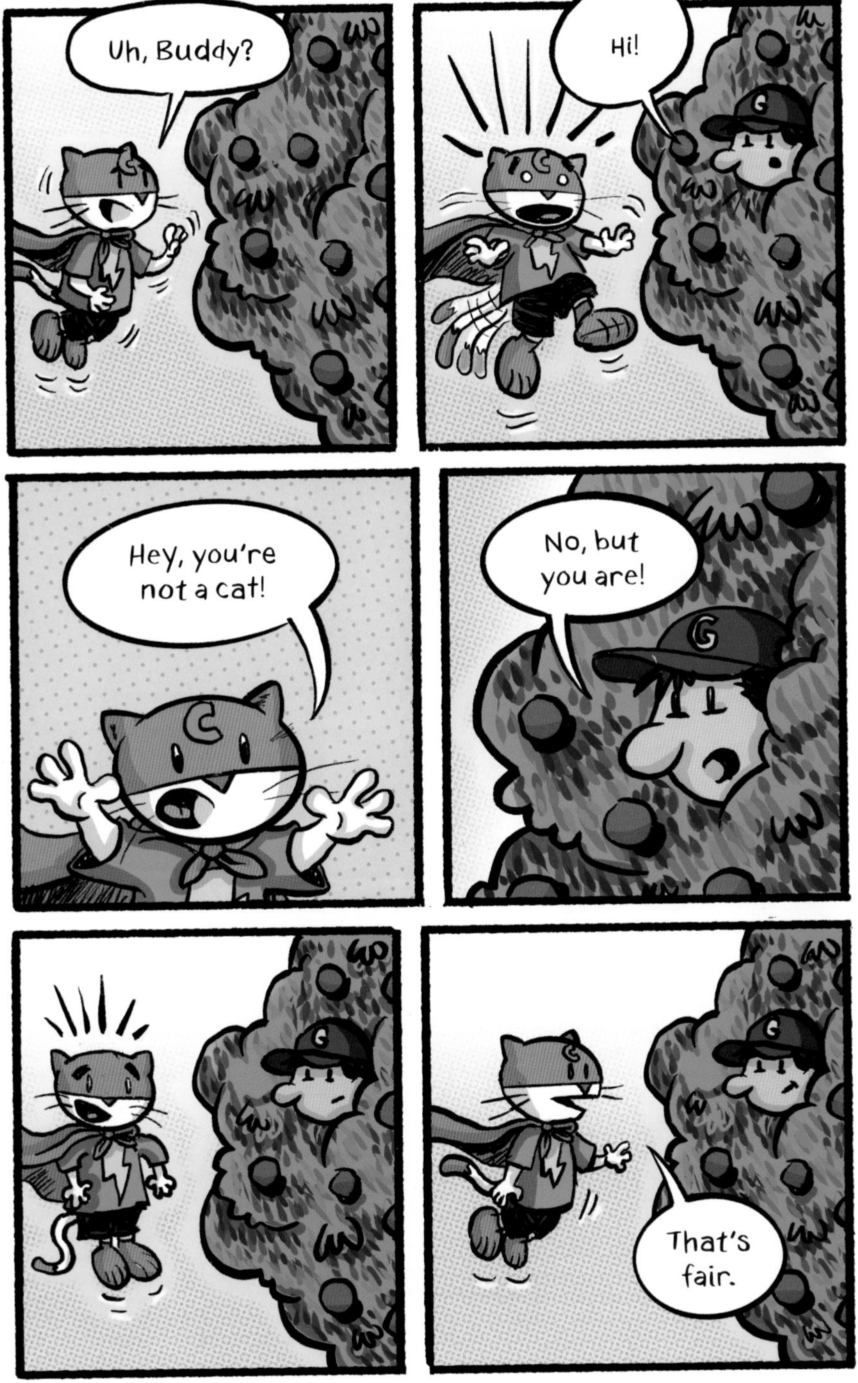

Uh, Buddy?
Hi!
Hey, you're not a cat!
No, but you are!
That's fair.

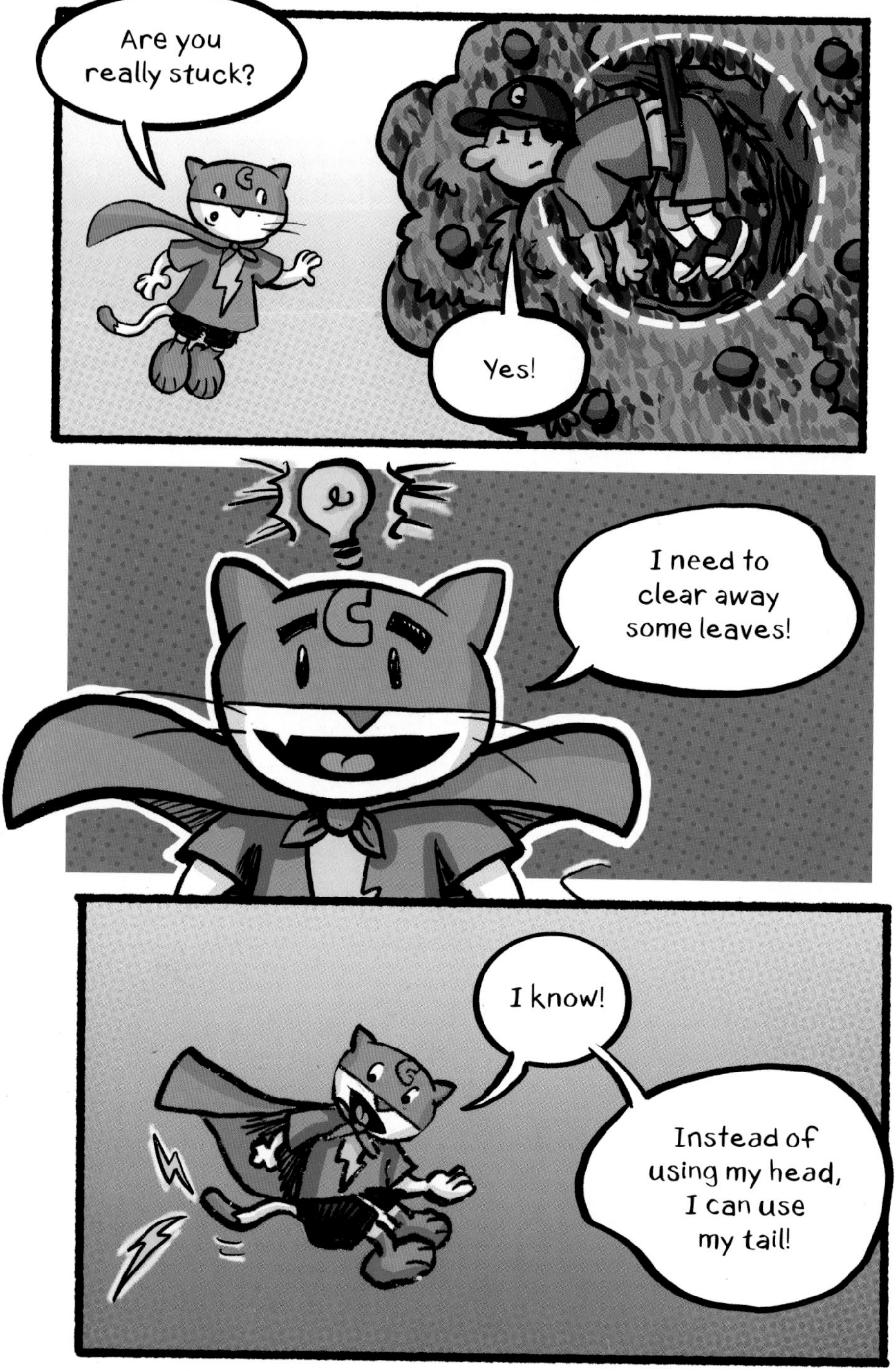
Are you really stuck?
Yes!
I need to clear away some leaves!
I know!
Instead of using my head, I can use my tail!

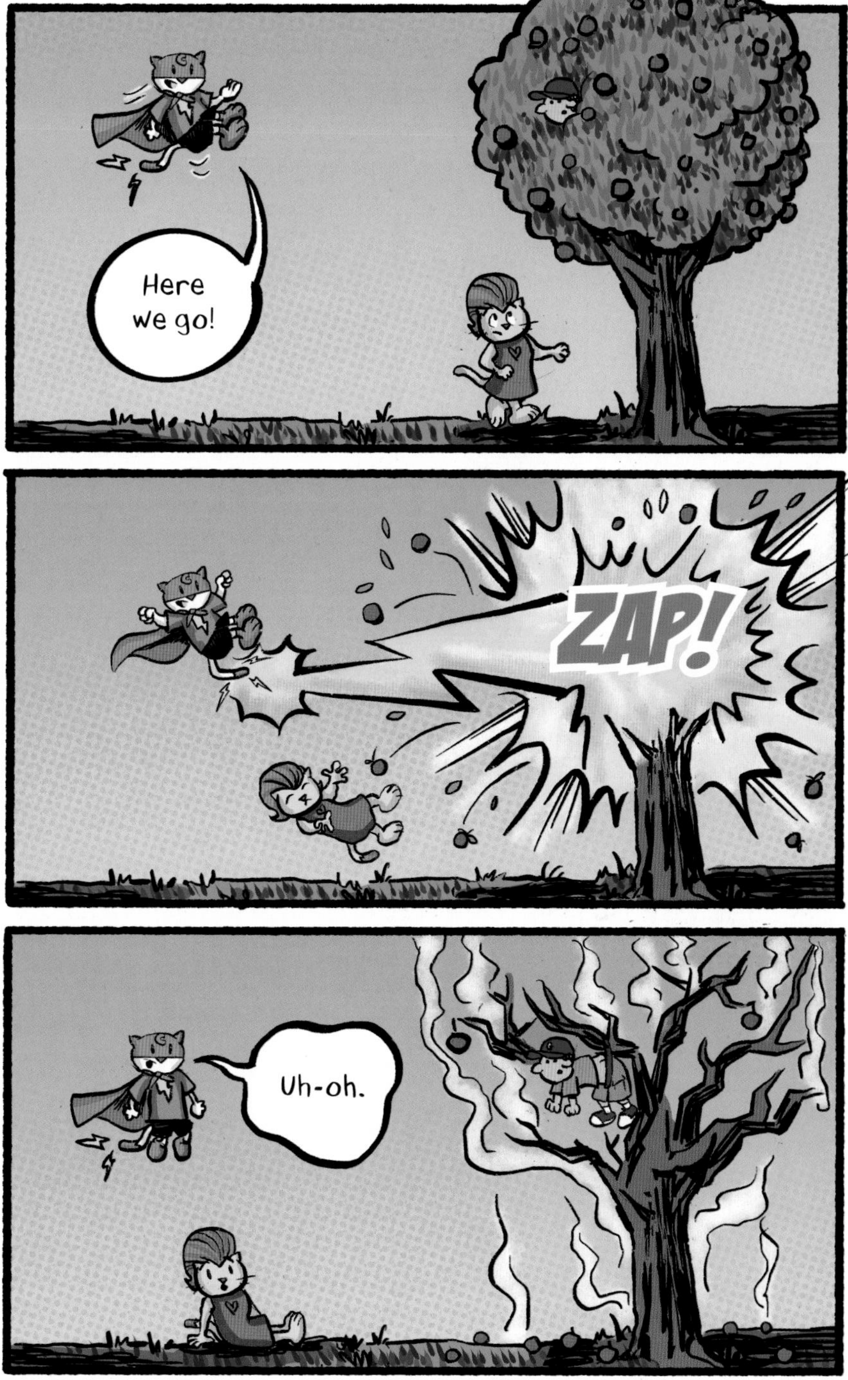
Here we go!
ZAP!
Uh-oh.

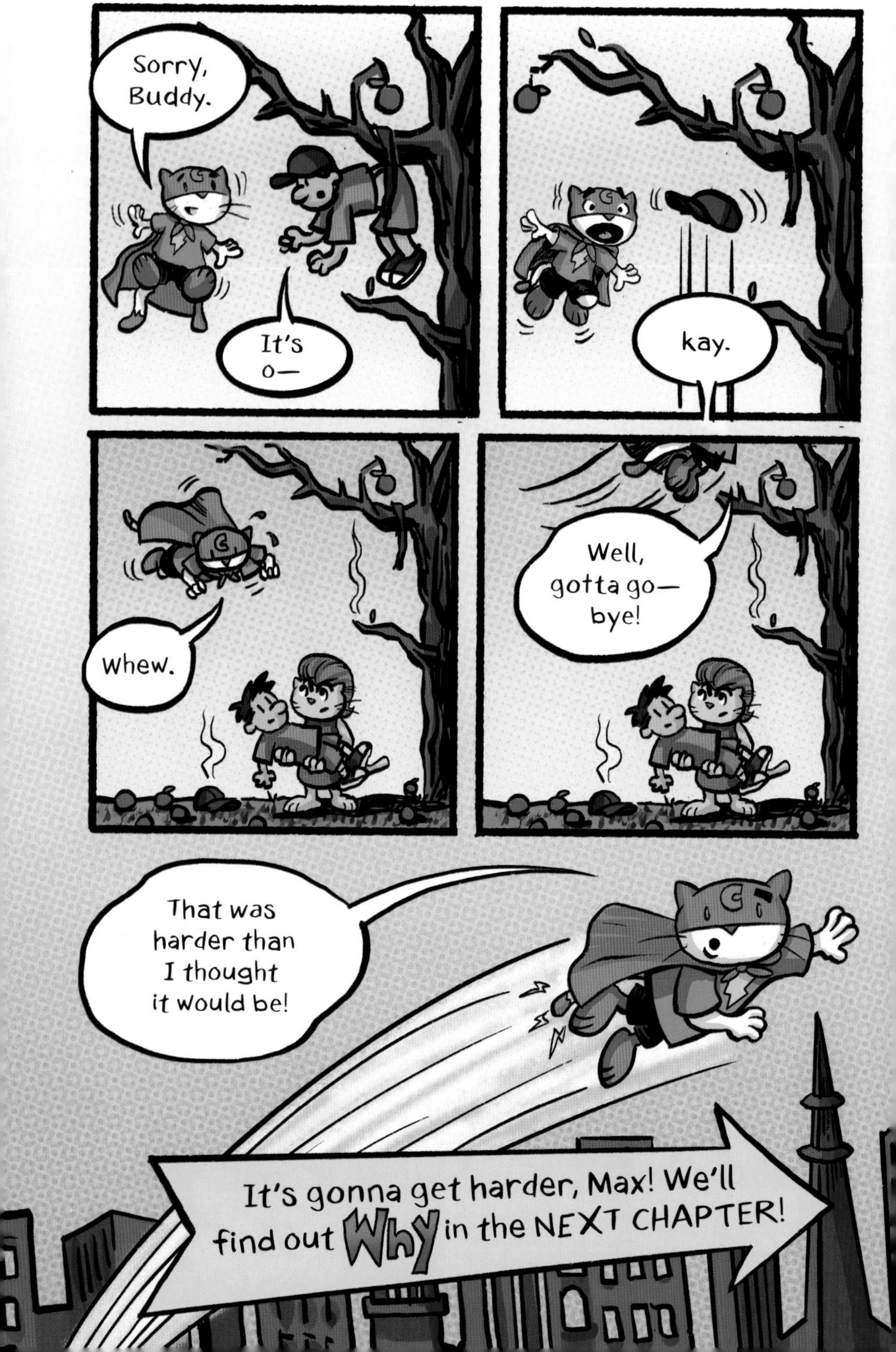
Sorry, Buddy.
It's o—
kay.
Whew.
Well, gotta go— bye!
That was harder than I thought it would be!
It's gonna get harder, Max! We'll find out Why in the NEXT CHAPTER!

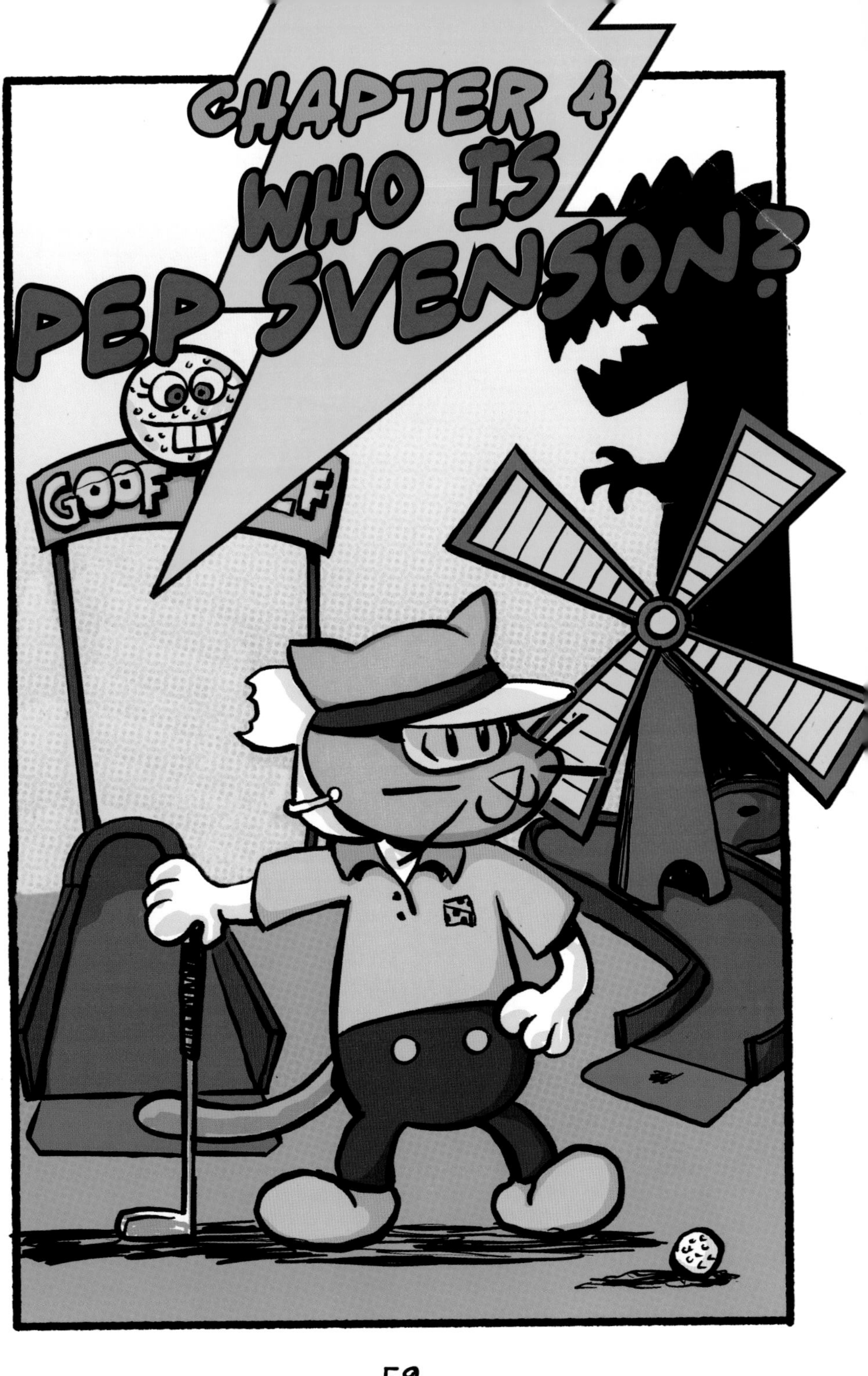
CHAPTER 4
WHO IS PEP SVENSON?
GOOF

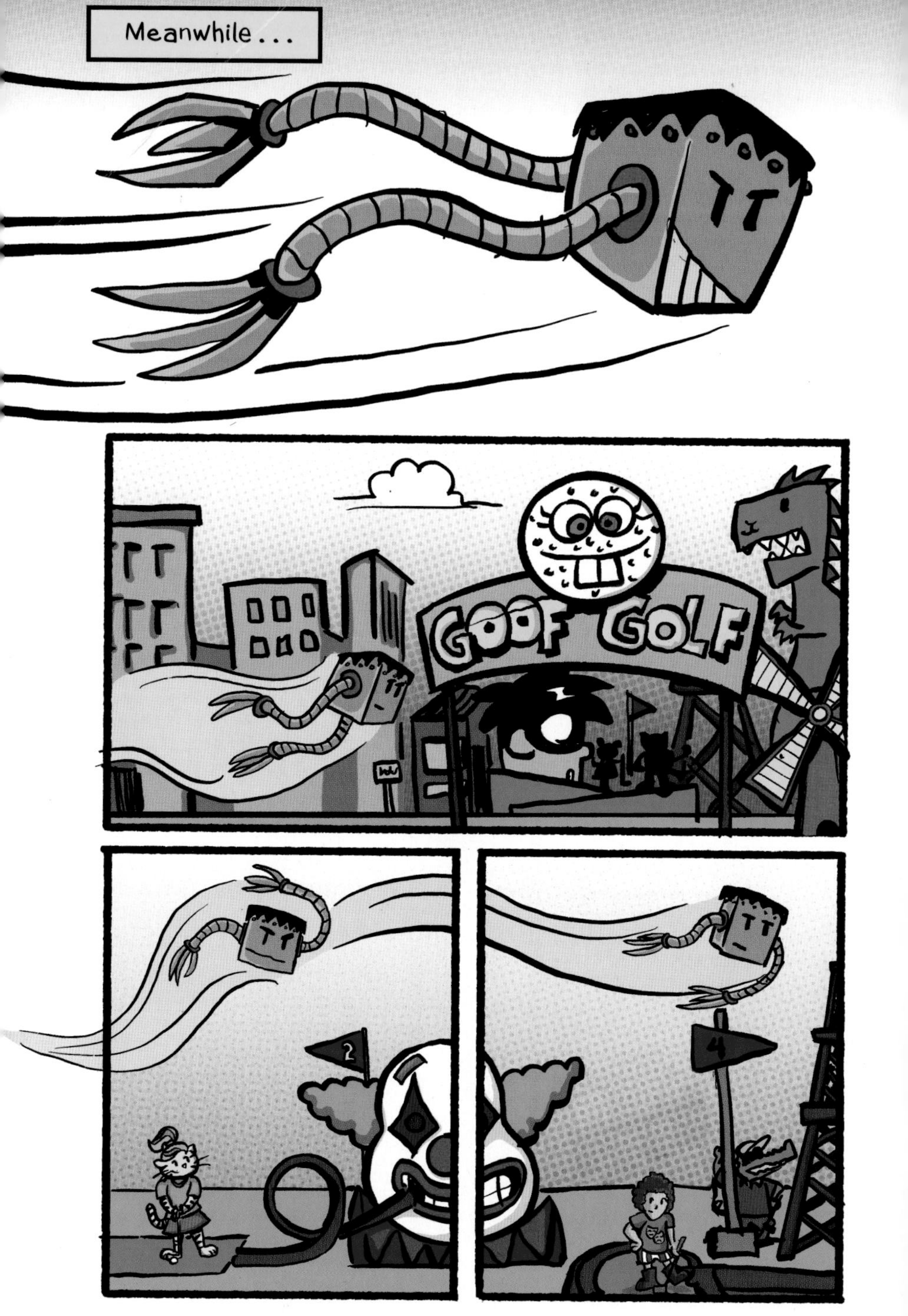
Meanwhile . . .
GOOF GOLF
2
4

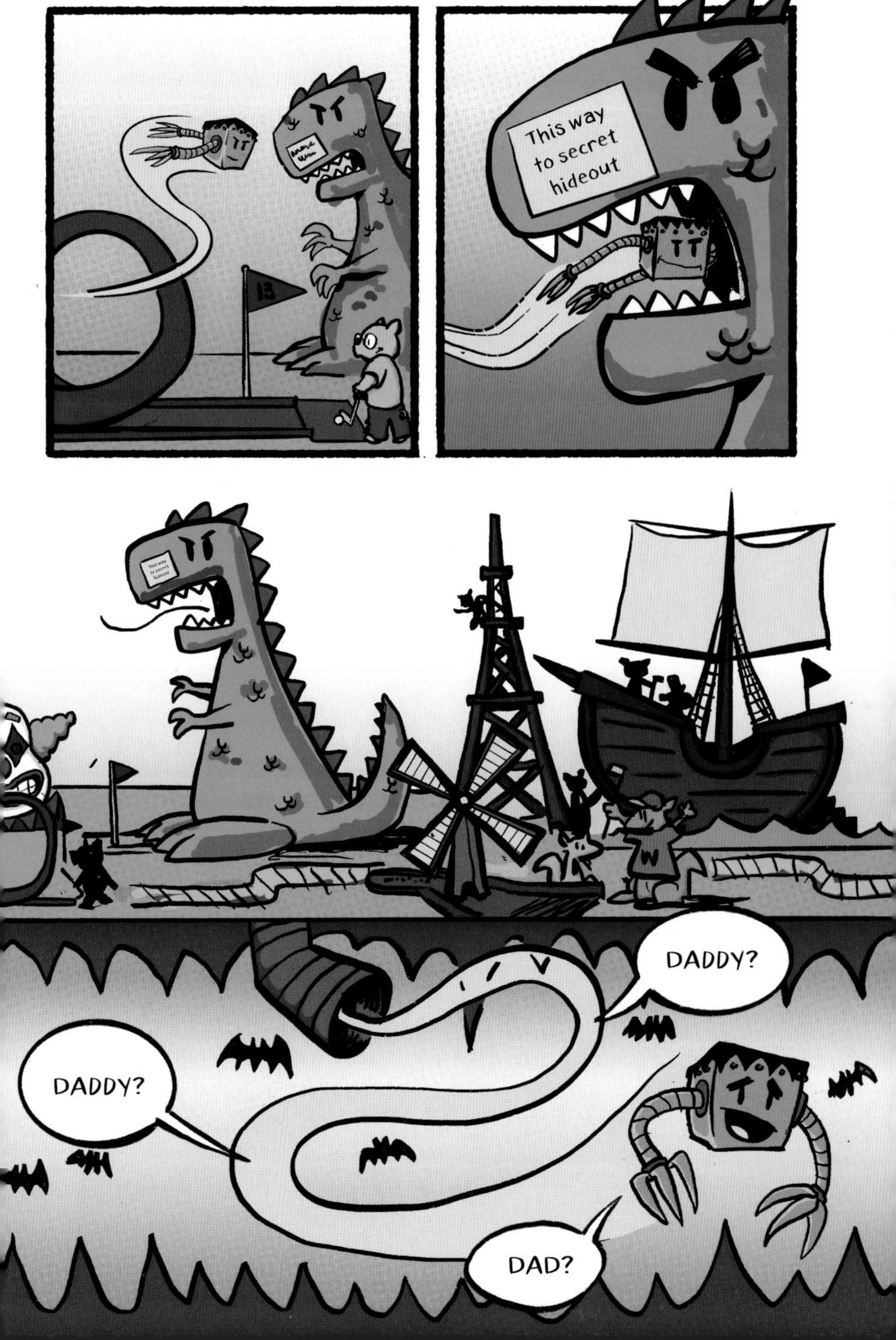
This way to secret hideout
DADDY?
DADDY?
DAD?

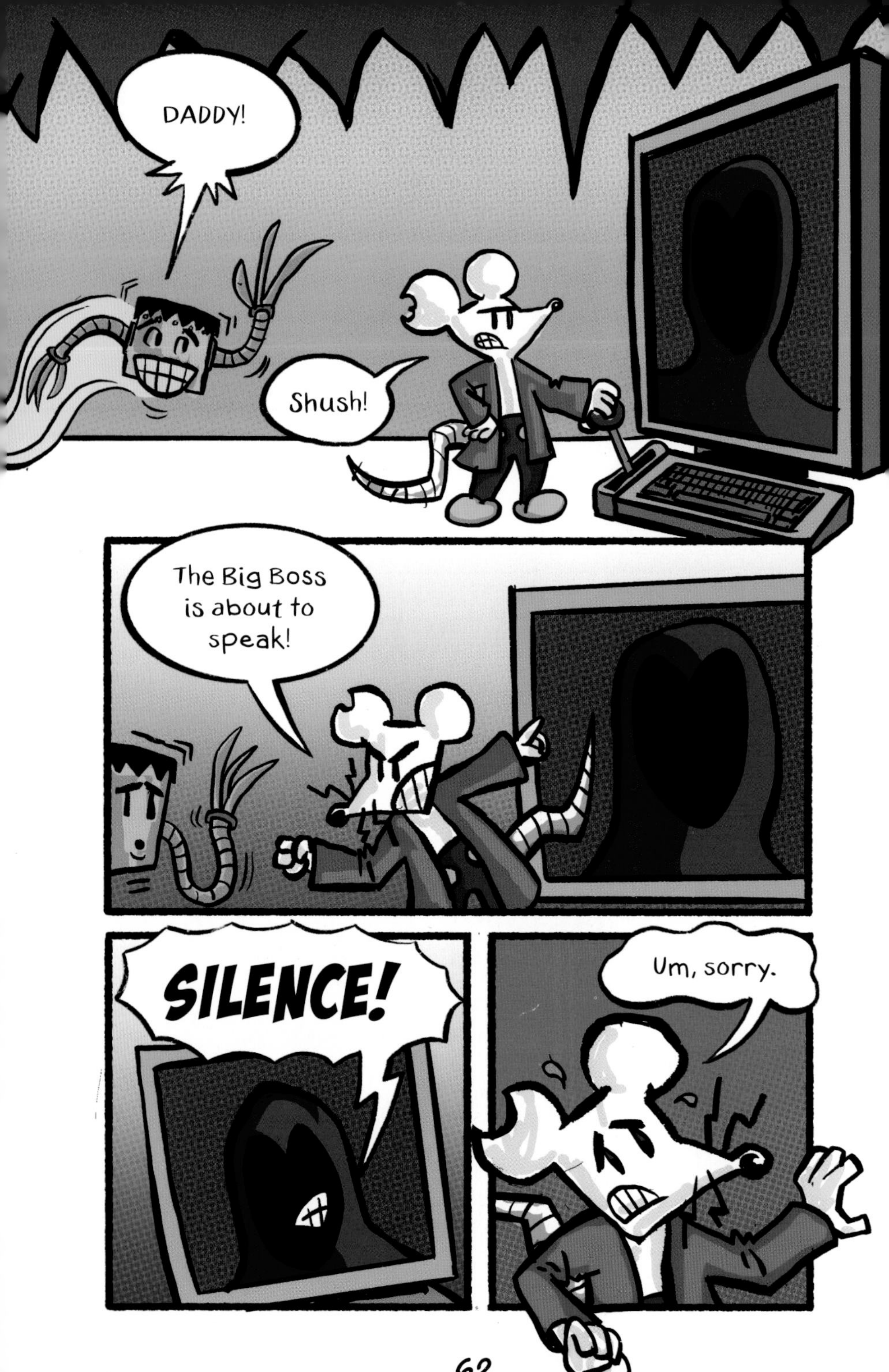
DADDY!
Shush!
The Big Boss is about to speak!
SILENCE!
Um, sorry.

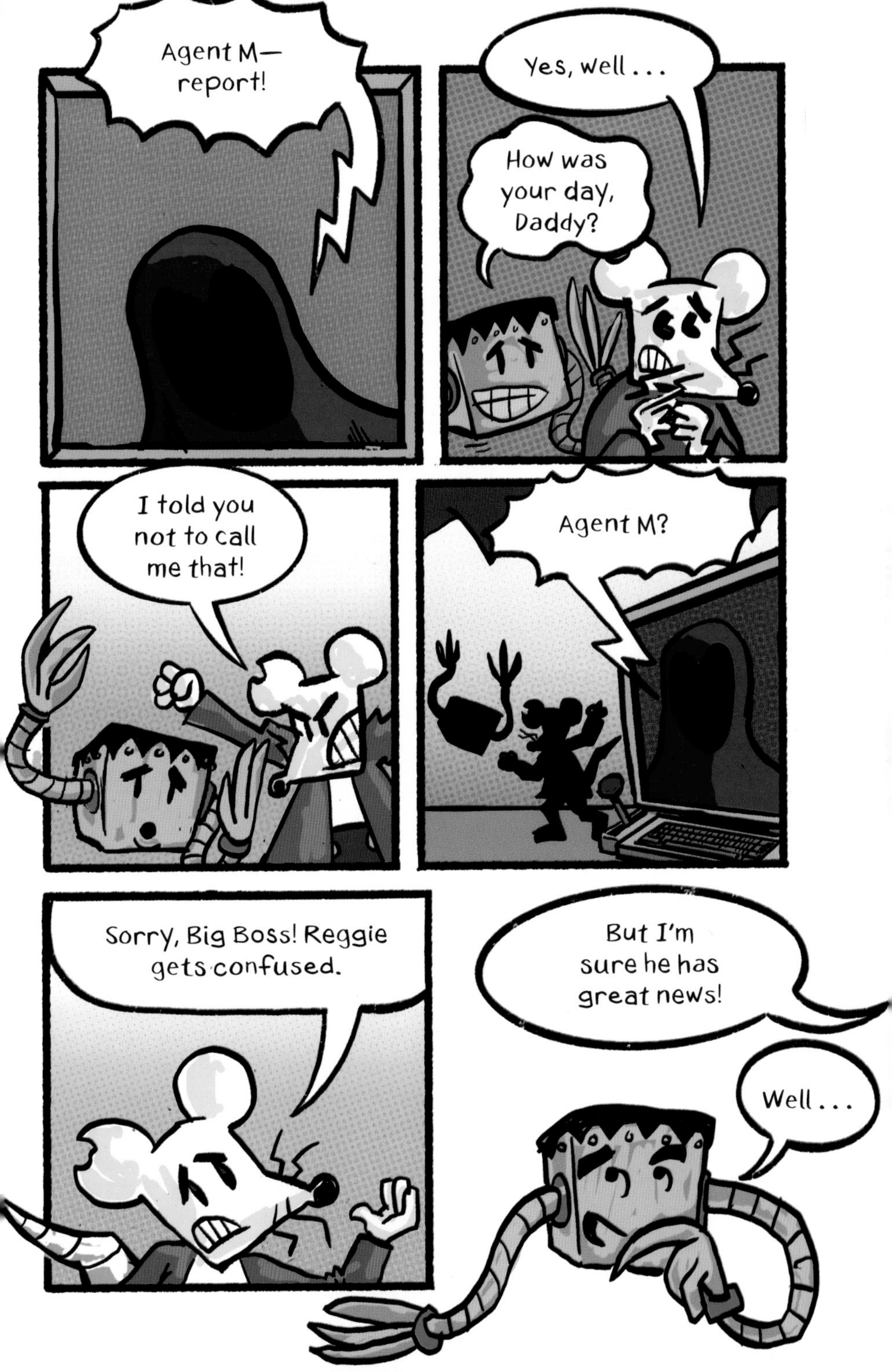
Agent M—
report!
Yes, well . . .
How was your day, Daddy?
I told you not to call me that!
Agent M?
Sorry, Big Boss! Reggie gets confused.
But I'm sure he has great news!
Well . . .

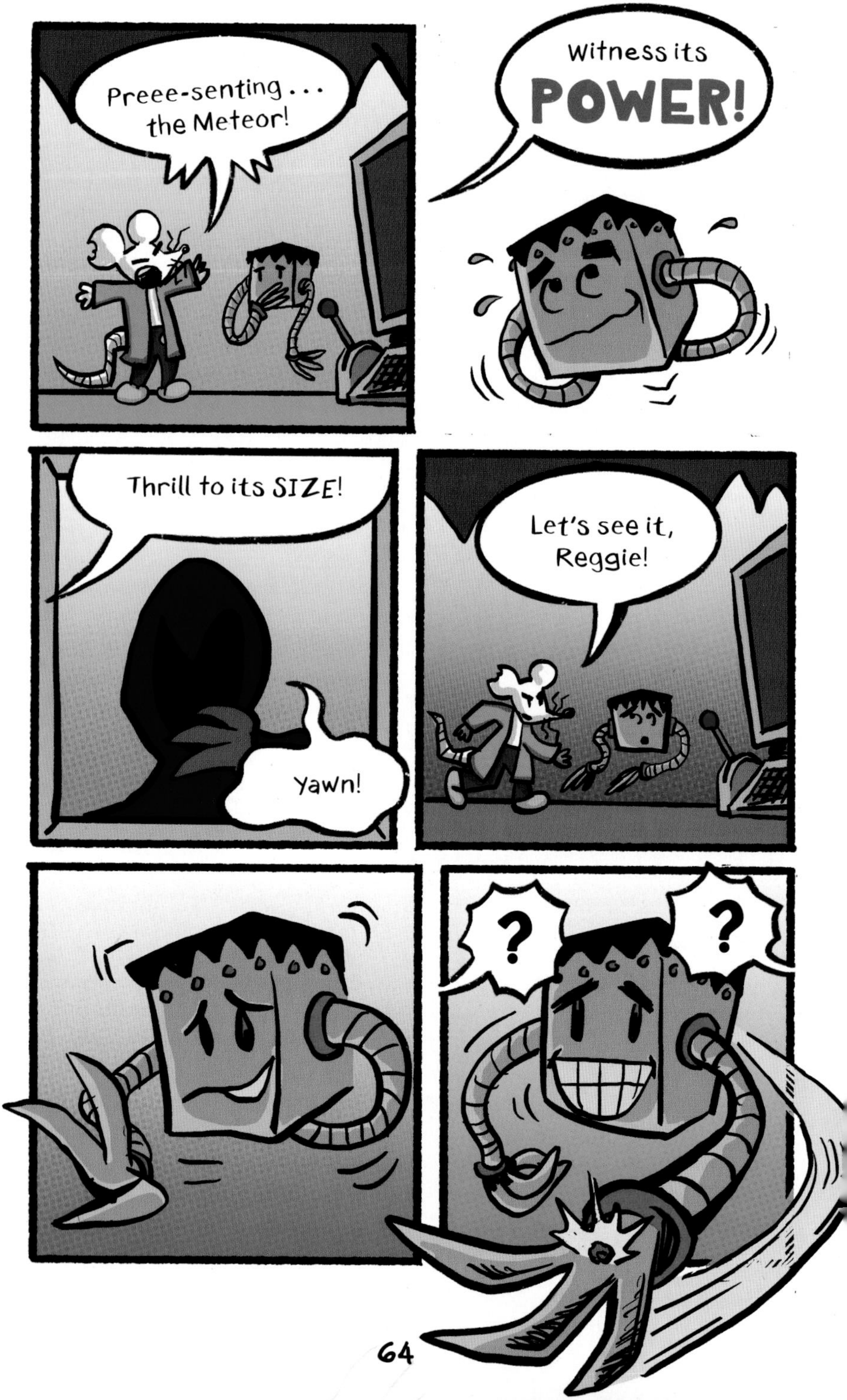
Preee-senting . . . the Meteor!
Witness its POWER!
Thrill to its SIZE!
Yawn!
Let's see it, Reggie!
?
?

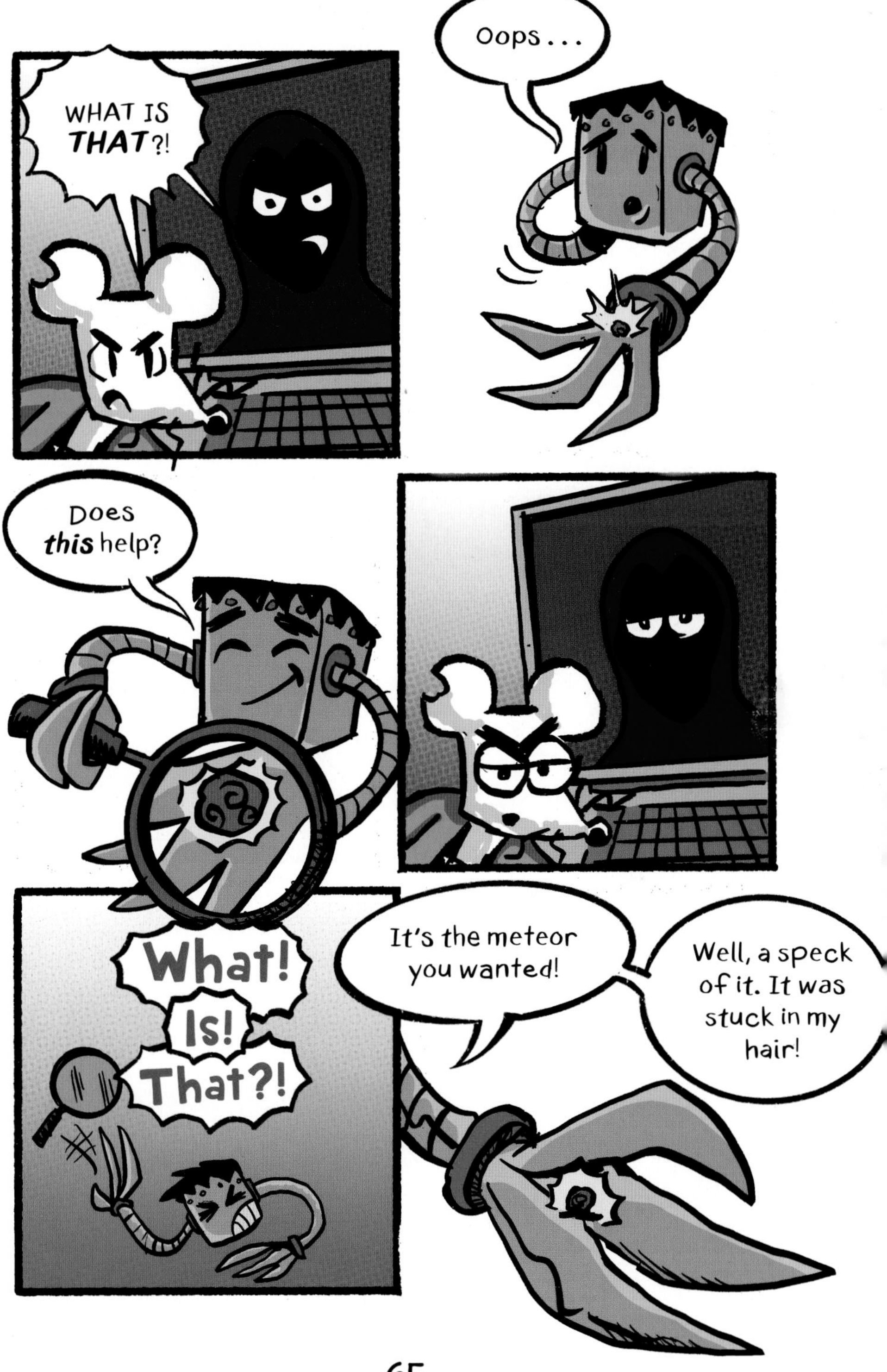
WHAT IS THAT?!
Oops . . .
Does this help?
What! Is! That?!
It's the meteor you wanted!
Well, a speck of it. It was stuck in my hair!

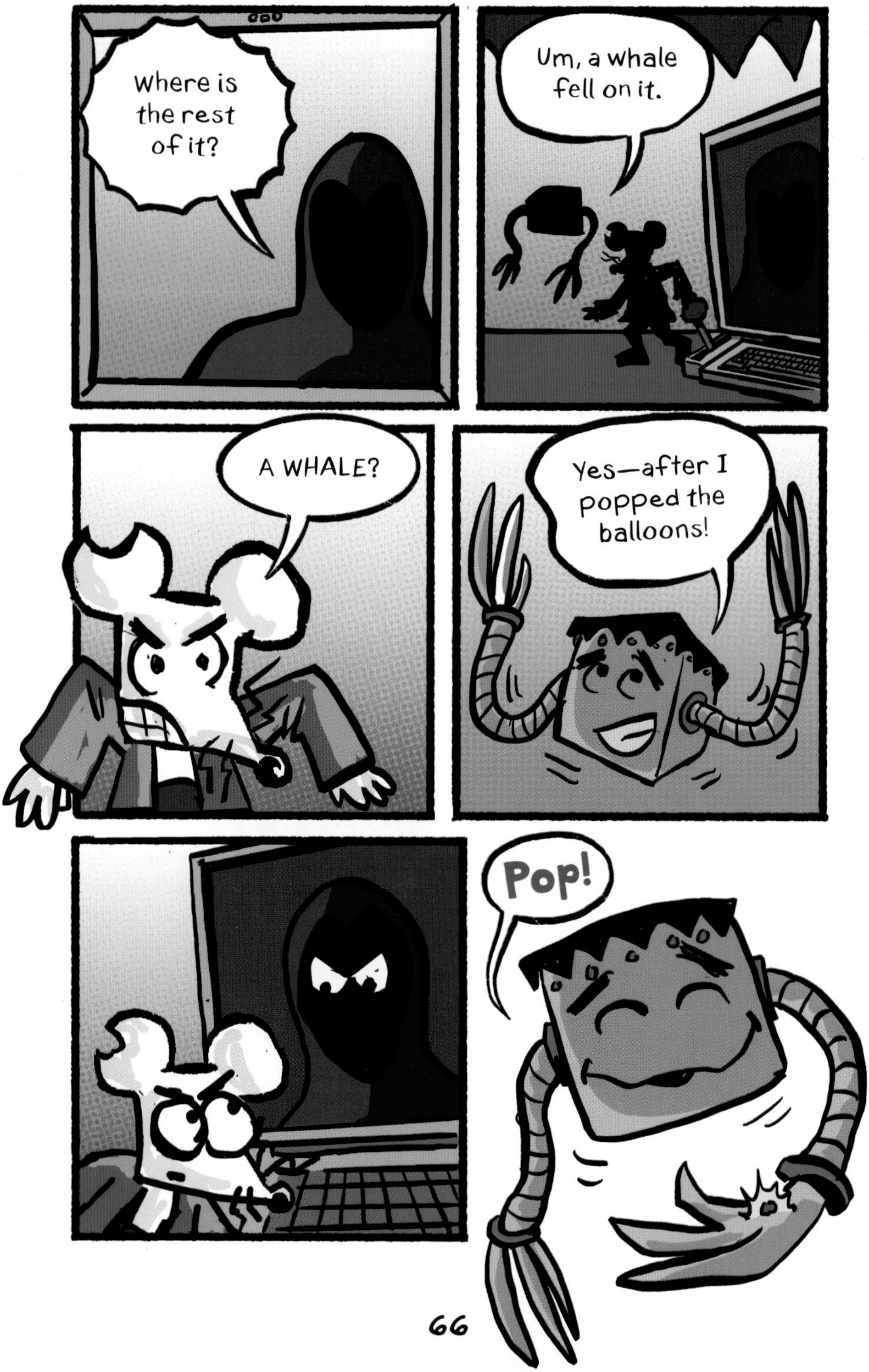
Where is the rest of it?
Um, a whale fell on it.
A WHALE?
Yes—after I popped the balloons!
Pop!

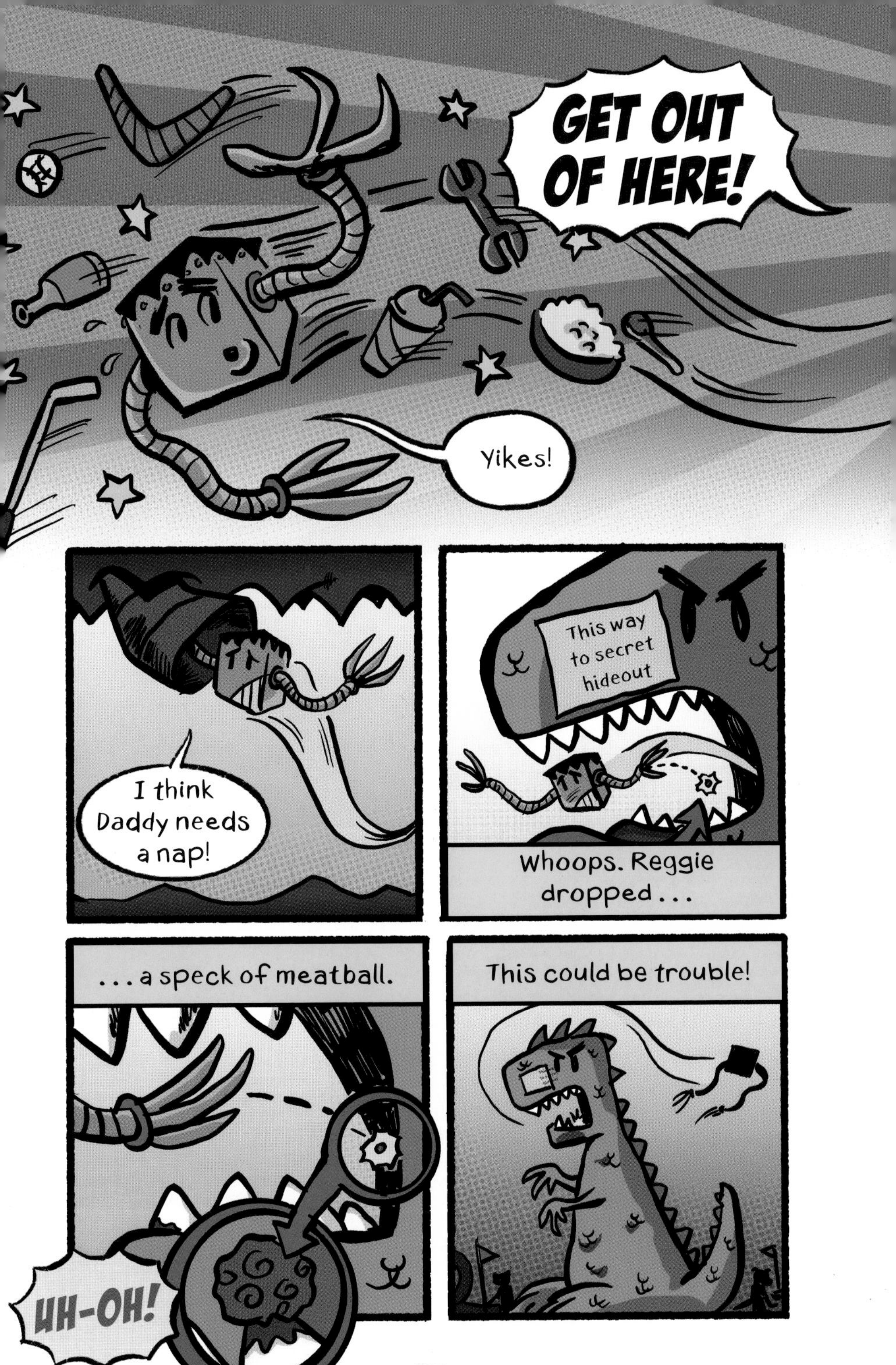
GET OUT OF HERE!
Yikes!
I think Daddy needs a nap!
This way to secret hideout
Whoops. Reggie dropped . . .
. . . a speck of meatball.
UH-OH!
This could be trouble!

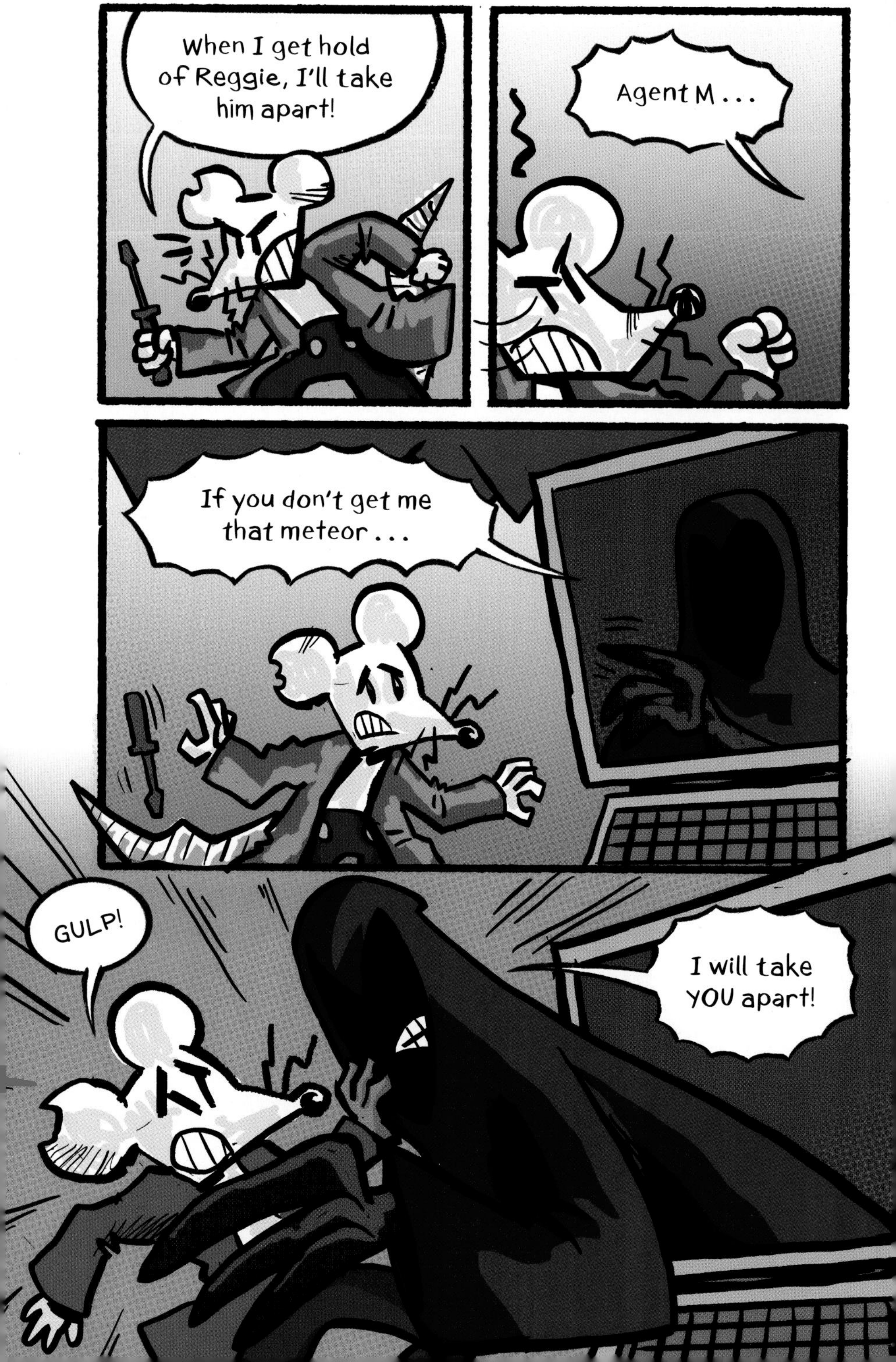
When I get hold of Reggie, I'll take him apart!
Agent M . . .
If you don't get me that meteor . . .
GULP!
I will take YOU apart!

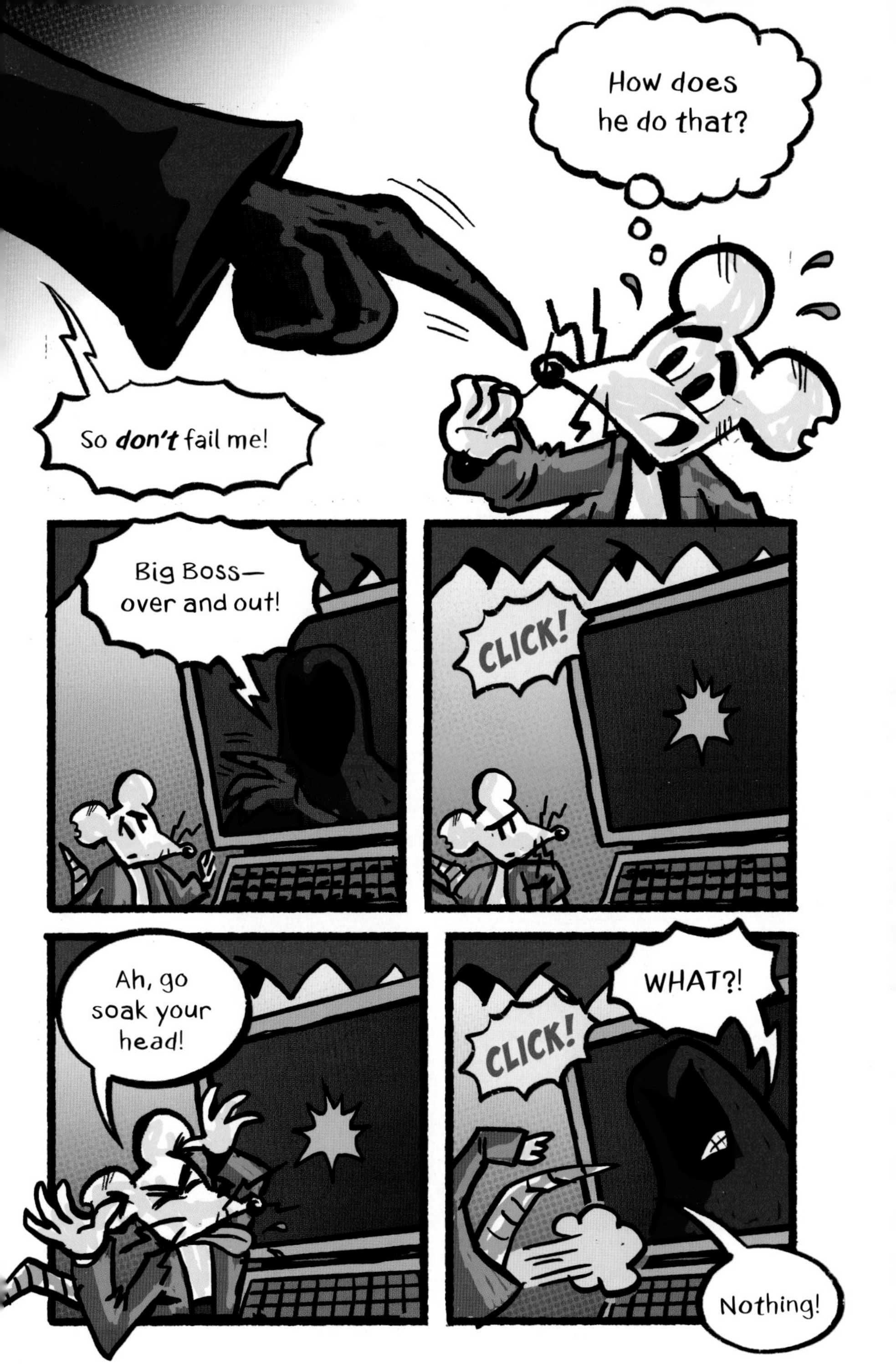
How does he do that?
So don't fail me!
Big Boss— over and out!
CLICK!
Ah, go soak your head!
WHAT?!
CLICK!
Nothing!

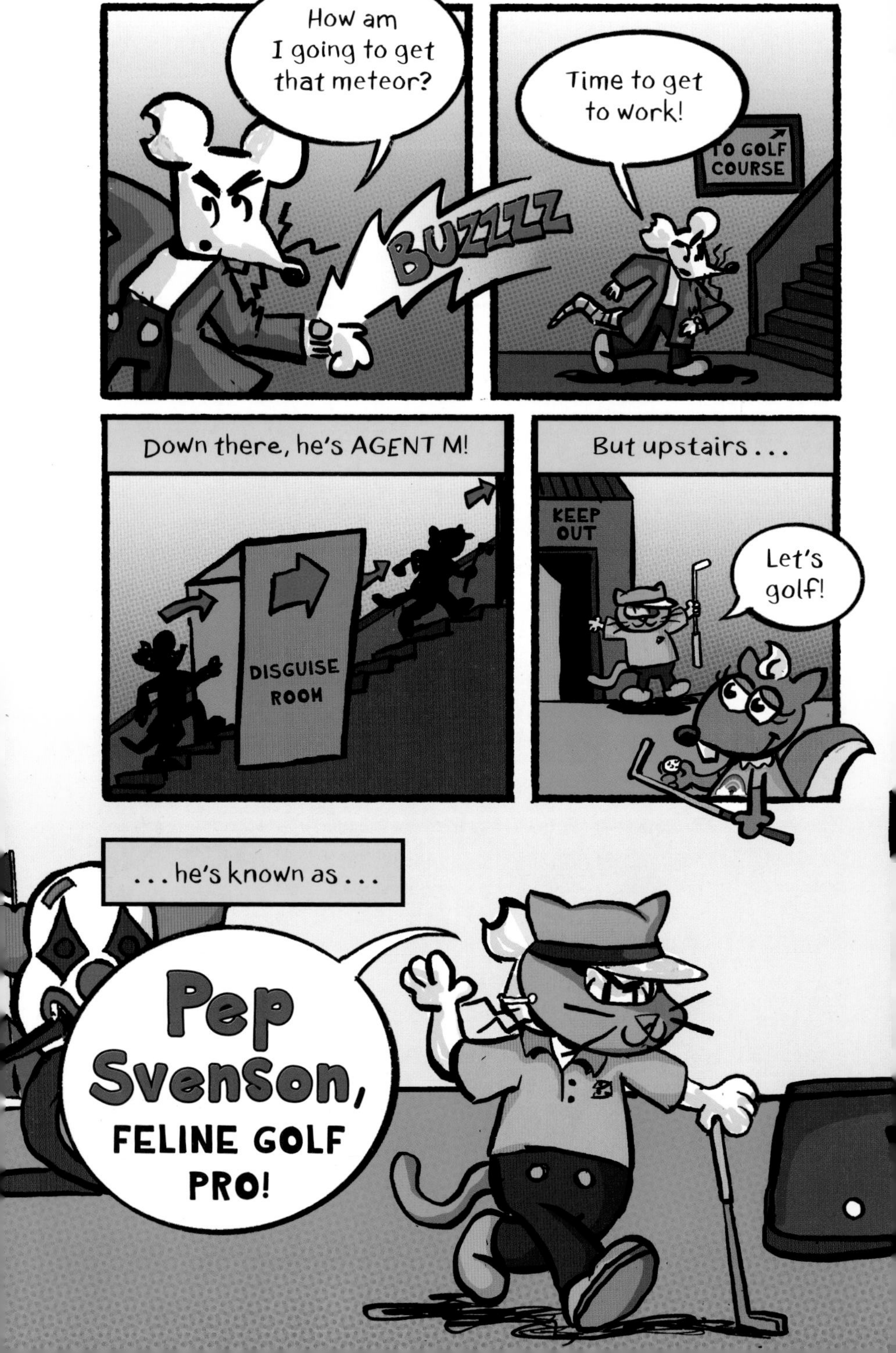
How am I going to get that meteor?
BUZZZZ
Time to get to work!
TO GOLF COURSE
Down there, he's AGENT M!
DISGUISE ROOM
But upstairs . . .
KEEP OUT
Let's golf!
. . . he's known as . . .
Pep Svenson, FELINE GOLF PRO!

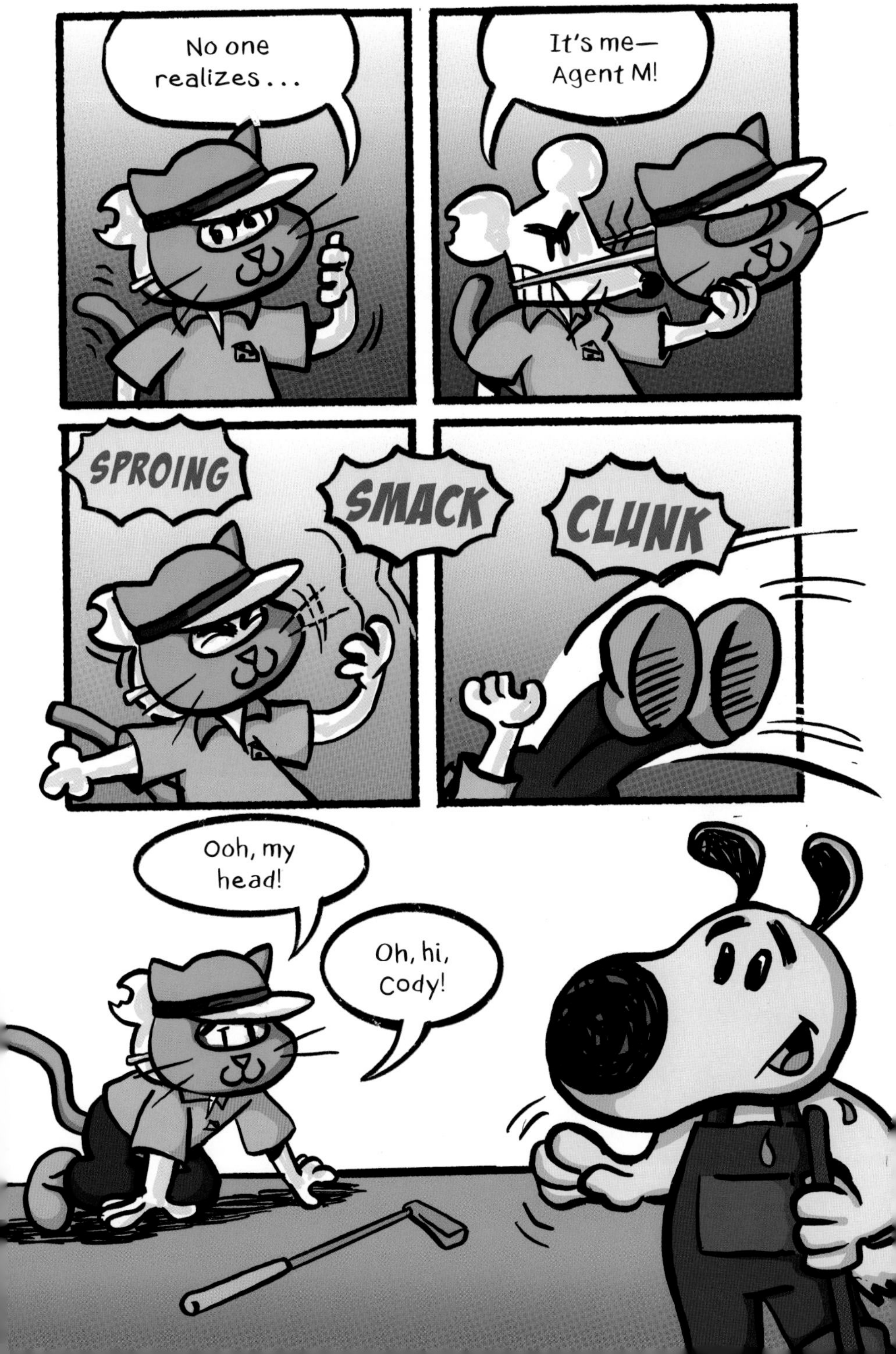
No one realizes . . .
It's me—Agent M!
SPROING
SMACK
CLUNK
Ooh, my head!
Oh, hi, Cody!

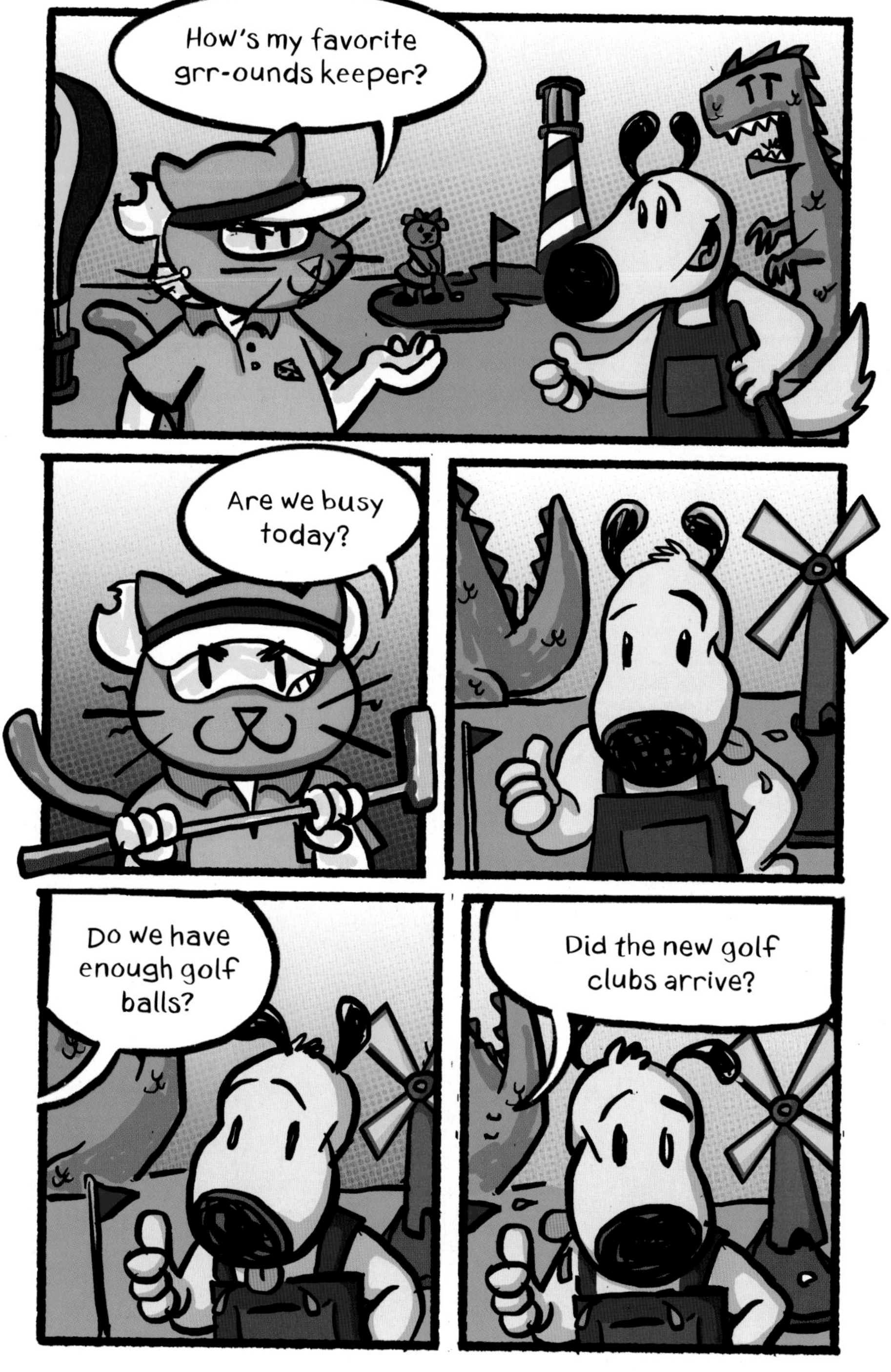
How's my favorite grr-ounds keeper?
Are we busy today?
Do we have enough golf balls?
Did the new golf clubs arrive?

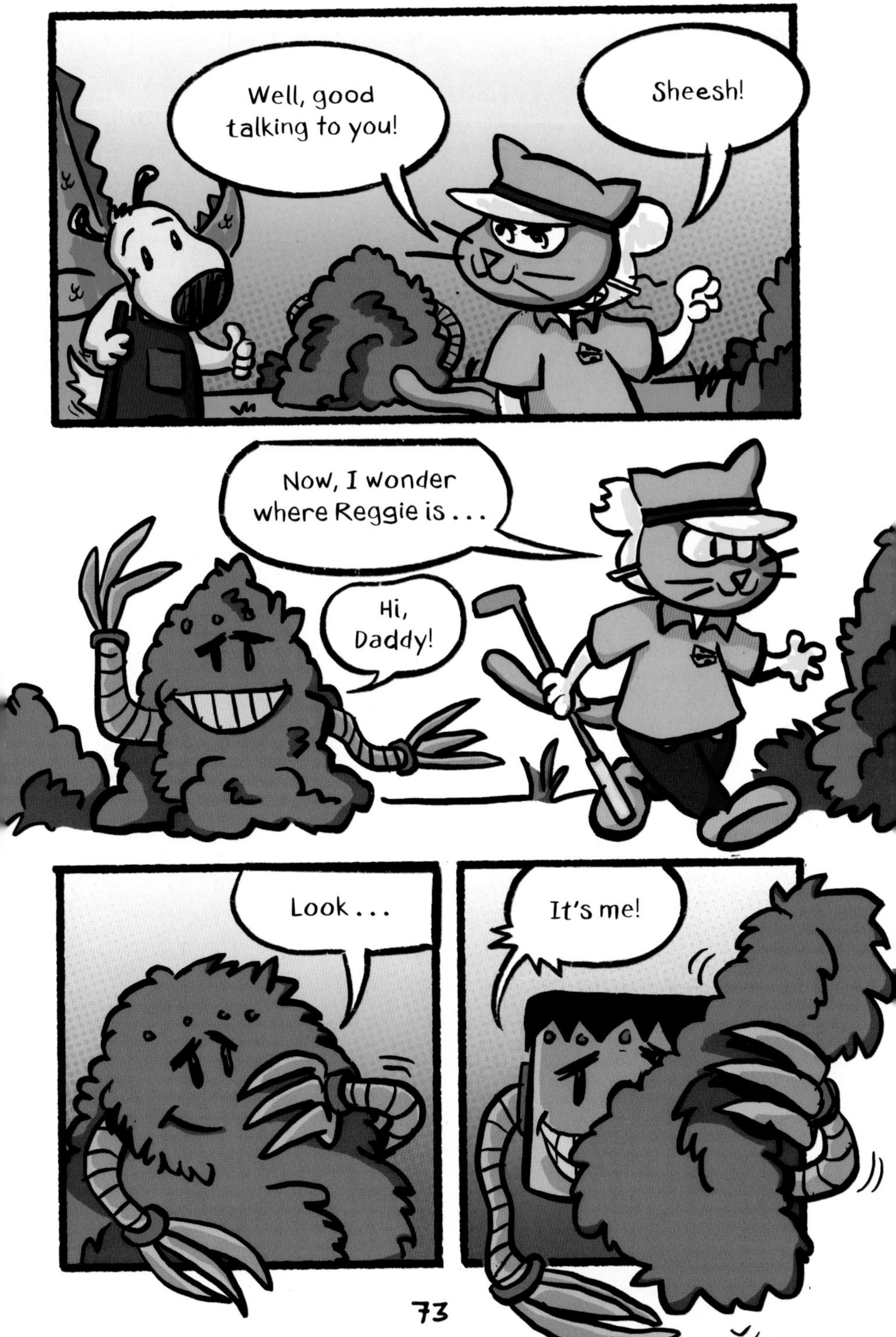
Well, good talking to you!
Sheesh!
Now, I wonder where Reggie is . . .
Hi, Daddy!
Look . . .
It's me!

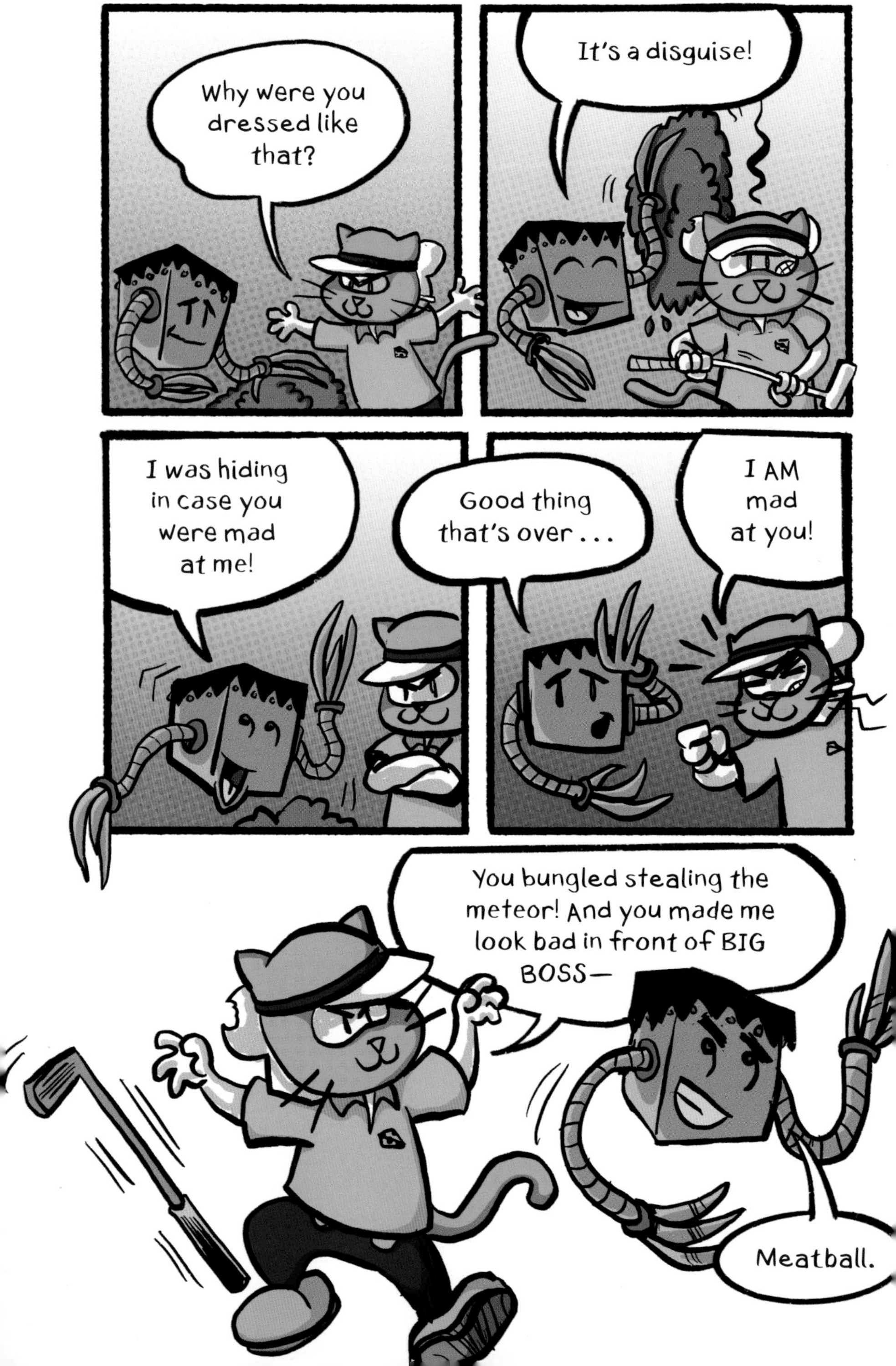
Why were you dressed like that?
It's a disguise!
I was hiding in case you were mad at me!
Good thing that's over . . .
I AM mad at you!
You bungled stealing the meteor! And you made me look bad in front of BIG BOSS—
Meatball.

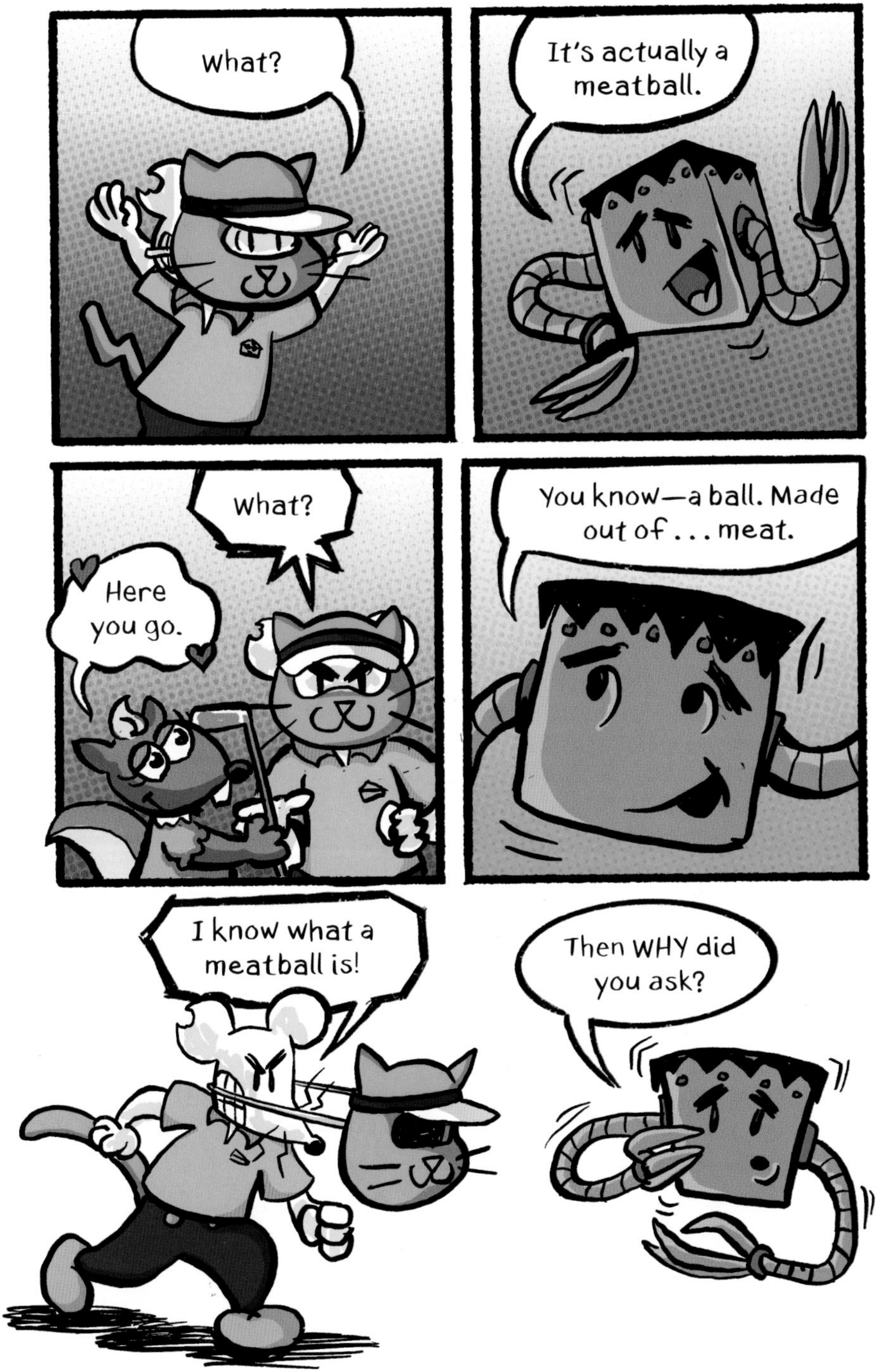
What?
It's actually a meatball.
What?
Here you go.
You know—a ball. Made out of . . . meat.
I know what a meatball is!
Then WHY did you ask?

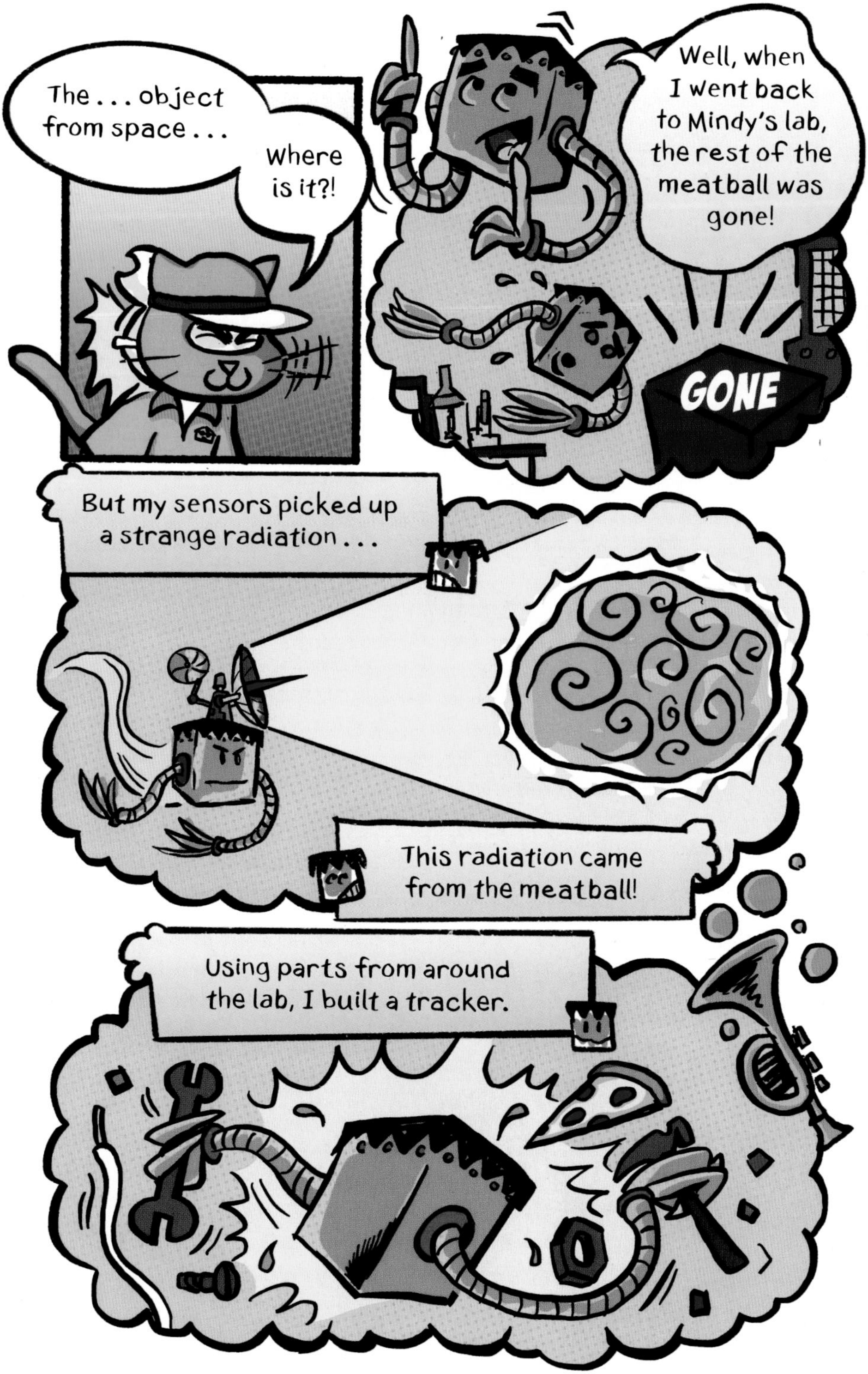
The . . . object from space . . .
Where is it?!
Well, when I went back to Mindy's lab, the rest of the meatball was gone!
GONE
But my sensors picked up a strange radiation . . .
This radiation came from the meatball!
Using parts from around the lab, I built a tracker.

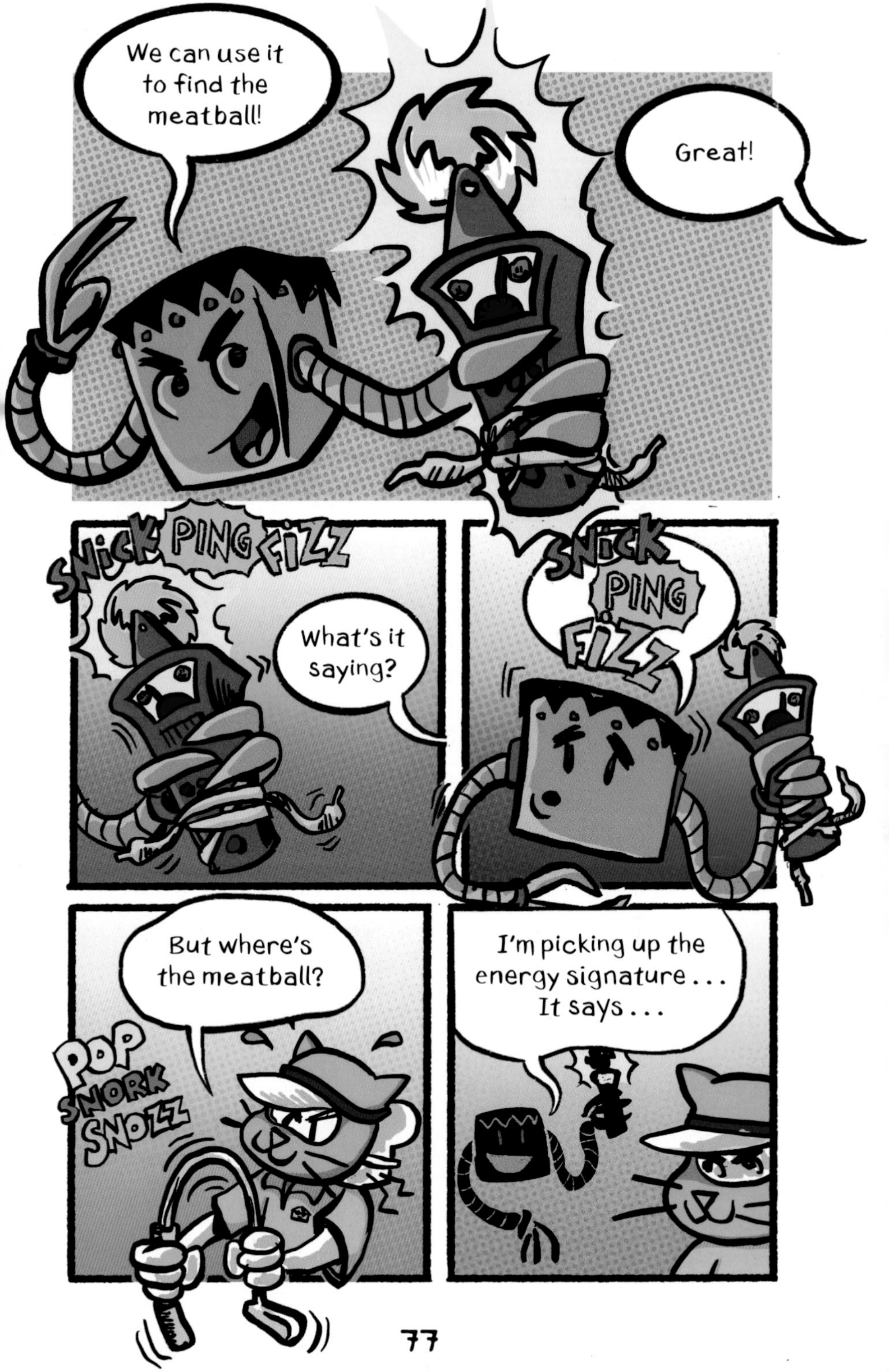
We can use it to find the meatball!
Great!
SNICK PING FIZZ
What's it saying?
SNICK
PING
FIZZ
But where's the meatball?
POP
SNORK
SNOZZ
I'm picking up the energy signature . . . It says . . .

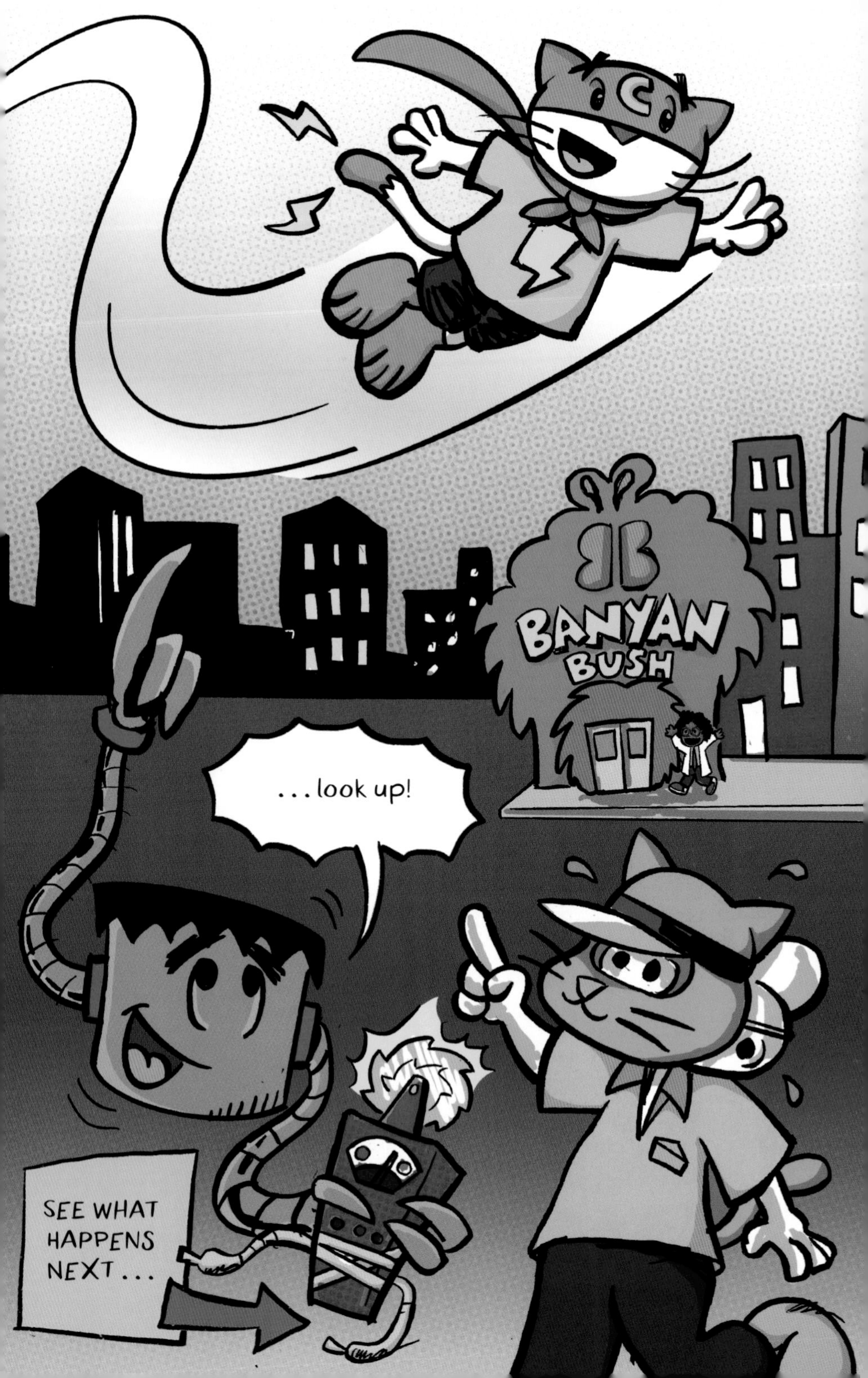
BANYAN BUSH
...look up!
SEE WHAT HAPPENS NEXT...

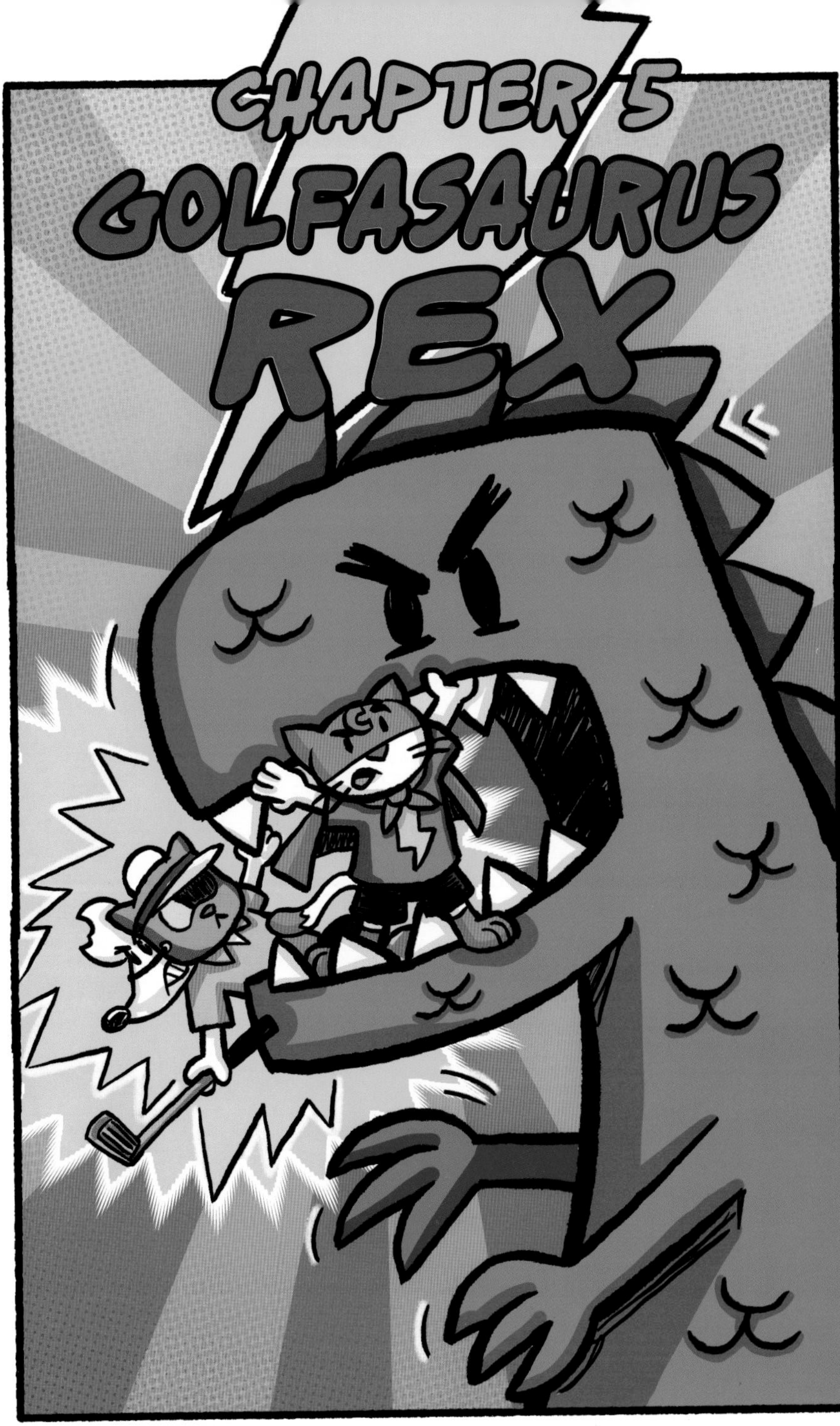
CHAPTER 5
GOLFASAURUS
REX

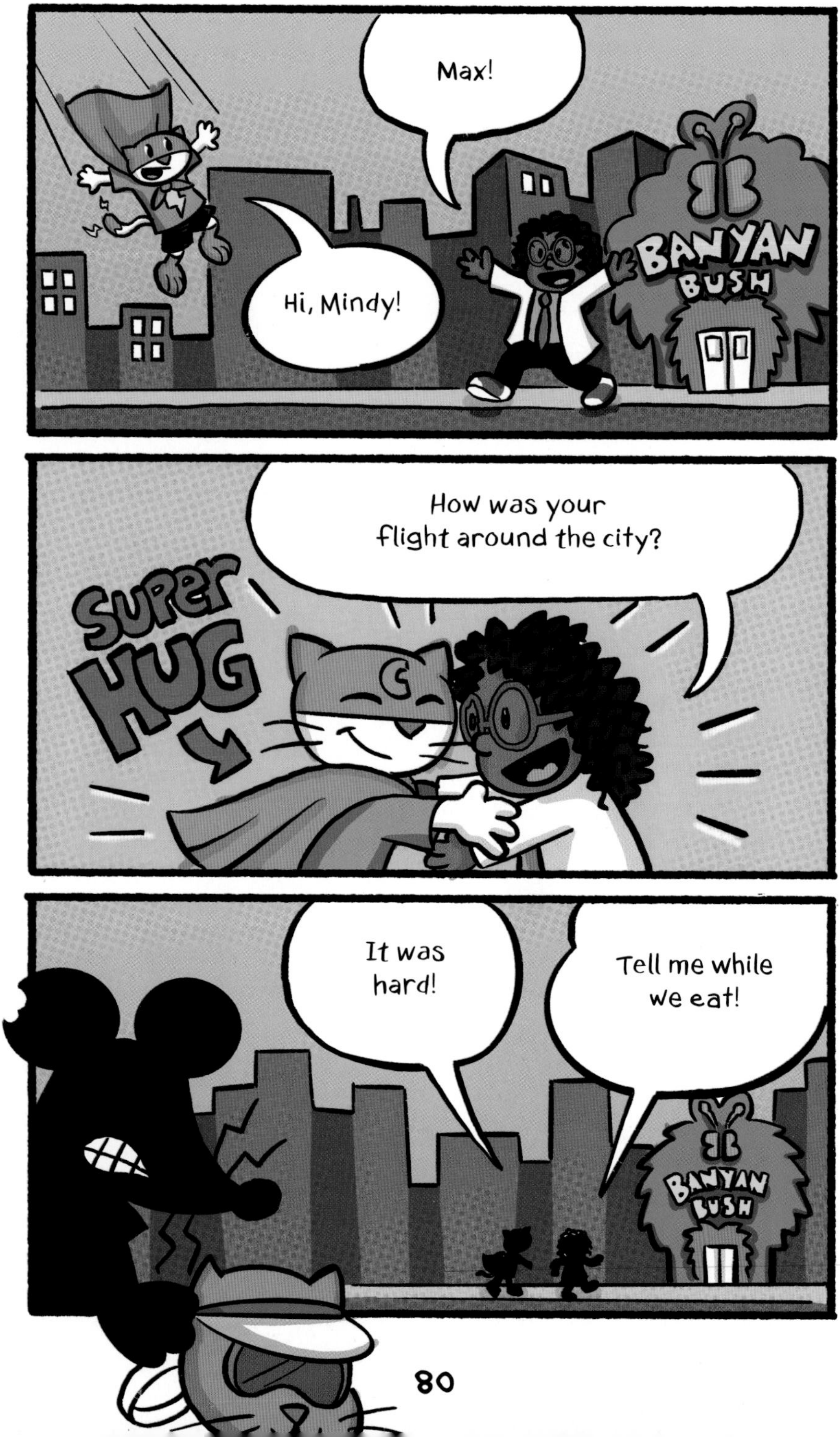
Max!
Hi, Mindy!
BANYAN BUSH
How was your flight around the city?
Super HUG
It was hard!
Tell me while we eat!
BANYAN BUSH

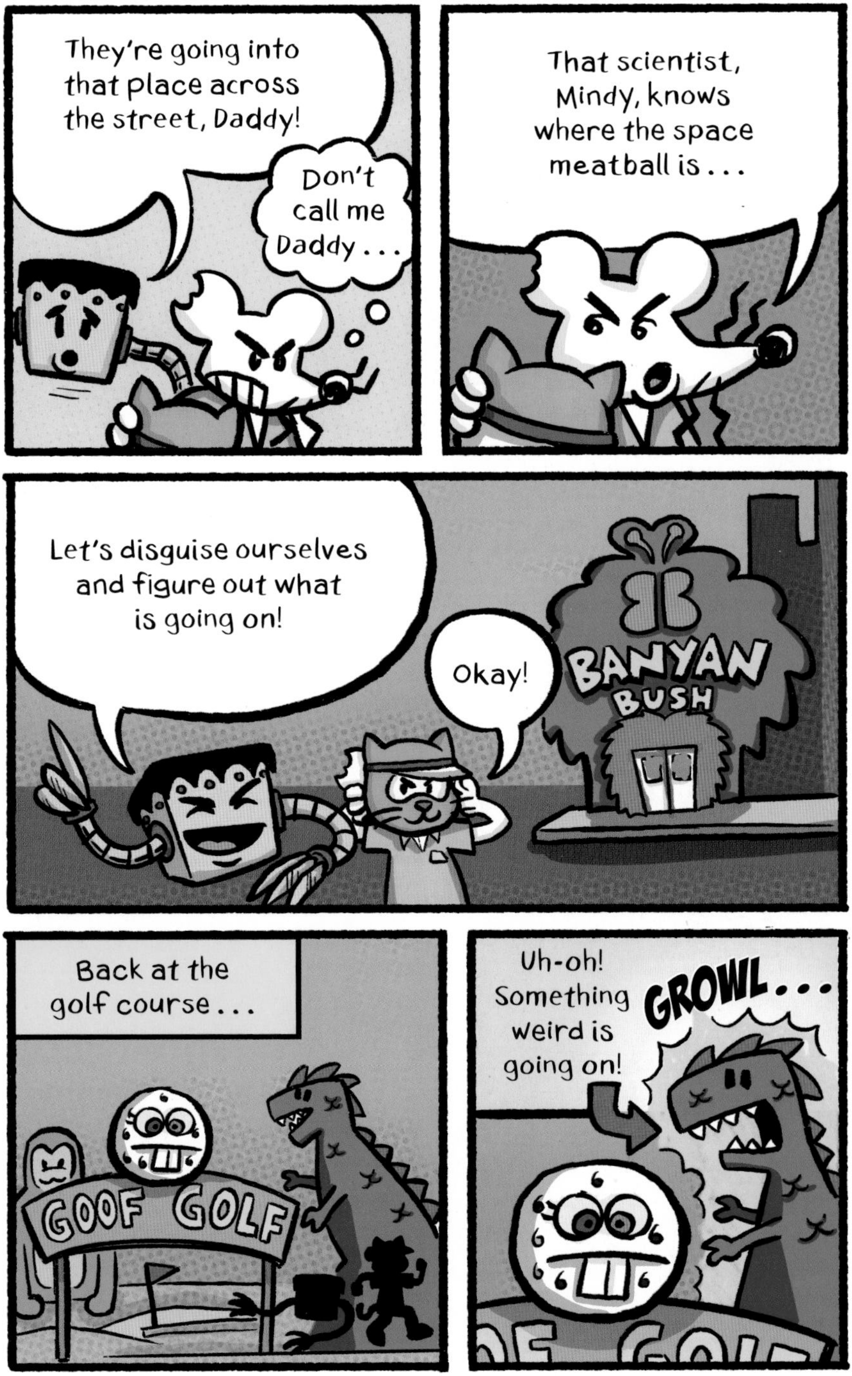

They're going into that place across the street, Daddy!
Don't call me Daddy . . .
That scientist, Mindy, knows where the space meatball is . . .
Let's disguise ourselves and figure out what is going on!
Okay!
BANYAN BUSH
Back at the golf course . . .
GOOF GOLF
Uh-oh! Something weird is going on!
GROWL . . .

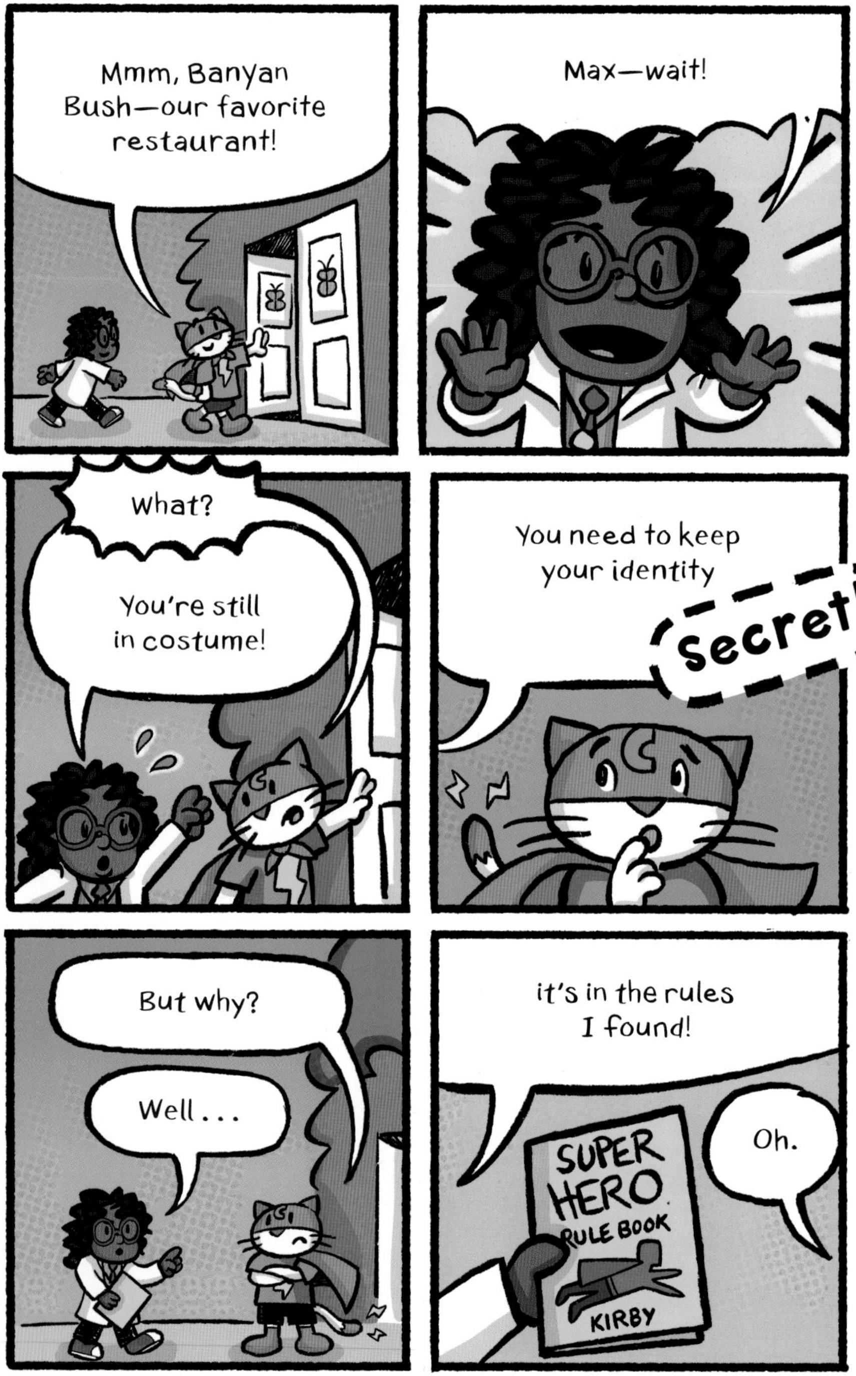
Mmm, Banyan Bush—our favorite restaurant!
Max—wait!
What?
You're still in costume!
You need to keep your identity
Secret!
But why?
Well . . .
it's in the rules I found!
SUPER HERO RULE BOOK
KIRBY
Oh.

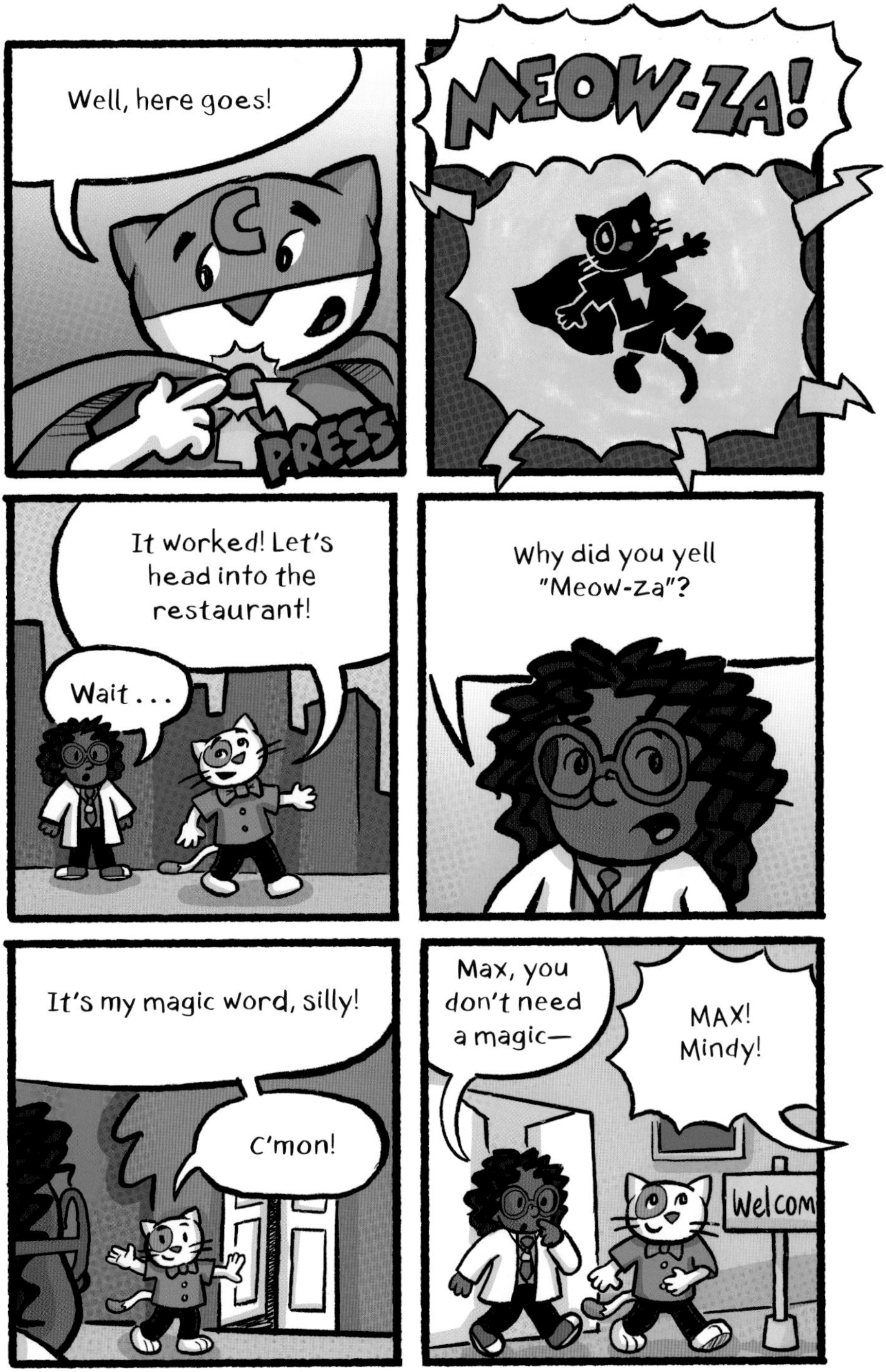
Well, here goes!
PRESS
MEOW-ZA!
It worked! Let's head into the restaurant!
Wait . . .
Why did you yell "Meow-Za"?
It's my magic word, silly!
C'mon!
Max, you don't need a magic—
MAX! Mindy!
Welcom

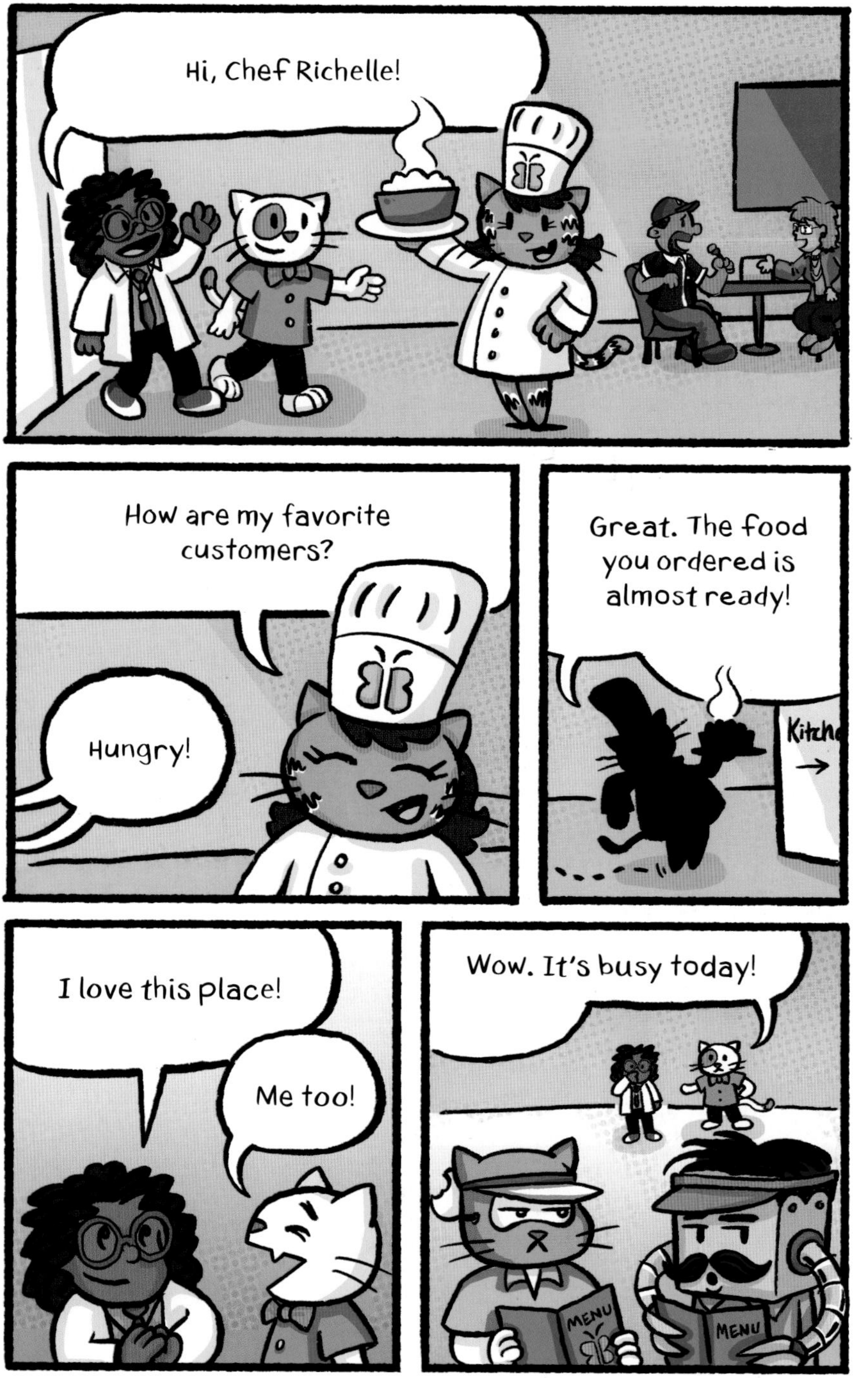
Hi, Chef Richelle!
How are my favorite customers?
Hungry!
Great. The food you ordered is almost ready!
I love this place!
Me too!
Wow. It's busy today!
MENU
MENU

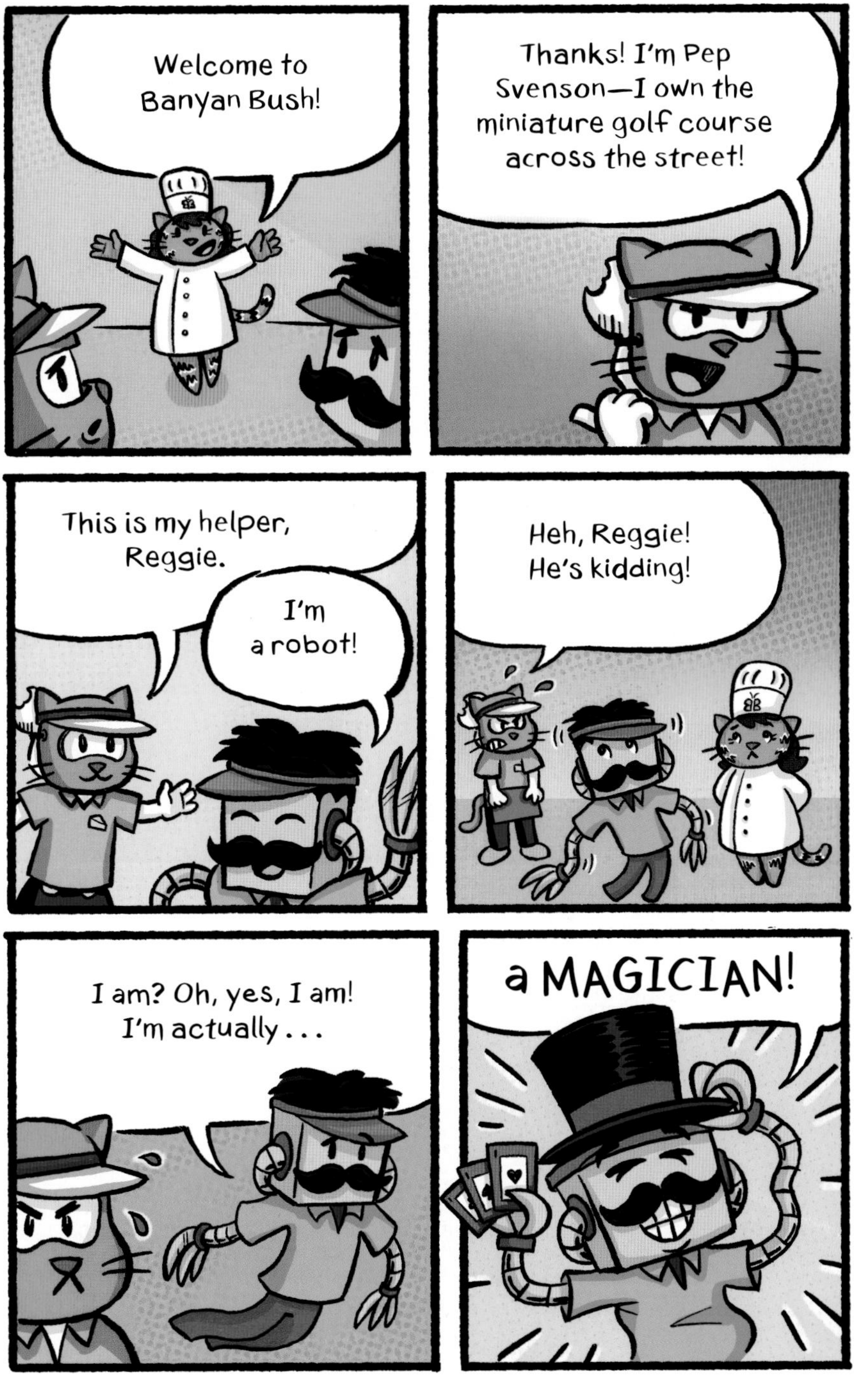
Welcome to Banyan Bush!
Thanks! I'm Pep Svenson—I own the miniature golf course across the street!
This is my helper, Reggie.
I'm a robot!
Heh, Reggie! He's kidding!
I am? Oh, yes, I am! I'm actually . . .
a MAGICIAN!

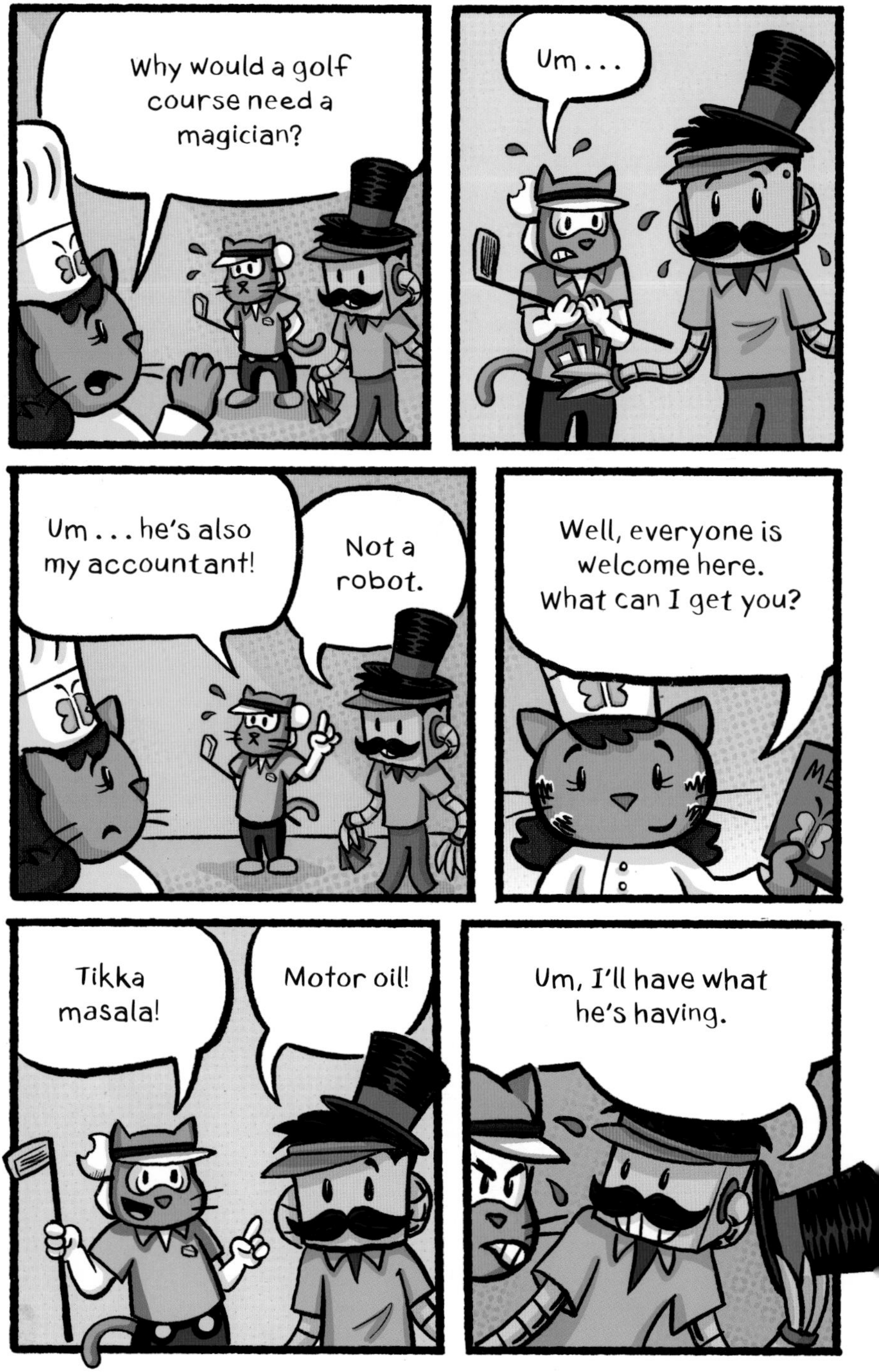
Why would a golf course need a magician?
Um . . .
Um . . . he's also my accountant!
Not a robot.
Well, everyone is welcome here. What can I get you?
Tikka masala!
Motor oil!
Um, I'll have what he's having.

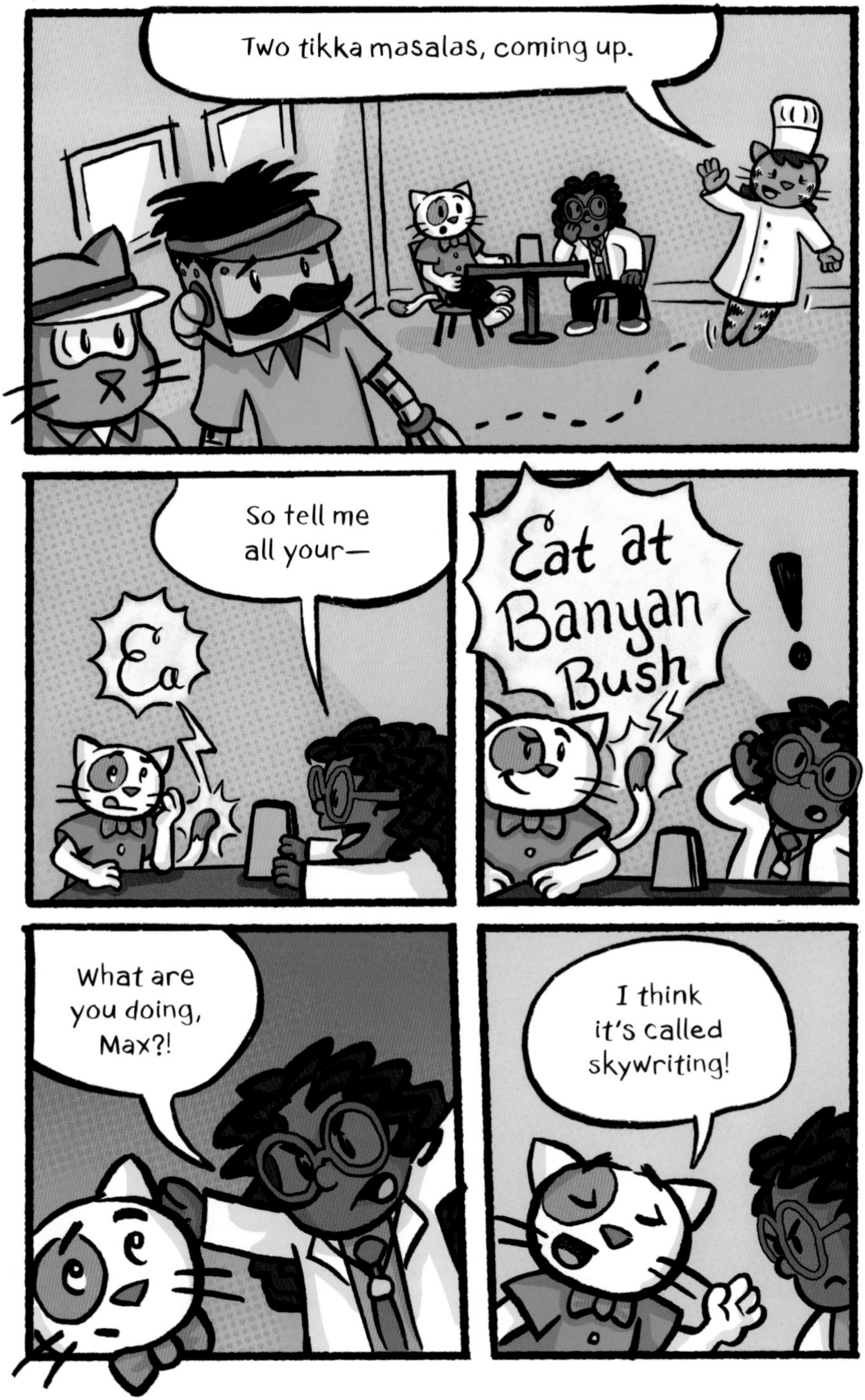
Two tikka masalas, coming up.
So tell me all your—
Ea
Eat at Banyan Bush
!
What are you doing, Max?!
I think it's called skywriting!

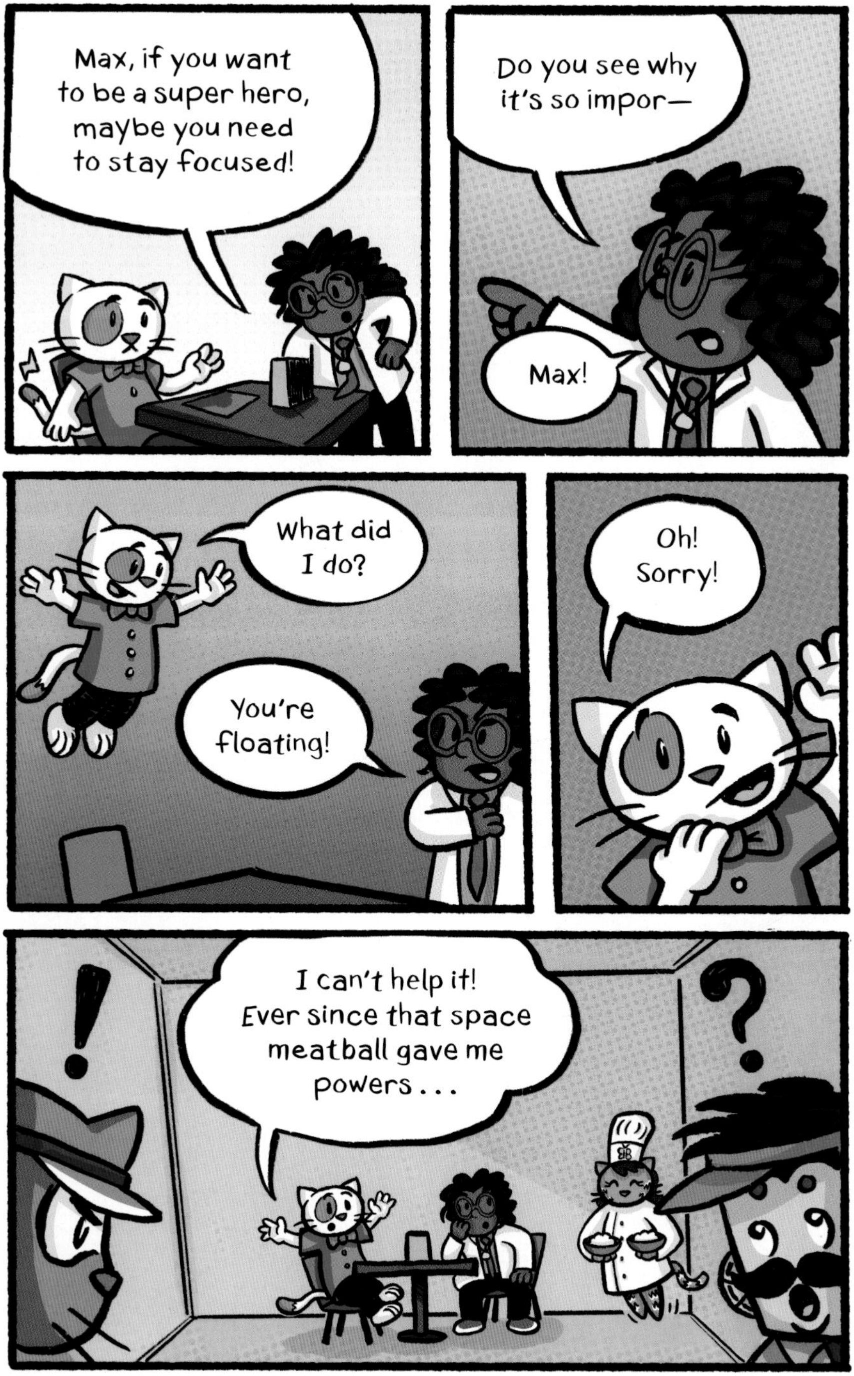
Max, if you want to be a super hero, maybe you need to stay focused!
Do you see why it's so impor—
Max!
What did I do?
You're floating!
Oh! Sorry!
!
I can't help it! Ever since that space meatball gave me powers . . .
?

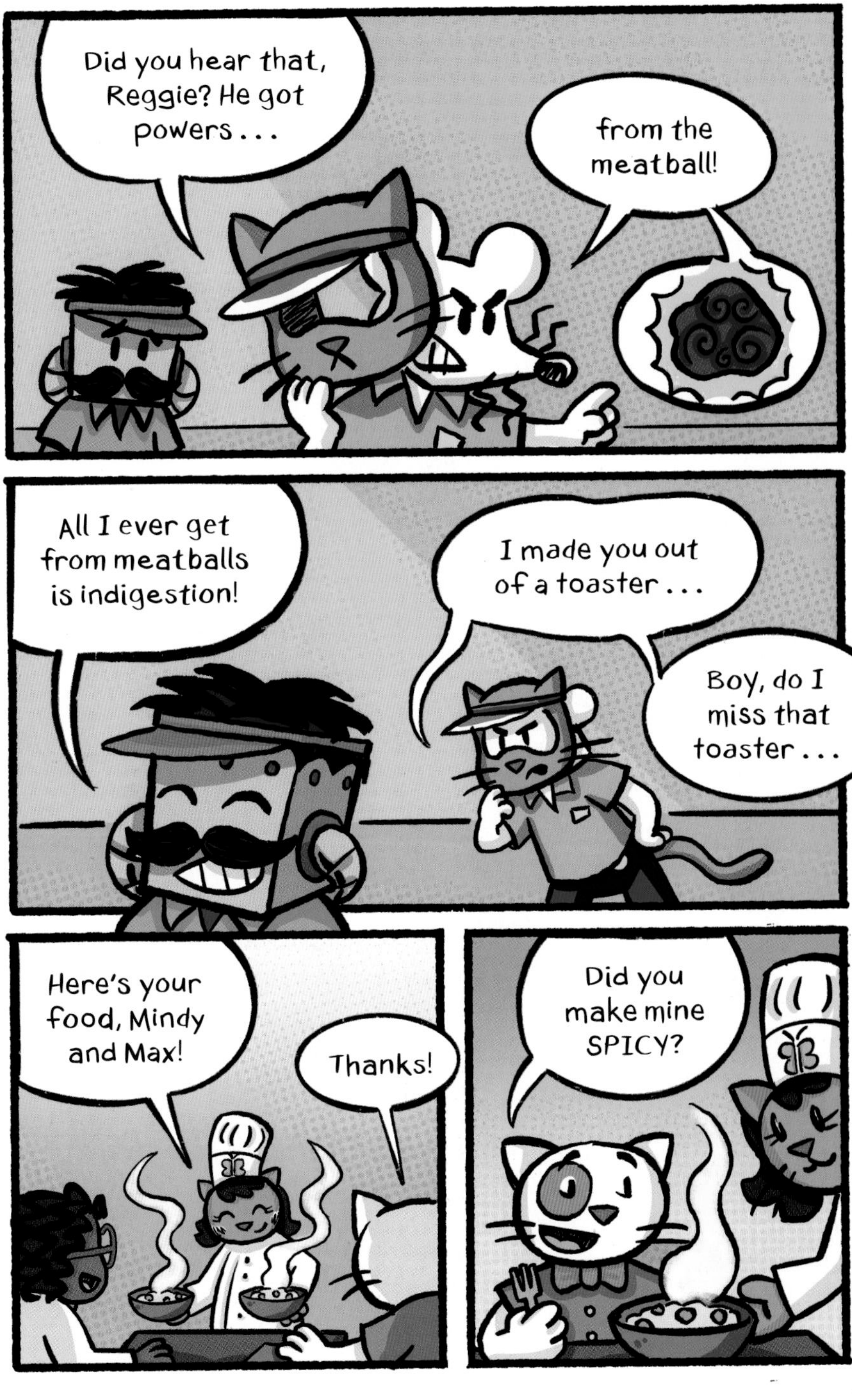
Did you hear that, Reggie? He got powers . . .
from the meatball!
All I ever get from meatballs is indigestion!
I made you out of a toaster . . .
Boy, do I miss that toaster . . .
Here's your food, Mindy and Max!
Thanks!
Did you make mine SPICY?

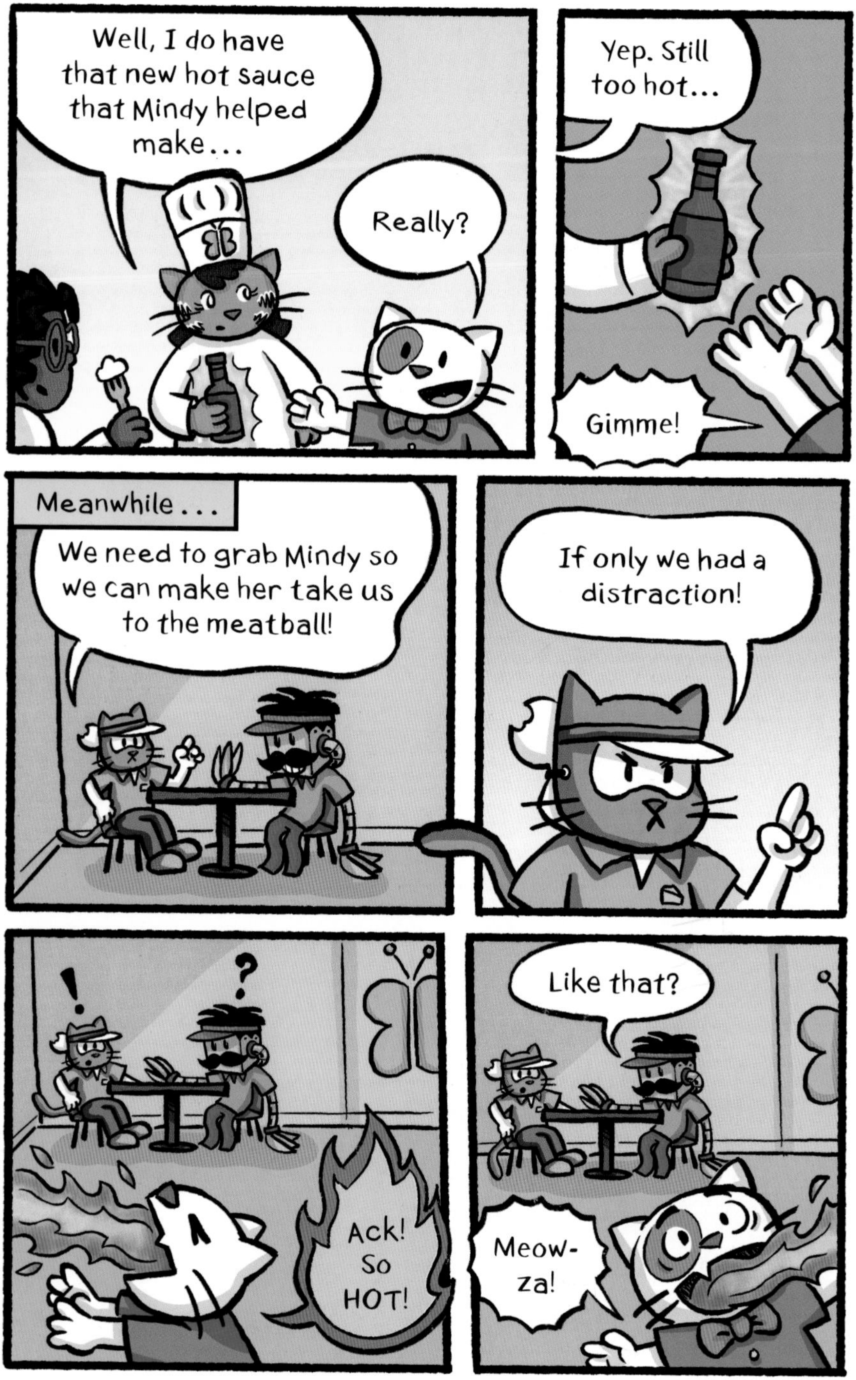
Well, I do have that new hot sauce that Mindy helped make...
Really?
Yep. Still too hot...
Gimme!
Meanwhile...
We need to grab Mindy so we can make her take us to the meatball!
If only we had a distraction!
!
?
Ack! So HOT!
Like that?
Meow-za!

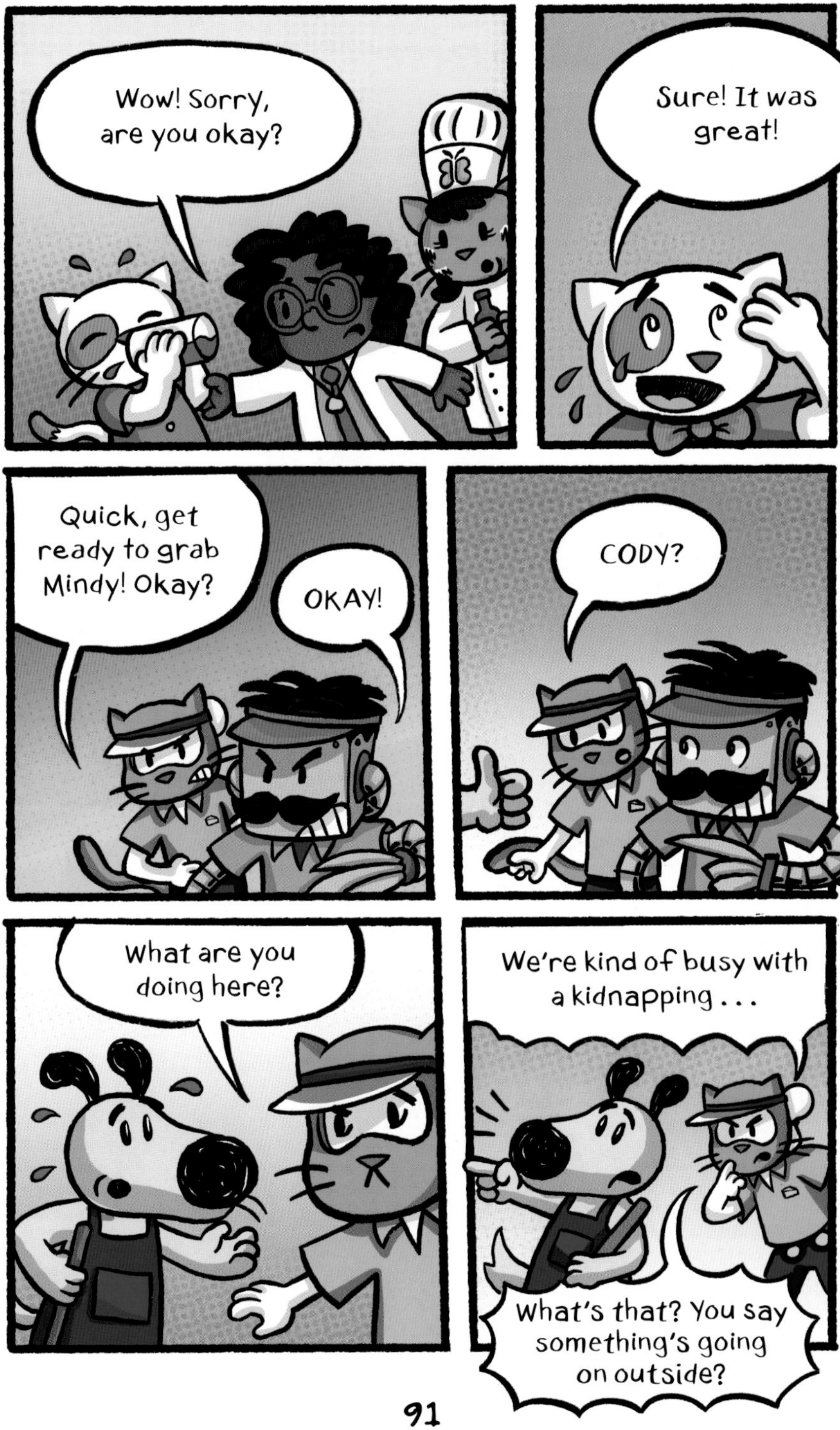
Wow! Sorry, are you okay?
Sure! It was great!
Quick, get ready to grab Mindy! Okay?
OKAY!
CODY?
What are you doing here?
We're kind of busy with a kidnapping . . .
What's that? You say something's going on outside?

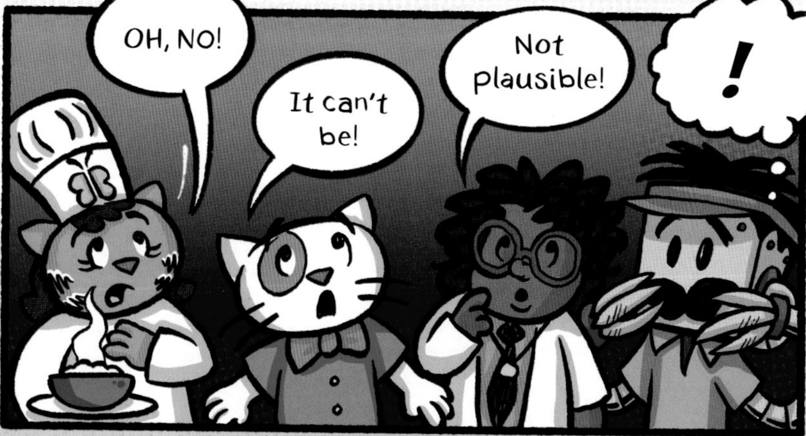
OH, NO!
It can't be!
Not plausible!
!

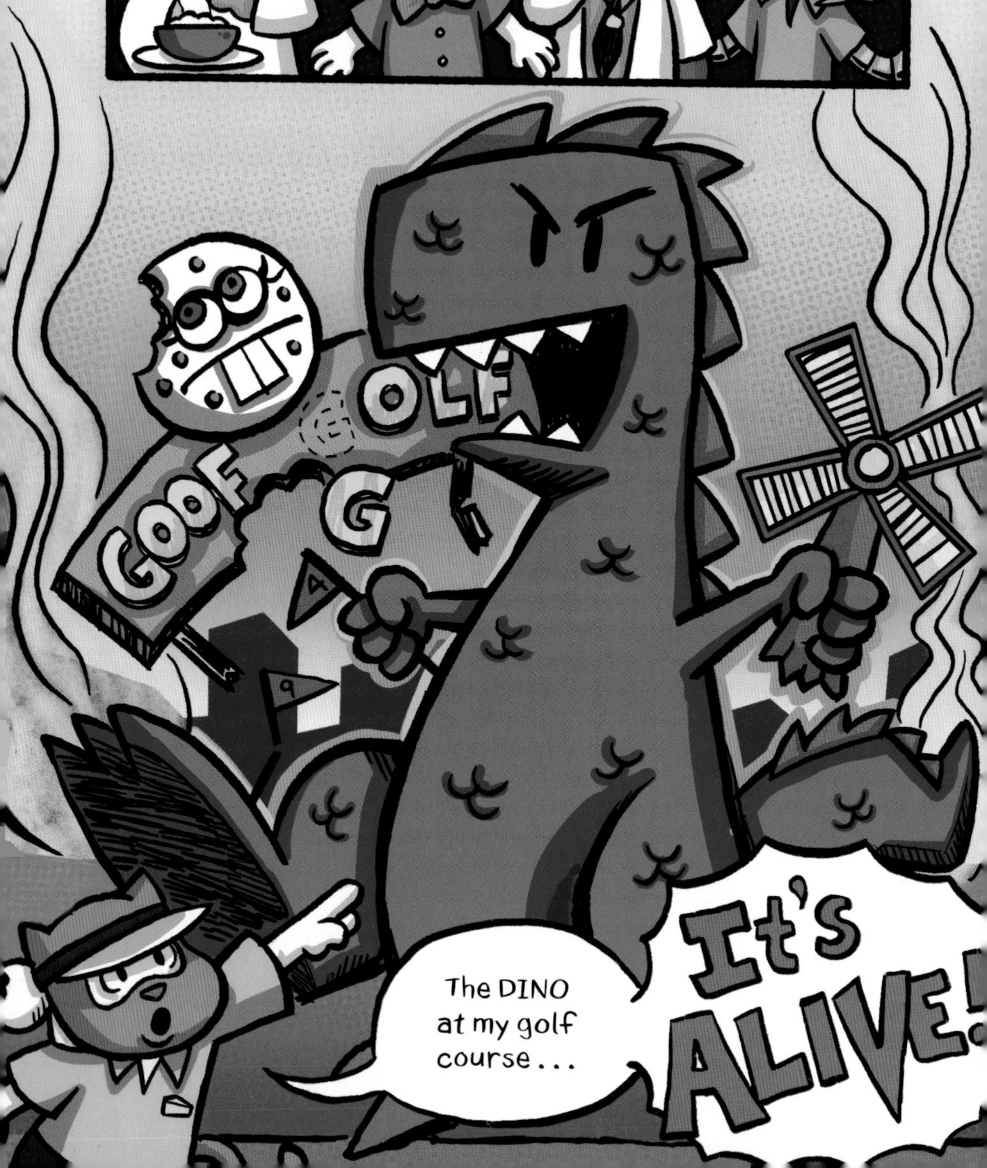
GOOF GOLF
The DINO at my golf course . . .
It's ALIVE!

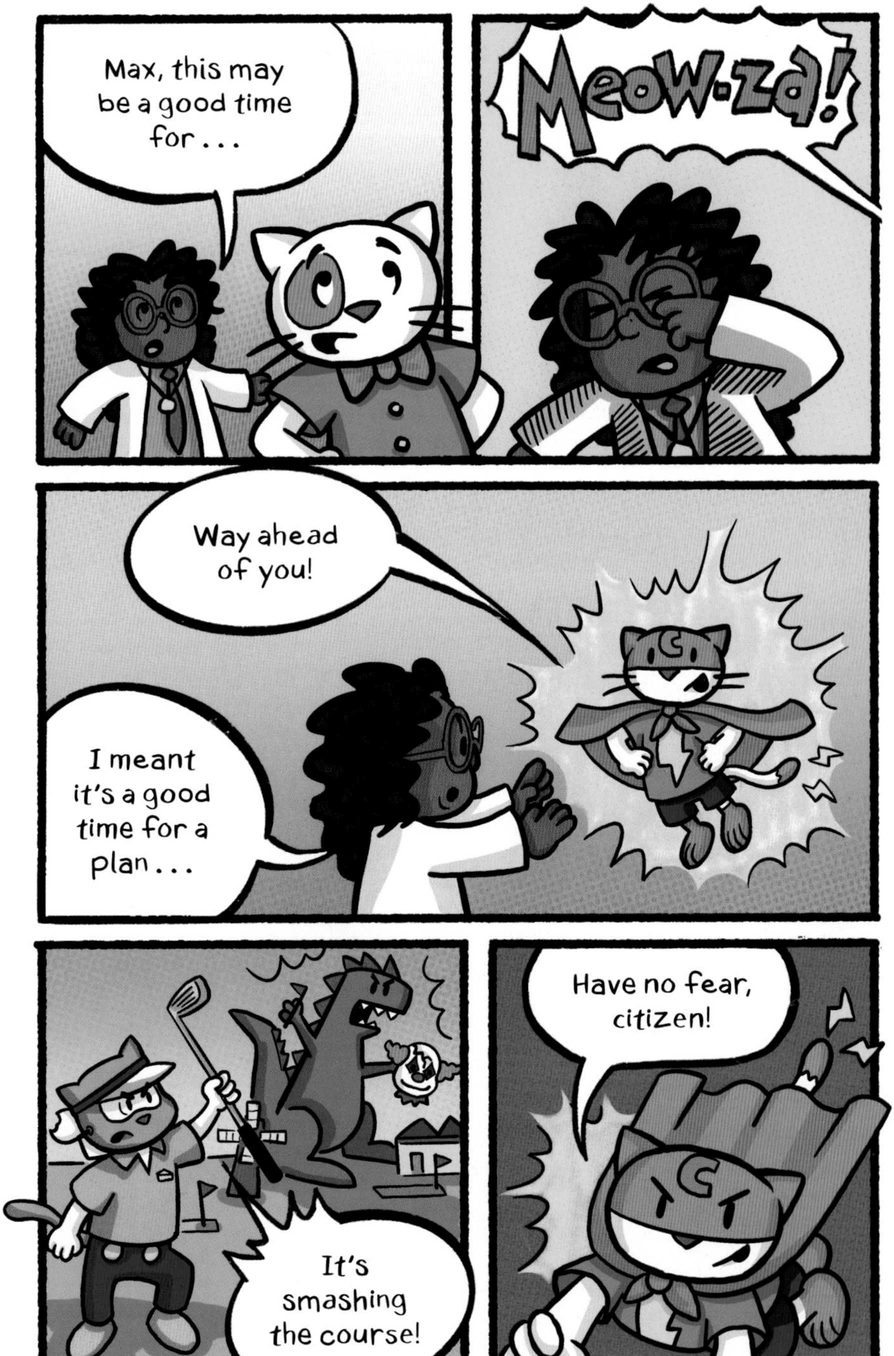
Max, this may be a good time for . . .
Meow-za!
Way ahead of you!
I meant it's a good time for a plan . . .
It's smashing the course!
Have no fear, citizen!

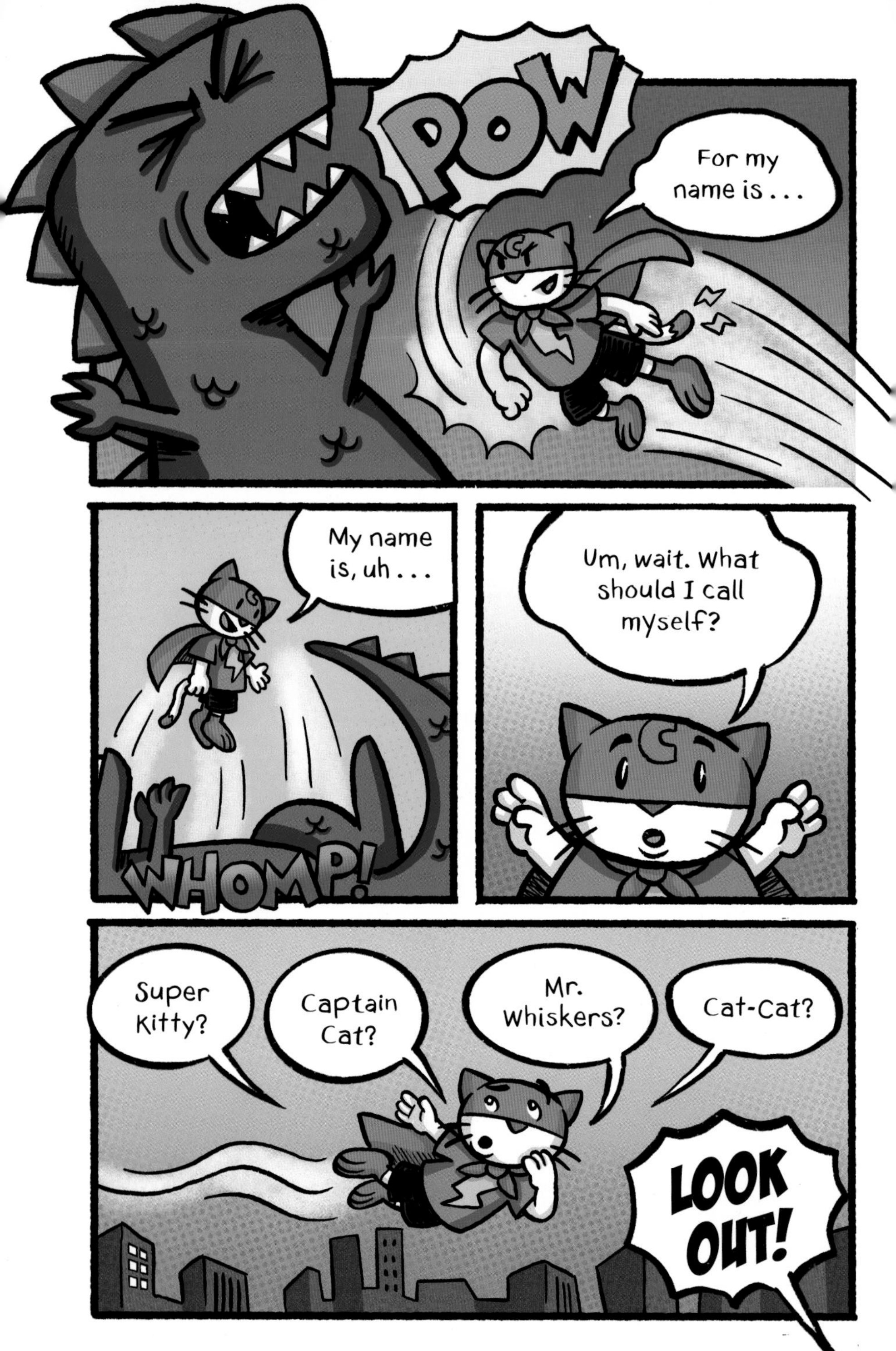
POW
For my name is . . .
My name is, uh . . .
WHOMP!
Um, wait. What should I call myself?
Super Kitty?
Captain Cat?
Mr. Whiskers?
Cat-Cat?
LOOK OUT!

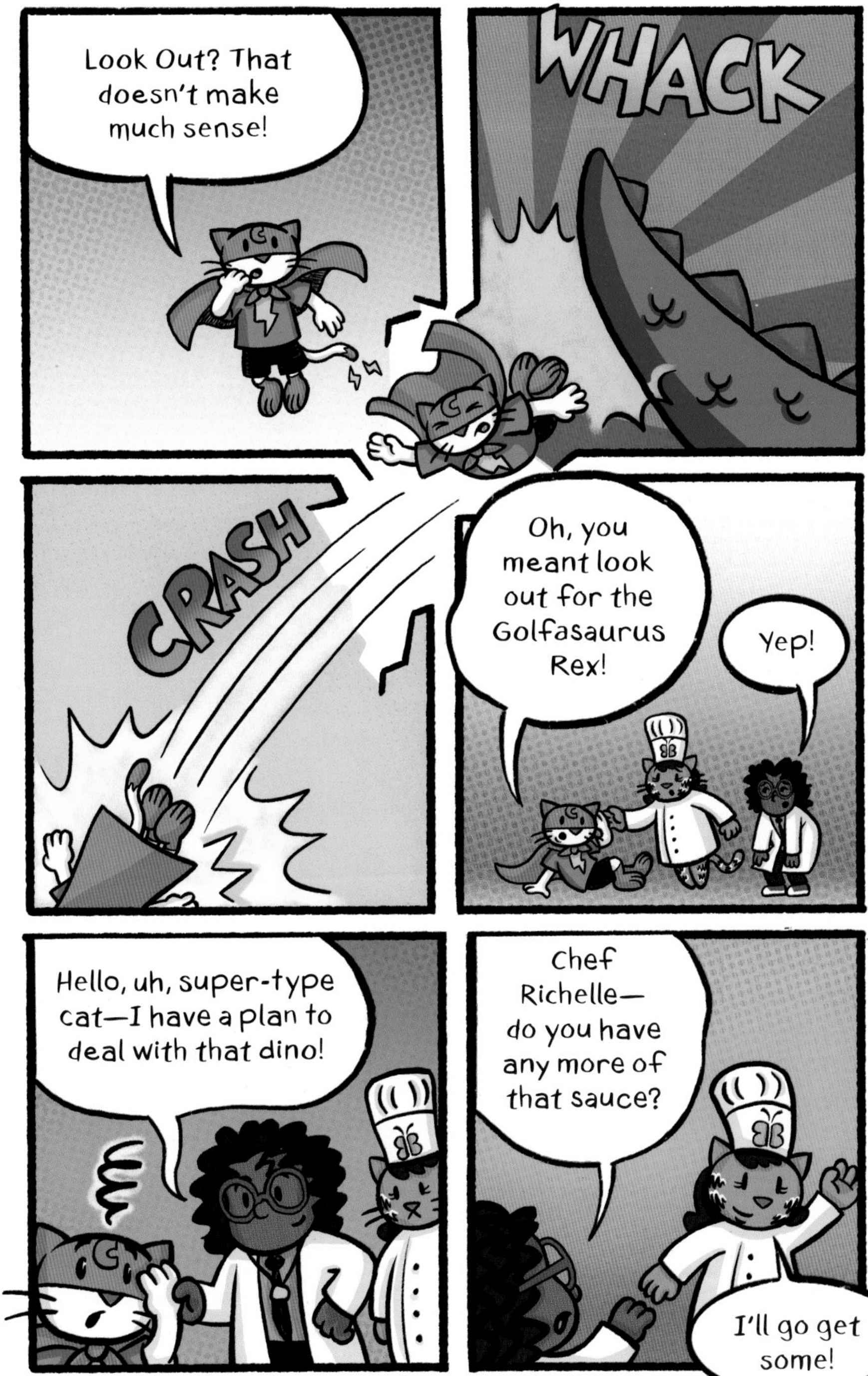

Look Out? That doesn't make much sense!
WHACK
CRASH
Oh, you meant look out for the Golfasaurus Rex!
Yep!
Hello, uh, super-type cat—I have a plan to deal with that dino!
Chef Richelle—do you have any more of that sauce?
I'll go get some!

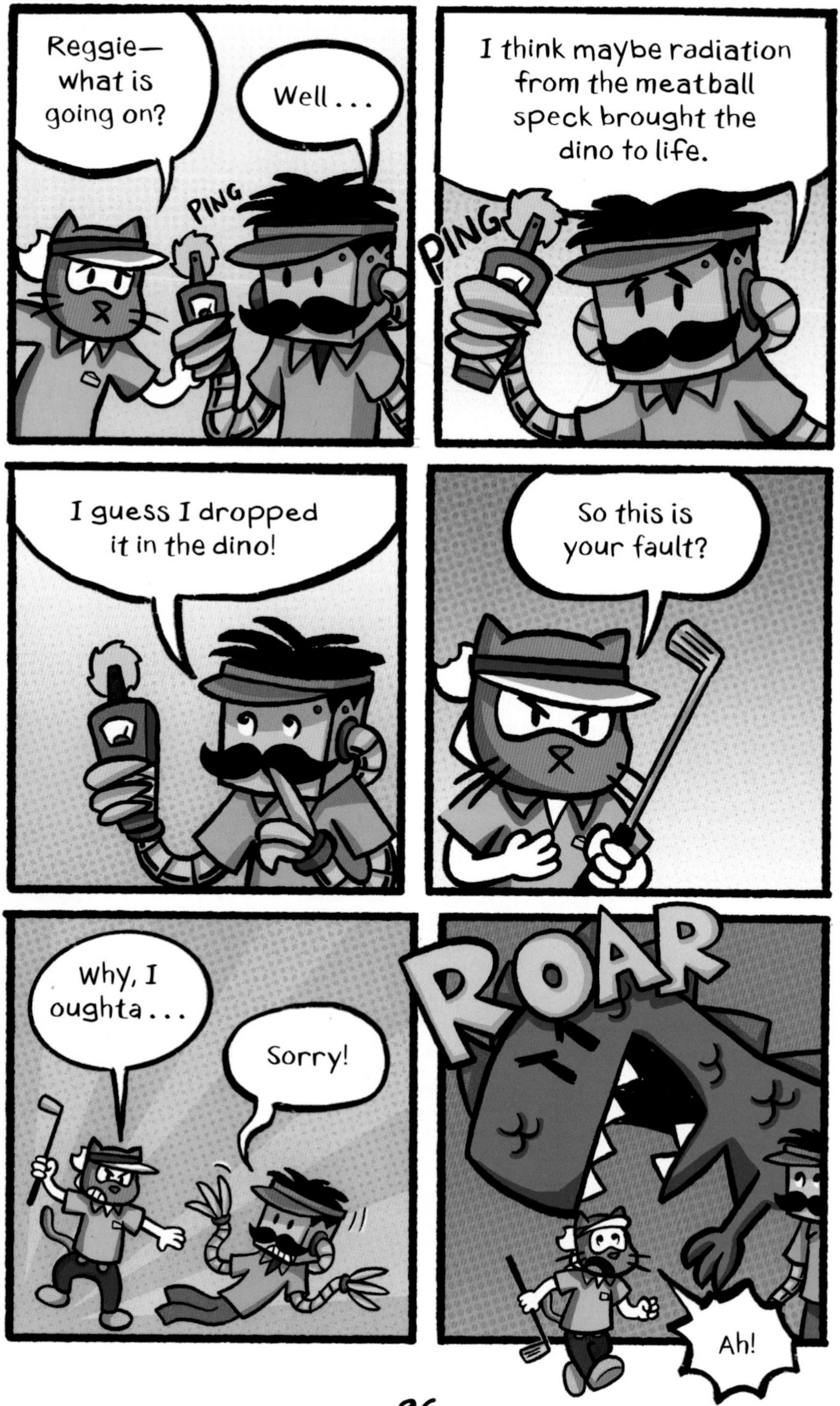
Reggie—
what is
going on?
PING
Well . . .
I think maybe radiation
from the meatball
speck brought the
dino to life.
PING
I guess I dropped
it in the dino!
So this is
your fault?
Why, I
oughta . . .
Sorry!
ROAR
Ah!

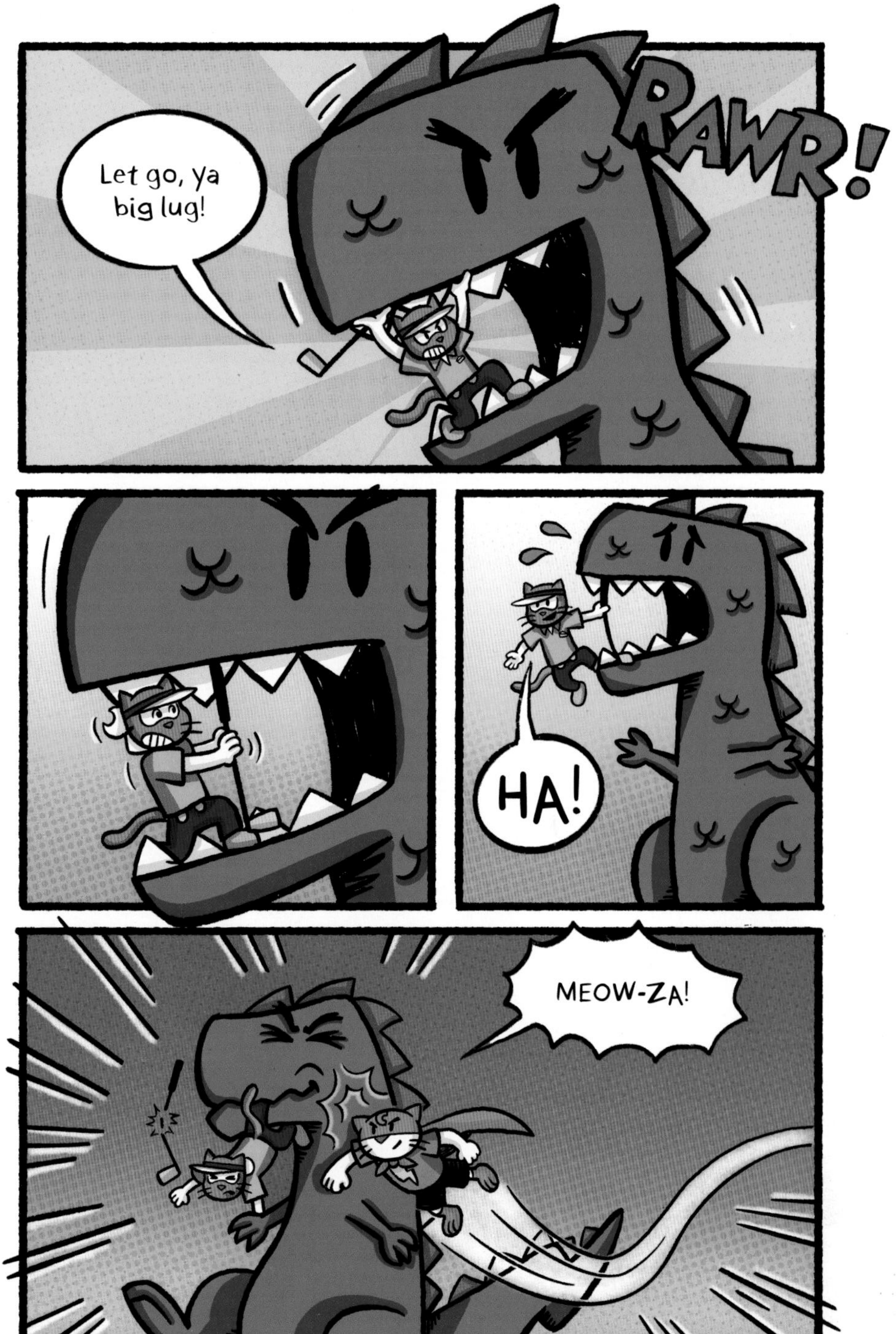
Let go, ya big lug!
RAWR!
HA!
MEOW-ZA!

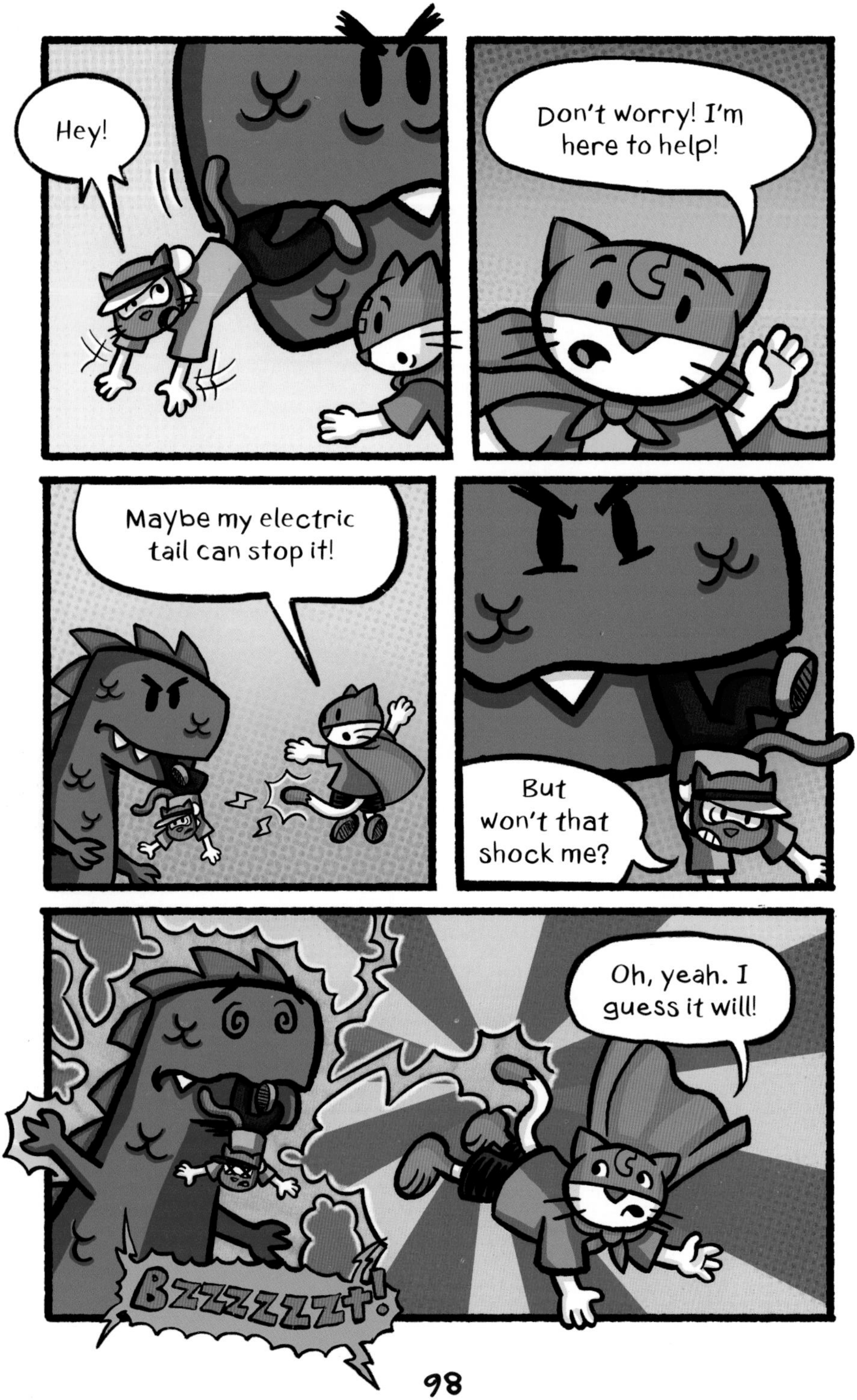
Hey!
Don't worry! I'm here to help!
Maybe my electric tail can stop it!
But won't that shock me?
Oh, yeah. I guess it will!
Bzzzzzzzt!

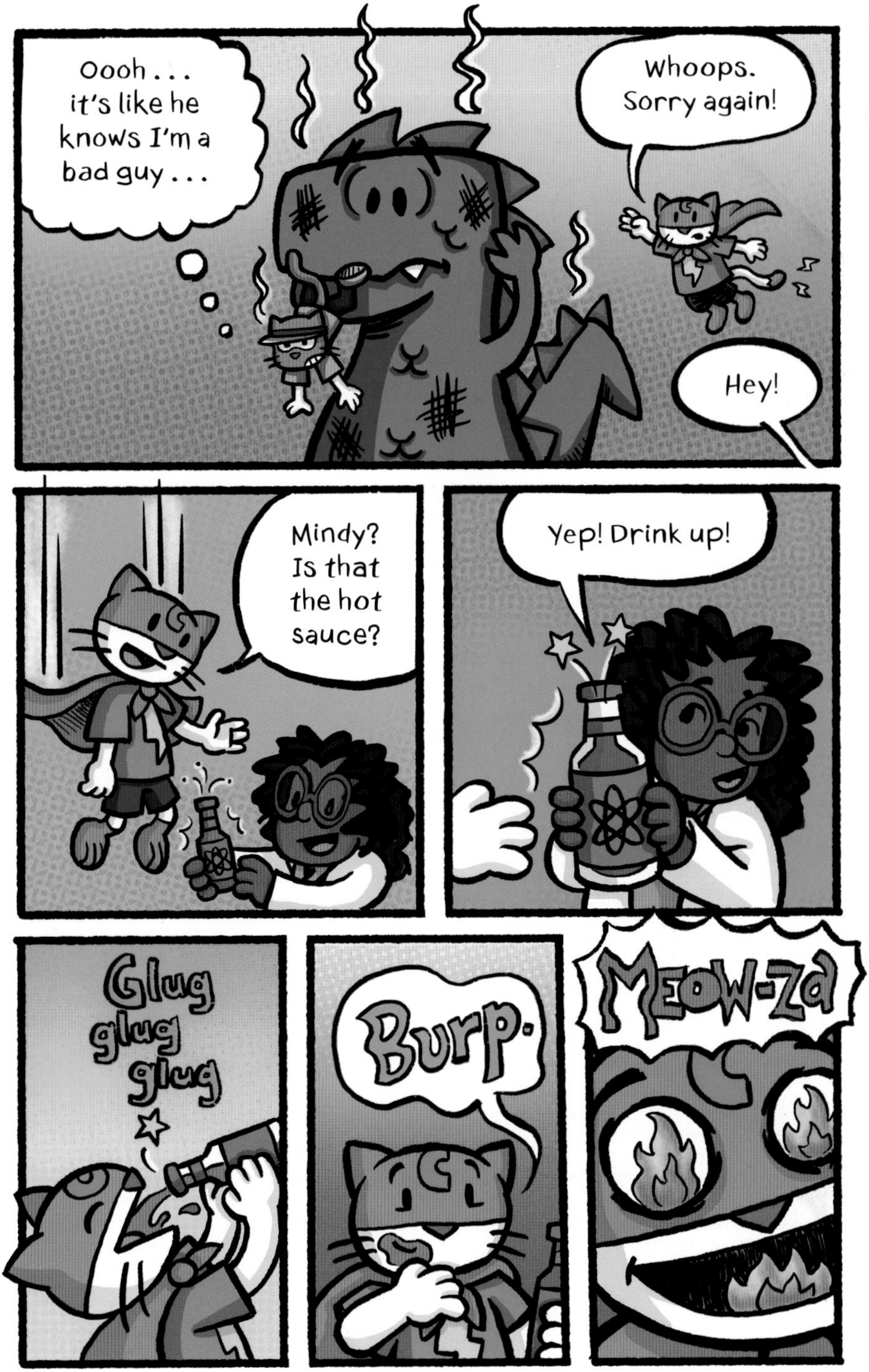
Oooh . . . it's like he knows I'm a bad guy . . .
Whoops. Sorry again!
Hey!
Mindy? Is that the hot sauce?
Yep! Drink up!
Glug glug glug
Burp.
MEOW-ZA

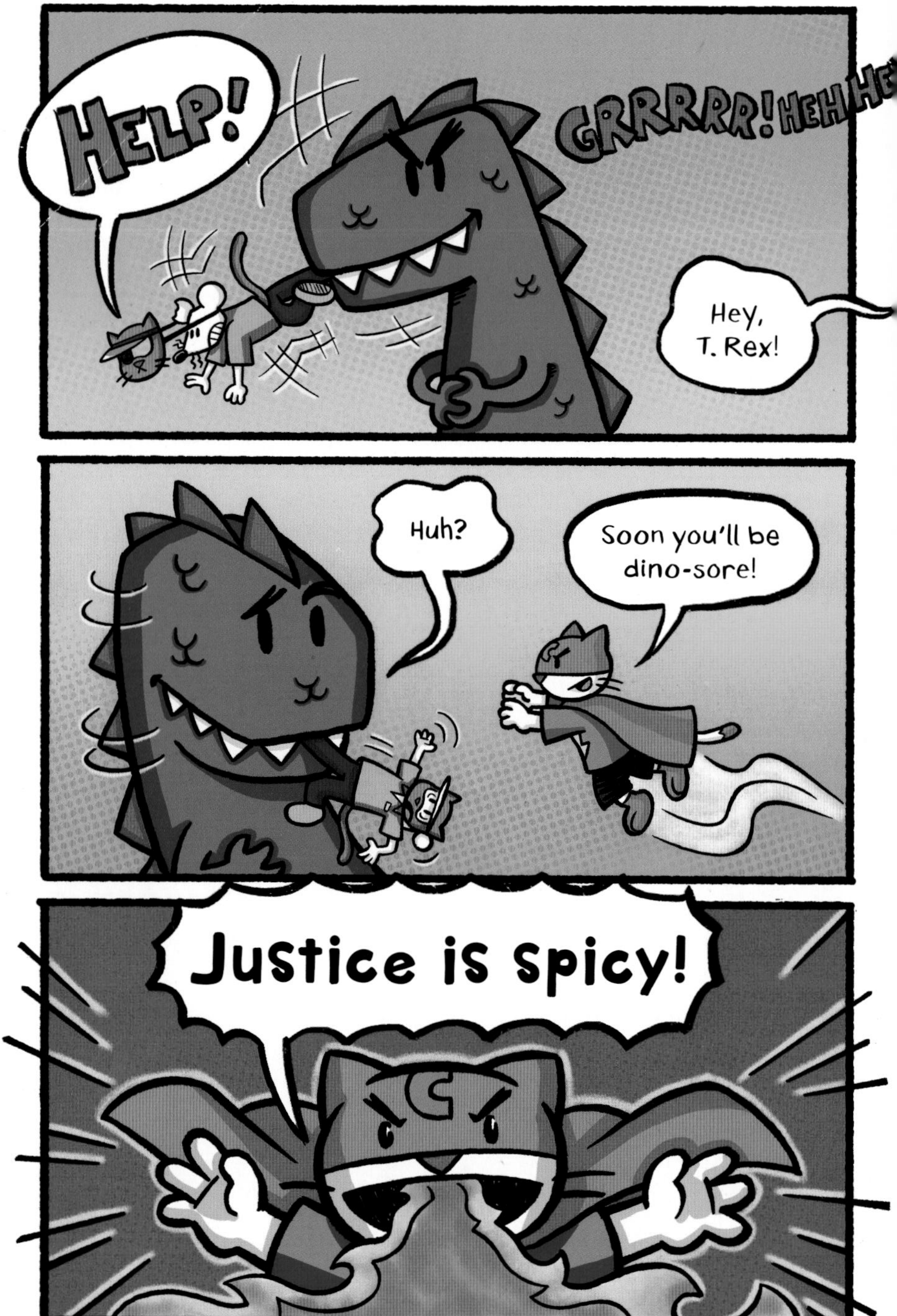
HELP!
GRRRRR! HEH HE
Hey, T. Rex!
Huh?
Soon you'll be dino-sore!
Justice is spicy!

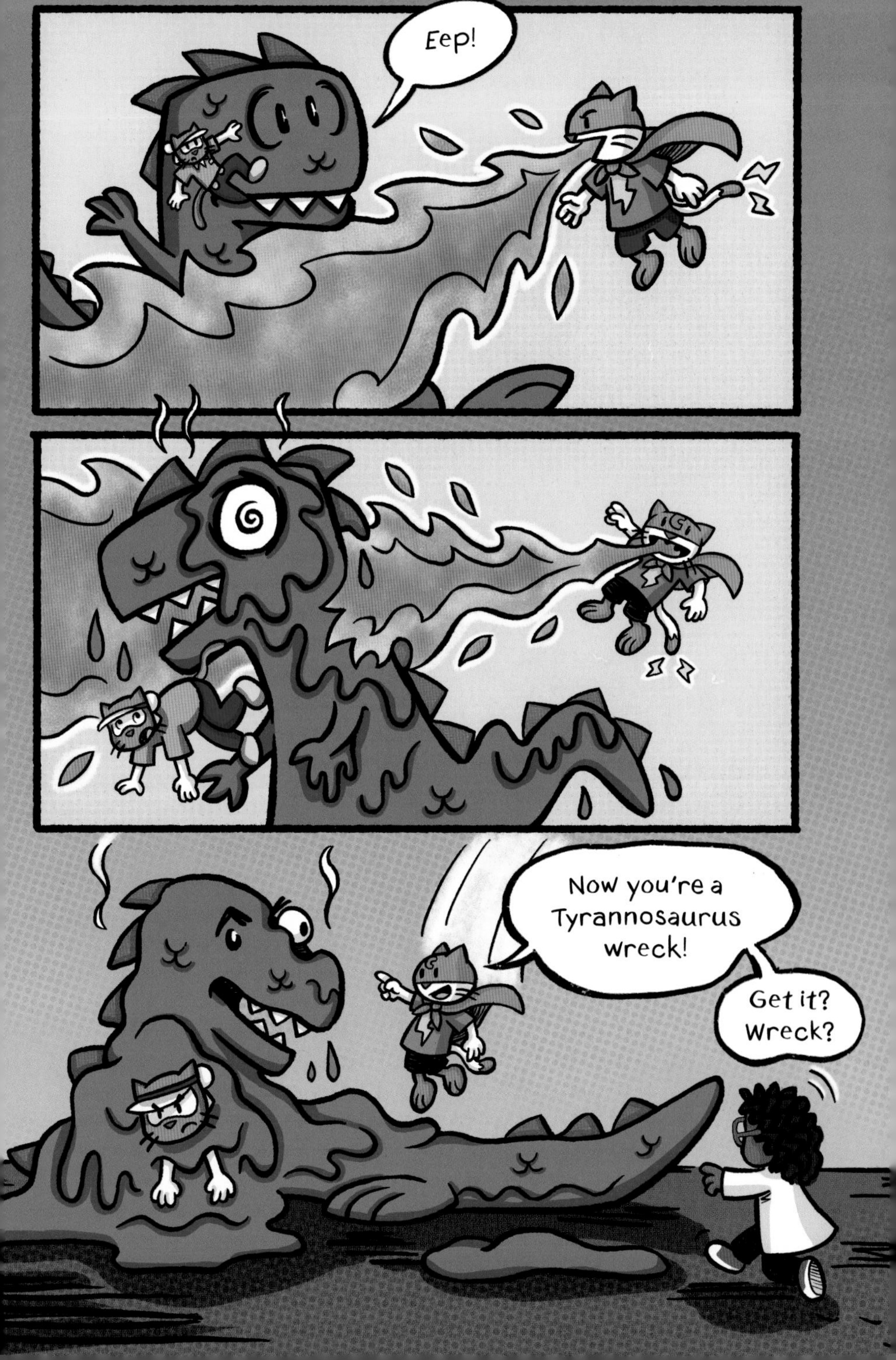
Eep!
Now you're a Tyrannosaurus wreck!
Get it? Wreck?

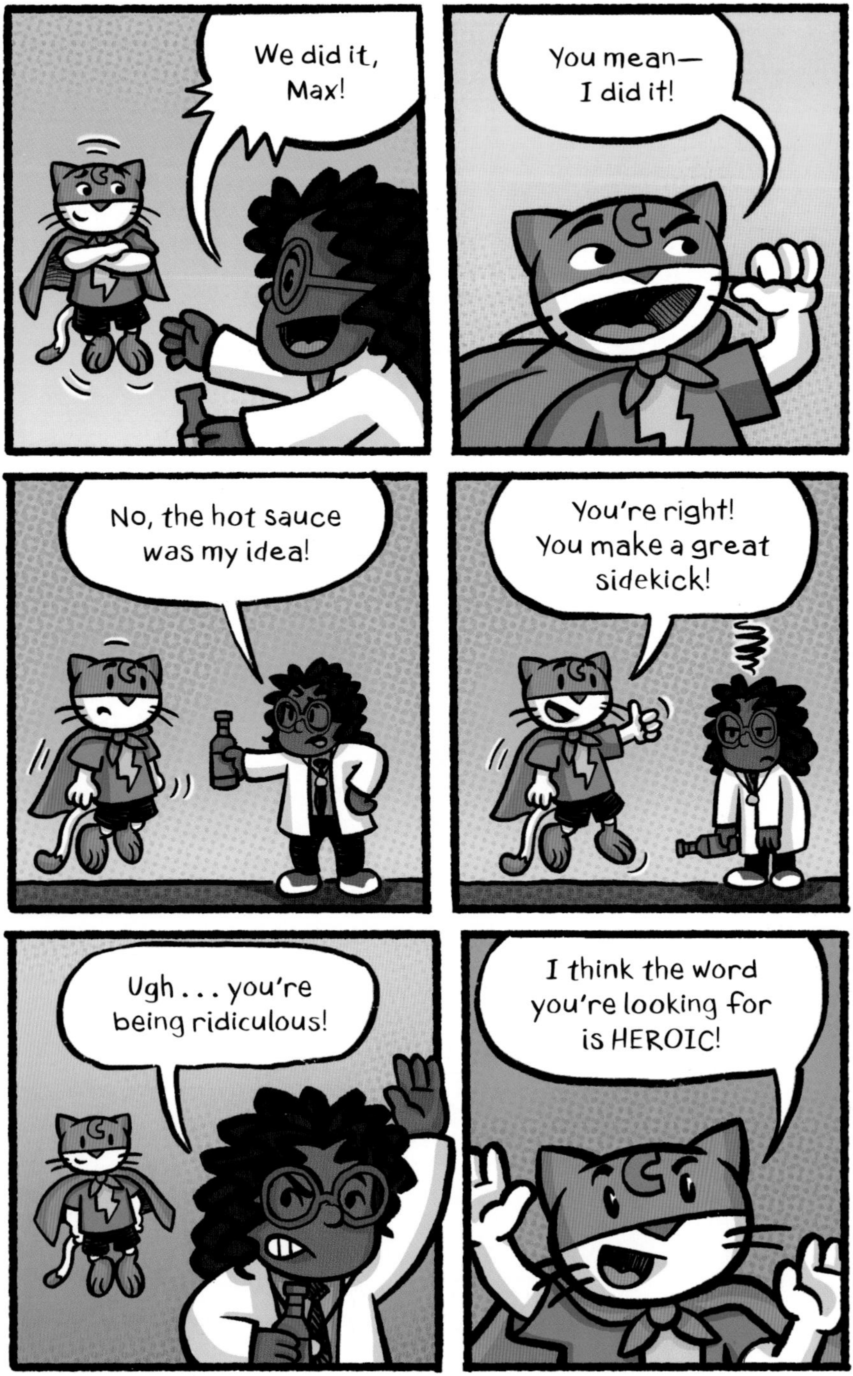
We did it, Max!
You mean— I did it!
No, the hot sauce was my idea!
You're right! You make a great sidekick!
Ugh . . . you're being ridiculous!
I think the word you're looking for is HEROIC!

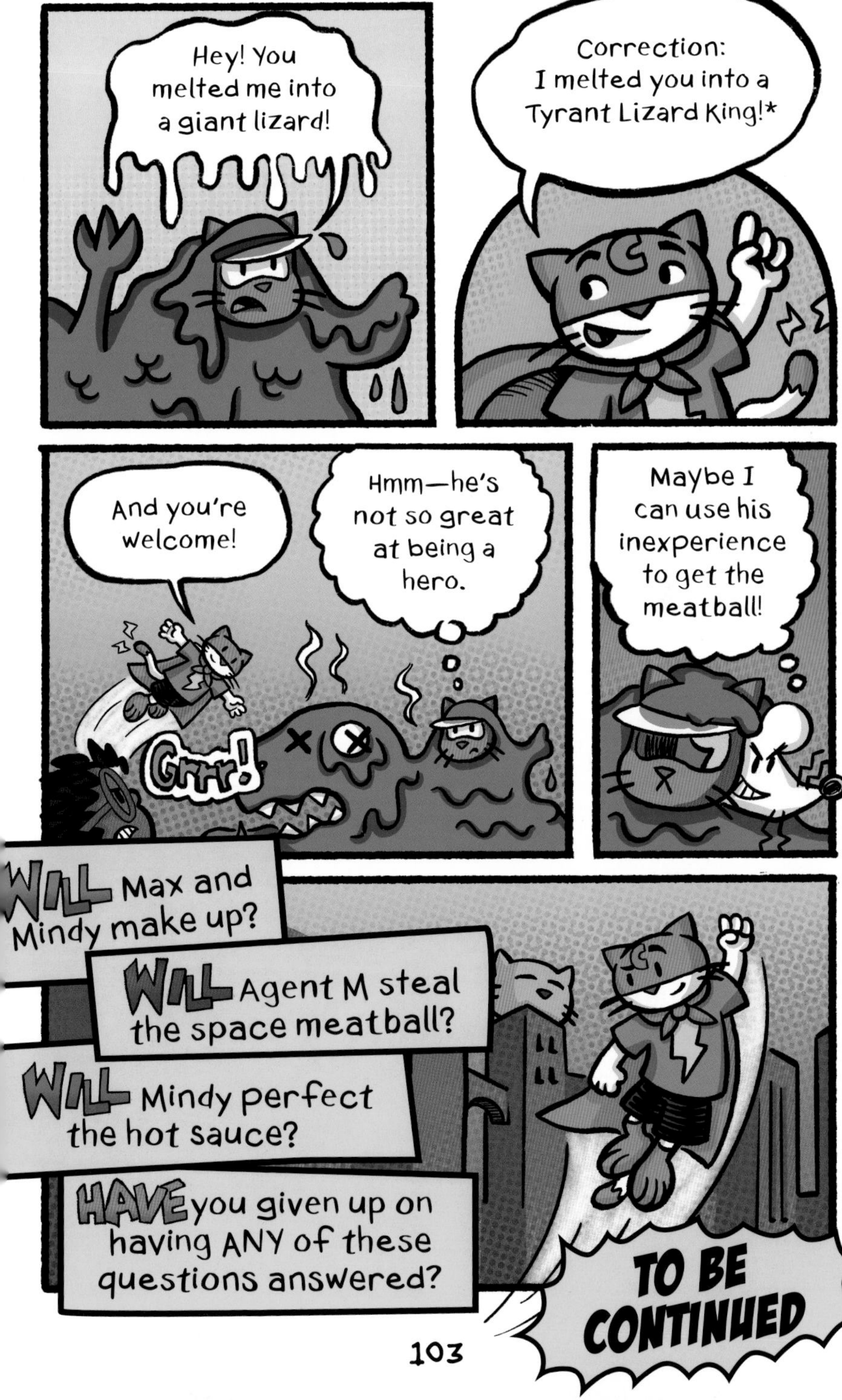
Hey! You melted me into a giant lizard!
Correction: I melted you into a Tyrant Lizard King!*
And you're welcome!
Hmm—he's not so great at being a hero.
Grrr!
Maybe I can use his inexperience to get the meatball!
WILL Max and Mindy make up?
WILL Agent M steal the space meatball?
WILL Mindy perfect the hot sauce?
HAVE you given up on having ANY of these questions answered?
TO BE CONTINUED

* "Tyrannosaurus rex" means "king of the tyrant lizards"!

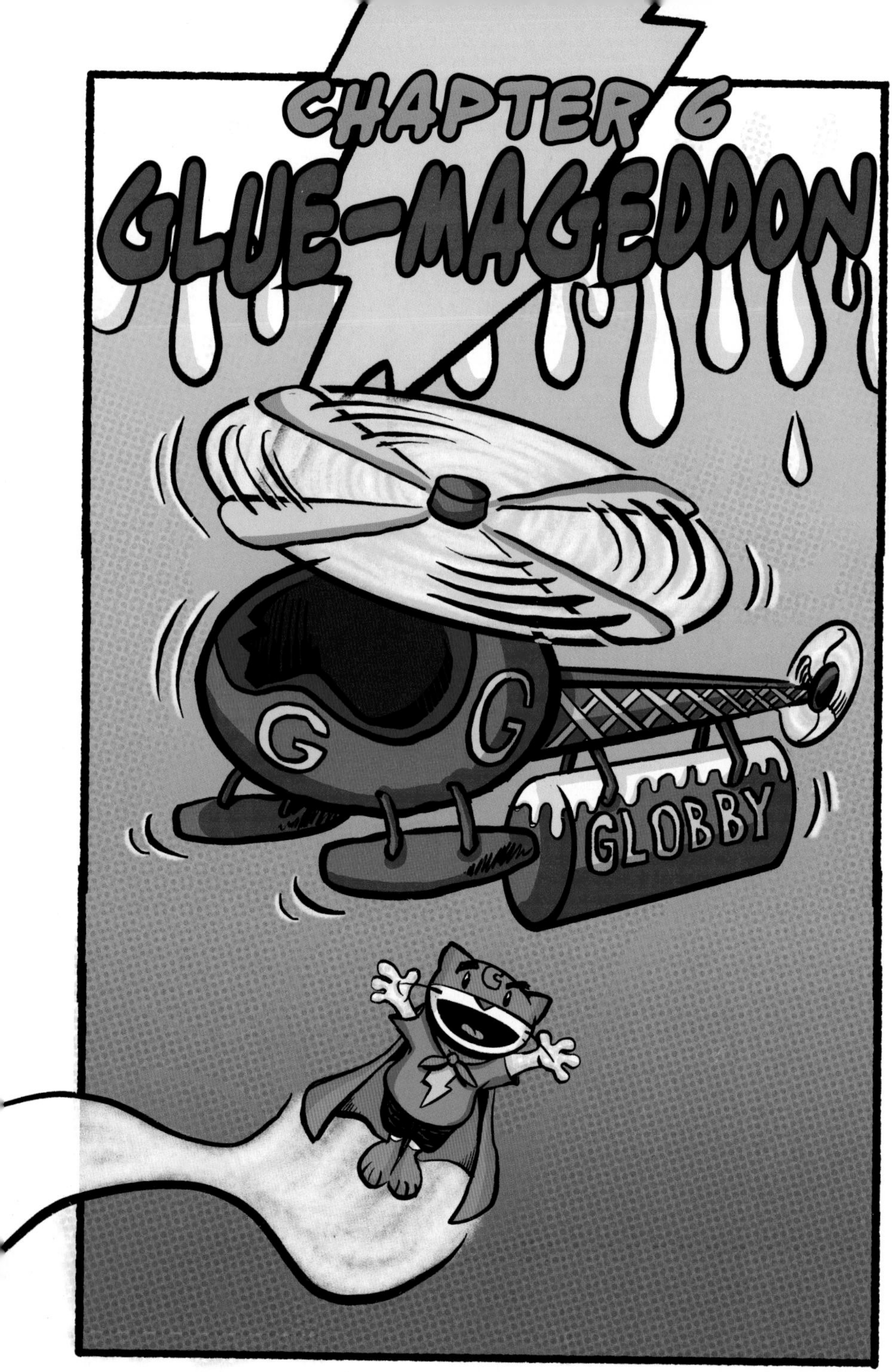
CHAPTER 6
GLUE-MAGEDDON
GLOBBY

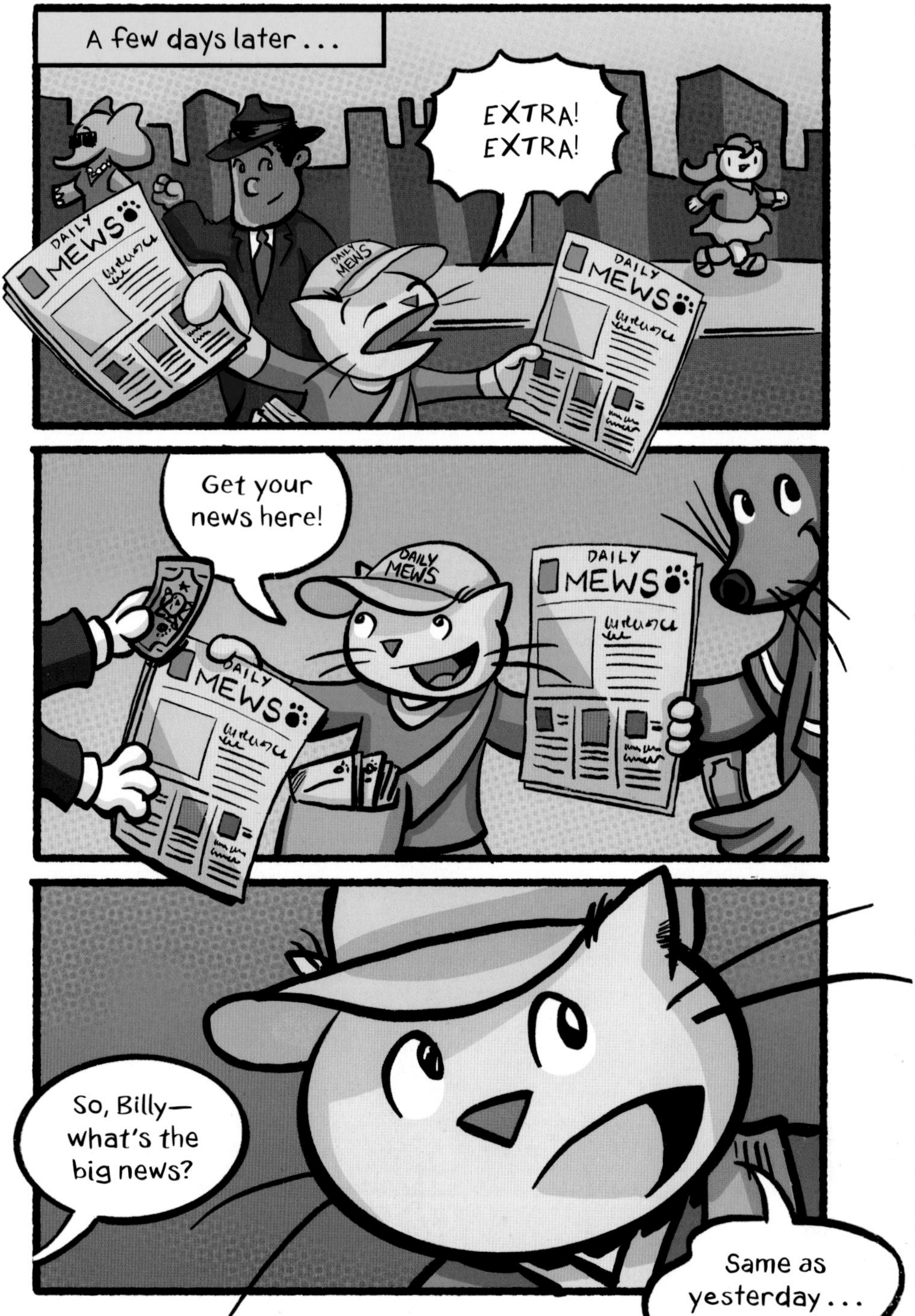
A few days later . . .
EXTRA! EXTRA!
DAILY MEWS
Get your news here!
DAILY MEWS
So, Billy— what's the big news?
Same as yesterday . . .

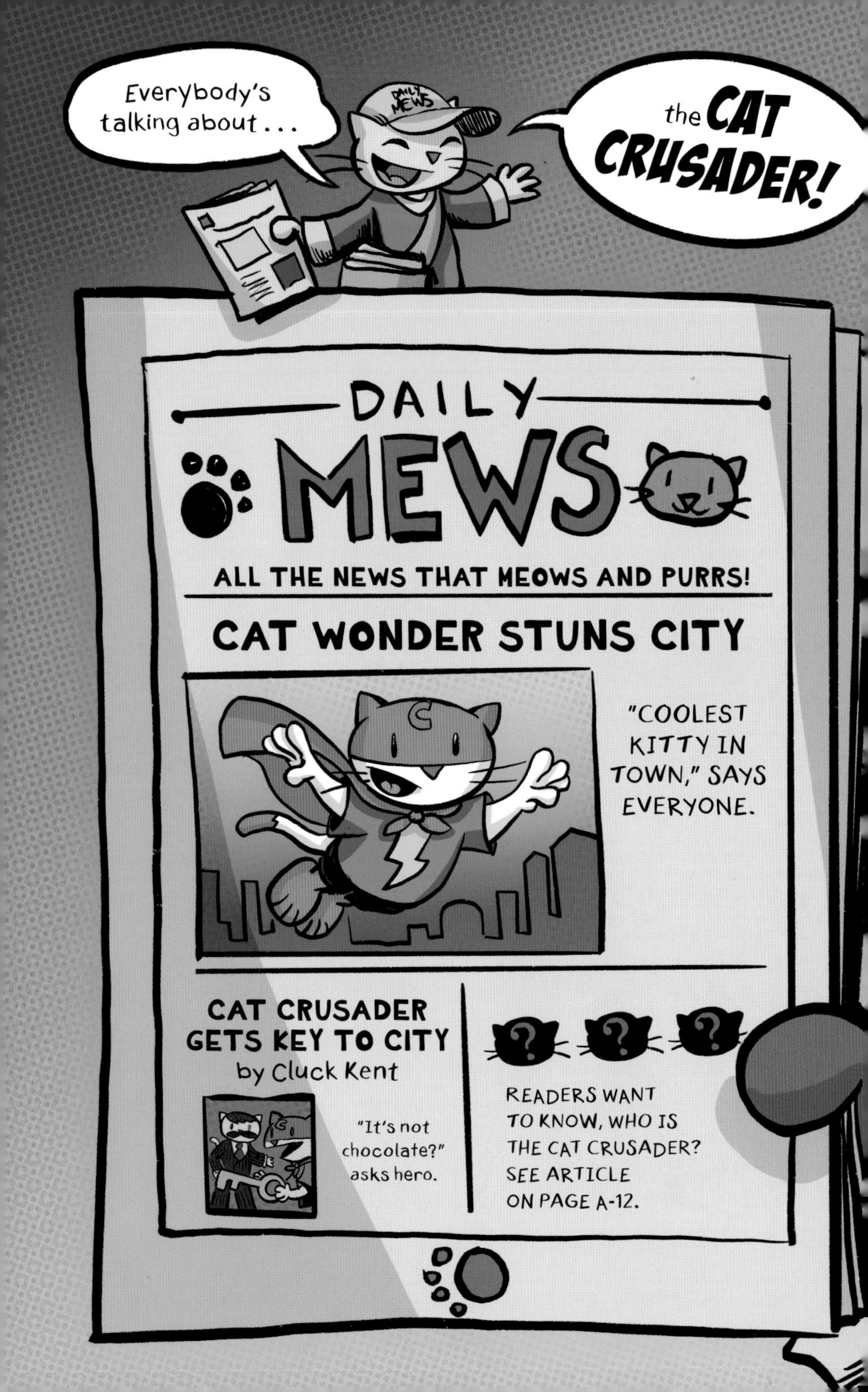
Everybody's talking about . . .
DAILY MEWS
the CAT CRUSADER!
DAILY MEWS
ALL THE NEWS THAT MEOWS AND PURRS!
CAT WONDER STUNS CITY
"COOLEST KITTY IN TOWN," SAYS EVERYONE.
CAT CRUSADER GETS KEY TO CITY
by Cluck Kent
"It's not chocolate?" asks hero.
READERS WANT TO KNOW, WHO IS THE CAT CRUSADER? SEE ARTICLE ON PAGE A-12.

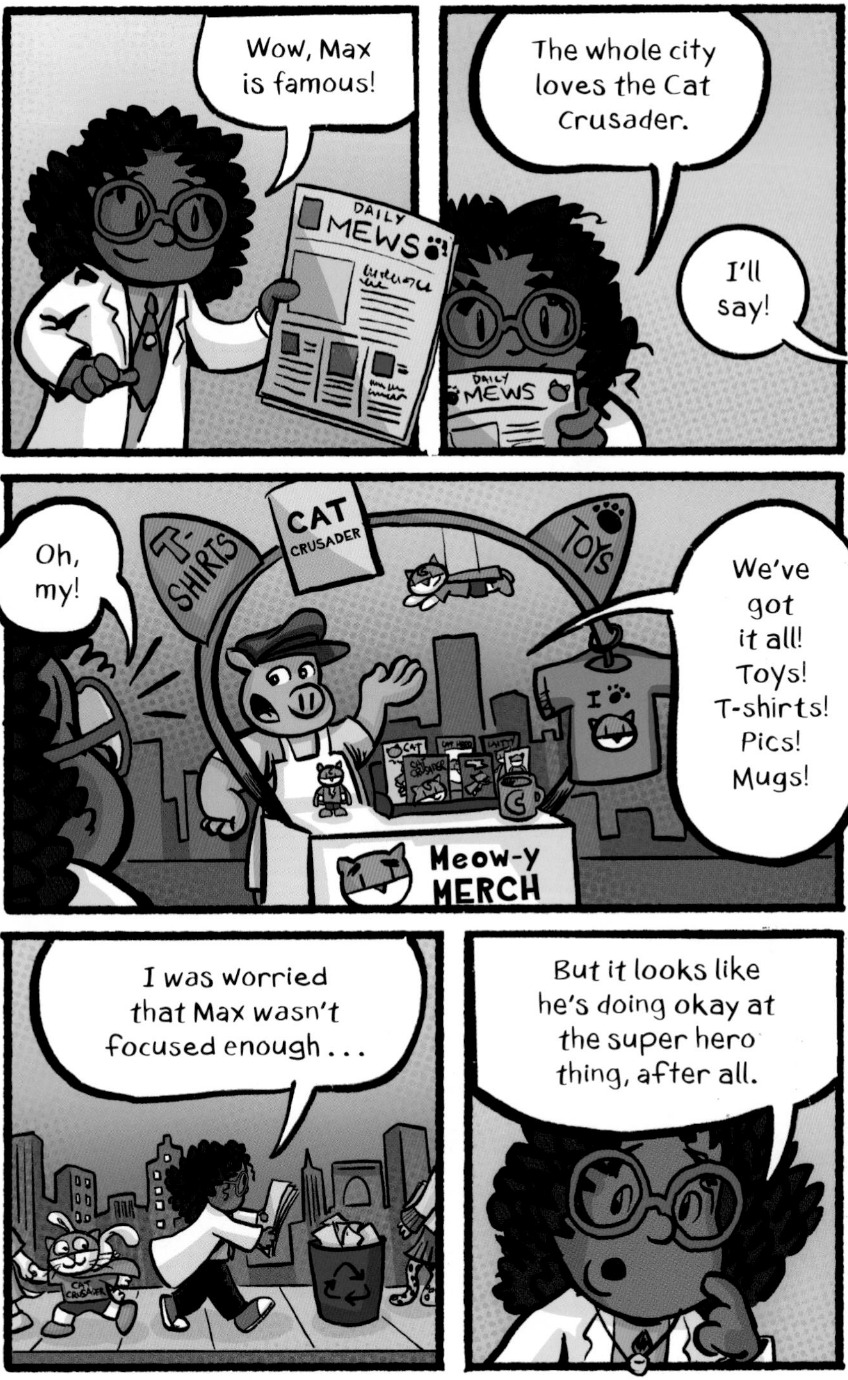
Wow, Max is famous!
DAILY MEWS
The whole city loves the Cat Crusader.
I'll say!
DAILY MEWS
Oh, my!
T-SHIRTS
CAT CRUSADER
TOYS
We've got it all! Toys! T-shirts! Pics! Mugs!
Meow-y MERCH
I was worried that Max wasn't focused enough . . .
CAT CRUSADER
But it looks like he's doing okay at the super hero thing, after all.

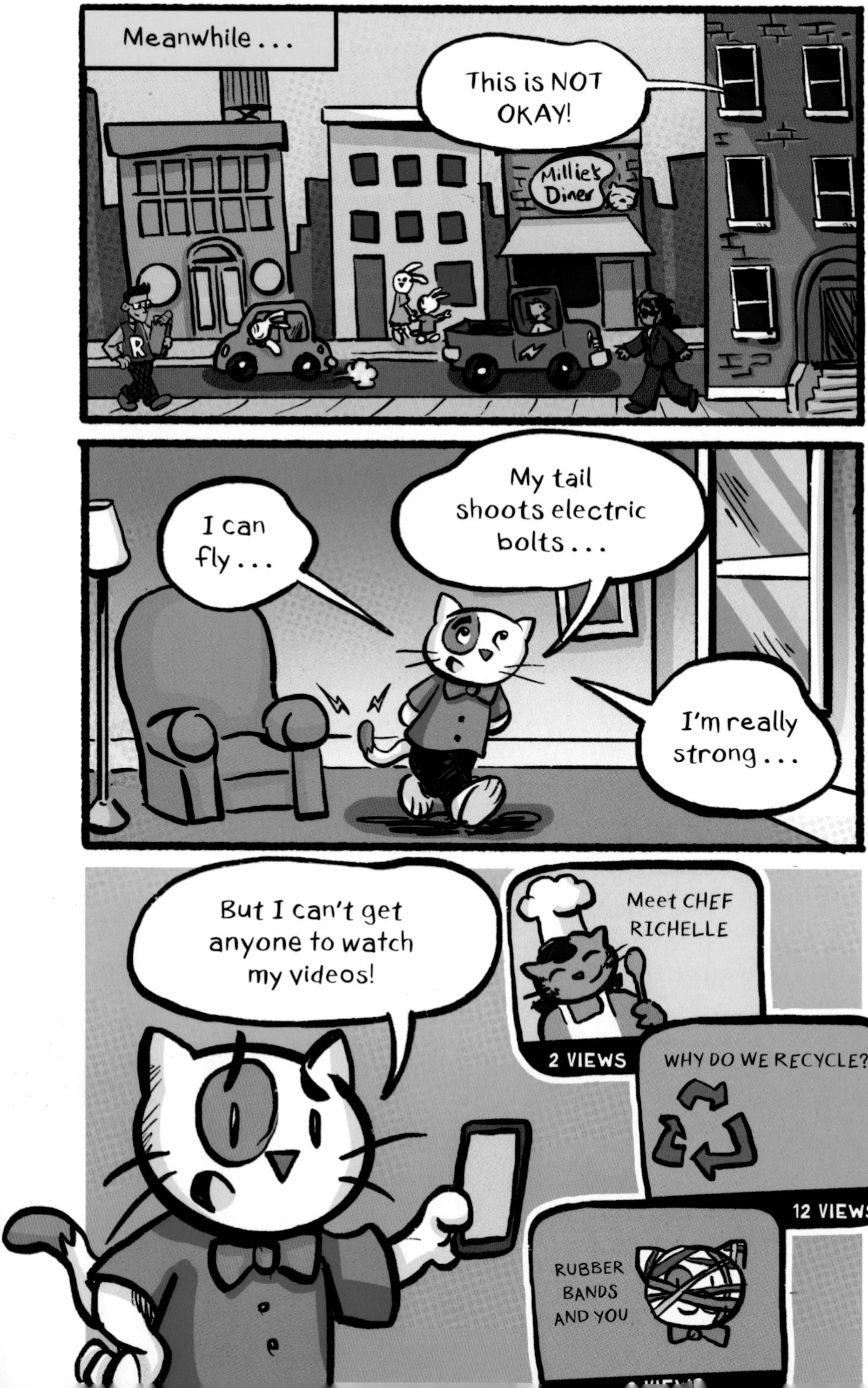
Meanwhile . . .
This is NOT OKAY!
Millie's Diner
I can fly . . .
My tail shoots electric bolts . . .
I'm really strong . . .
But I can't get anyone to watch my videos!
Meet CHEF RICHELLE
2 VIEWS
WHY DO WE RECYCLE?
12 VIEWS
RUBBER BANDS AND YOU

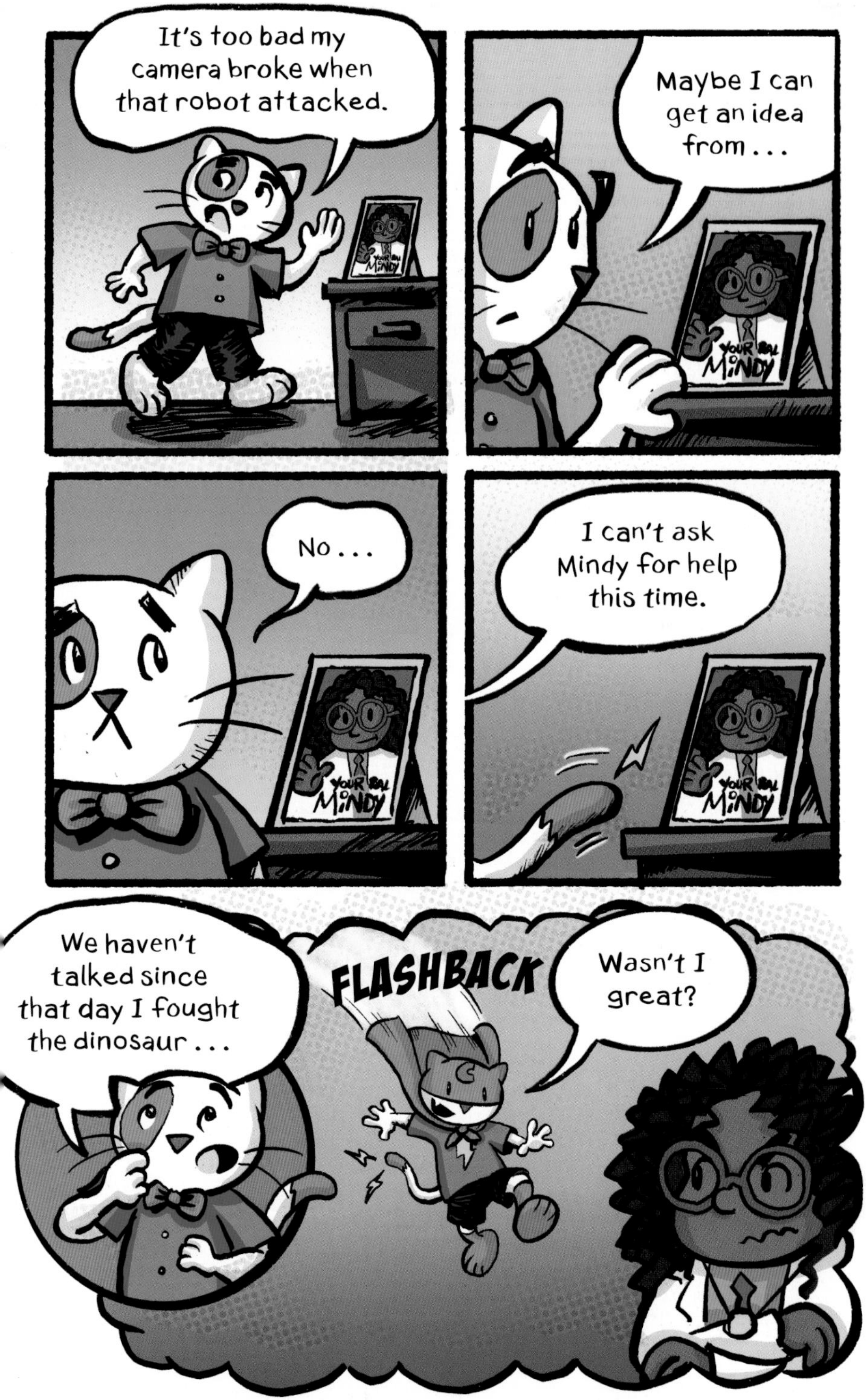
It's too bad my camera broke when that robot attacked.
YOUR PAL MINDY
Maybe I can get an idea from . . .
YOUR PAL MINDY
No . . .
YOUR PAL MINDY
I can't ask Mindy for help this time.
YOUR PAL MINDY
We haven't talked since that day I fought the dinosaur . . .
FLASHBACK
Wasn't I great?

Mindy thought I was too "brash"...

You could have been hurt...

which led to a long discussion:

"Brash" means "self-assured in a brazen way"... blah blah...

And that's when I said:

Maybe you're just jealous!

And Mindy said:

My scientific opinion is you're a jerk!

Then we both stormed off.

Fine!

Fine!

Except...

Wait—what does "brazen" mean?

Bold and unashamed!

Oh. Thanks.

Sure...

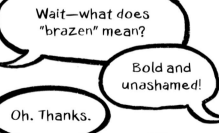

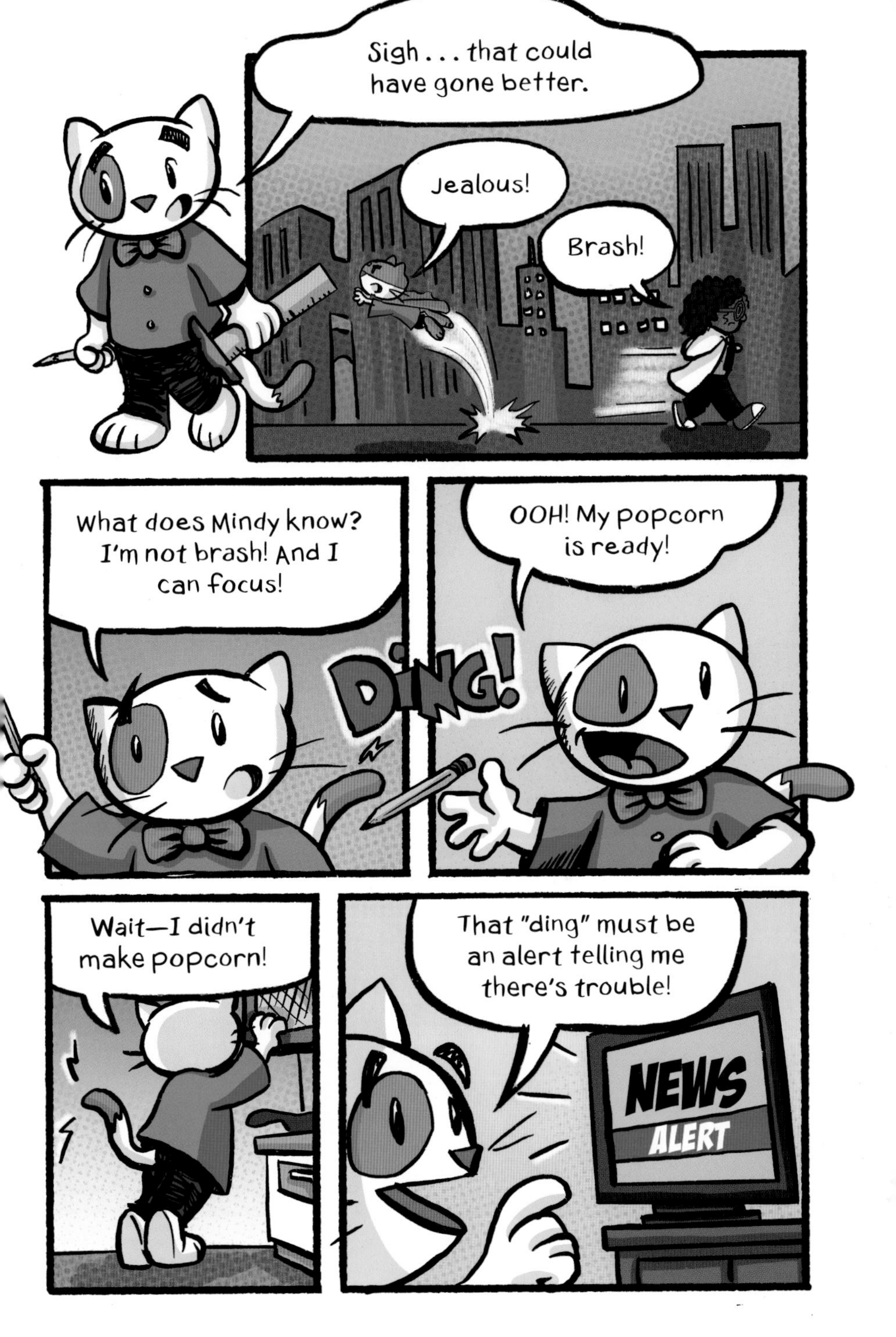
Sigh . . . that could have gone better.
Jealous!
Brash!
What does Mindy know? I'm not brash! And I can focus!
DING!
OOH! My popcorn is ready!
Wait—I didn't make popcorn!
That "ding" must be an alert telling me there's trouble!
NEWS
ALERT

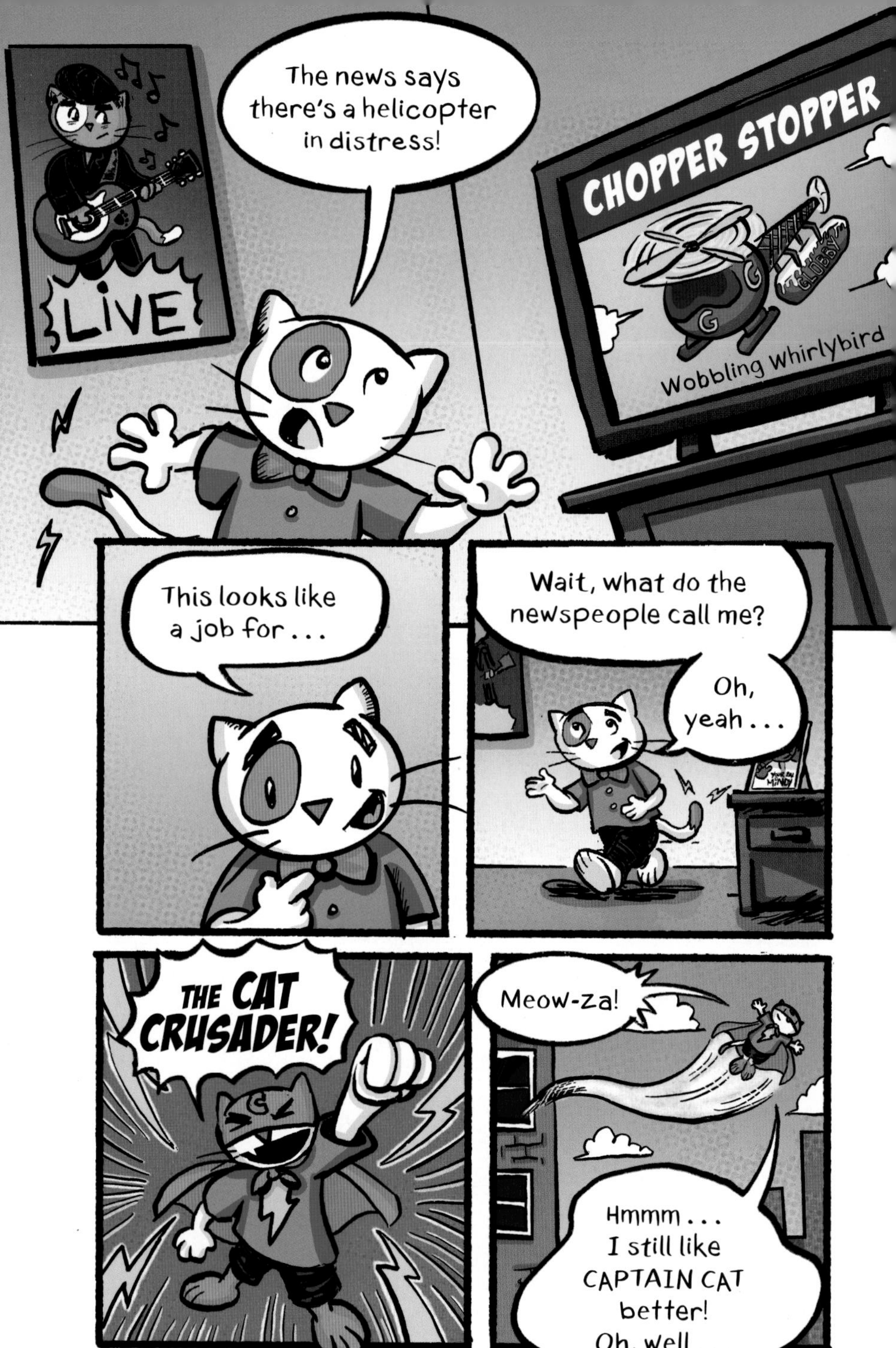
LIVE
The news says there's a helicopter in distress!
CHOPPER STOPPER
Wobbling Whirlybird
This looks like a job for . . .
Wait, what do the newspeople call me?
Oh, yeah . . .
THE CAT CRUSADER!
Meow-za!
Hmmm . . . I still like CAPTAIN CAT better! Oh, well . . .

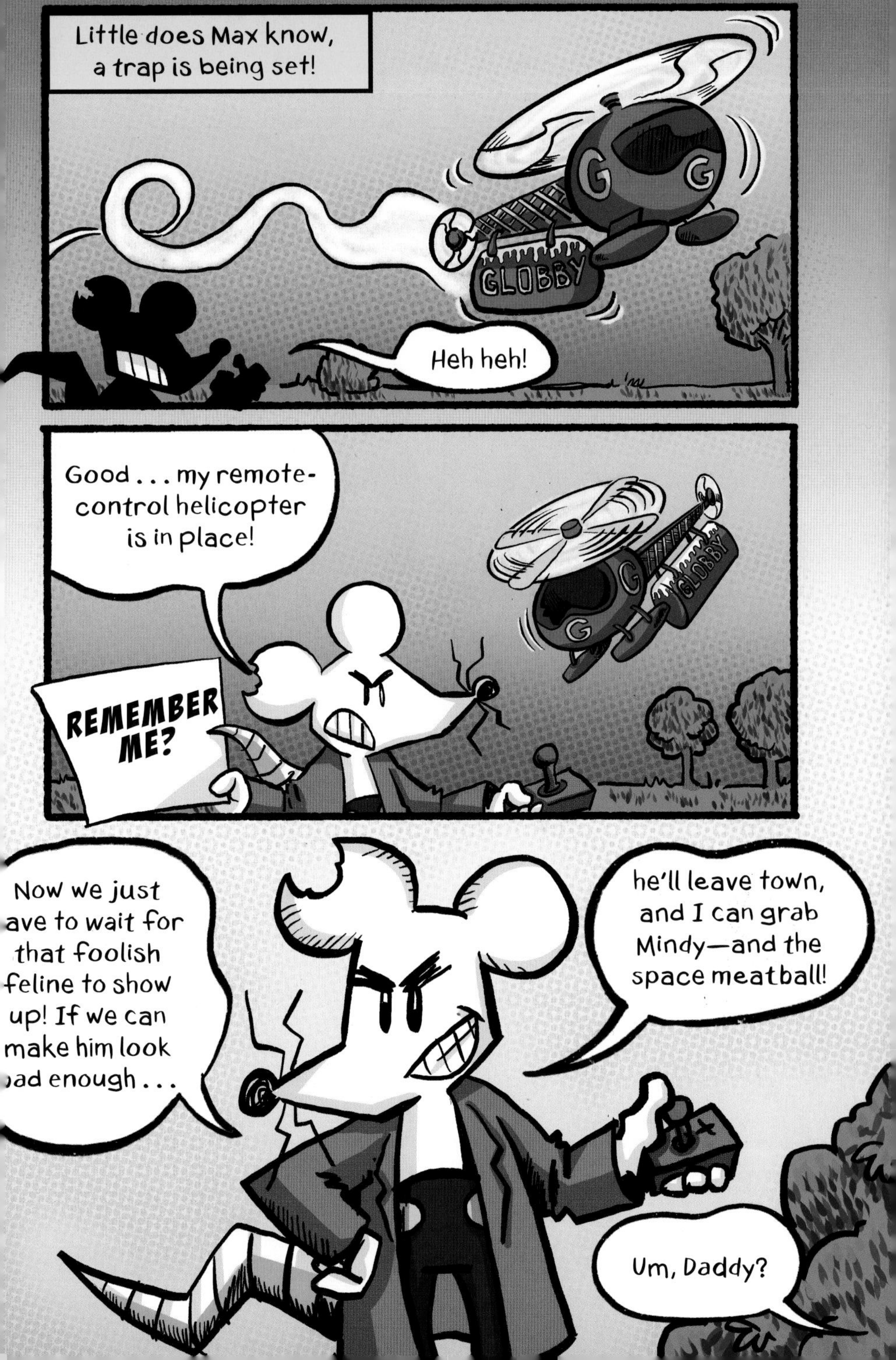
Little does Max know, a trap is being set!
Heh heh!
Good . . . my remote-control helicopter is in place!
GLOBBY
REMEMBER ME?
Now we just ave to wait for that foolish feline to show up! If we can make him look ad enough . . .
he'll leave town, and I can grab Mindy—and the space meatball!
Um, Daddy?

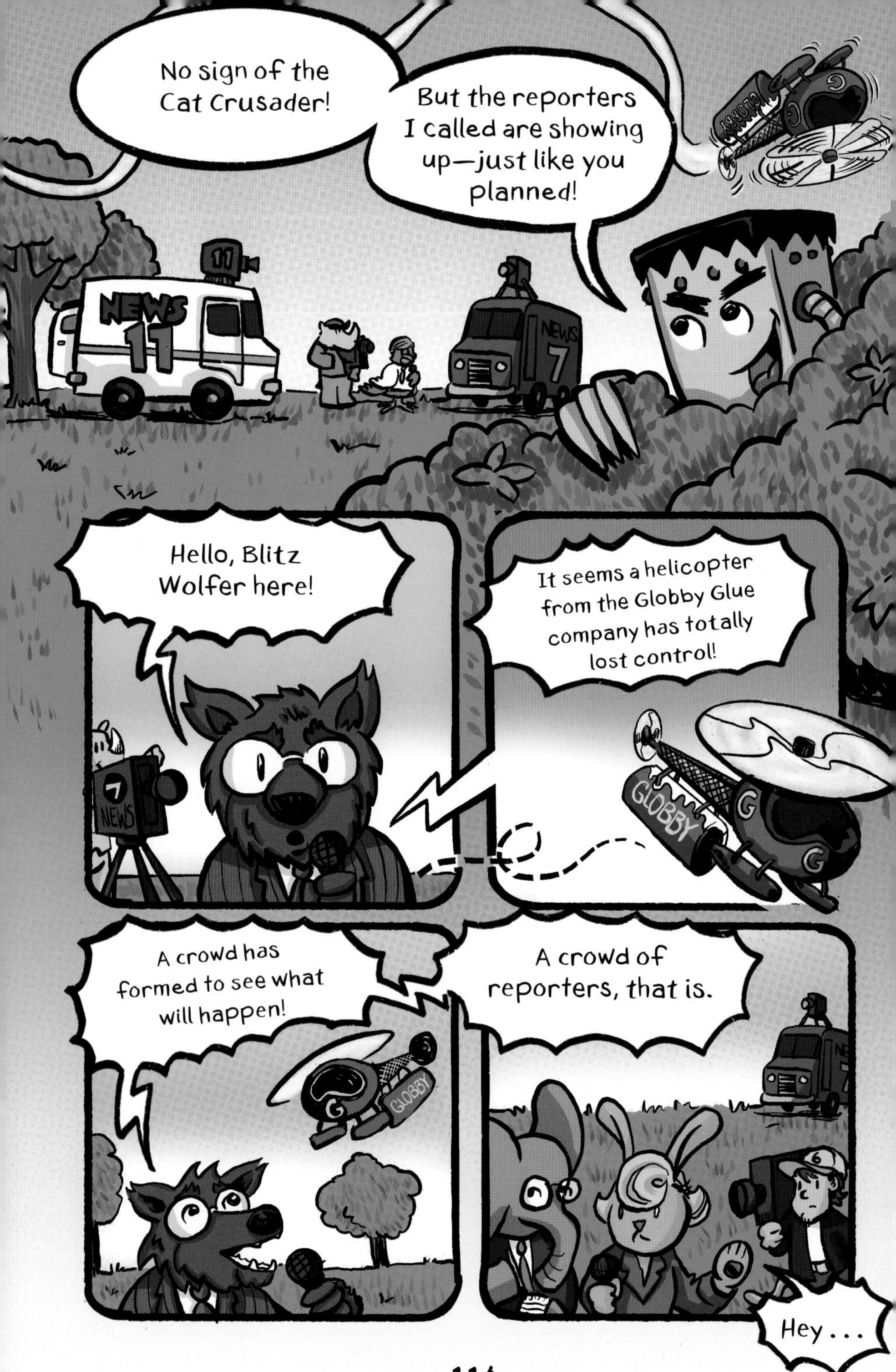
No sign of the Cat Crusader!
But the reporters I called are showing up—just like you planned!
NEWS 11
NEWS 7
GLOBBY
Hello, Blitz Wolfer here!
It seems a helicopter from the Globby Glue company has totally lost control!
GLOBBY
A crowd has formed to see what will happen!
A crowd of reporters, that is.
Hey . . .

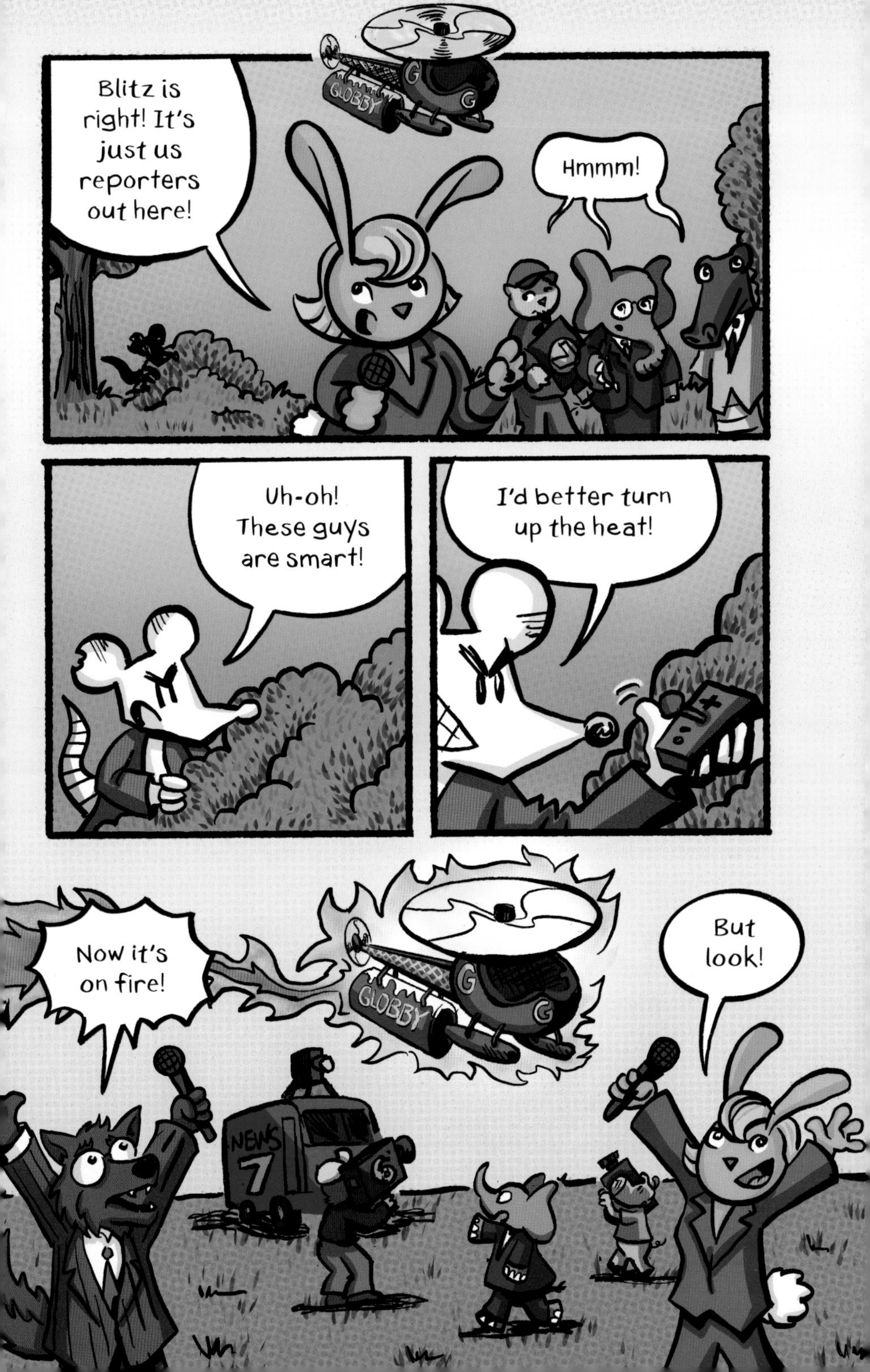
Blitz is right! It's just us reporters out here!
Hmmm!
GLOBBY
Uh-oh! These guys are smart!
I'd better turn up the heat!
Now it's on fire!
GLOBBY
NEWS 7
But look!

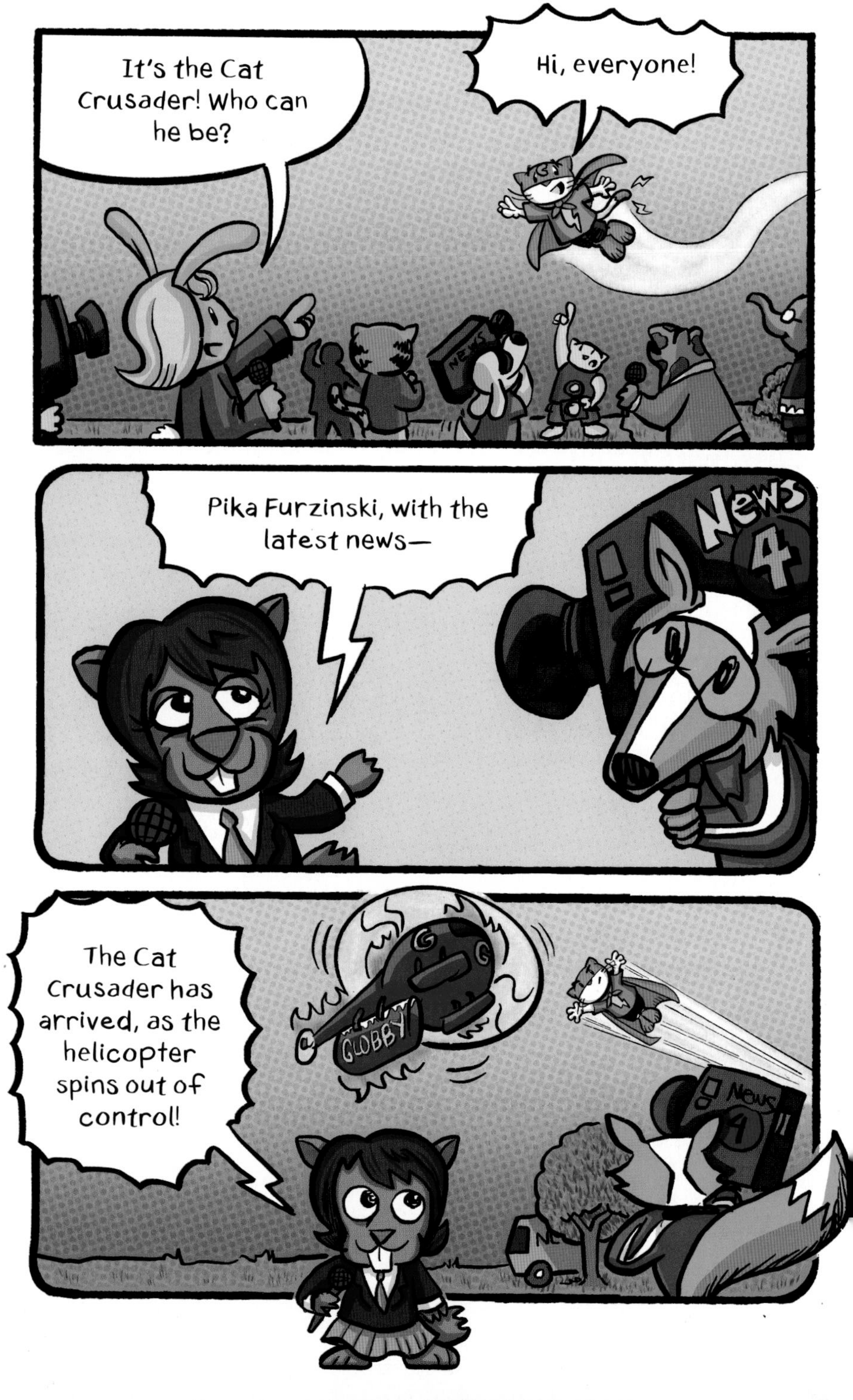
It's the Cat Crusader! Who can he be?
Hi, everyone!
NEWS
Pika Furzinski, with the latest news—
News 4
The Cat Crusader has arrived, as the helicopter spins out of control!
GLOBBY
News 4

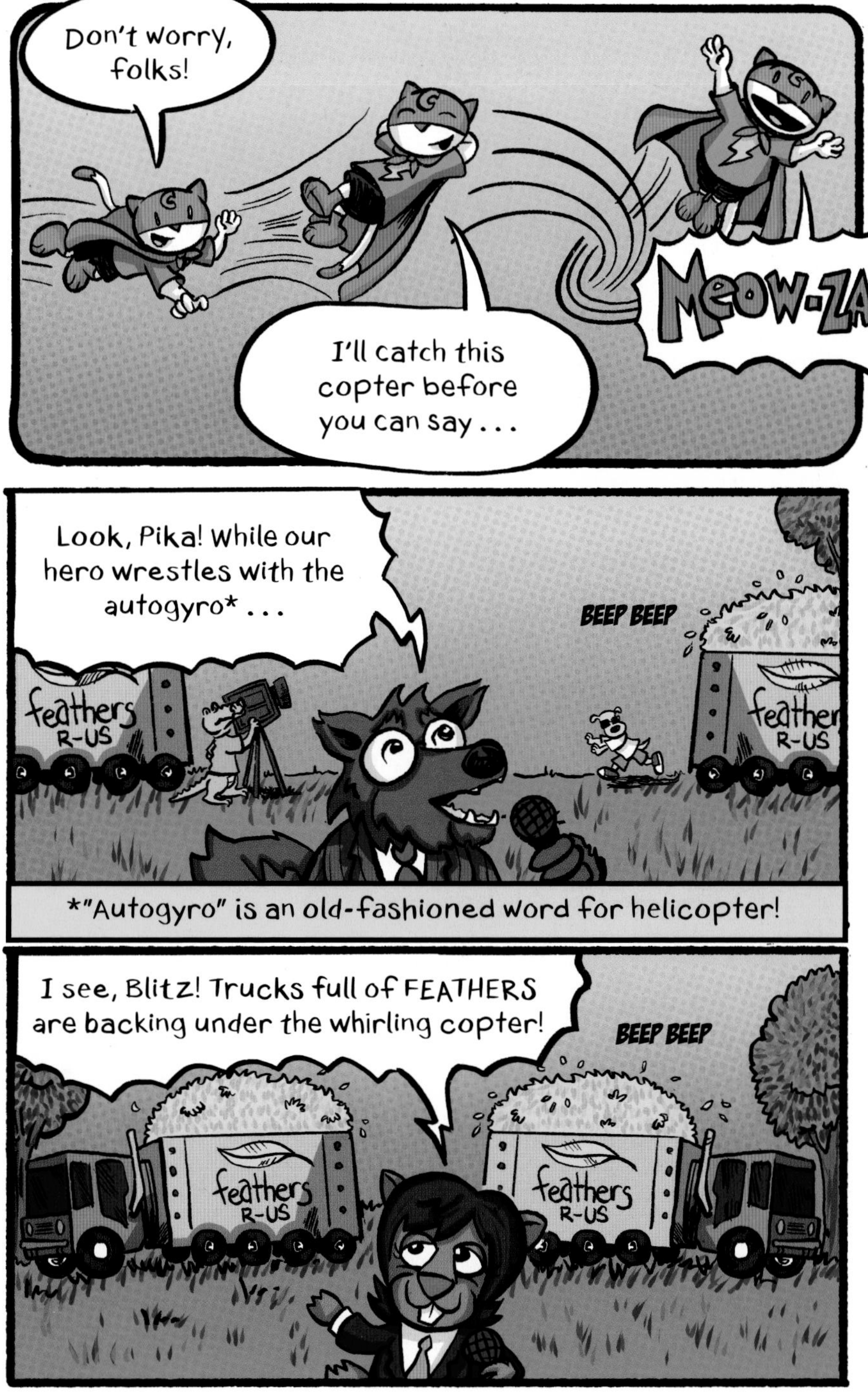
Don't worry, folks!
I'll catch this copter before you can say . . .
MEOW-ZA!
Look, Pika! While our hero wrestles with the autogyro* . . .
BEEP BEEP
feathers R-US
feathers R-US
*"Autogyro" is an old-fashioned word for helicopter!
I see, Blitz! Trucks full of FEATHERS are backing under the whirling copter!
BEEP BEEP
feathers R-US
feathers R-US

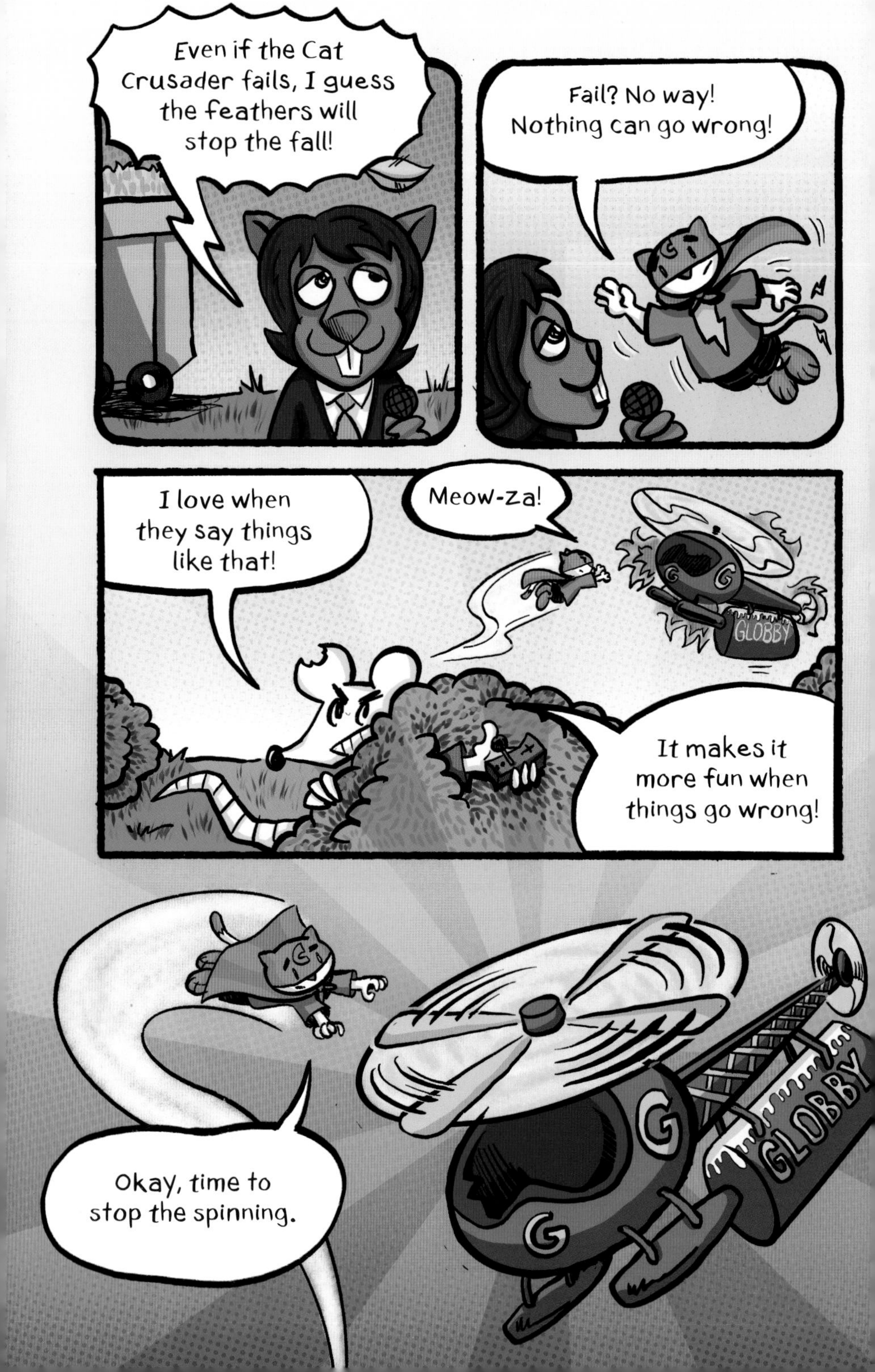
Even if the Cat Crusader fails, I guess the feathers will stop the fall!
Fail? No way! Nothing can go wrong!
I love when they say things like that!
Meow-za!
GLOBBY
It makes it more fun when things go wrong!
Okay, time to stop the spinning.
GLOBBY

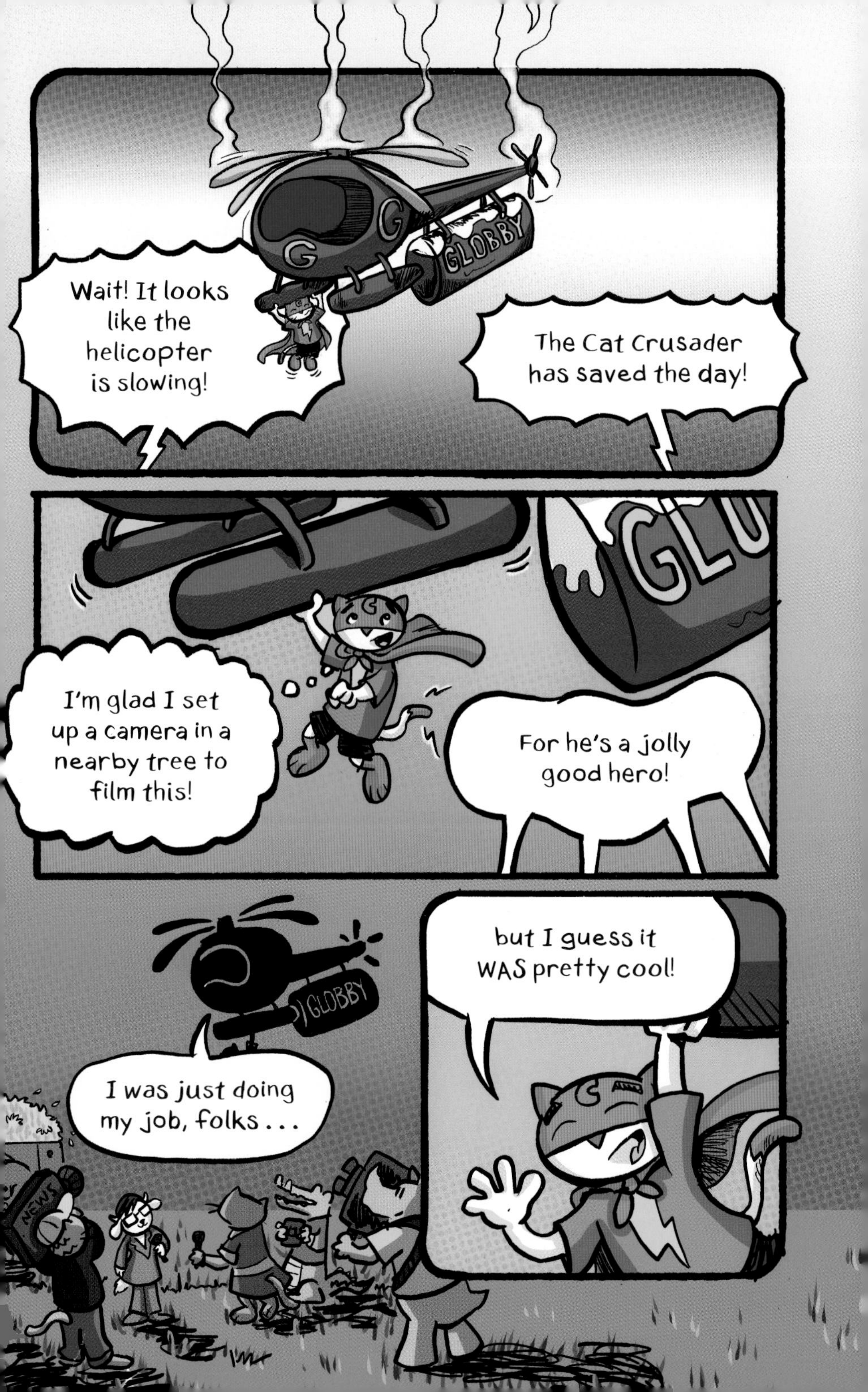
GLOBBY
Wait! It looks like the helicopter is slowing!
The Cat Crusader has saved the day!
GLU
I'm glad I set up a camera in a nearby tree to film this!
For he's a jolly good hero!
GLOBBY
I was just doing my job, folks . . .
but I guess it WAS pretty cool!
NEWS

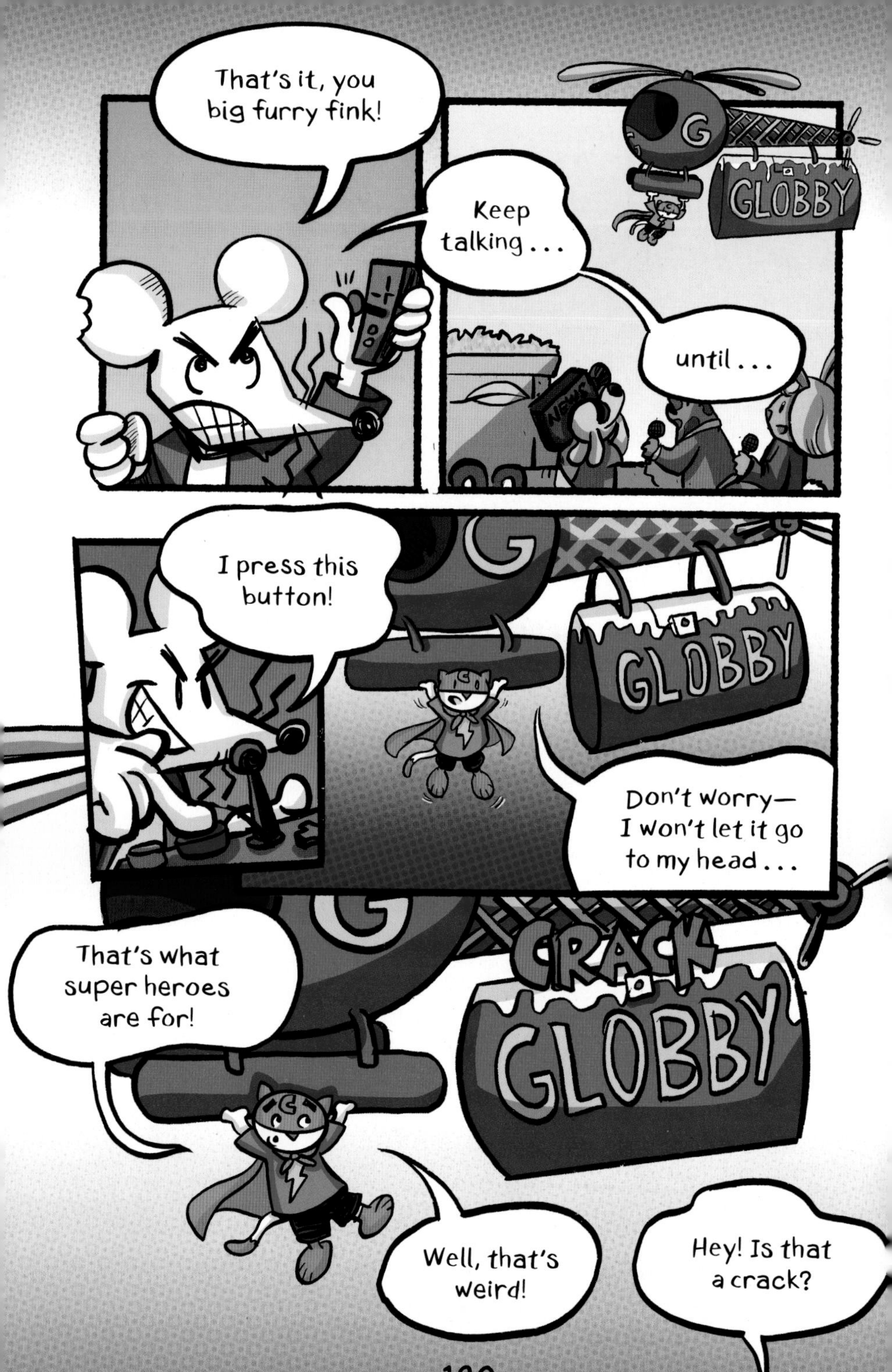
That's it, you big furry fink!
Keep talking . . .
until . . .
NEWS
GLOBBY
I press this button!
GLOBBY
Don't worry— I won't let it go to my head . . .
That's what super heroes are for!
CRACK
GLOBBY
Well, that's weird!
Hey! Is that a crack?

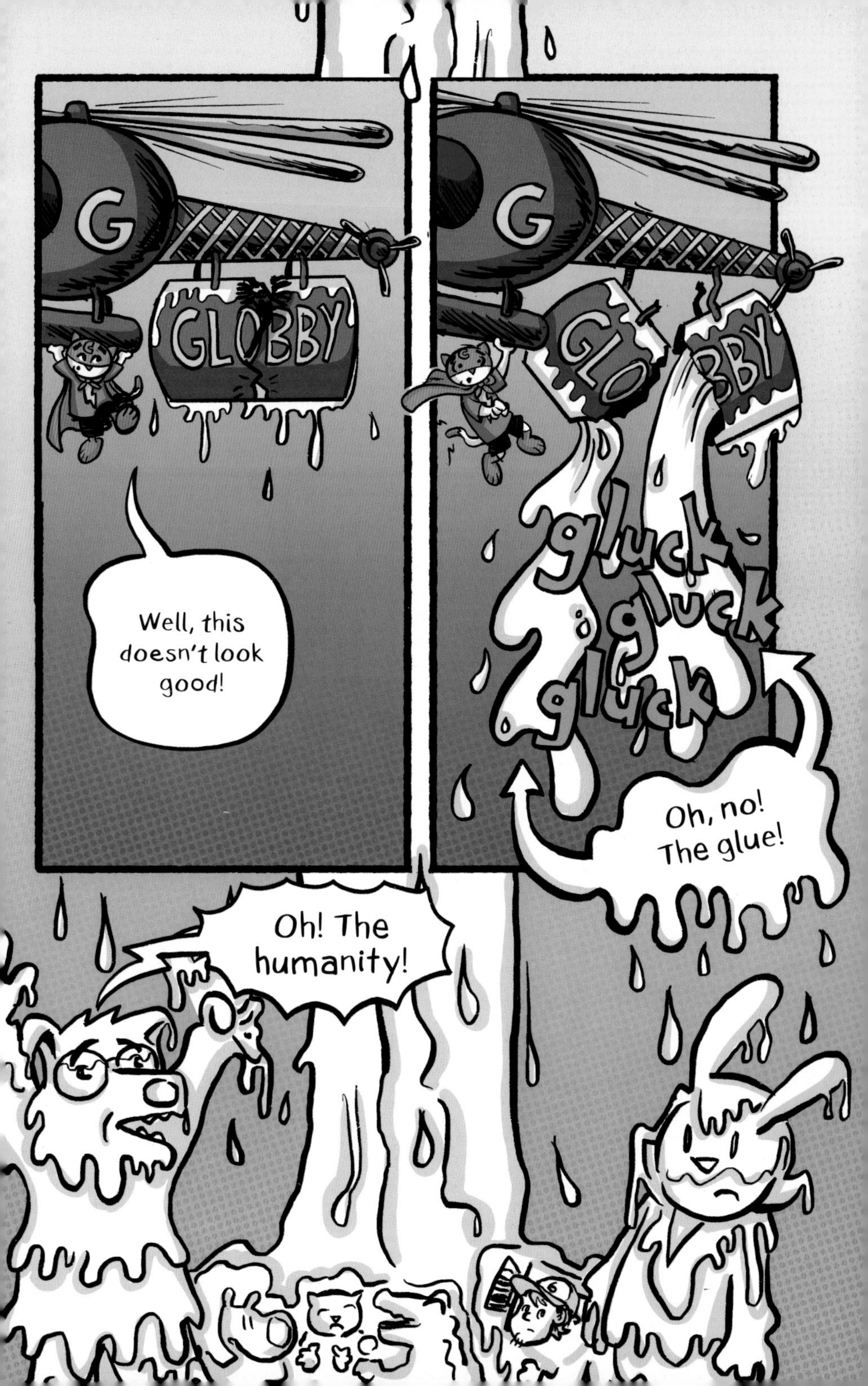
GLOBBY
Well, this doesn't look good!
GLO BBY
gluck gluck gluck
Oh, no! The glue!
Oh! The humanity!

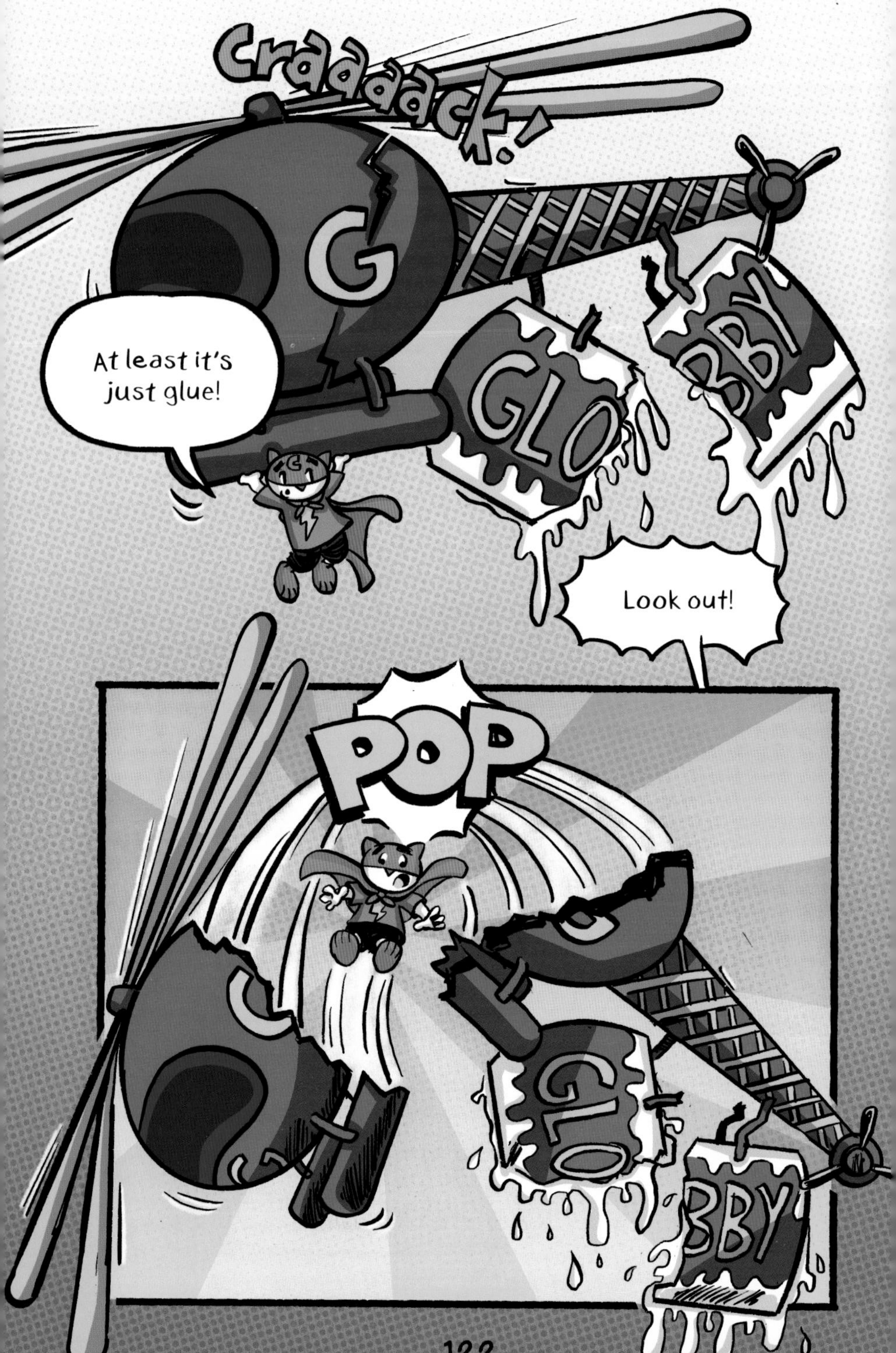
Craaaack!
At least it's just glue!
GLO
BBY
Look out!
POP
GLO
BBY

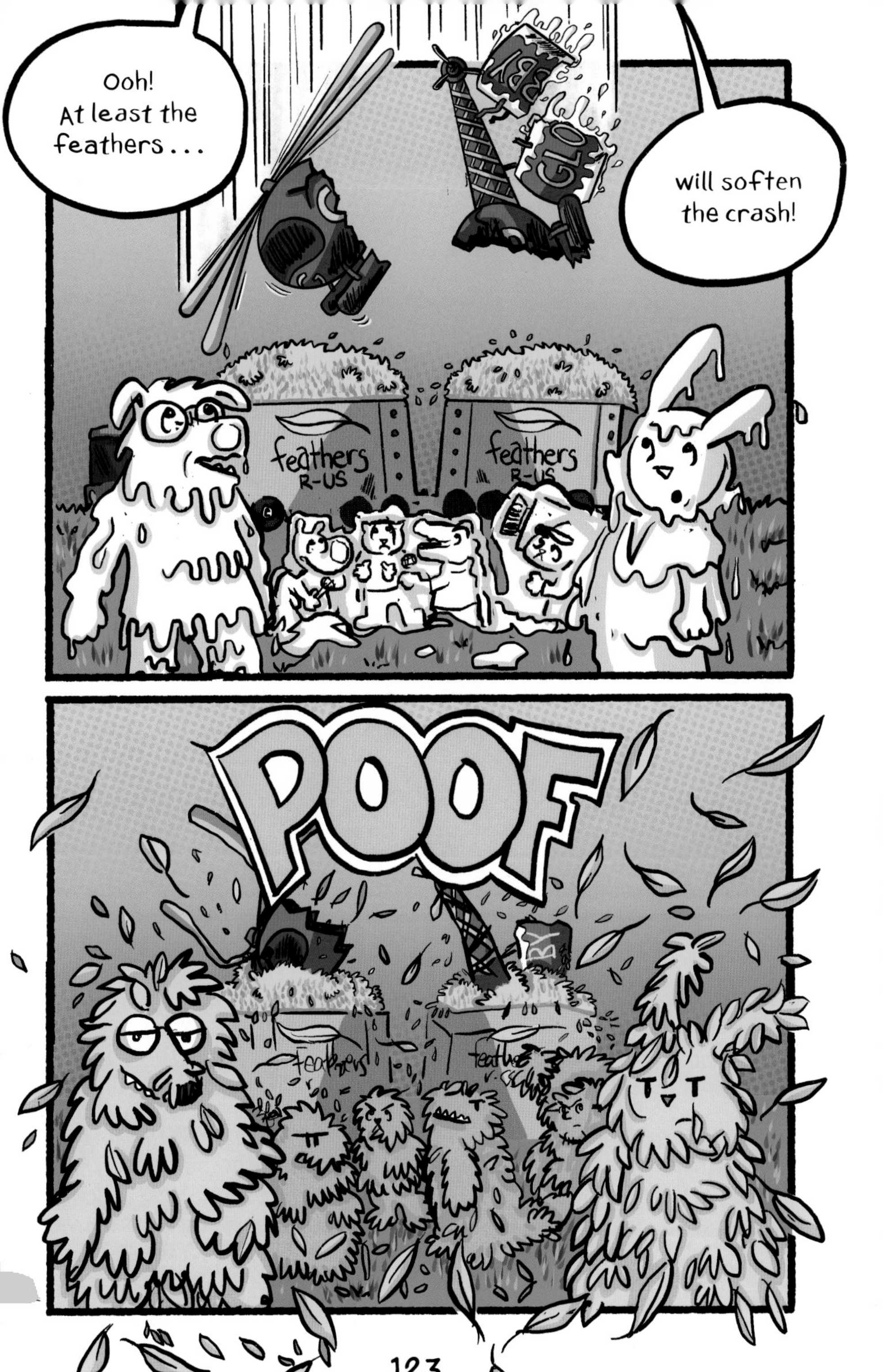
Ooh! At least the feathers . . .
will soften the crash!
feathers R-US
feathers R-US
POOF

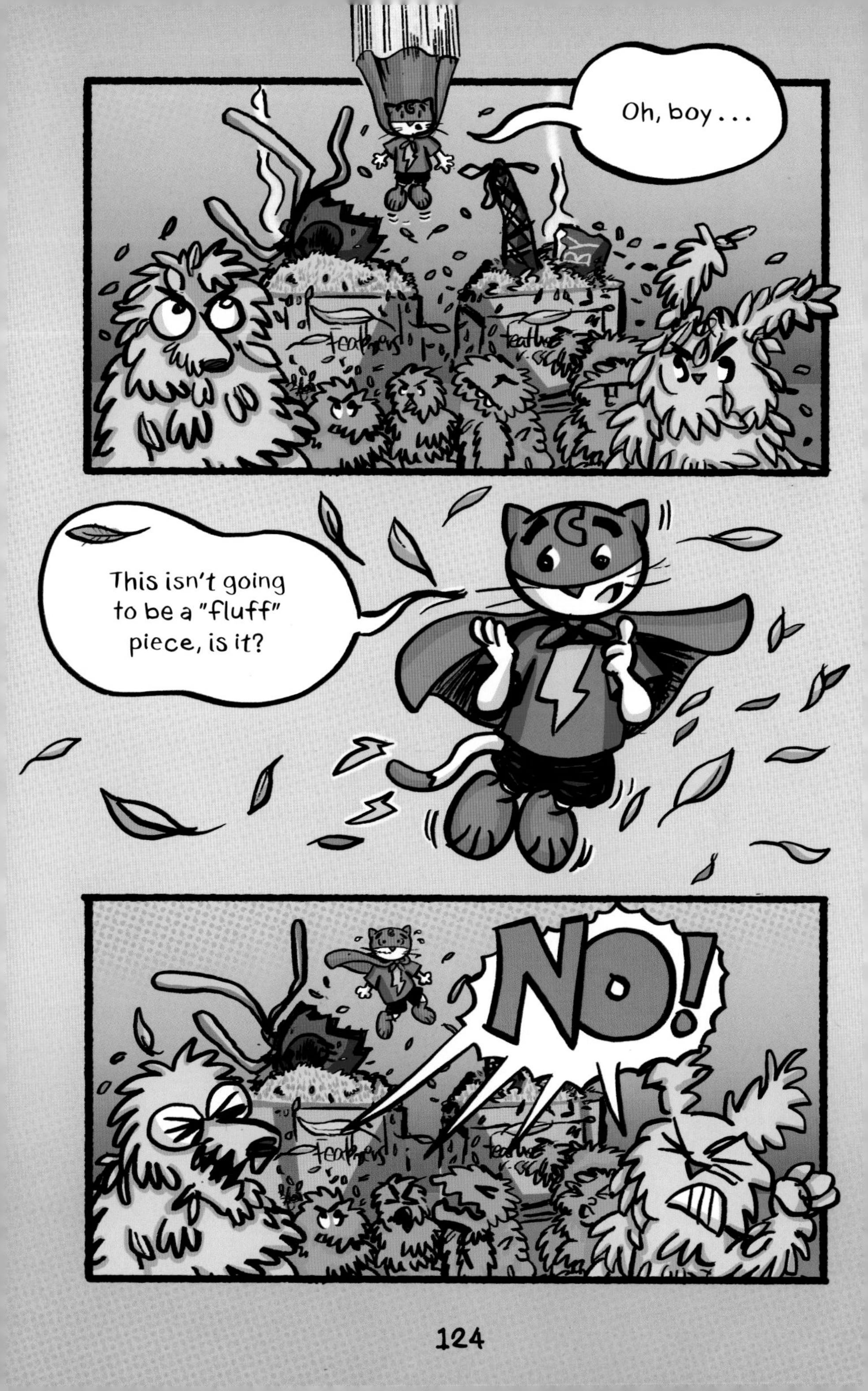
Oh, boy . . .
This isn't going to be a "fluff" piece, is it?
NO!

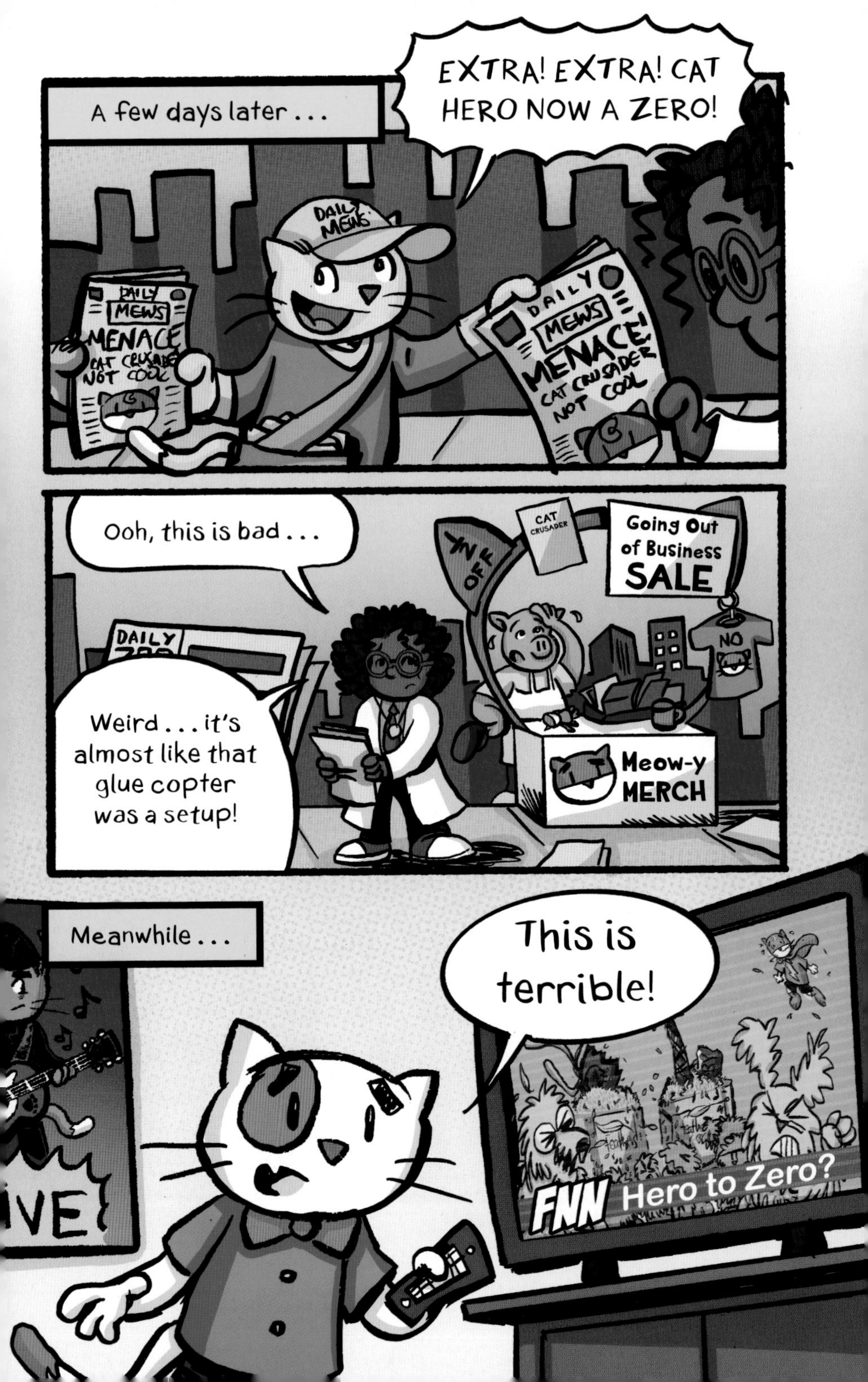
A few days later . . .
EXTRA! EXTRA! CAT HERO NOW A ZERO!
DAILY MEWS
DAILY MEWS MENACE CAT CRUSADER NOT COOL
DAILY MEWS MENACE! CAT CRUSADER NOT COOL
Ooh, this is bad . . .
Weird . . . it's almost like that glue copter was a setup!
DAILY
CAT CRUSADER
OFF
Going Out of Business SALE
NO
Meow-y MERCH
Meanwhile . . .
This is terrible!
FNN Hero to Zero?

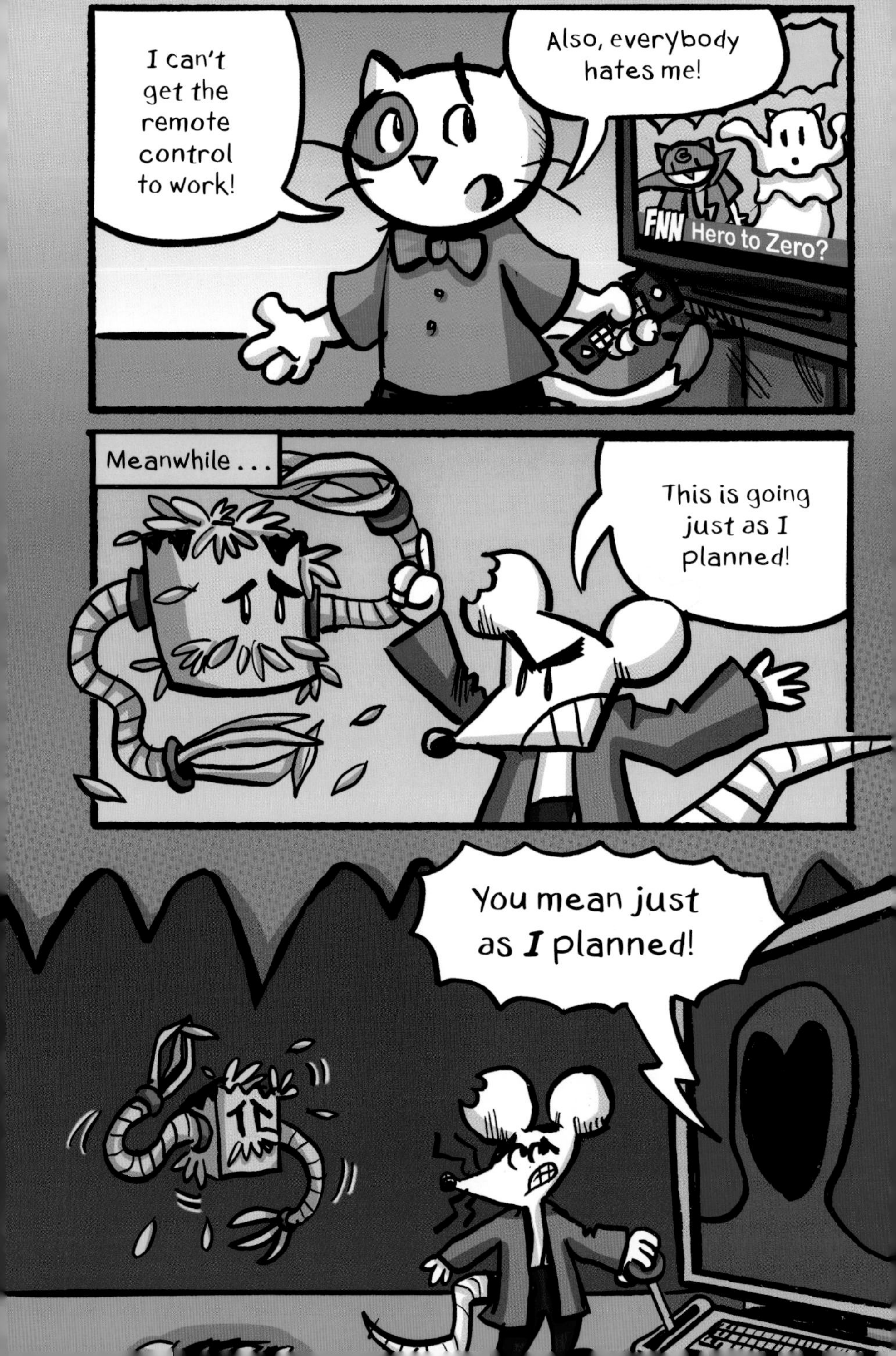

I can't get the remote control to work!
Also, everybody hates me!
FNN Hero to Zero?
Meanwhile . . .
This is going just as I planned!
You mean just as *I* planned!

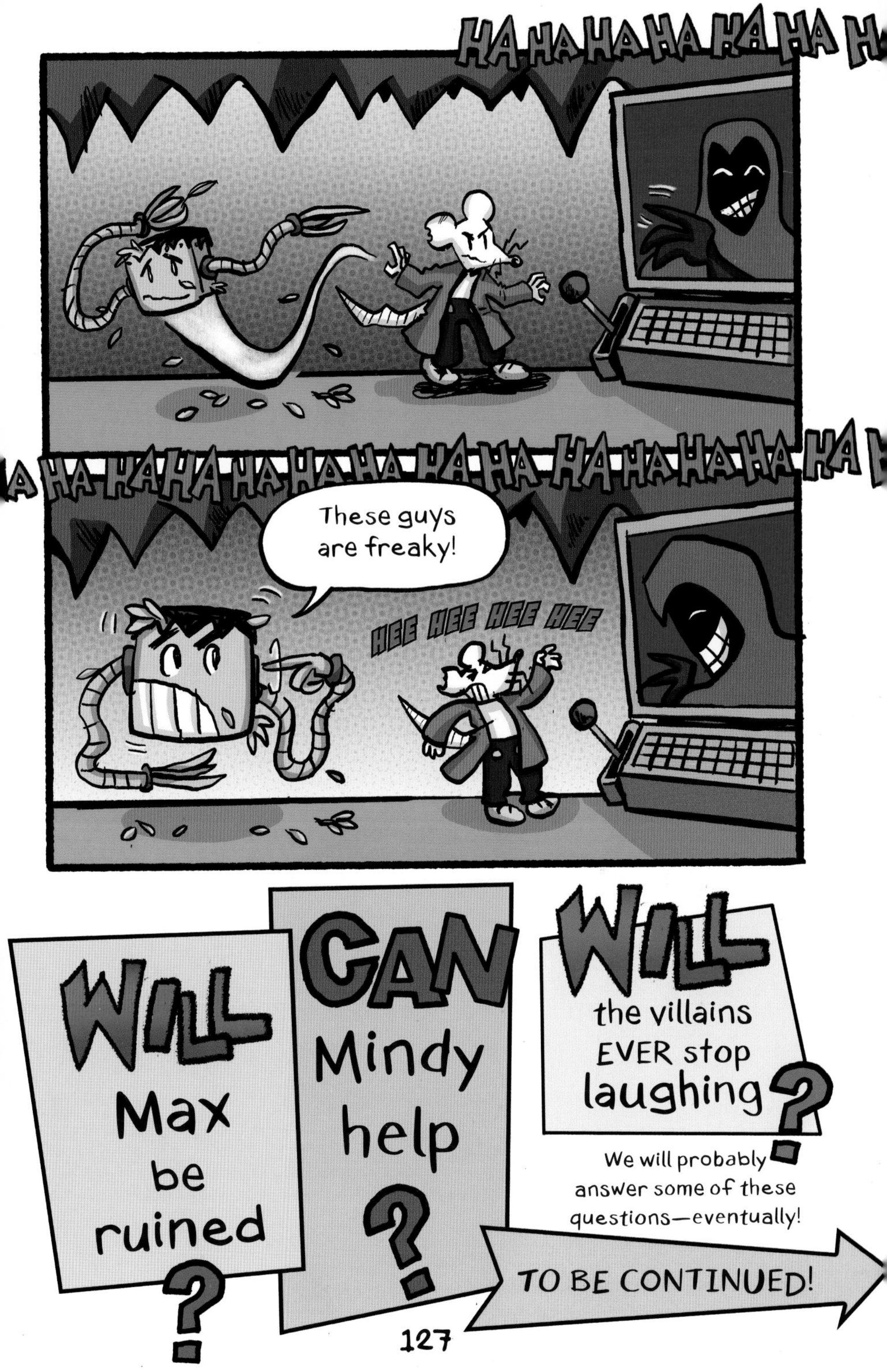
HA HA HA HA HA HA HA
HA HA HA HA HA HA HA HA HA HA HA HA HA HA HA HA HA HA
These guys are freaky!
HEE HEE HEE HEE
WILL Max be ruined?
CAN Mindy help?
WILL the villains EVER stop laughing?
We will probably answer some of these questions—eventually!
TO BE CONTINUED!

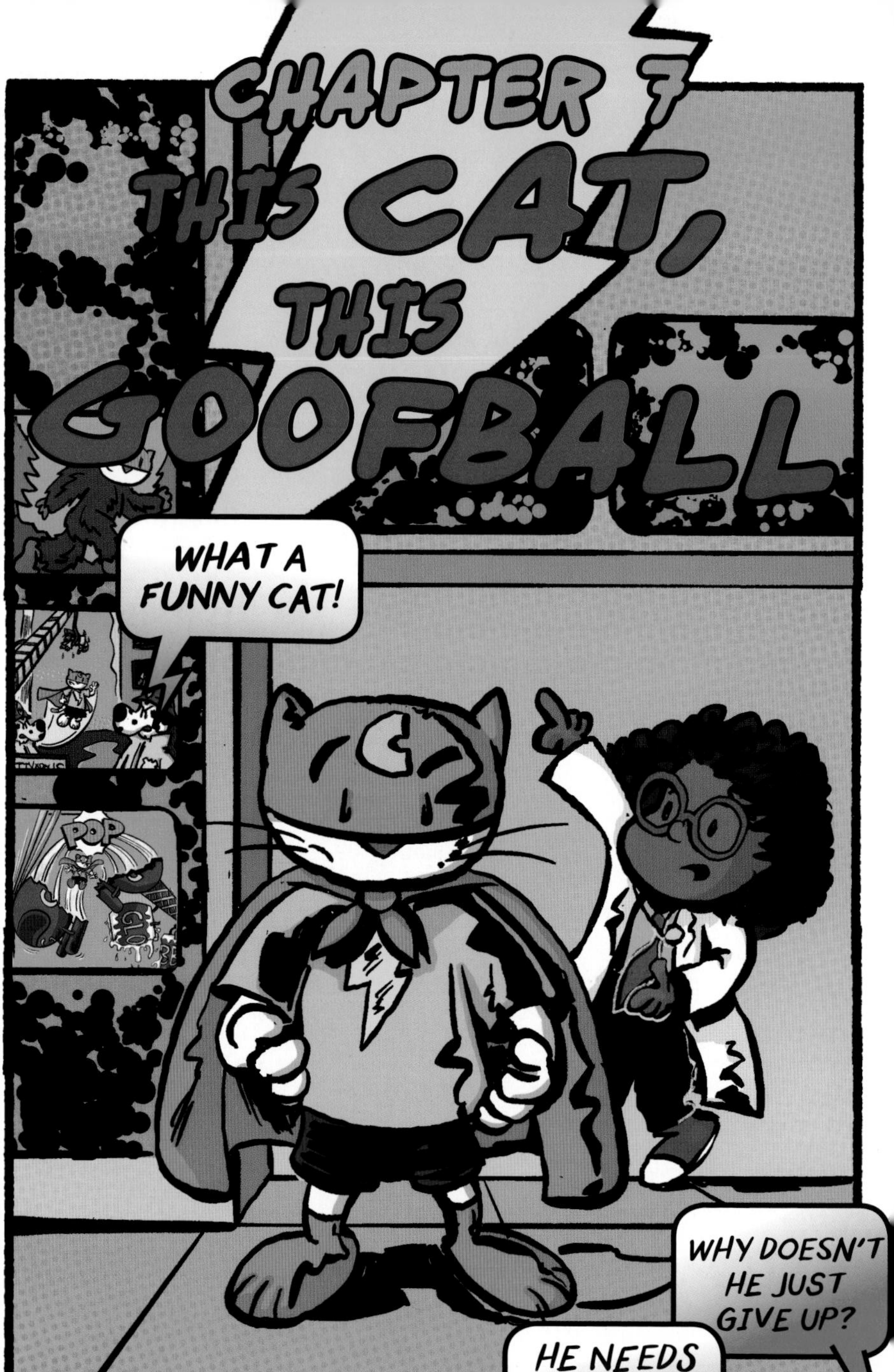
CHAPTER 7
THIS CAT, THIS GOOFBALL
WHAT A FUNNY CAT!
POP
WHY DOESN'T HE JUST GIVE UP?
HE NEEDS TO GET A NEW JOB!

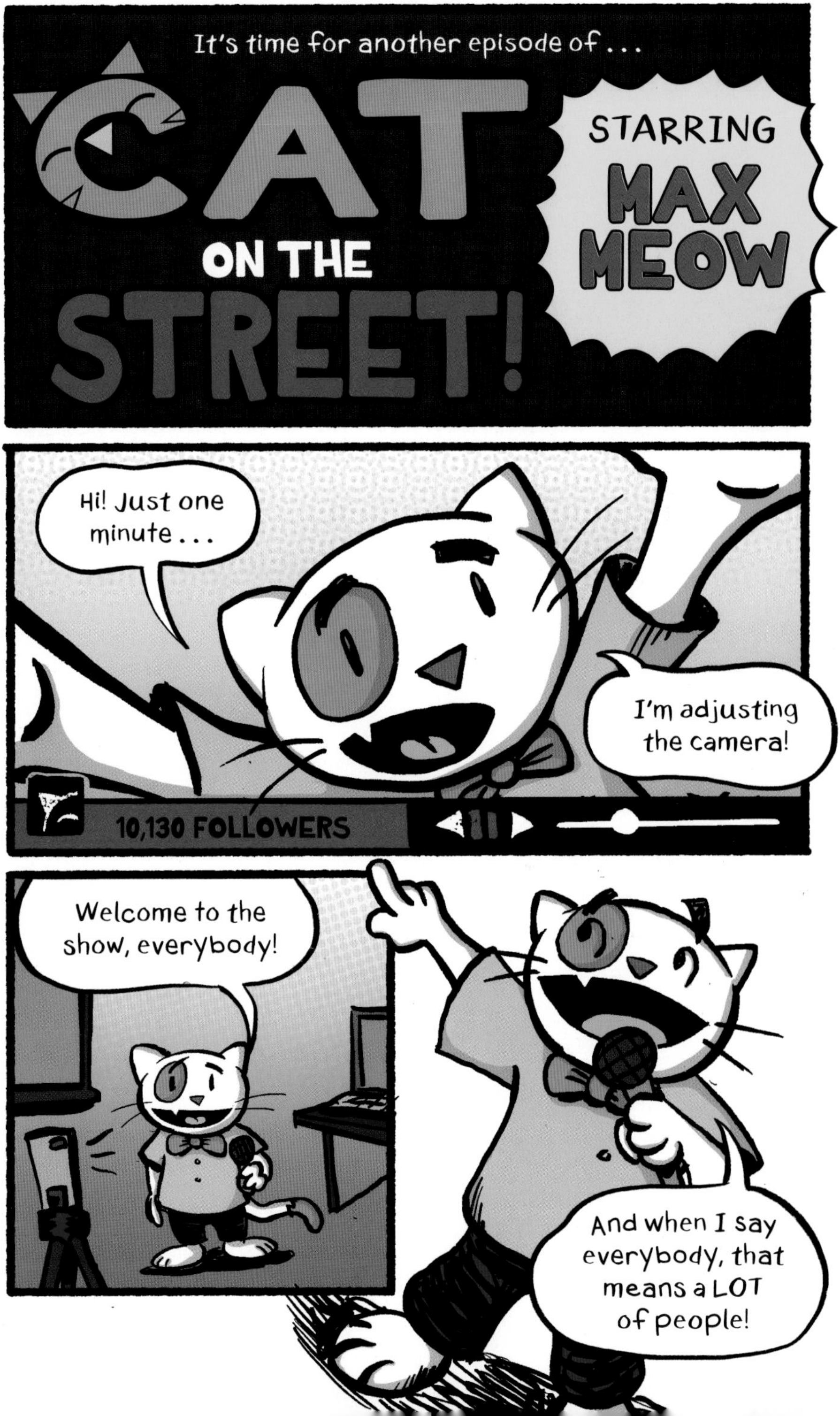

It's time for another episode of . . .
CAT ON THE STREET!
STARRING MAX MEOW
Hi! Just one minute . . .
I'm adjusting the camera!
10,130 FOLLOWERS
Welcome to the show, everybody!
And when I say everybody, that means a LOT of people!

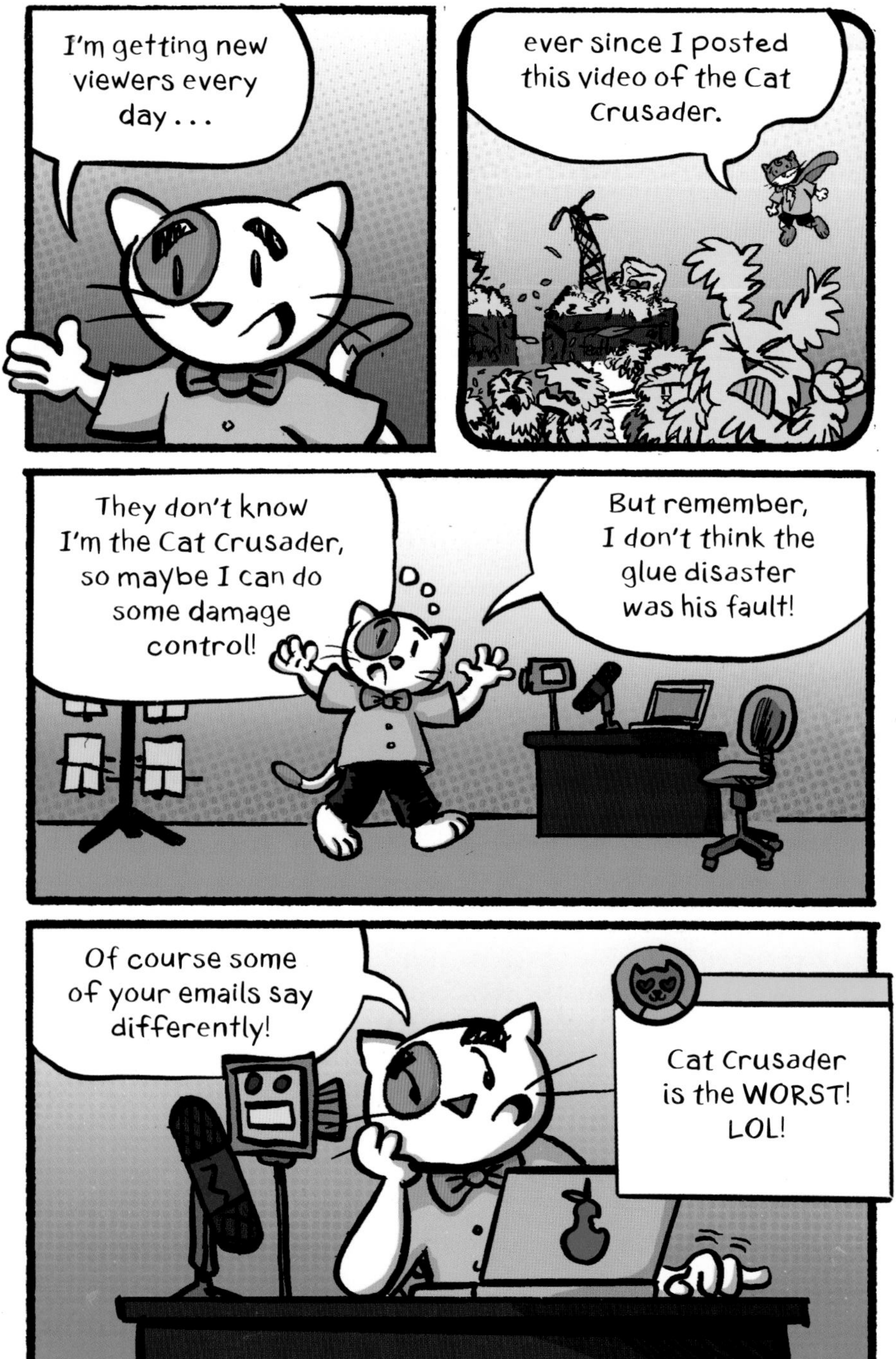
I'm getting new viewers every day . . .
ever since I posted this video of the Cat Crusader.
They don't know I'm the Cat Crusader, so maybe I can do some damage control!
But remember, I don't think the glue disaster was his fault!
Of course some of your emails say differently!
Cat Crusader is the WORST! LOL!

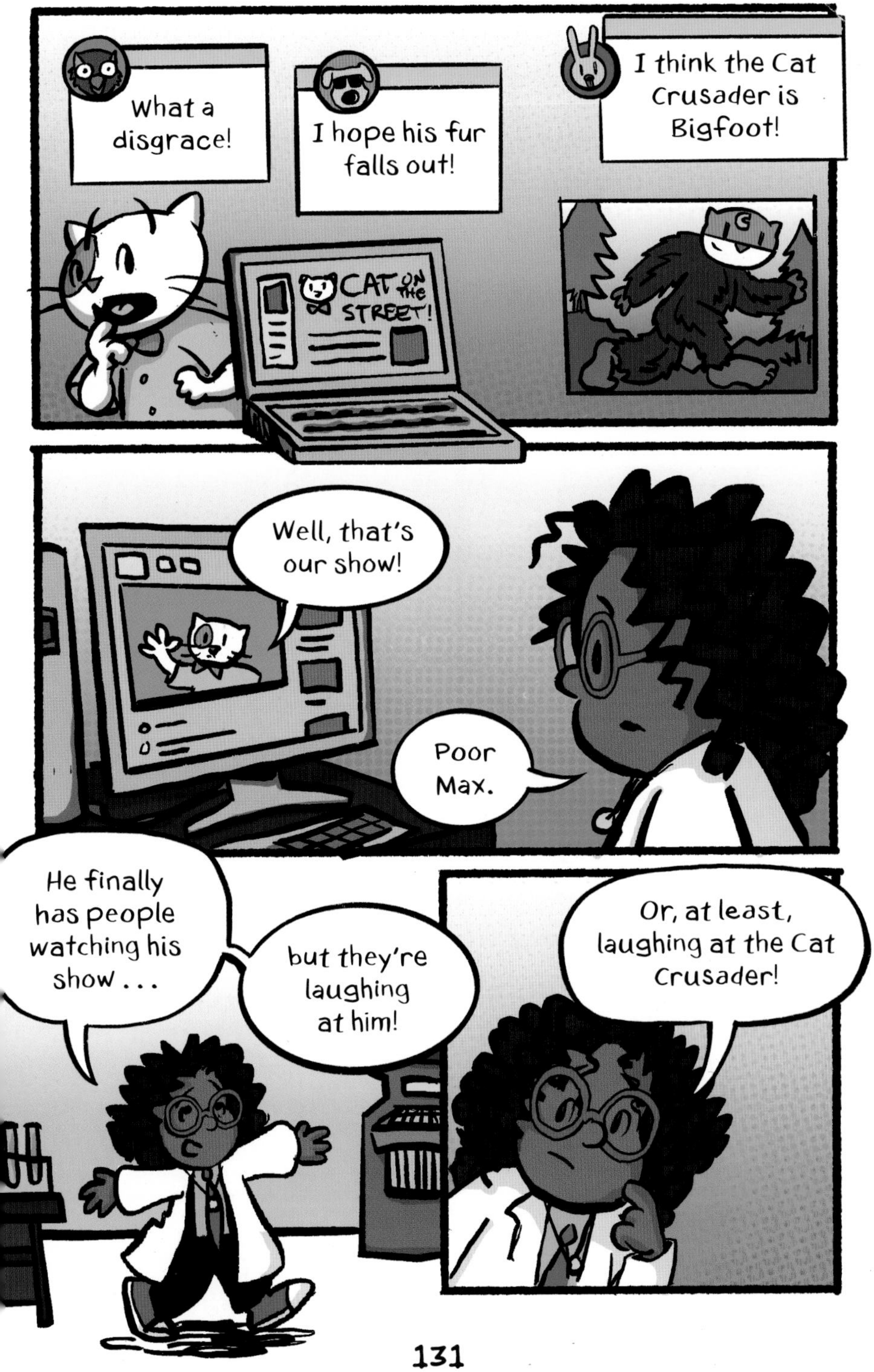

What a disgrace!
I hope his fur falls out!
I think the Cat Crusader is Bigfoot!
CAT ON THE STREET!
Well, that's our show!
Poor Max.
He finally has people watching his show . . .
but they're laughing at him!
Or, at least, laughing at the Cat Crusader!

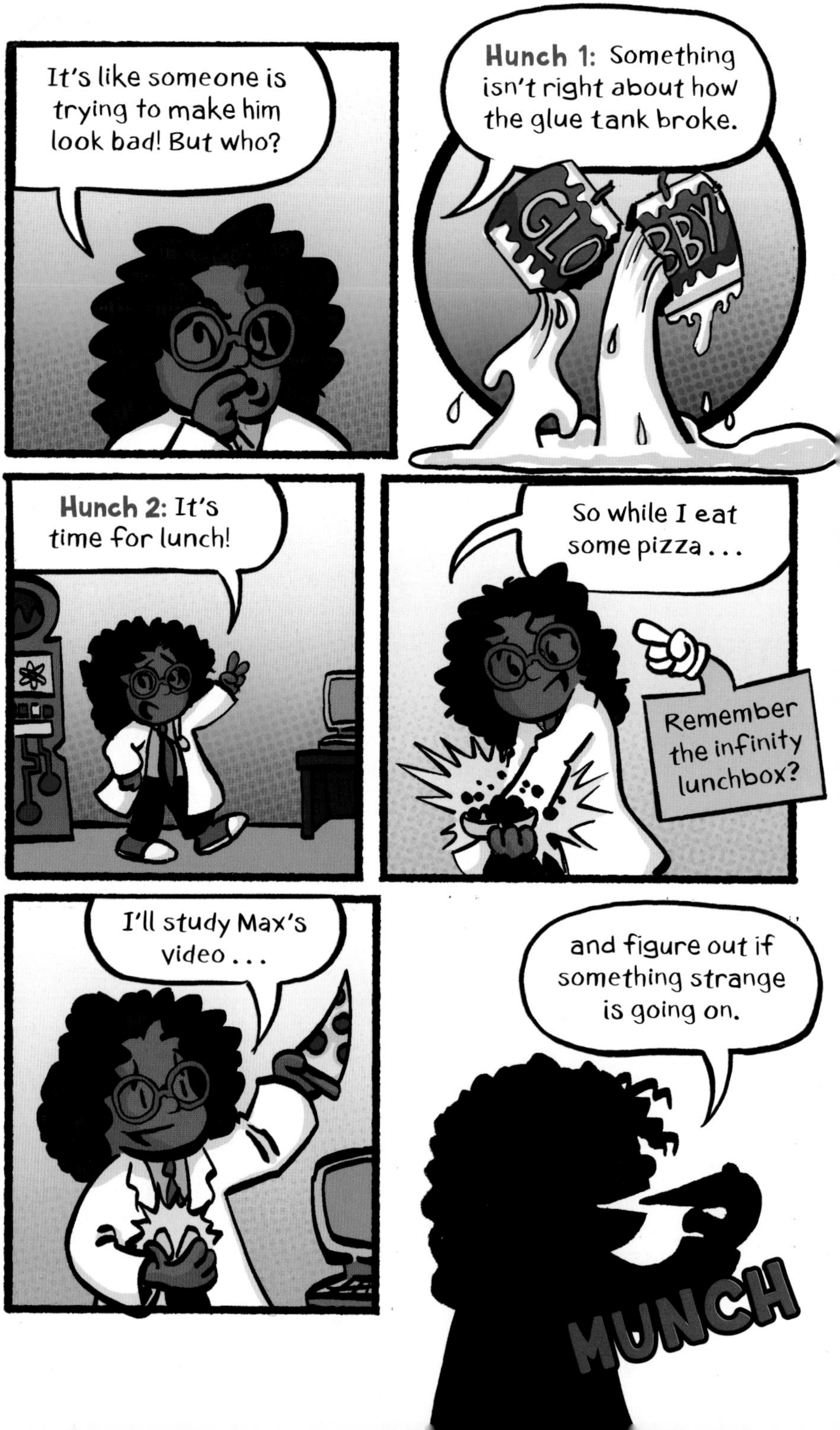
It's like someone is trying to make him look bad! But who?
Hunch 1: Something isn't right about how the glue tank broke.
GLO
BBY
Hunch 2: It's time for lunch!
So while I eat some pizza . . .
Remember the infinity lunchbox?
I'll study Max's video . . .
and figure out if something strange is going on.
MUNCH

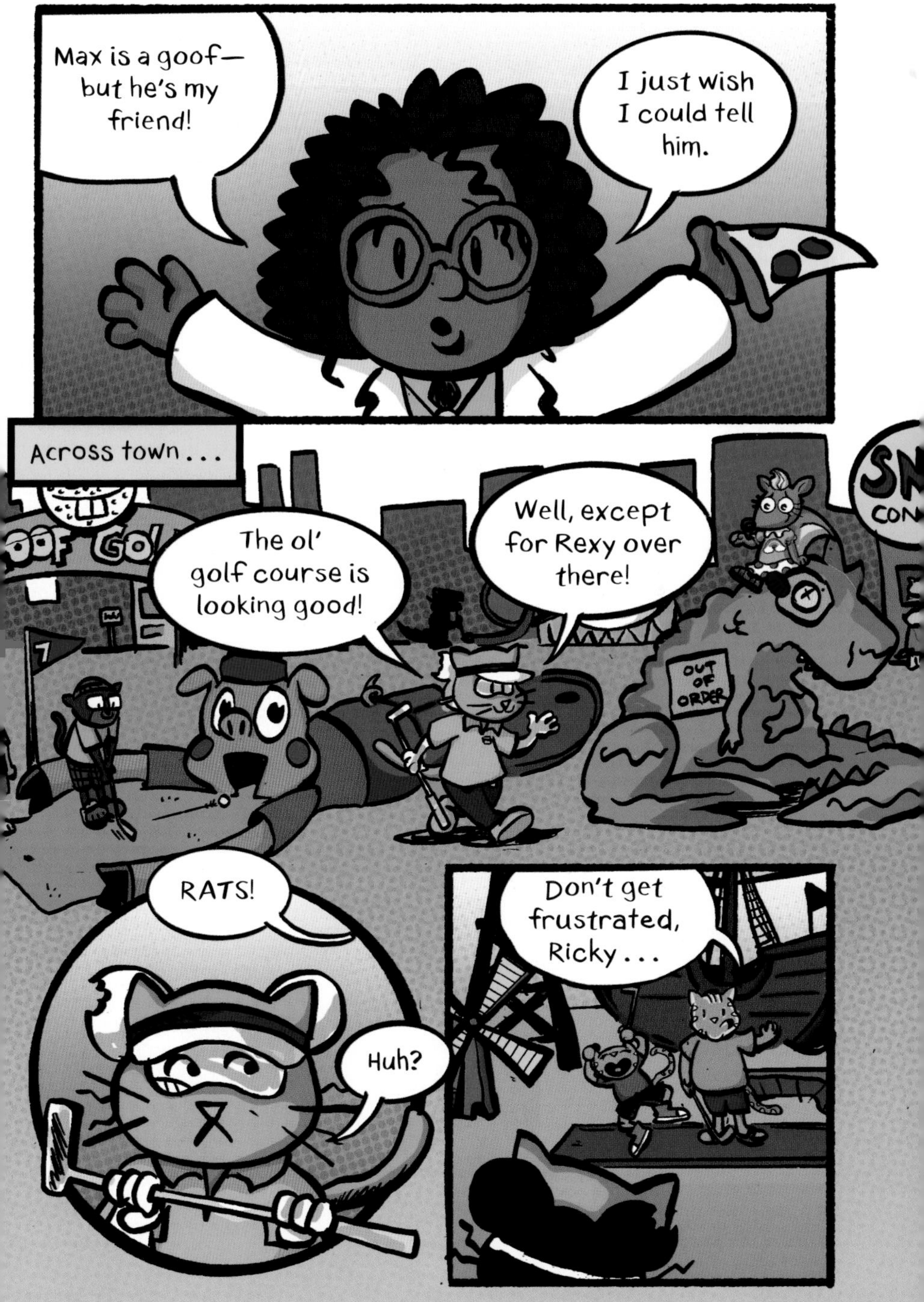
Max is a goof— but he's my friend!
I just wish I could tell him.
Across town . . .
The ol' golf course is looking good!
Well, except for Rexy over there!
OUT OF ORDER
RATS!
Huh?
Don't get frustrated, Ricky . . .

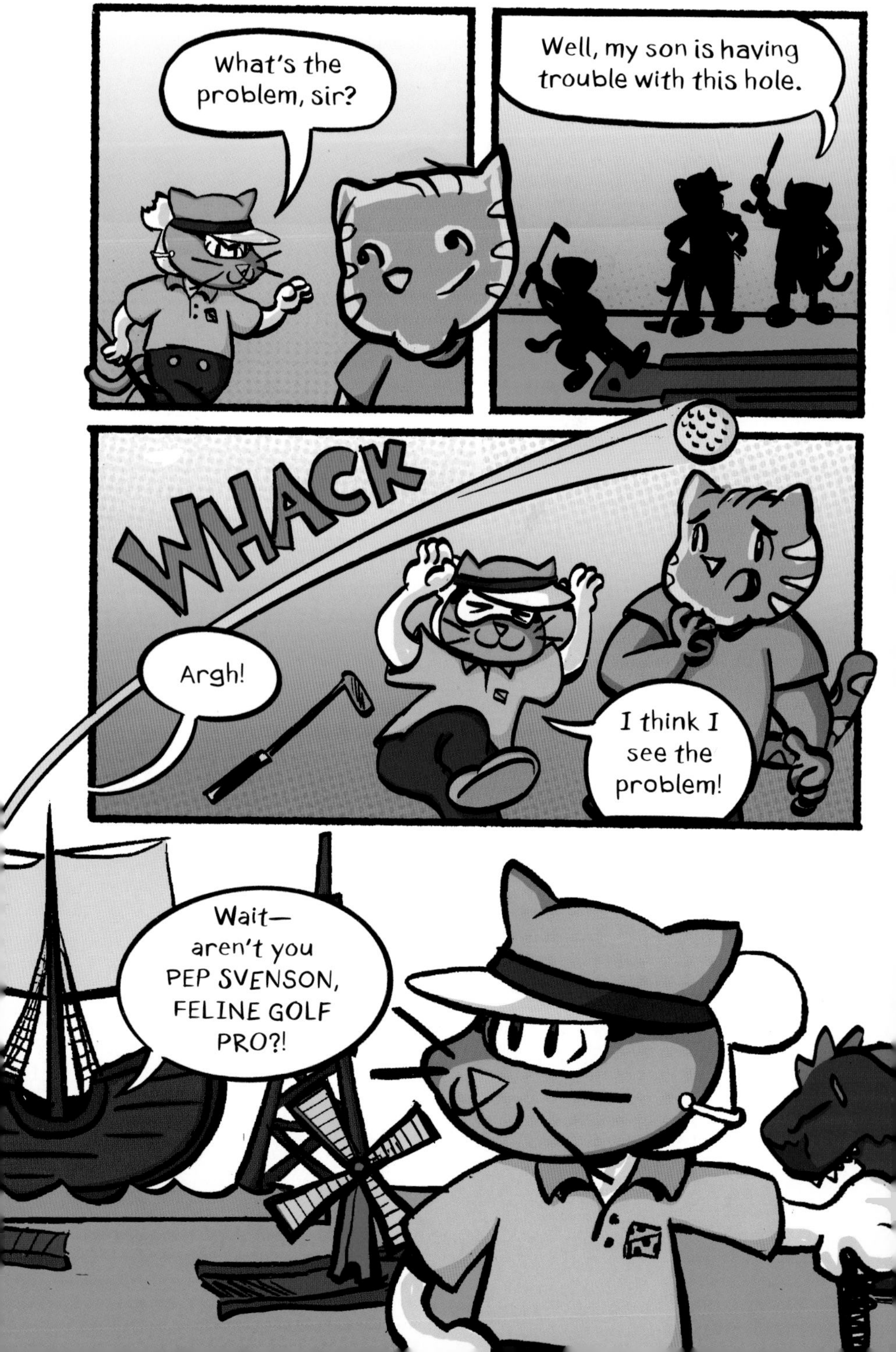
What's the problem, sir?
Well, my son is having trouble with this hole.
WHACK
Argh!
I think I see the problem!
Wait— aren't you PEP SVENSON, FELINE GOLF PRO?!

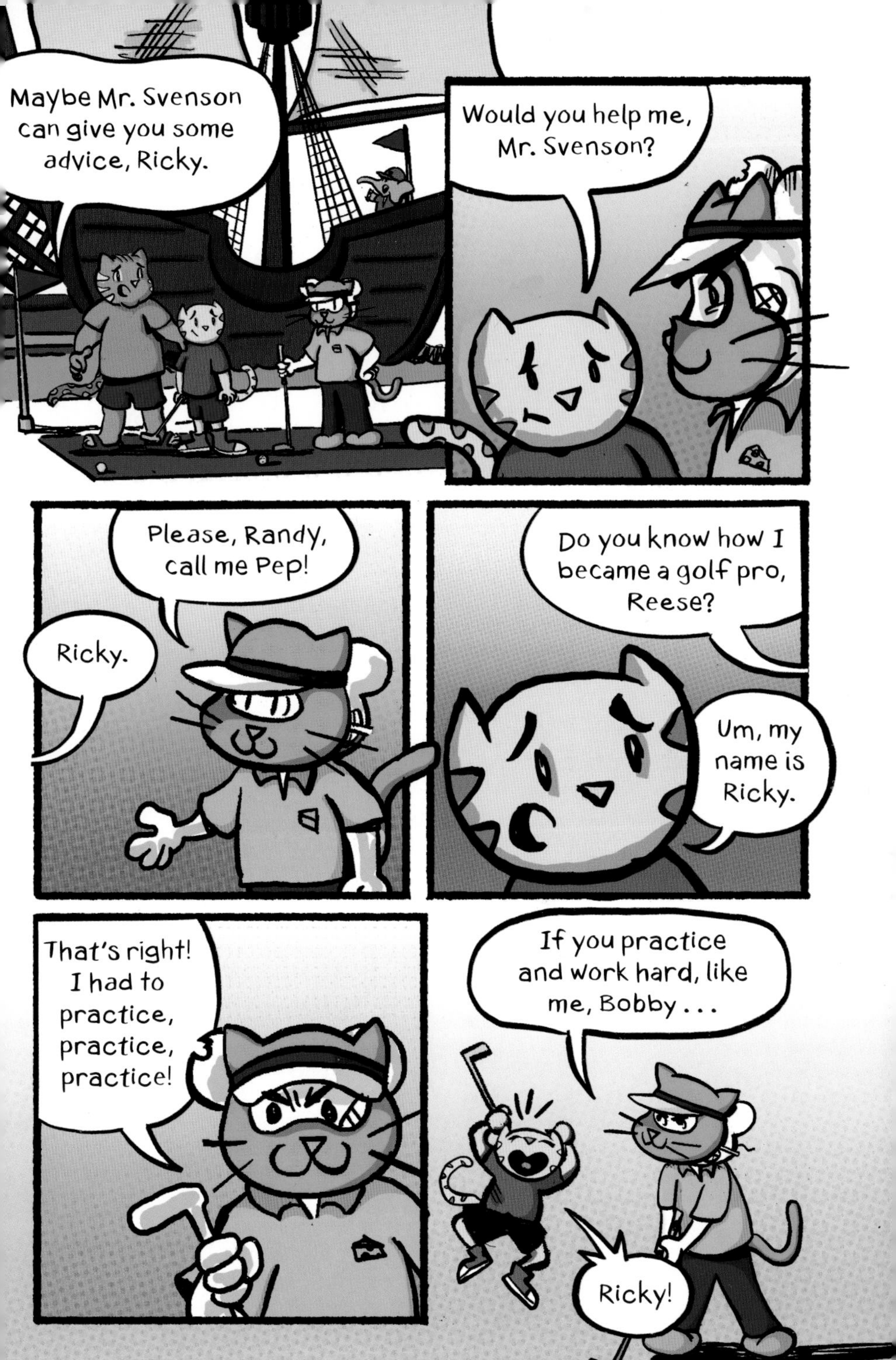
Maybe Mr. Svenson can give you some advice, Ricky.
Would you help me, Mr. Svenson?
Please, Randy, call me Pep!
Ricky.
Do you know how I became a golf pro, Reese?
Um, my name is Ricky.
That's right! I had to practice, practice, practice!
If you practice and work hard, like me, Bobby . . .
Ricky!

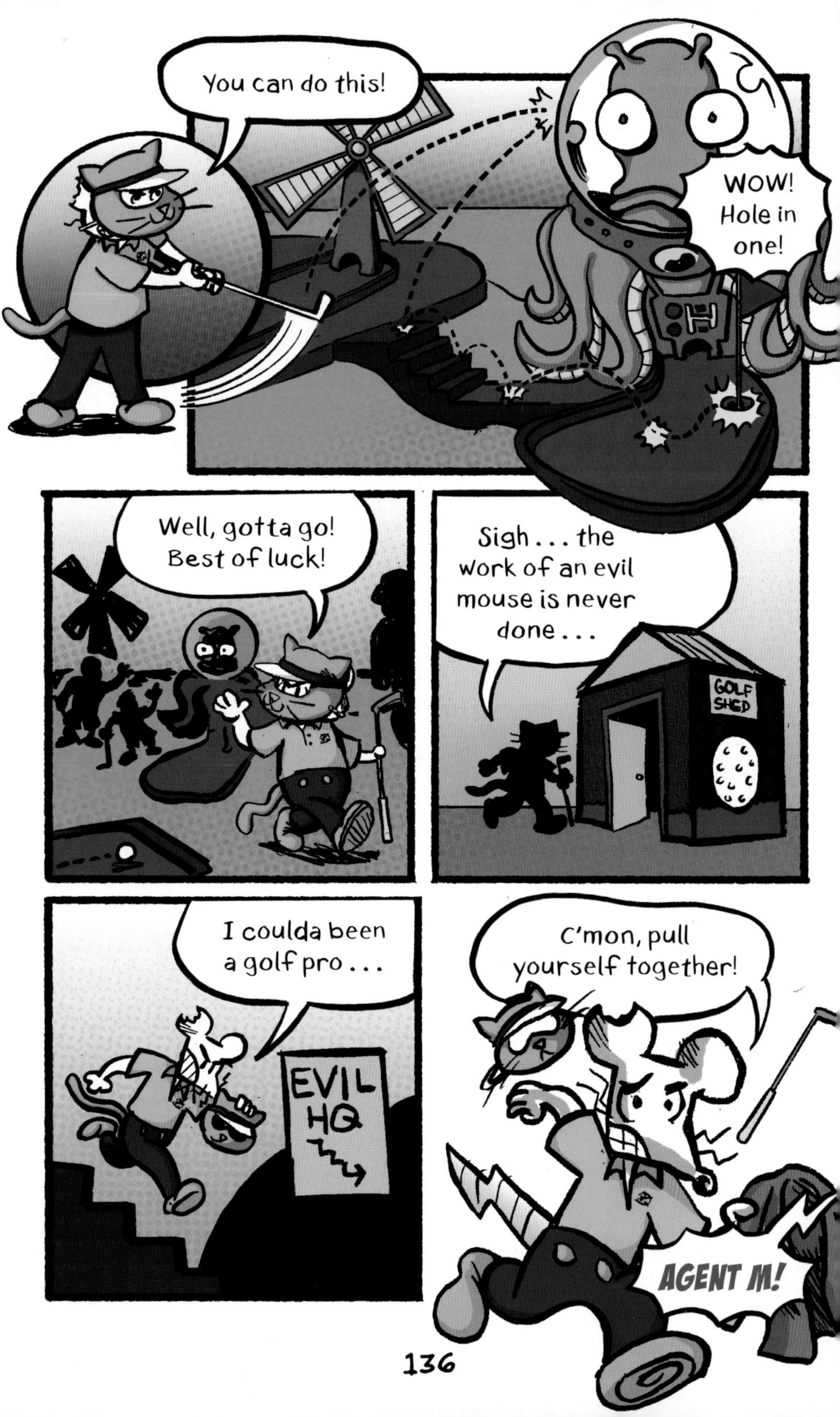
You can do this!
M
WOW! Hole in one!
Well, gotta go! Best of luck!
Sigh . . . the work of an evil mouse is never done . . .
GOLF SHED
I coulda been a golf pro . . .
EVIL HQ
C'mon, pull yourself together!
AGENT M!

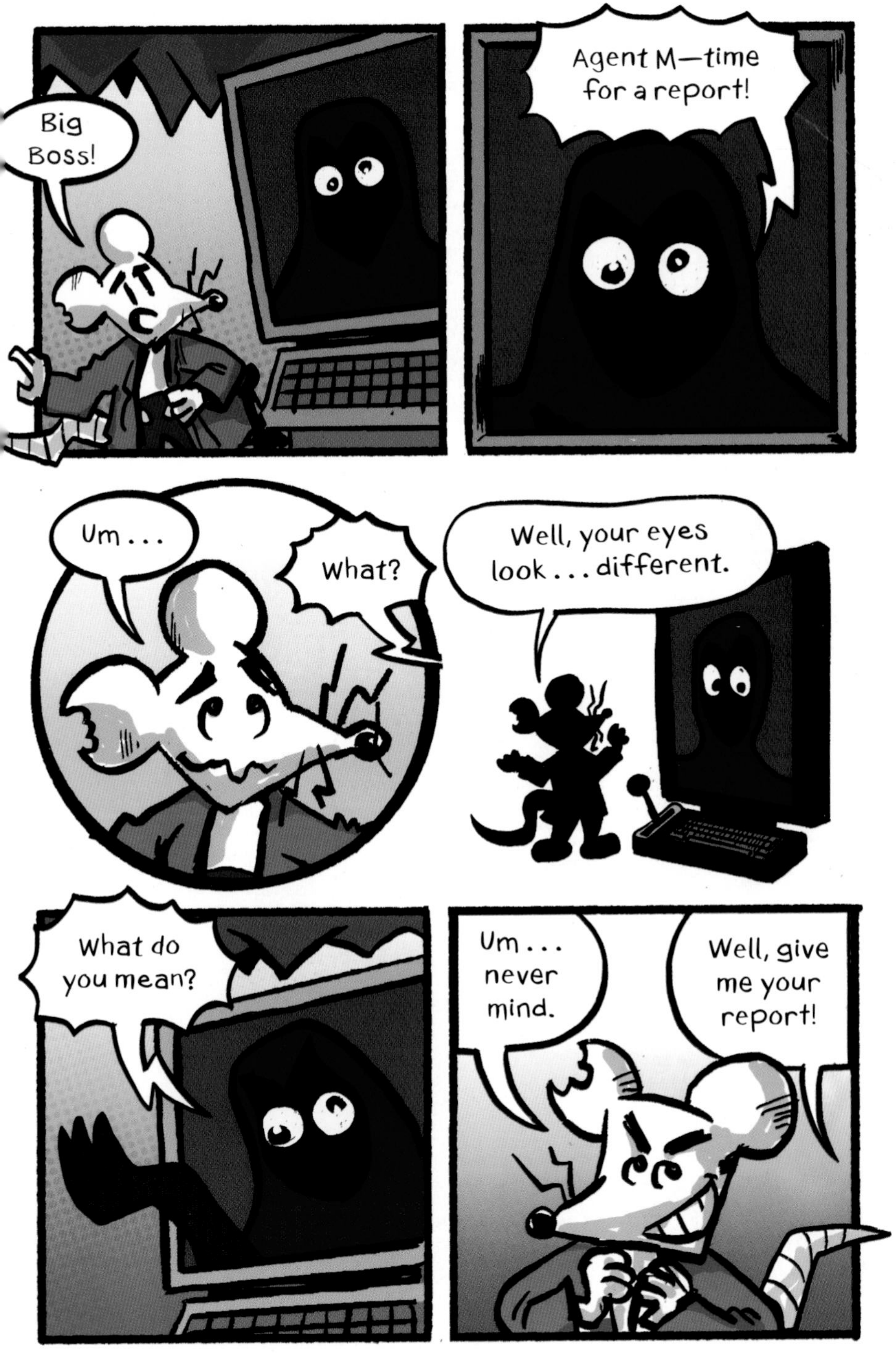
Big Boss!
Agent M—time for a report!
Um . . .
What?
Well, your eyes look . . . different.
What do you mean?
Um . . . never mind.
Well, give me your report!

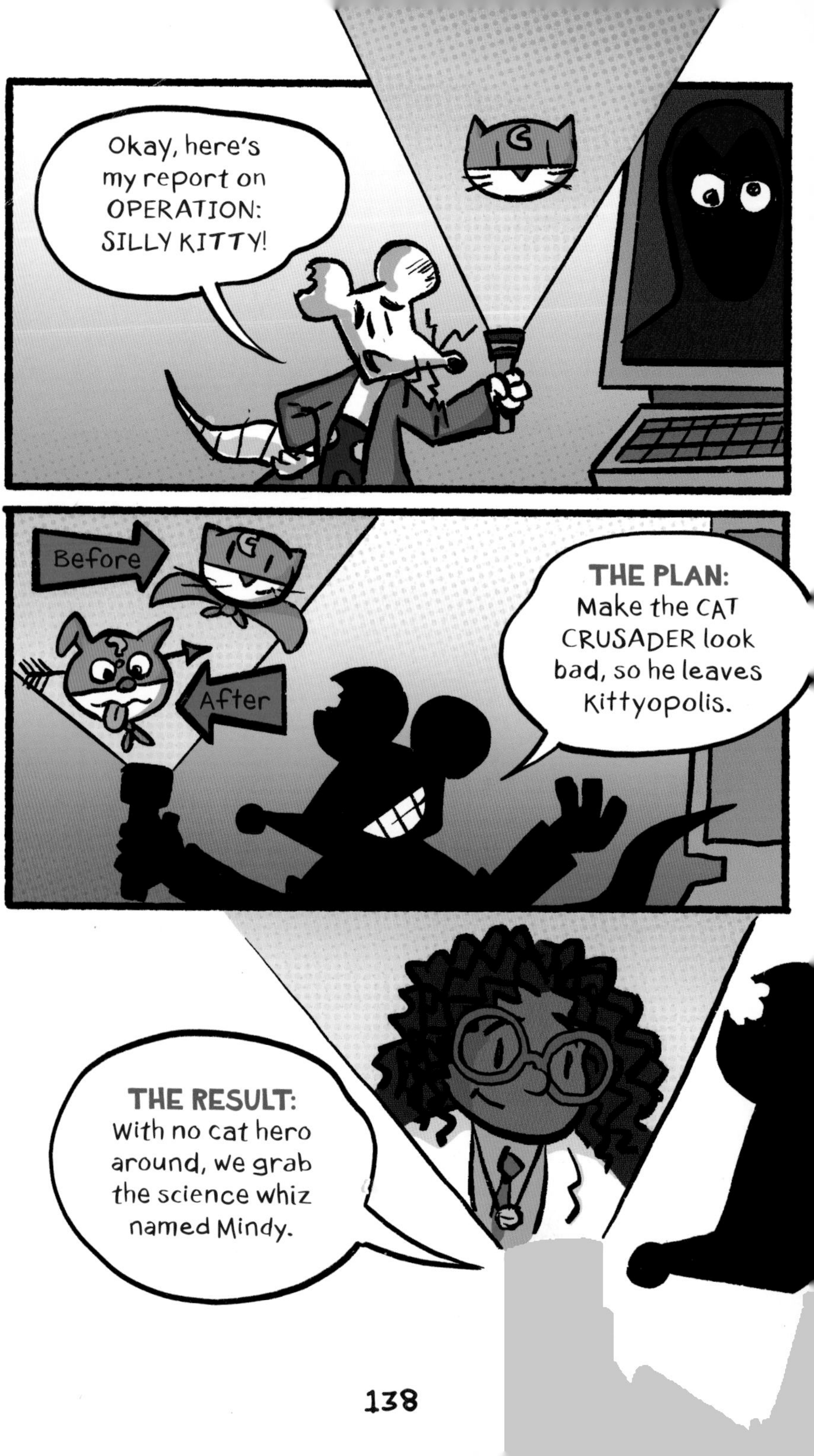
Okay, here's my report on OPERATION: SILLY KITTY!
Before
After
THE PLAN: Make the CAT CRUSADER look bad, so he leaves Kittyopolis.
THE RESULT: With no cat hero around, we grab the science whiz named Mindy.

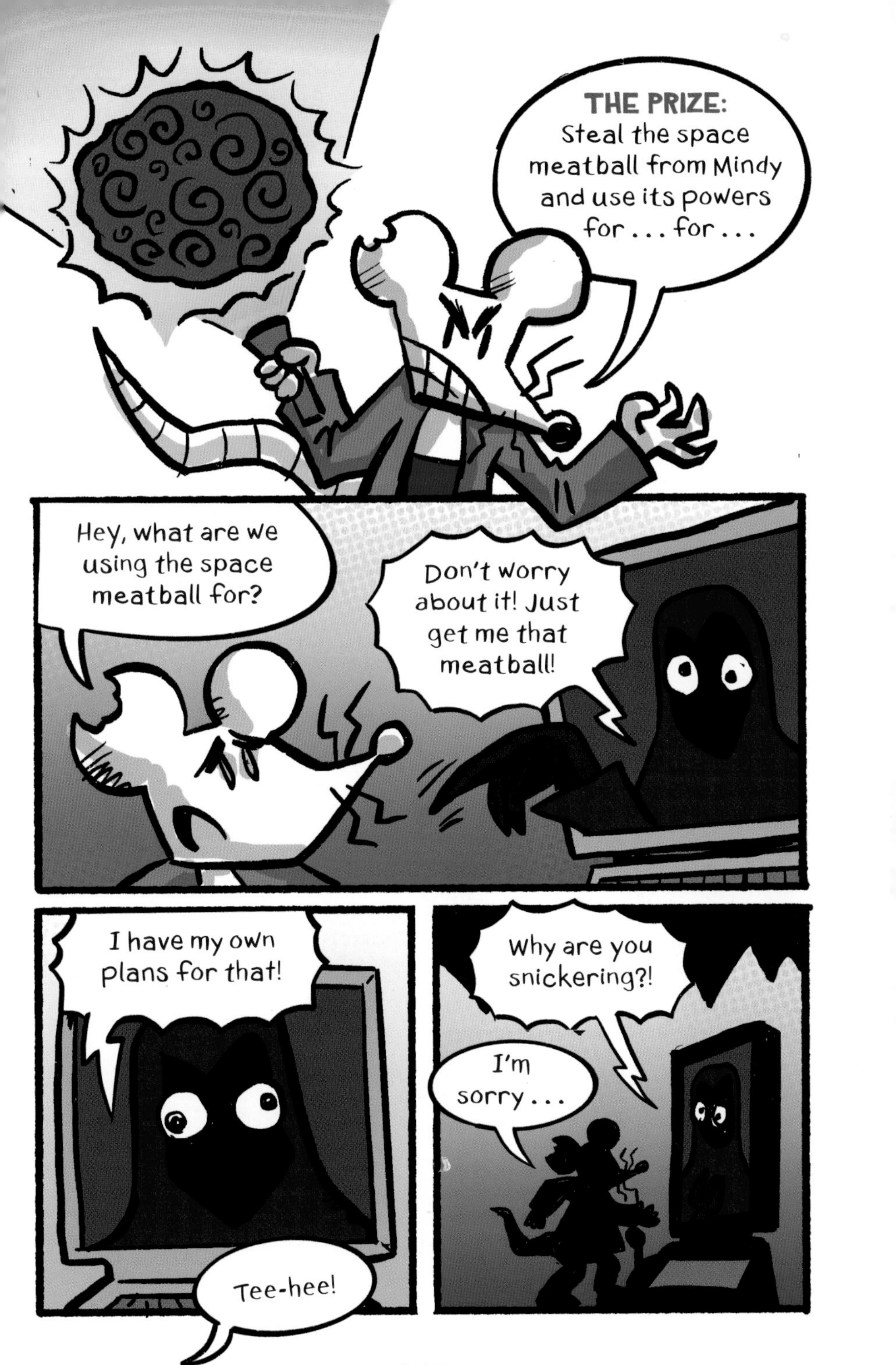
THE PRIZE: Steal the space meatball from Mindy and use its powers for . . . for . . .
Hey, what are we using the space meatball for?
Don't worry about it! Just get me that meatball!
I have my own plans for that!
Tee-hee!
Why are you snickering?!
I'm sorry . . .

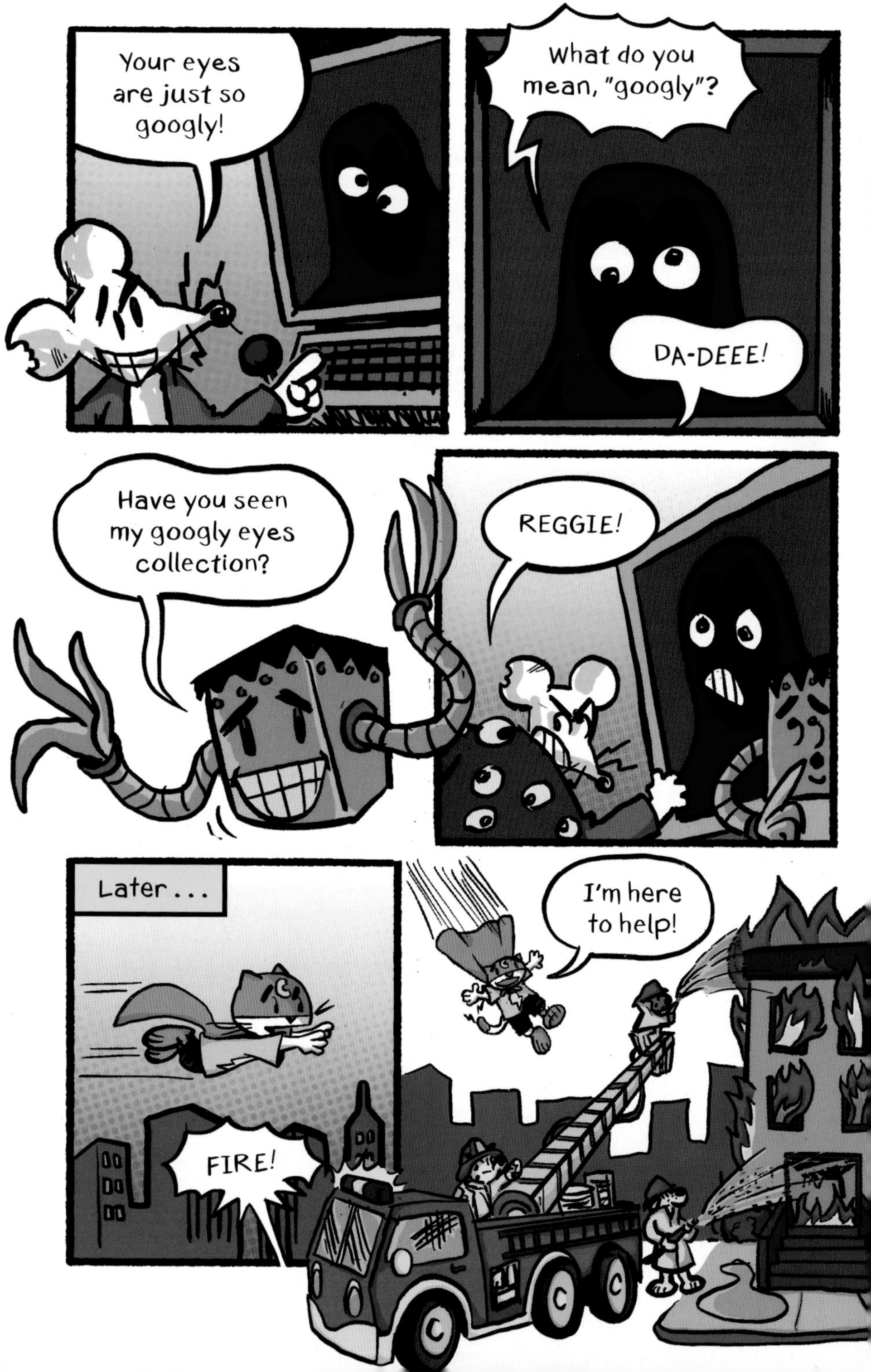

Your eyes are just so googly!
What do you mean, "googly"?
DA-DEEE!
Have you seen my googly eyes collection?
REGGIE!
Later . . .
FIRE!
I'm here to help!

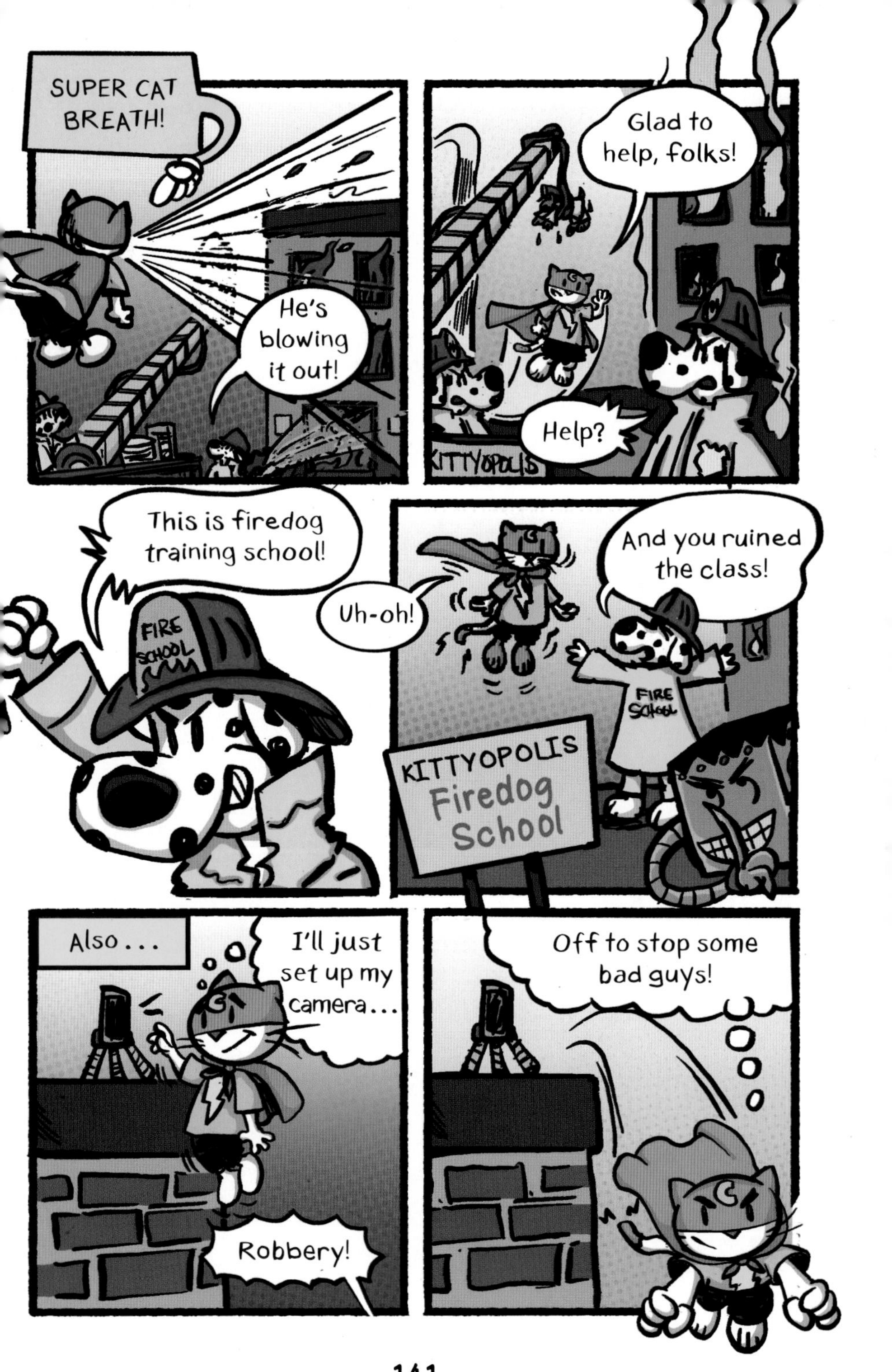
SUPER CAT BREATH!
He's blowing it out!
Glad to help, folks!
Help?
KITTYOPOLIS
This is firedog training school!
FIRE SCHOOL
Uh-oh!
And you ruined the class!
FIRE SCHOOL
KITTYOPOLIS Firedog School
Also . . .
I'll just set up my camera . . .
Robbery!
Off to stop some bad guys!

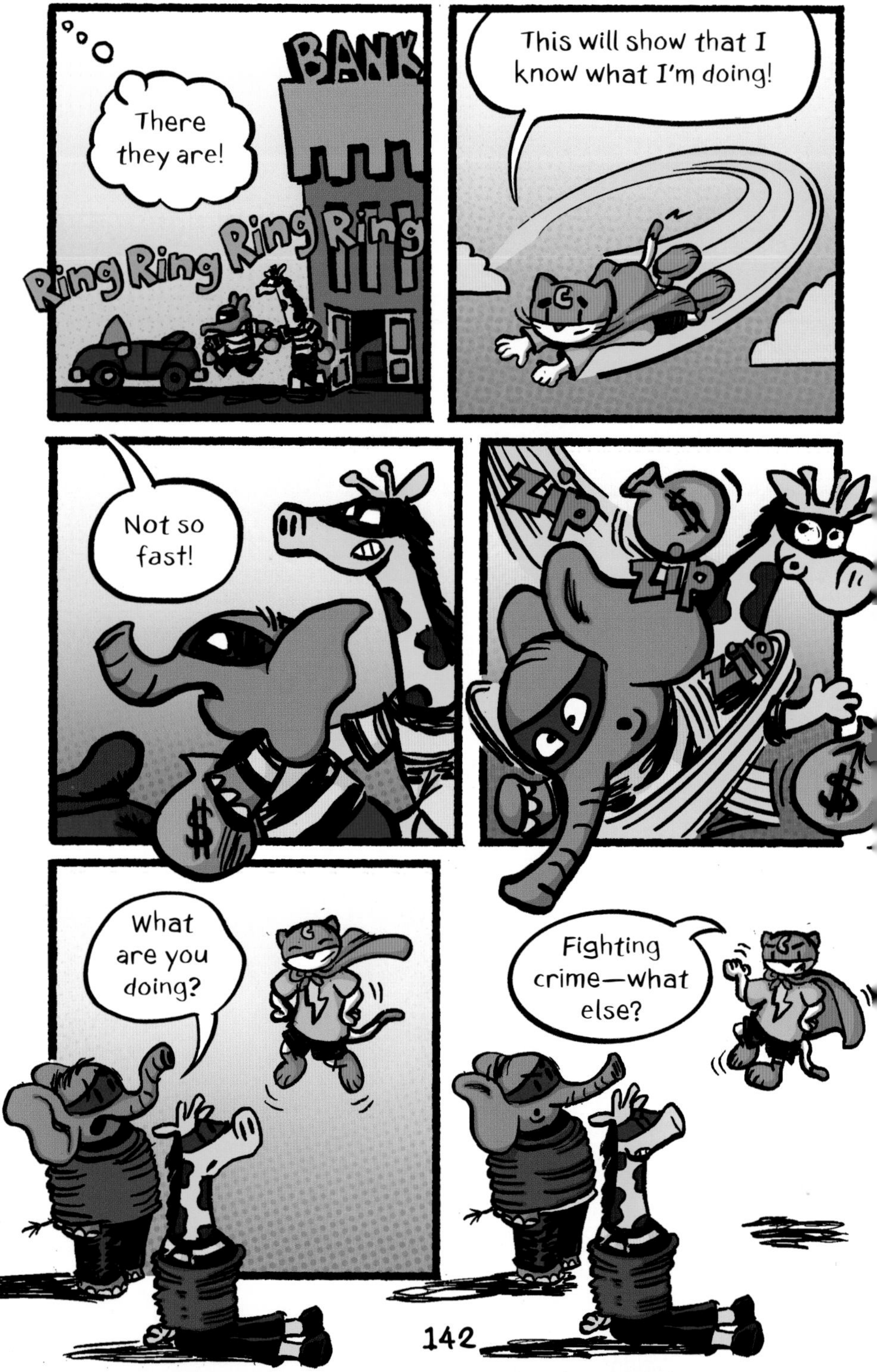
There they are!
BANK
Ring Ring Ring Ring
This will show that I know what I'm doing!
Not so fast!
Zip
Zip
Zip
What are you doing?
Fighting crime—what else?

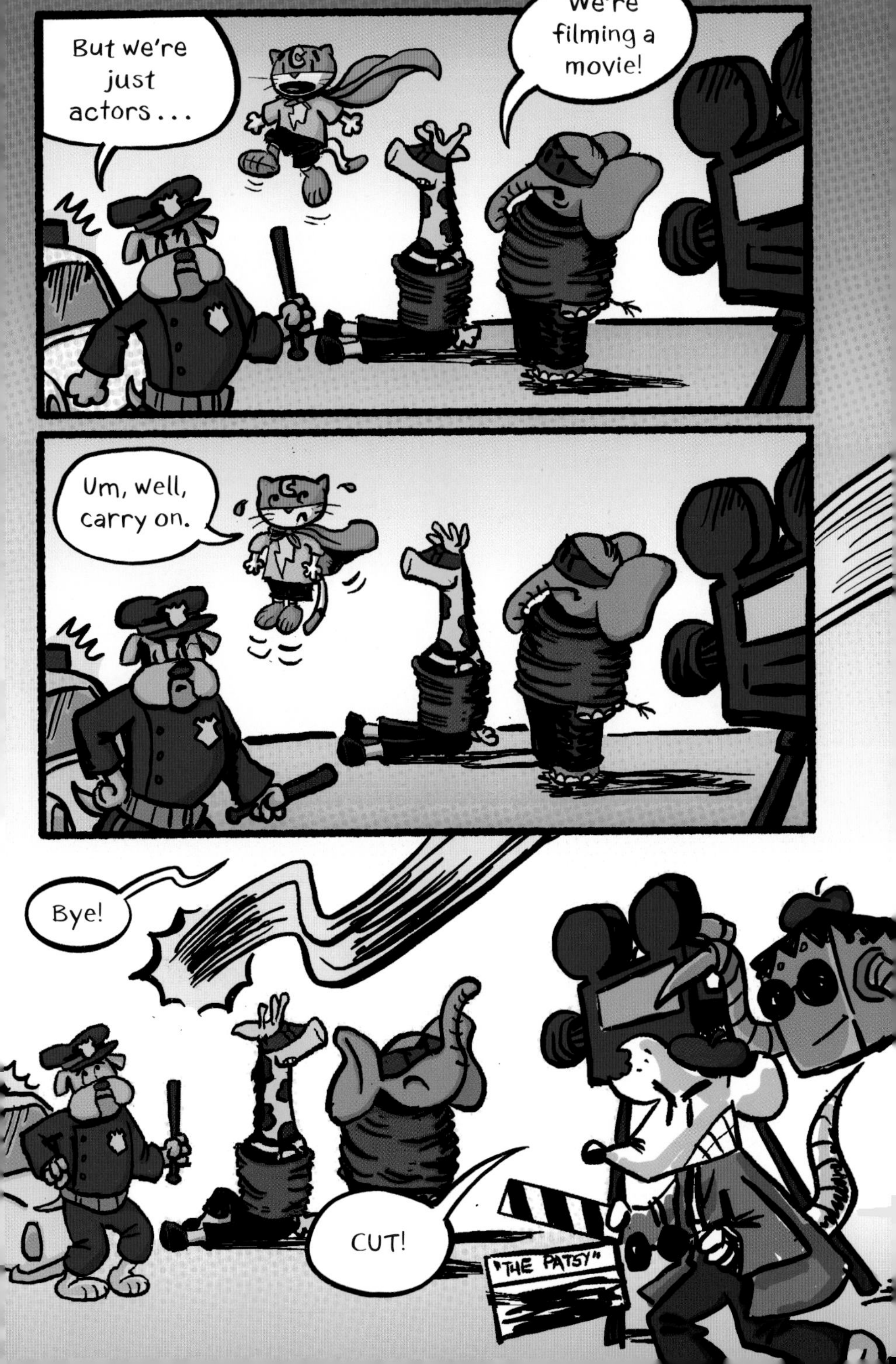
But we're just actors . . .
We're filming a movie!
Um, well, carry on.
Bye!
CUT!
"THE PATSY"

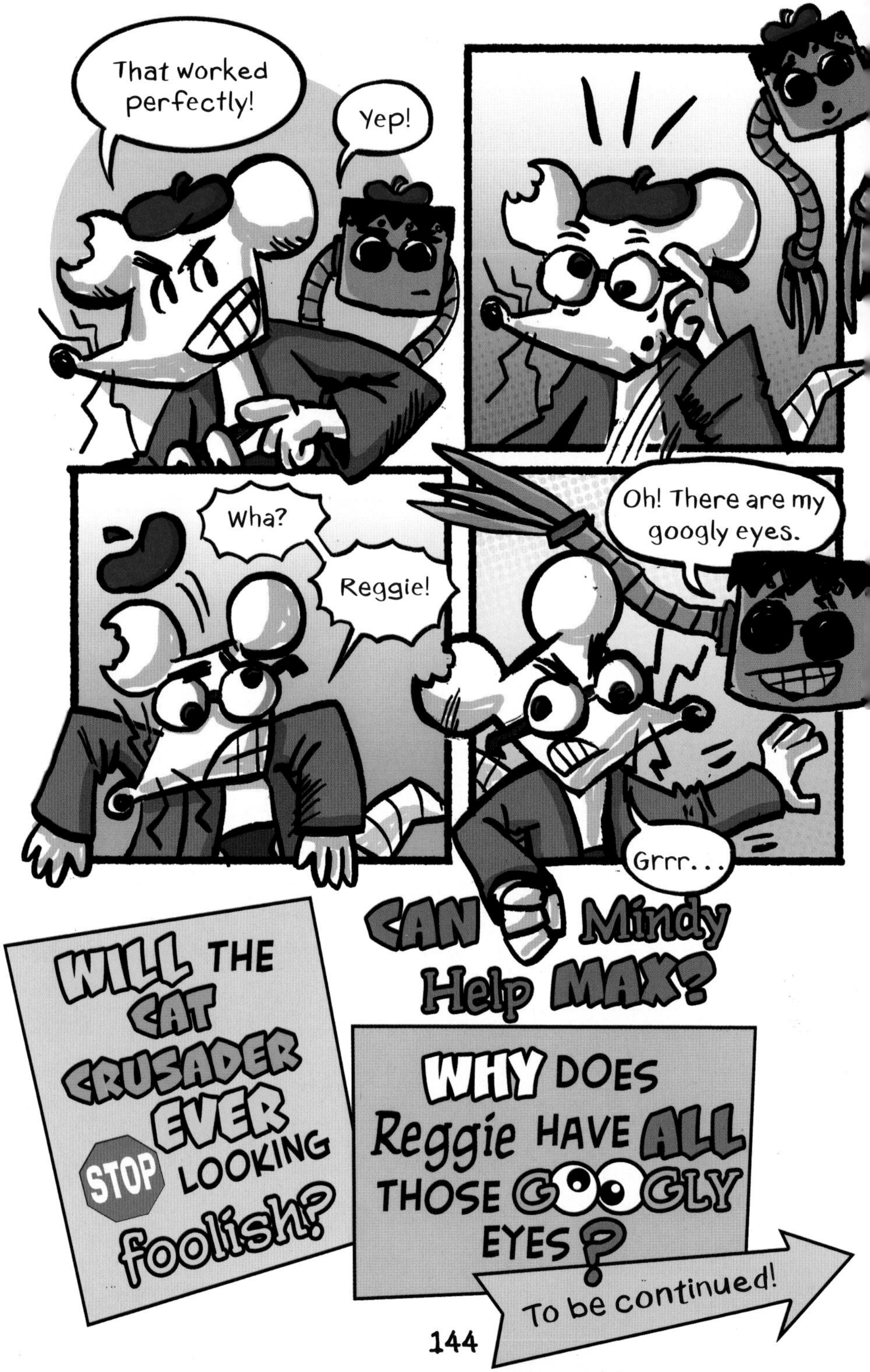
That worked perfectly!
Yep!
Wha?
Reggie!
Oh! There are my googly eyes.
Grrr...
CAN Mindy Help MAX?
WILL THE CAT CRUSADER EVER STOP LOOKING foolish?
WHY DOES Reggie HAVE ALL THOSE GOOGLY EYES?
To be continued!

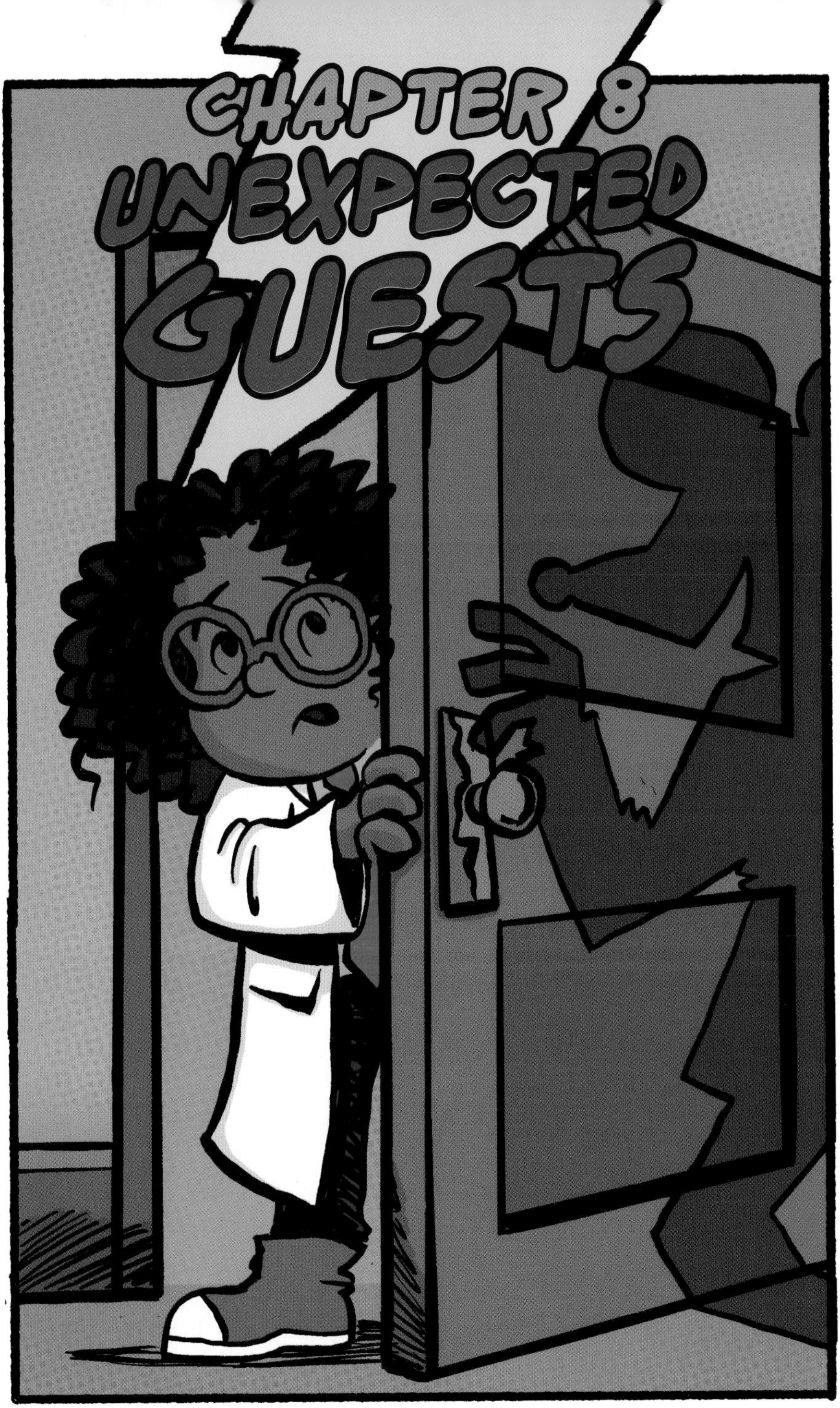
CHAPTER 8
UNEXPECTED GUESTS

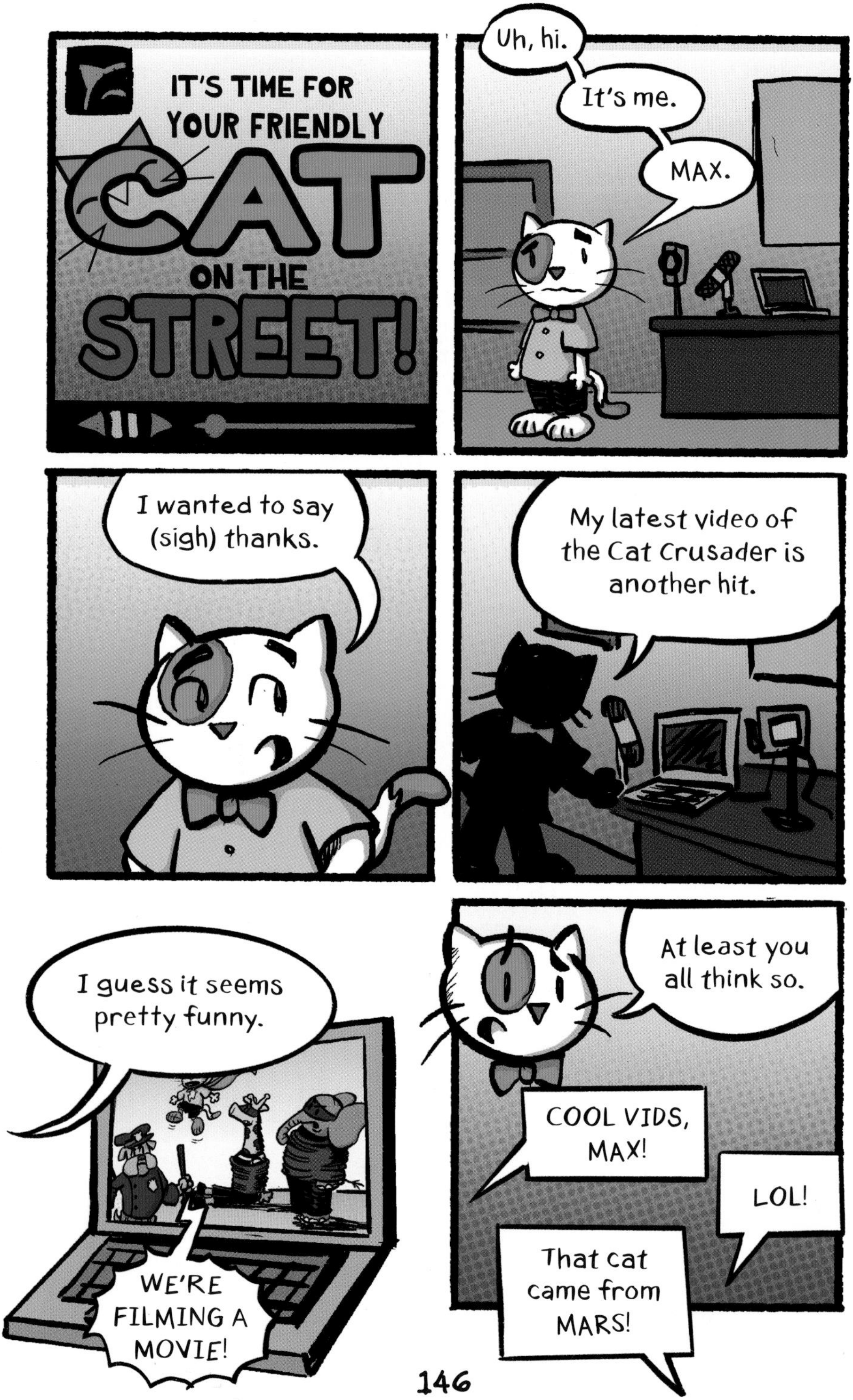
IT'S TIME FOR YOUR FRIENDLY CAT ON THE STREET!
Uh, hi.
It's me.
MAX.
I wanted to say (sigh) thanks.
My latest video of the Cat Crusader is another hit.
I guess it seems pretty funny.
WE'RE FILMING A MOVIE!
At least you all think so.
COOL VIDS, MAX!
LOL!
That cat came from MARS!

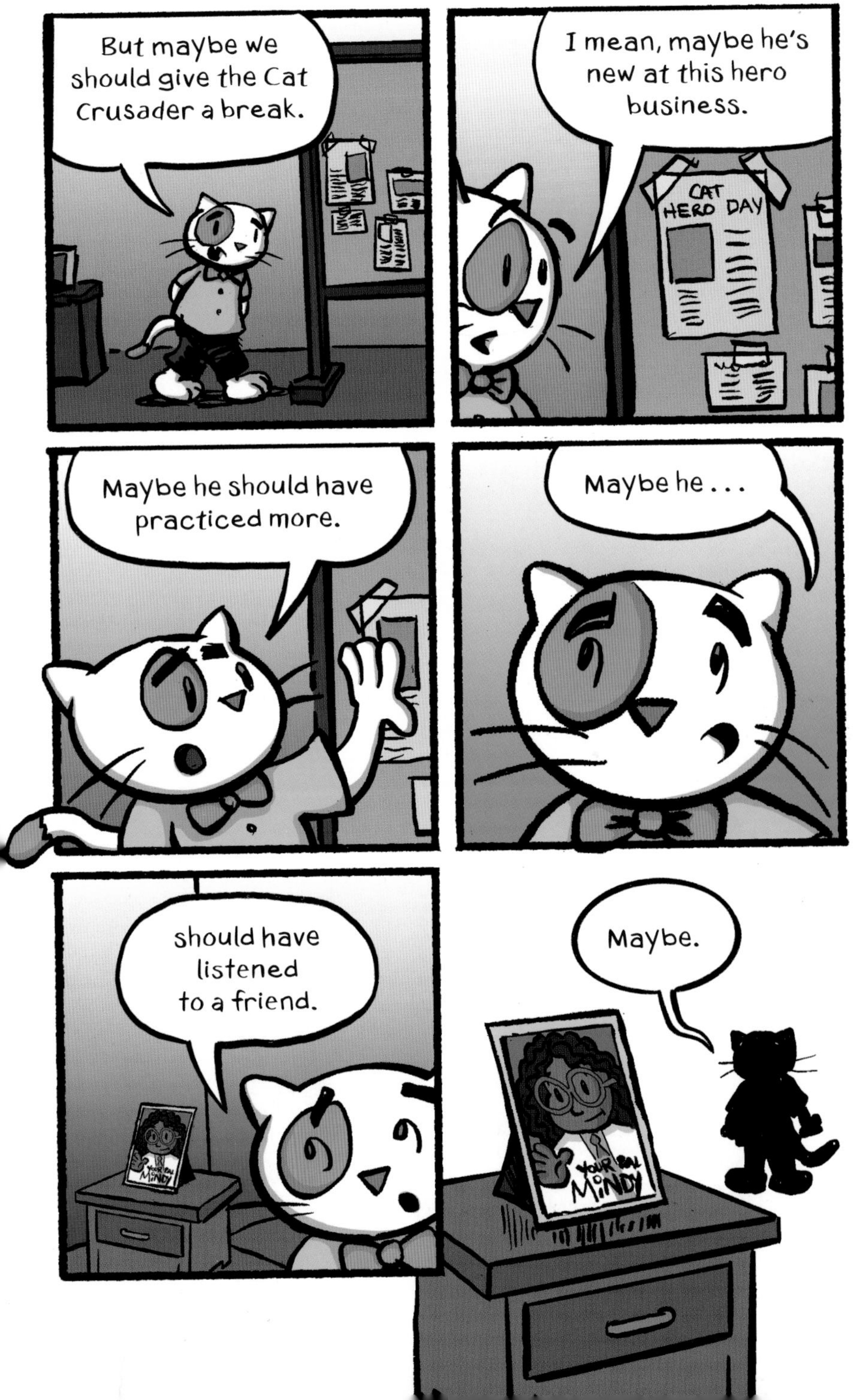
But maybe we should give the Cat Crusader a break.
I mean, maybe he's new at this hero business.
CAT HERO DAY
Maybe he should have practiced more.
Maybe he . . .
should have listened to a friend.
YOUR PAL MINDY
Maybe.

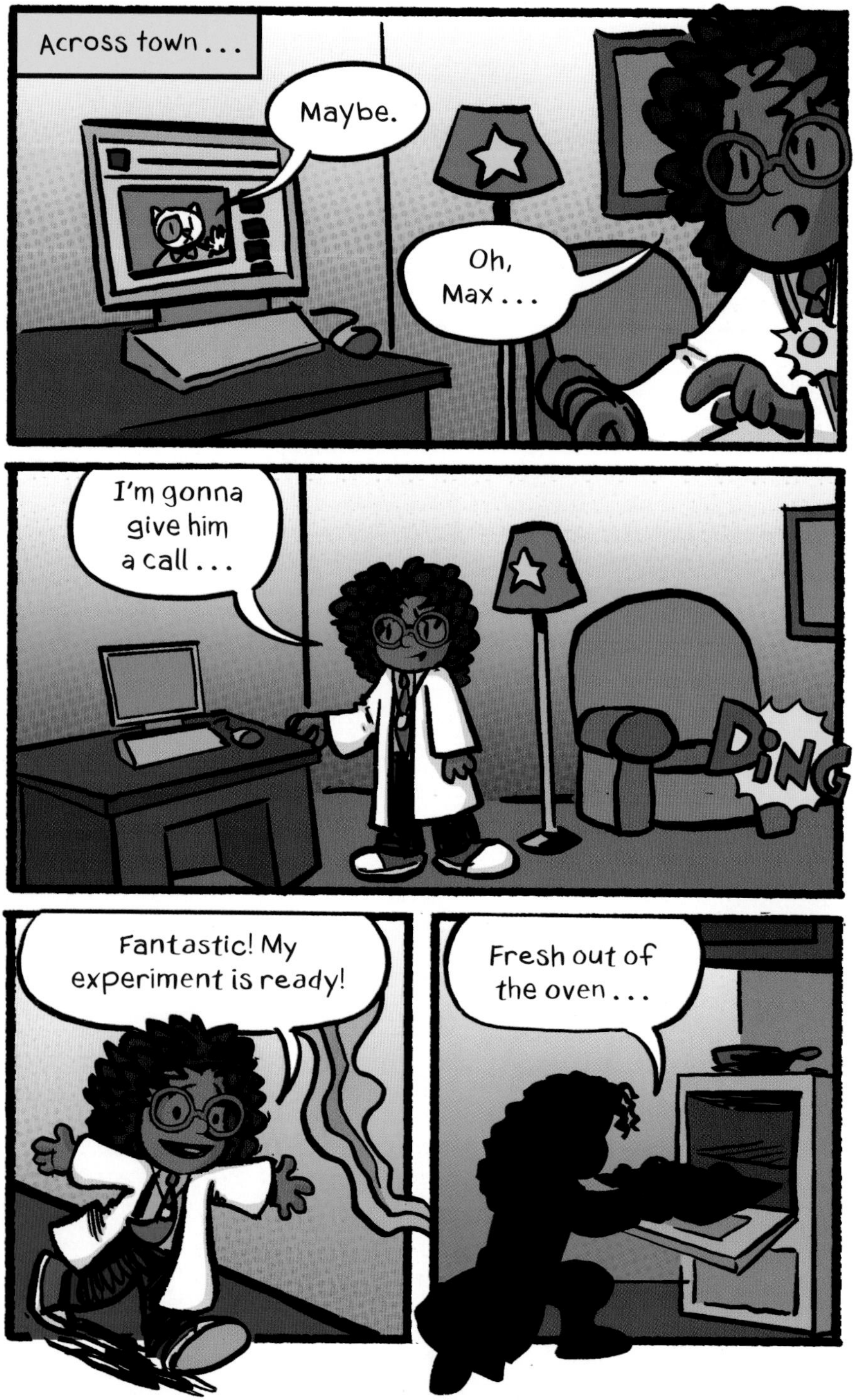
Across town . . .
Maybe.
Oh, Max . . .
I'm gonna give him a call . . .
DING
Fantastic! My experiment is ready!
Fresh out of the oven . . .

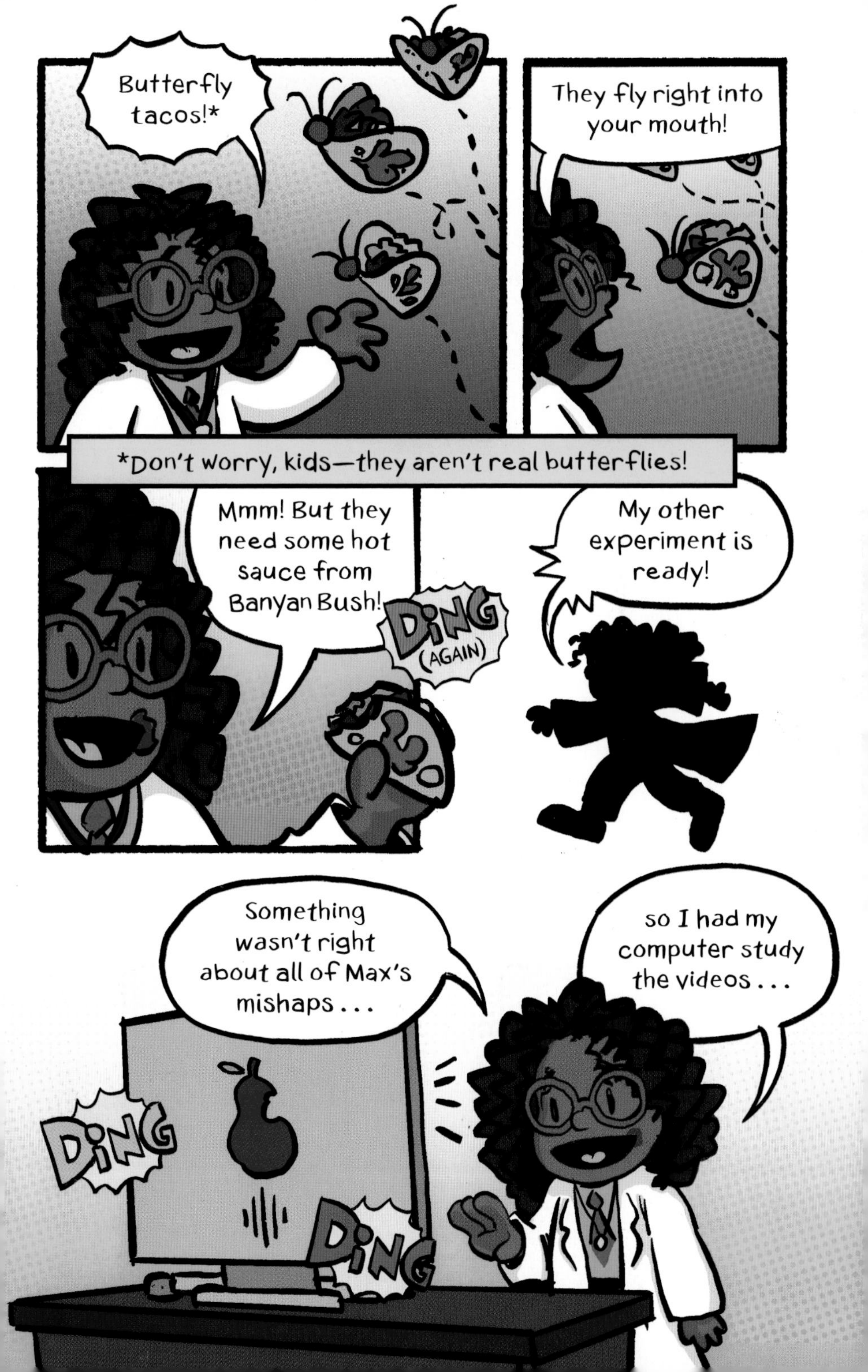
Butterfly tacos!*
They fly right into your mouth!
*Don't worry, kids—they aren't real butterflies!
Mmm! But they need some hot sauce from Banyan Bush!
DiNG (AGAIN)
My other experiment is ready!
Something wasn't right about all of Max's mishaps . . .
so I had my computer study the videos . . .
DiNG
DiNG

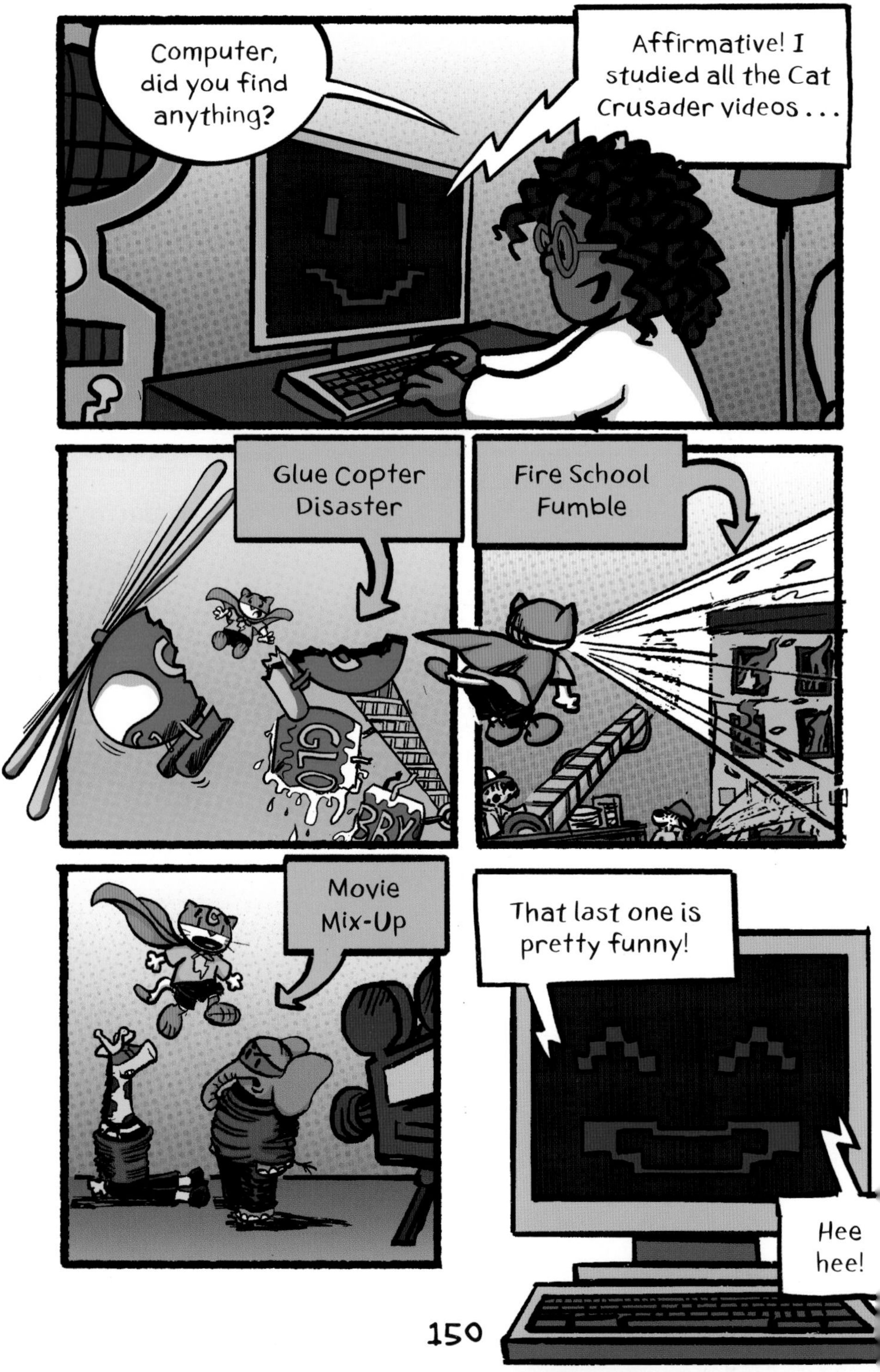
Computer, did you find anything?
Affirmative! I studied all the Cat Crusader videos . . .
Glue Copter Disaster
Fire School Fumble
Movie Mix-Up
That last one is pretty funny!
Hee hee!

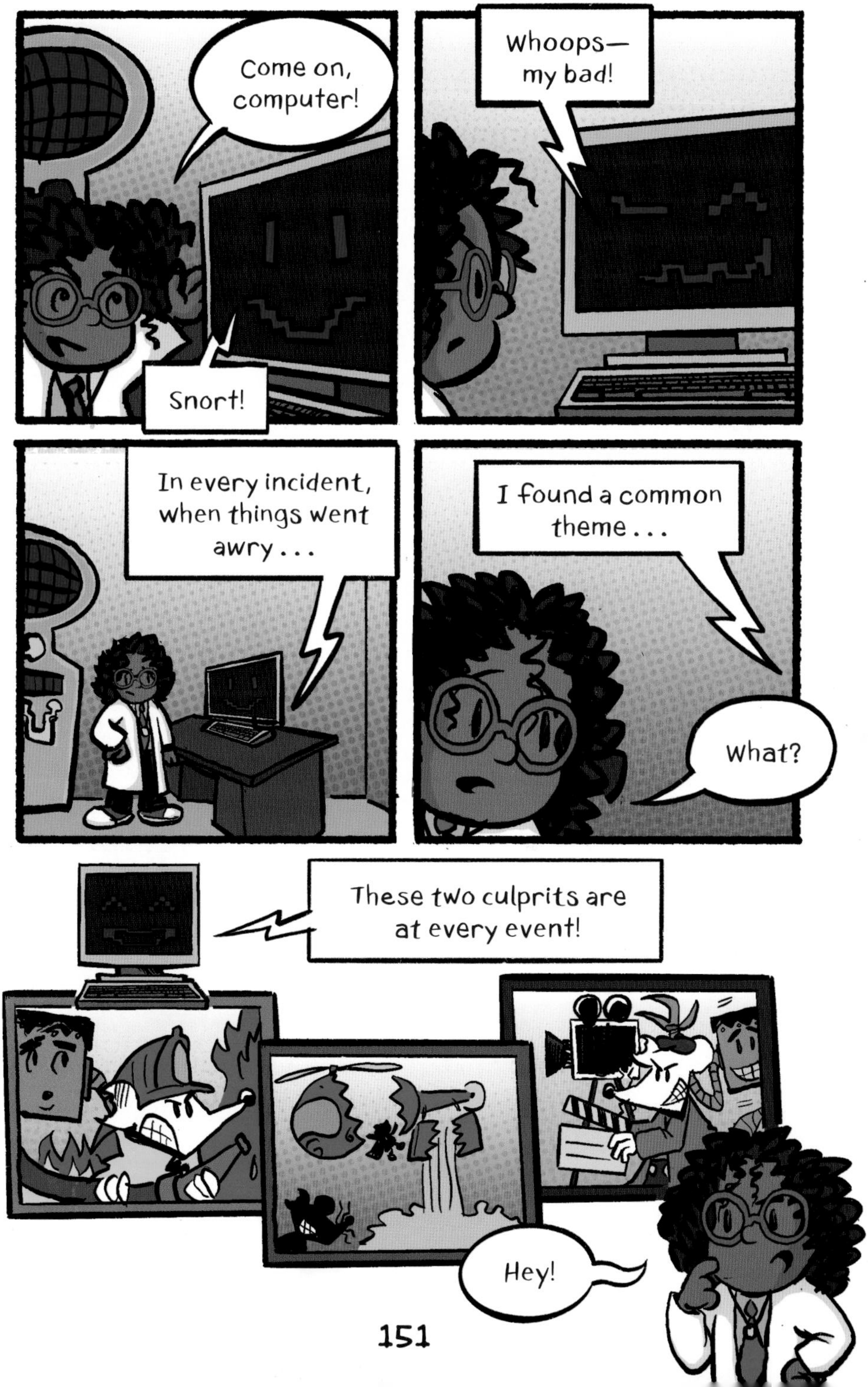
Come on, computer!
Snort!
Whoops— my bad!
In every incident, when things went awry . . .
I found a common theme . . .
What?
These two culprits are at every event!
Hey!

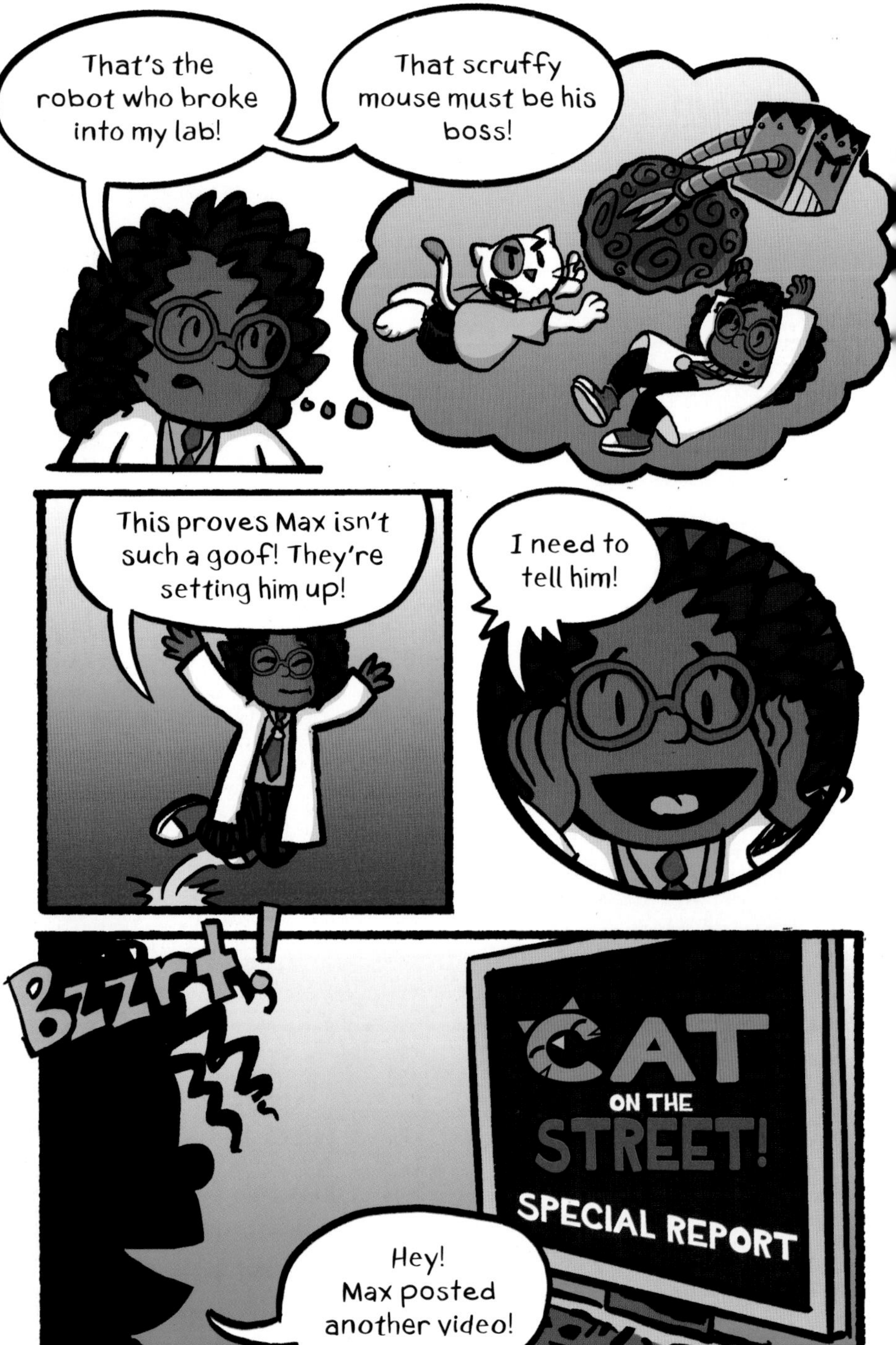

That's the robot who broke into my lab!
That scruffy mouse must be his boss!
This proves Max isn't such a goof! They're setting him up!
I need to tell him!
Bzzrt!
CAT ON THE STREET!
SPECIAL REPORT
Hey! Max posted another video!

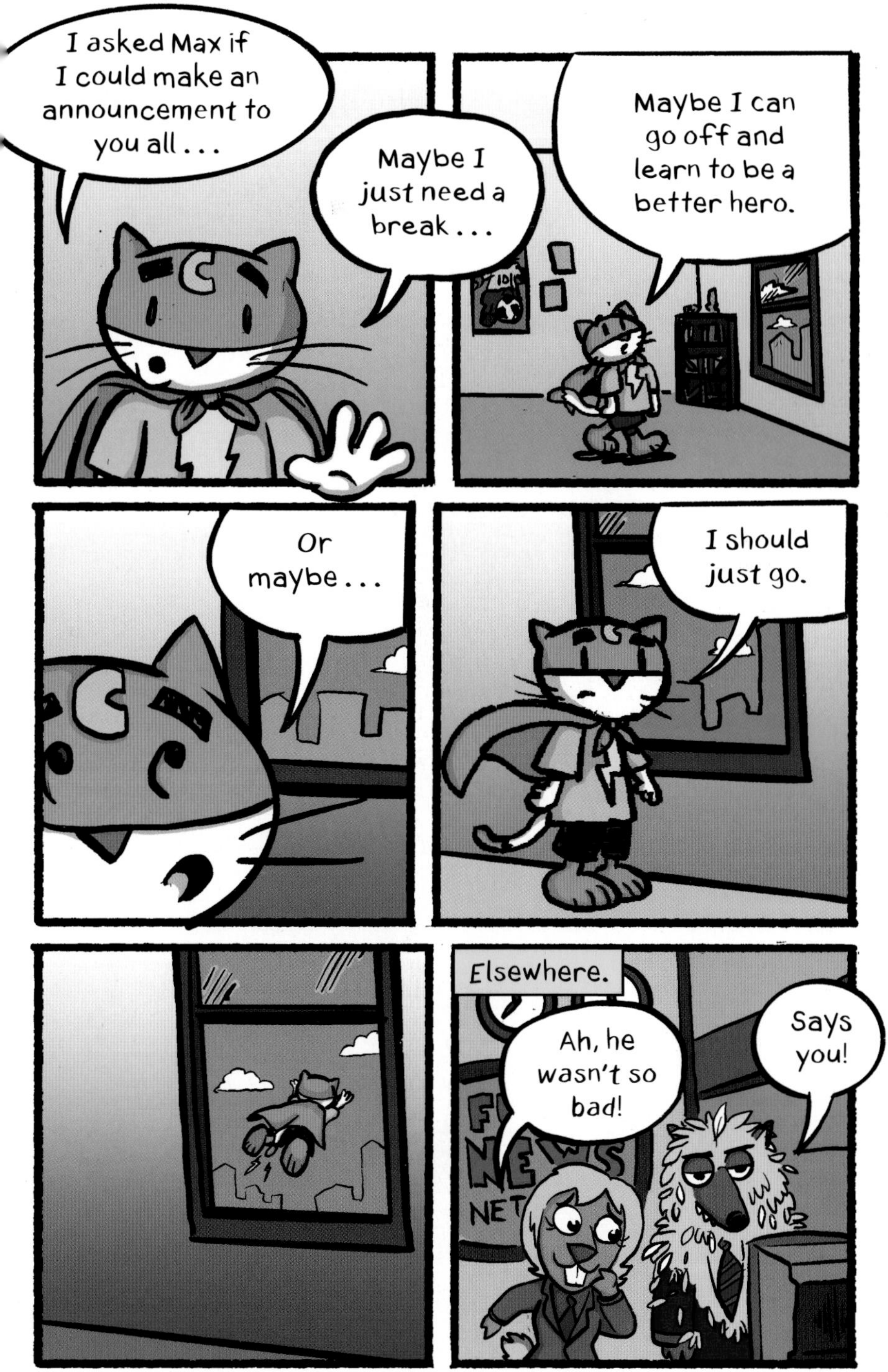
I asked Max if I could make an announcement to you all . . .
Maybe I just need a break . . .
Maybe I can go off and learn to be a better hero.
Or maybe . . .
I should just go.
Elsewhere.
Ah, he wasn't so bad!
Says you!

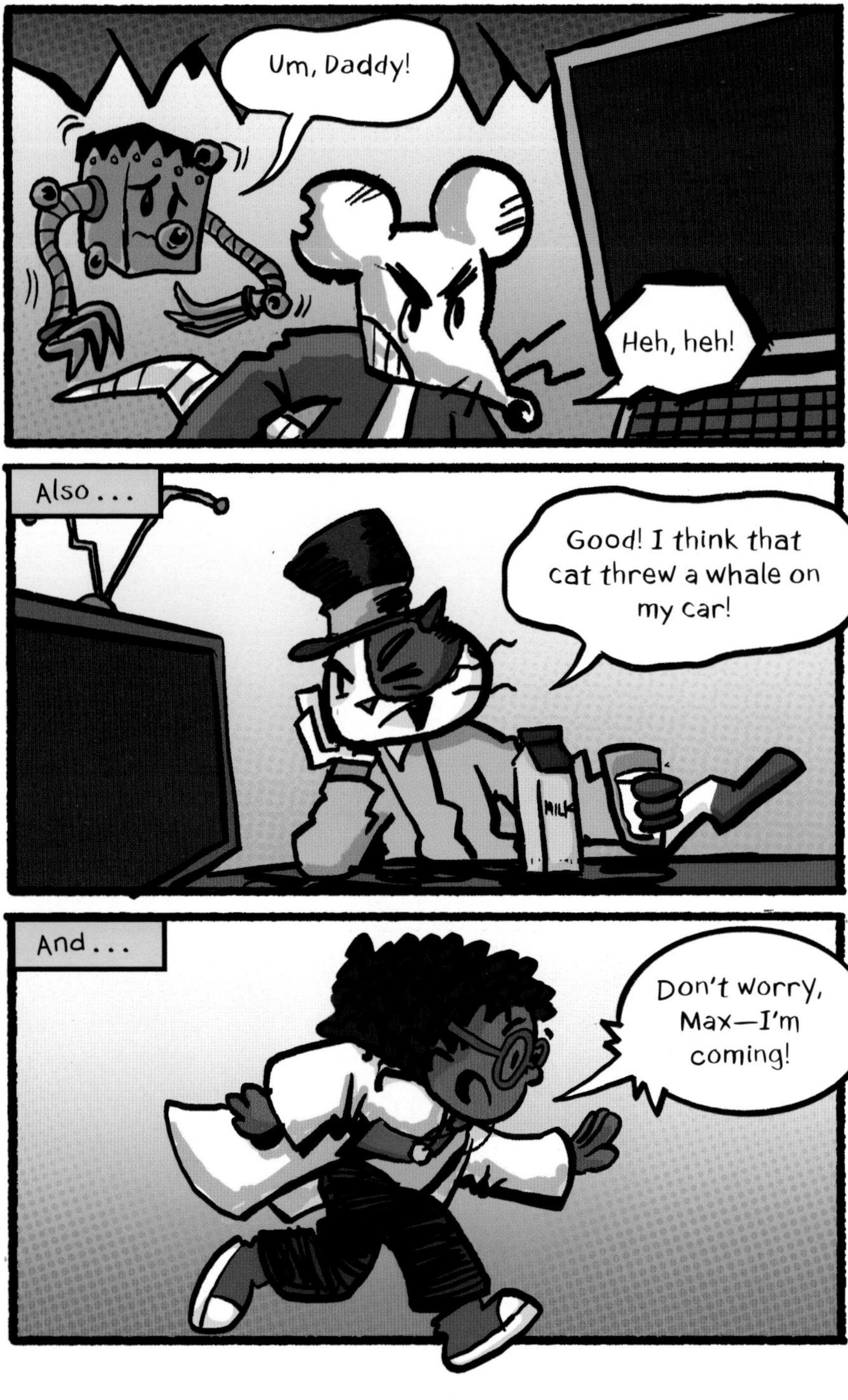
Um, Daddy!
Heh, heh!
Also . . .
Good! I think that cat threw a whale on my car!
MILK
And . . .
Don't worry, Max—I'm coming!

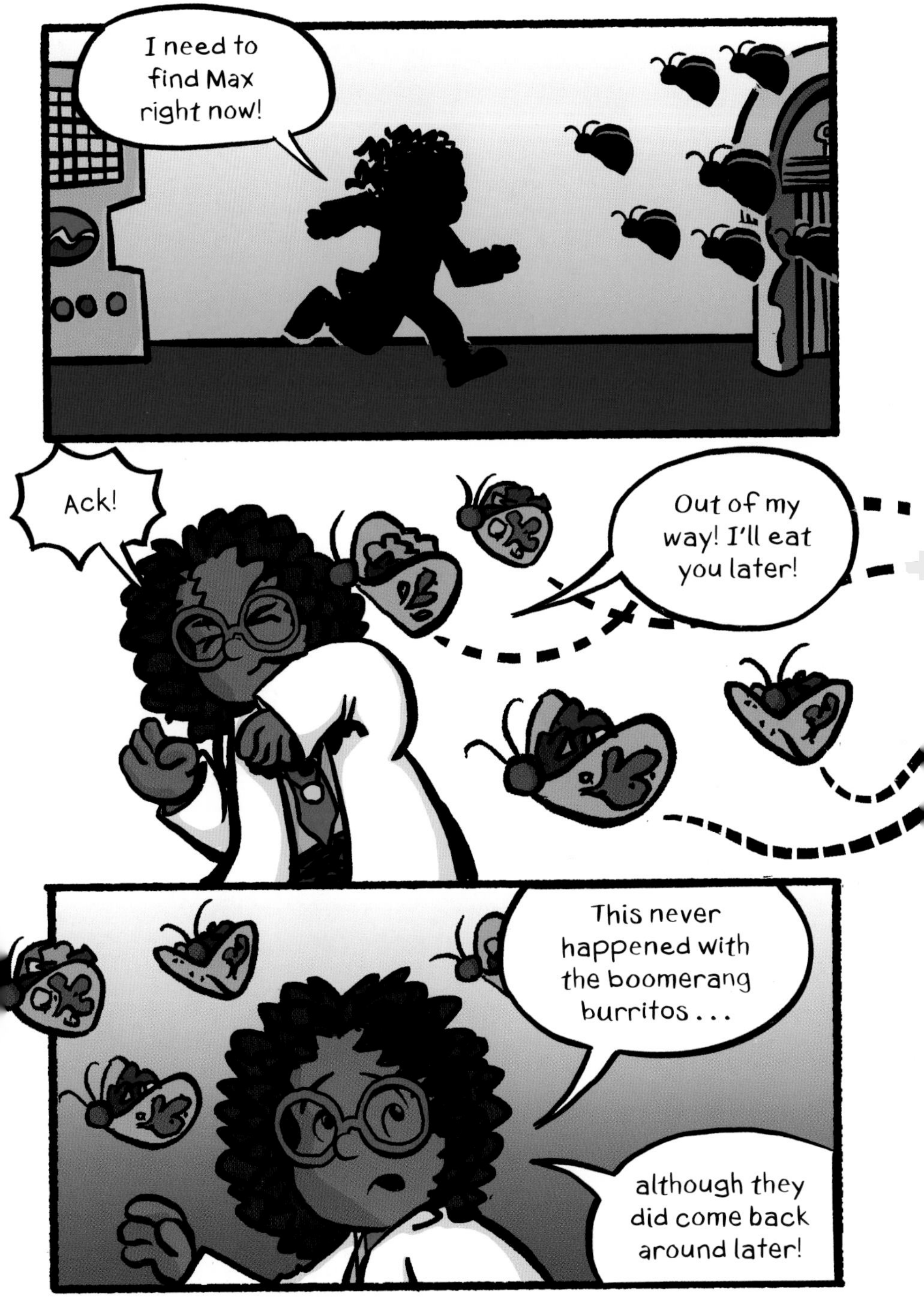
I need to find Max right now!
Ack!
Out of my way! I'll eat you later!
This never happened with the boomerang burritos . . .
although they did come back around later!

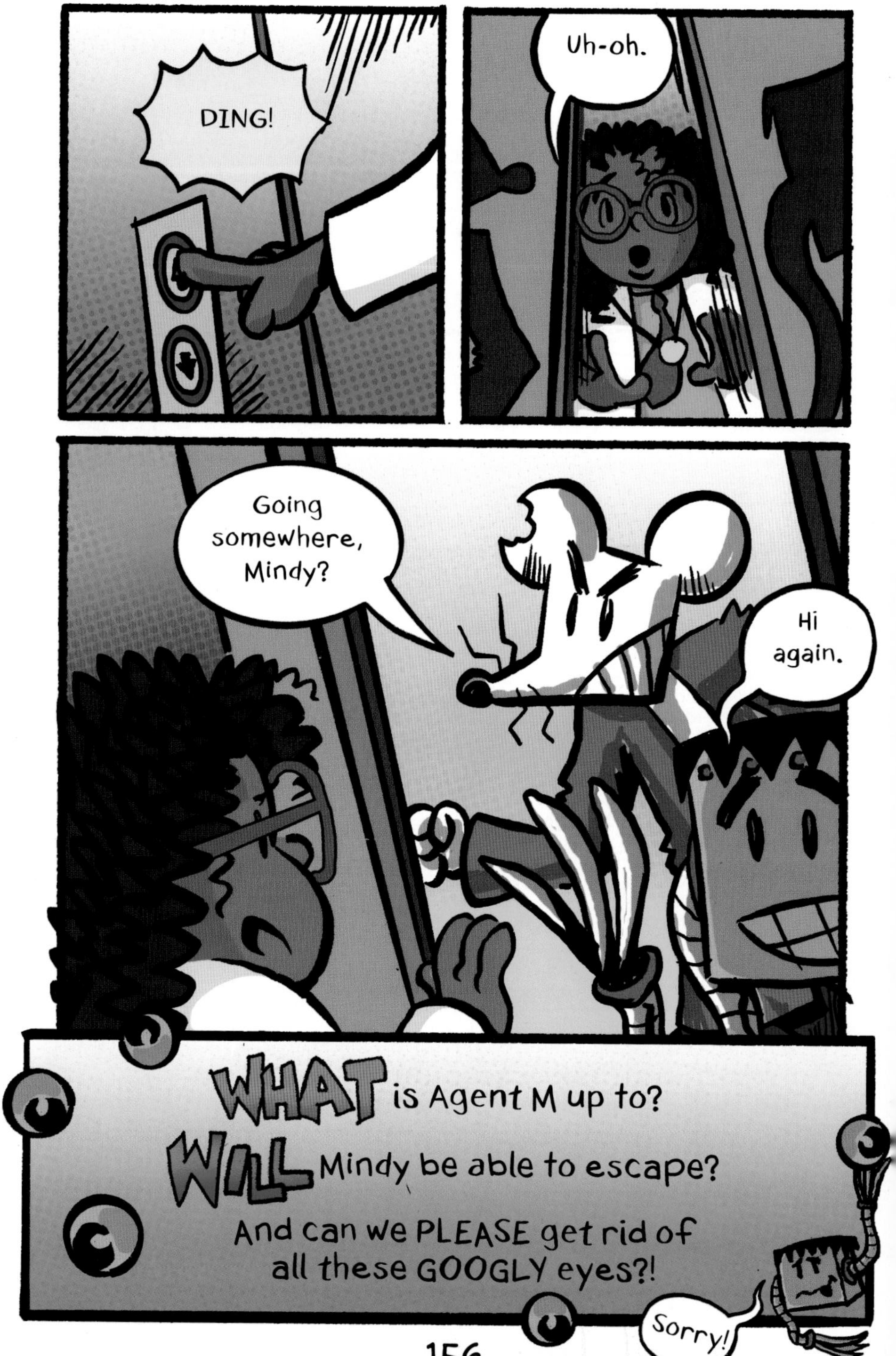
DING!
Uh-oh.
Going somewhere, Mindy?
Hi again.
WHAT is Agent M up to?
WILL Mindy be able to escape?
And can we PLEASE get rid of all these GOOGLY eyes?!
Sorry!

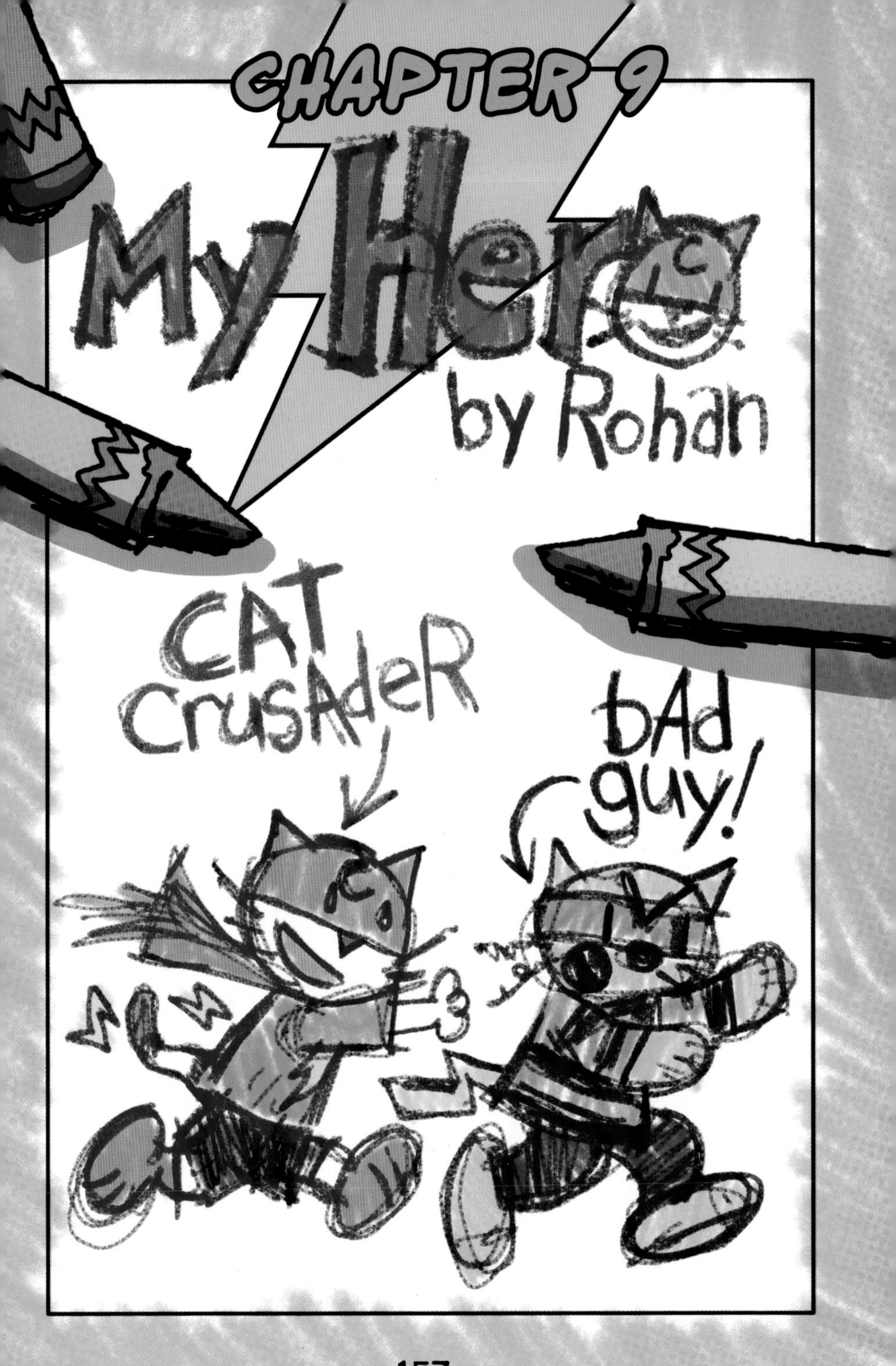
CHAPTER 9
My Hero
by Rohan
CAT Crusader
bAd guy!

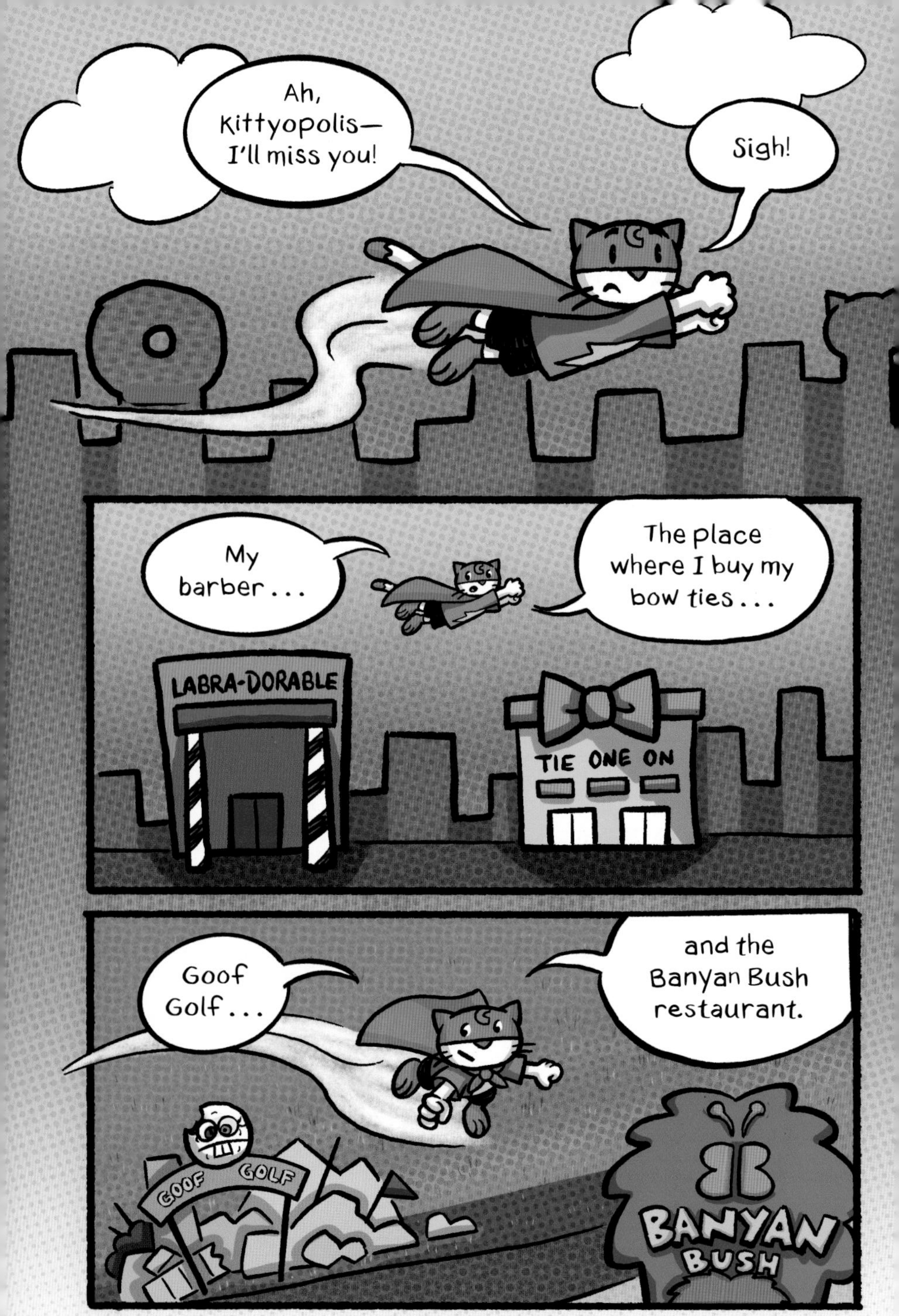
Ah, Kittyopolis— I'll miss you!
Sigh!
My barber . . .
The place where I buy my bow ties . . .
LABRA-DORABLE
TIE ONE ON
Goof Golf . . .
and the Banyan Bush restaurant.
GOOF GOLF
BANYAN BUSH

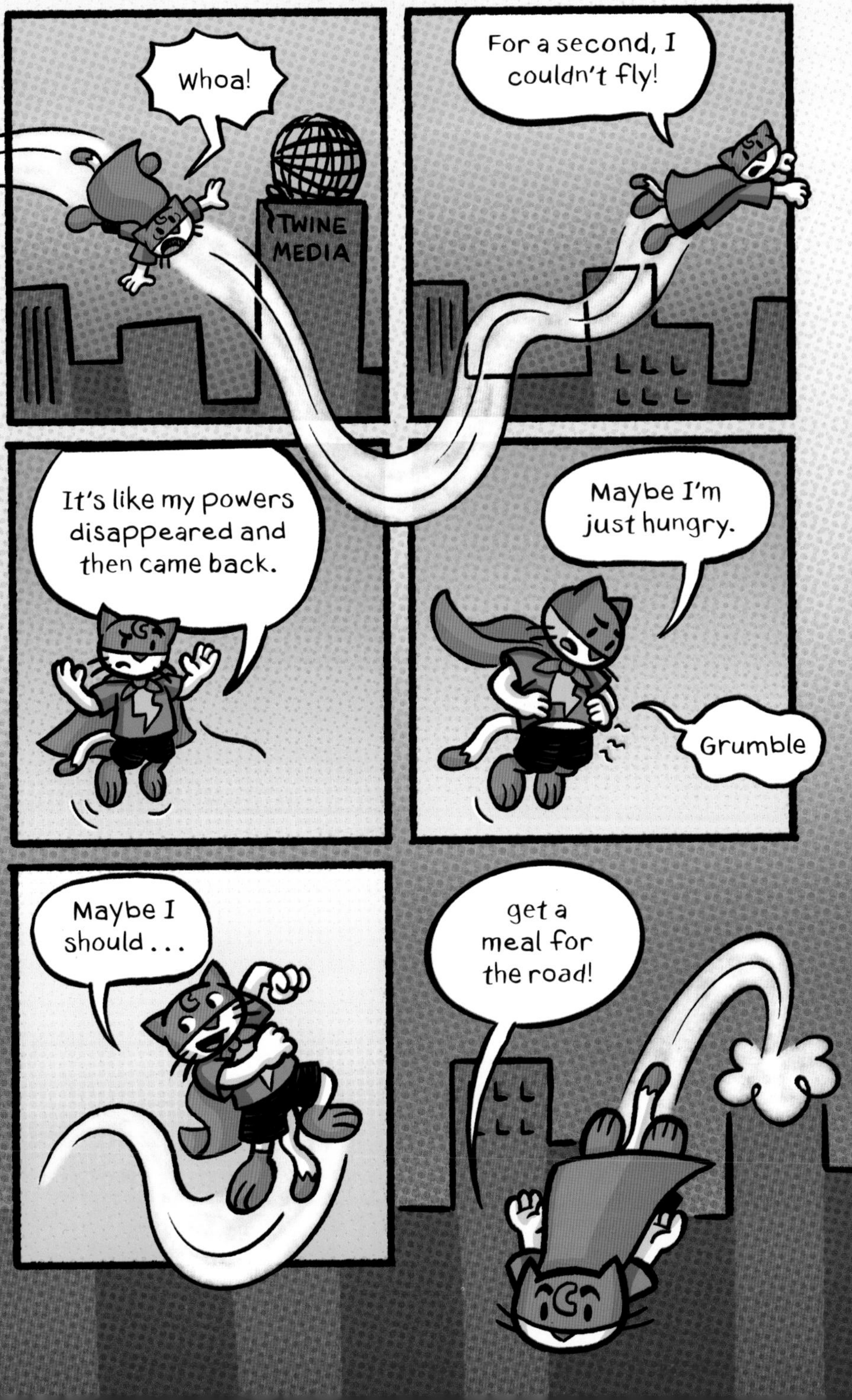
Whoa!
TWINE MEDIA
For a second, I couldn't fly!
It's like my powers disappeared and then came back.
Maybe I'm just hungry.
Grumble
Maybe I should . . .
get a meal for the road!

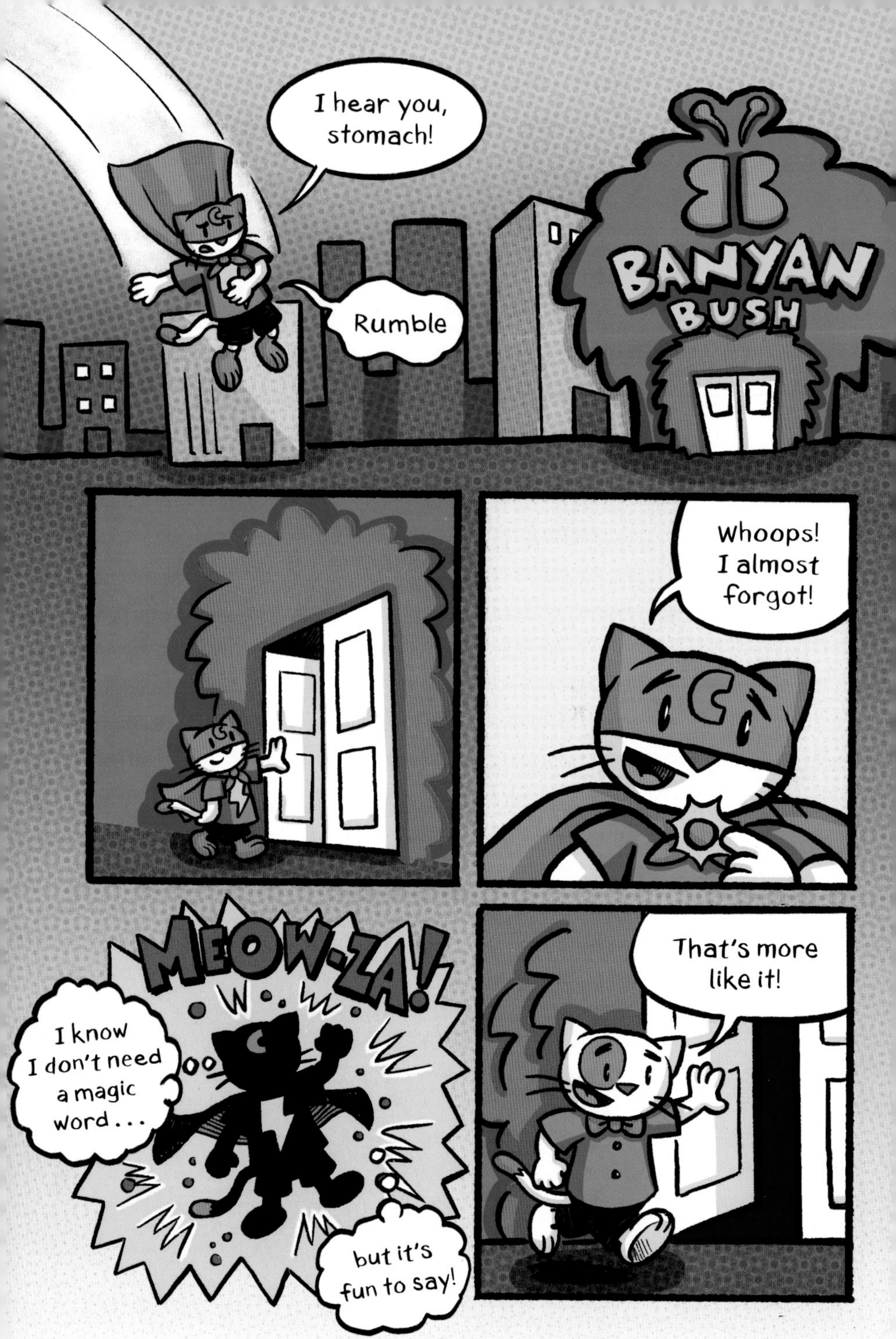
I hear you, stomach!
Rumble
BANYAN BUSH
Whoops! I almost forgot!
MEOW-ZA!
I know I don't need a magic word . . .
but it's fun to say!
That's more like it!

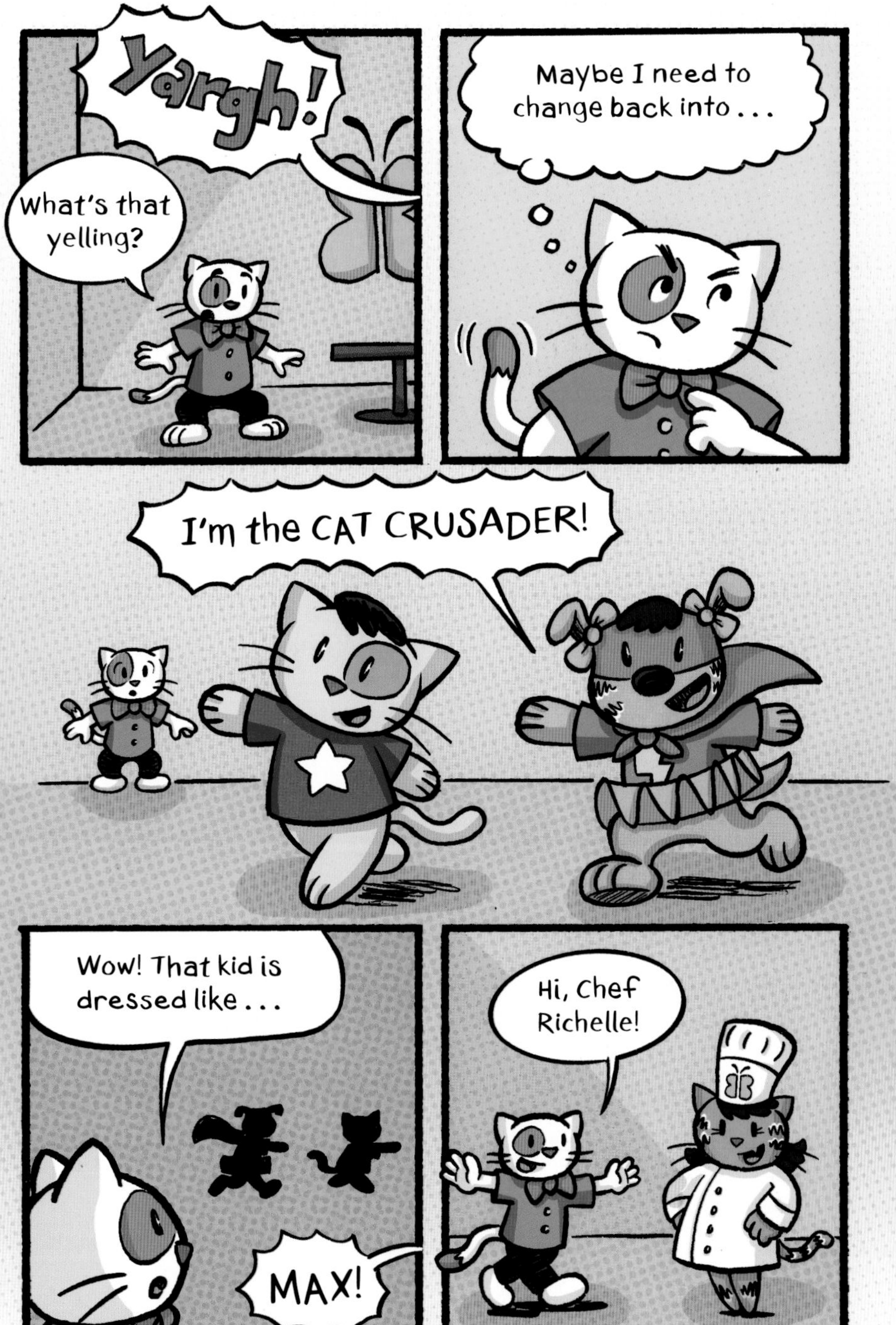
Yargh!
What's that yelling?
Maybe I need to change back into . . .
I'm the CAT CRUSADER!
Wow! That kid is dressed like . . .
MAX!
Hi, Chef Richelle!

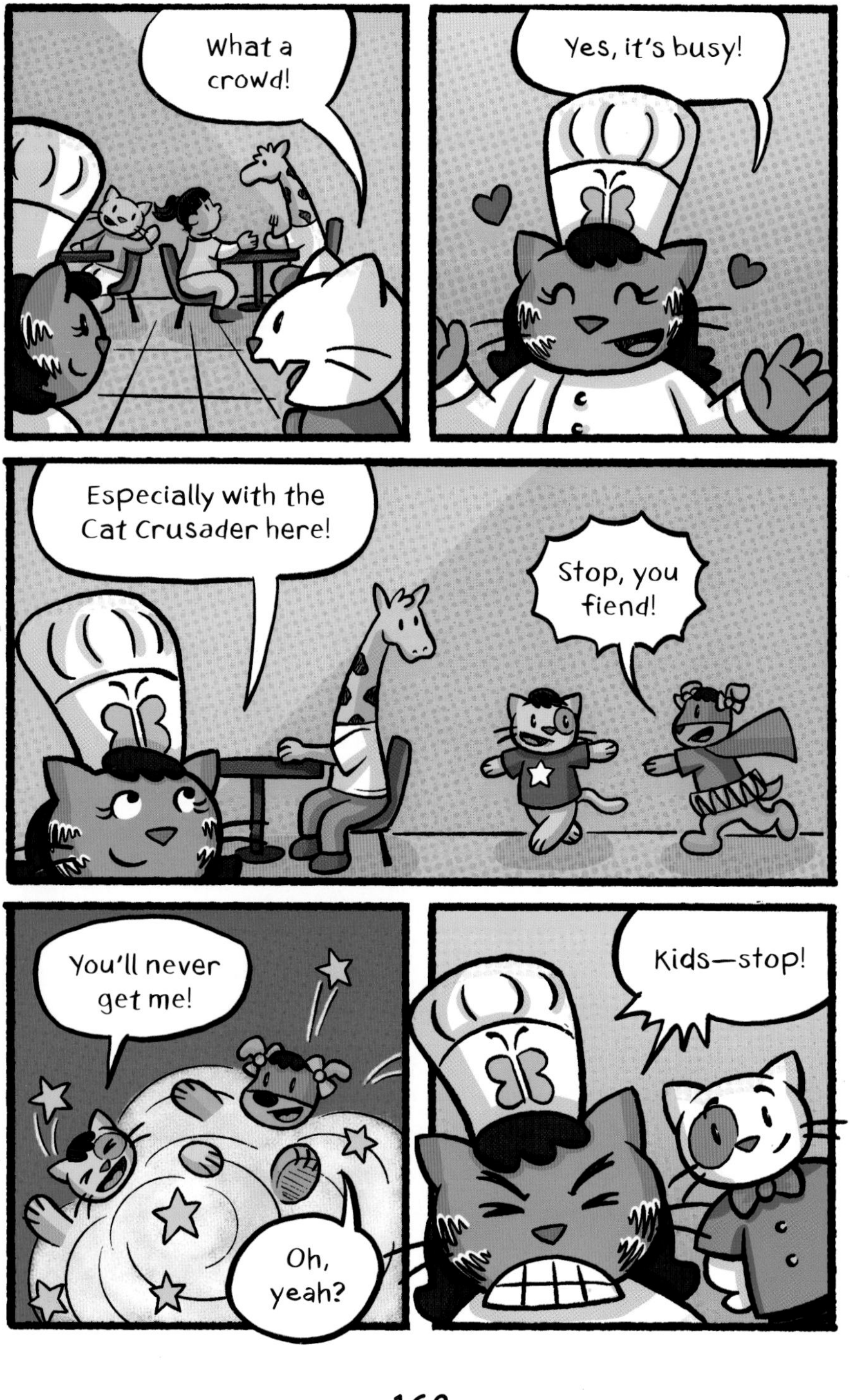
What a crowd!
Yes, it's busy!
Especially with the Cat Crusader here!
Stop, you fiend!
You'll never get me!
Oh, yeah?
Kids—stop!

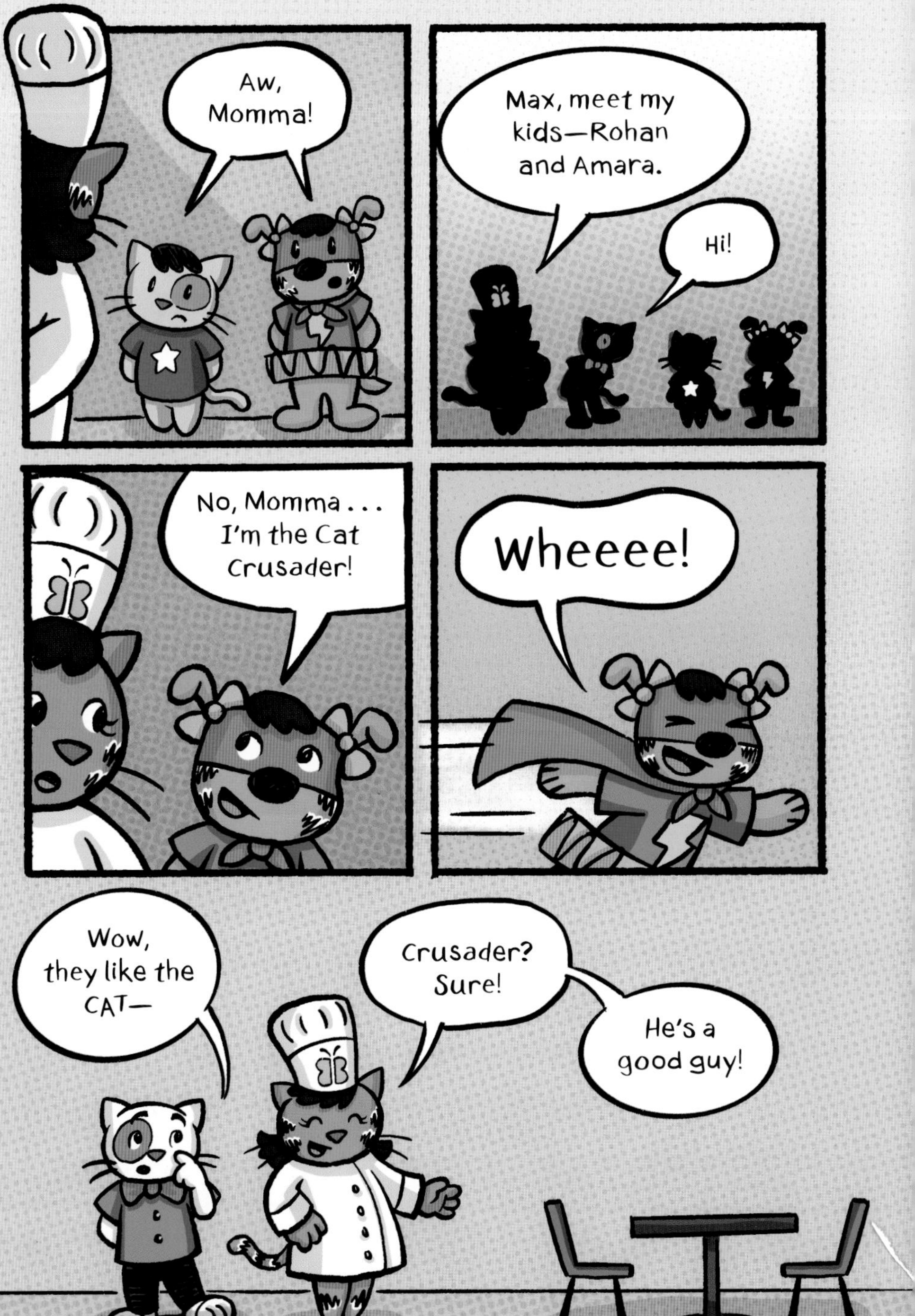
Aw, Momma!
Max, meet my kids—Rohan and Amara.
Hi!
No, Momma . . . I'm the Cat Crusader!
Wheeee!
Wow, they like the CAT—
Crusader? Sure!
He's a good guy!

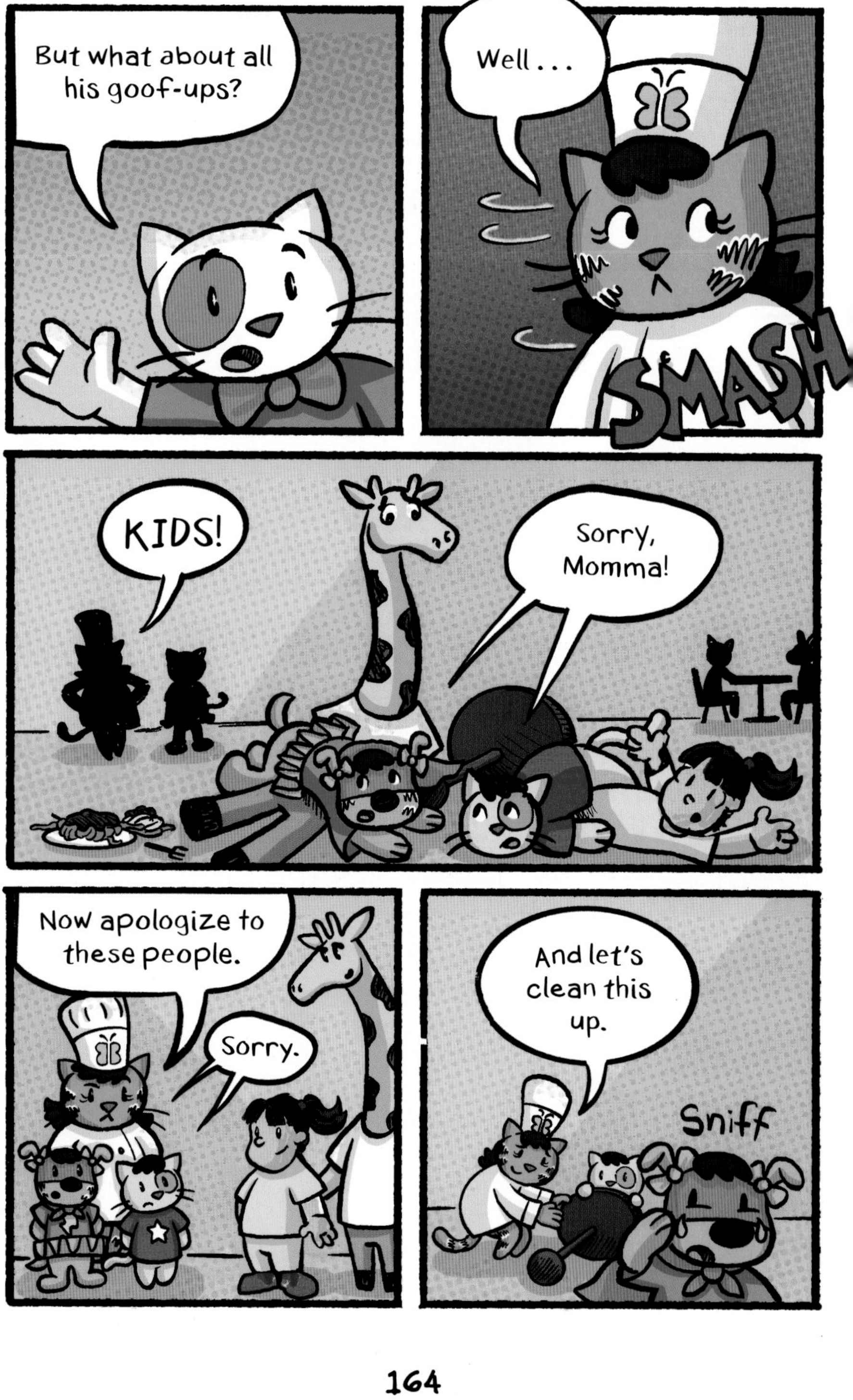
But what about all his goof-ups?
Well...
SMASH
KIDS!
Sorry, Momma!
Now apologize to these people.
Sorry.
And let's clean this up.
Sniff

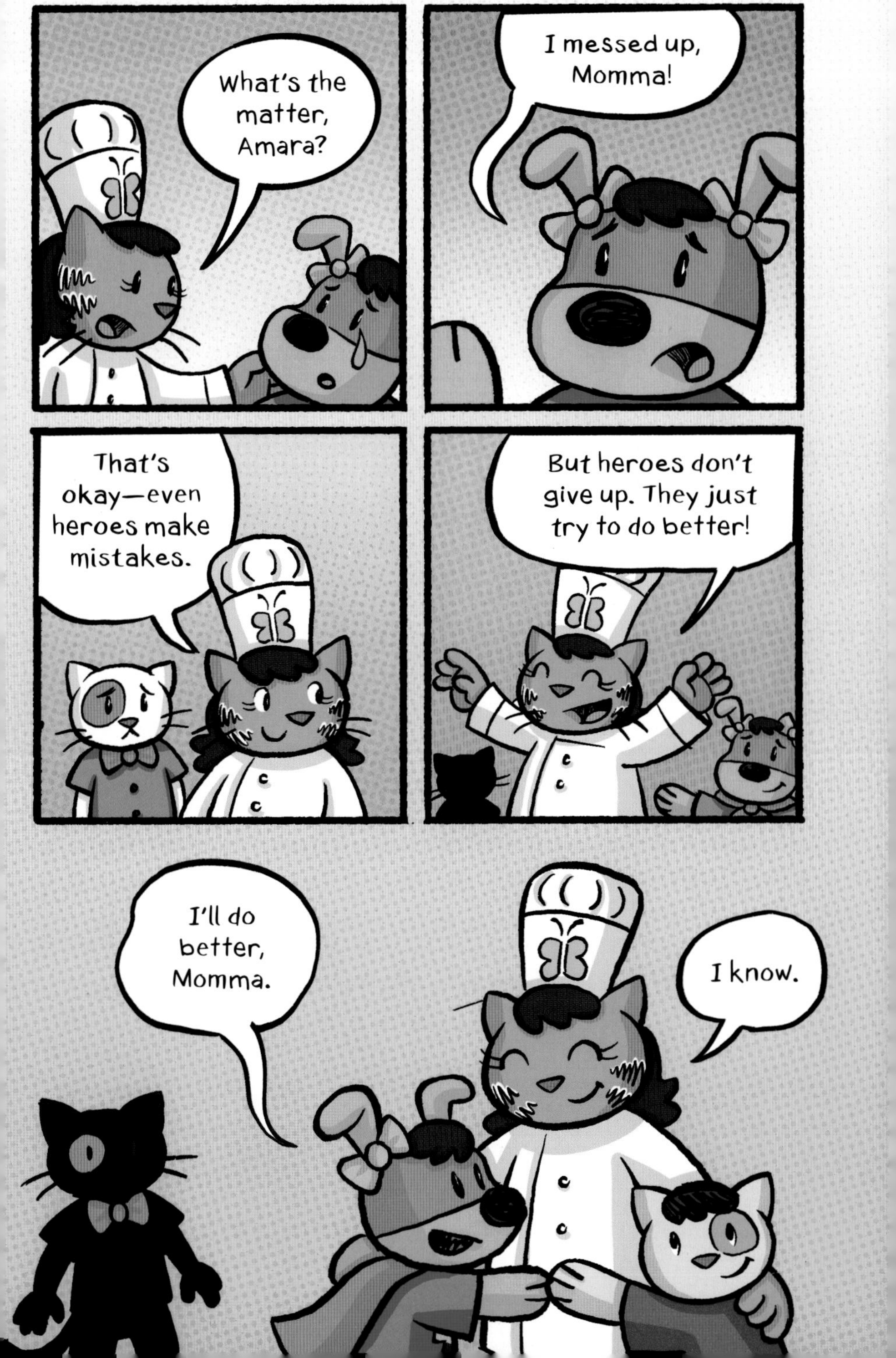
What's the matter, Amara?
I messed up, Momma!
That's okay—even heroes make mistakes.
But heroes don't give up. They just try to do better!
I'll do better, Momma.
I know.

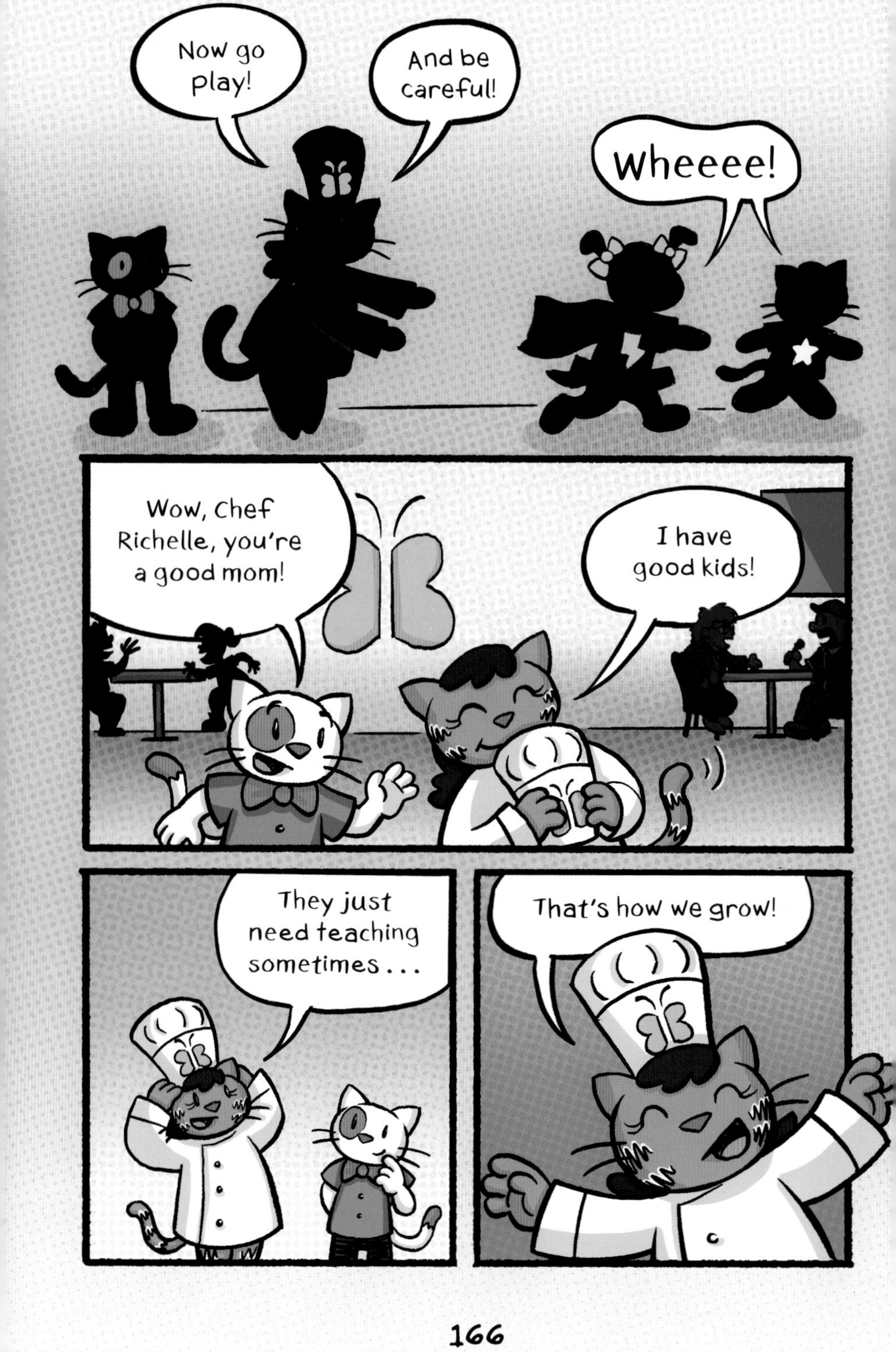
Now go play!
And be careful!
Wheeee!
Wow, Chef Richelle, you're a good mom!
I have good kids!
They just need teaching sometimes . . .
That's how we grow!

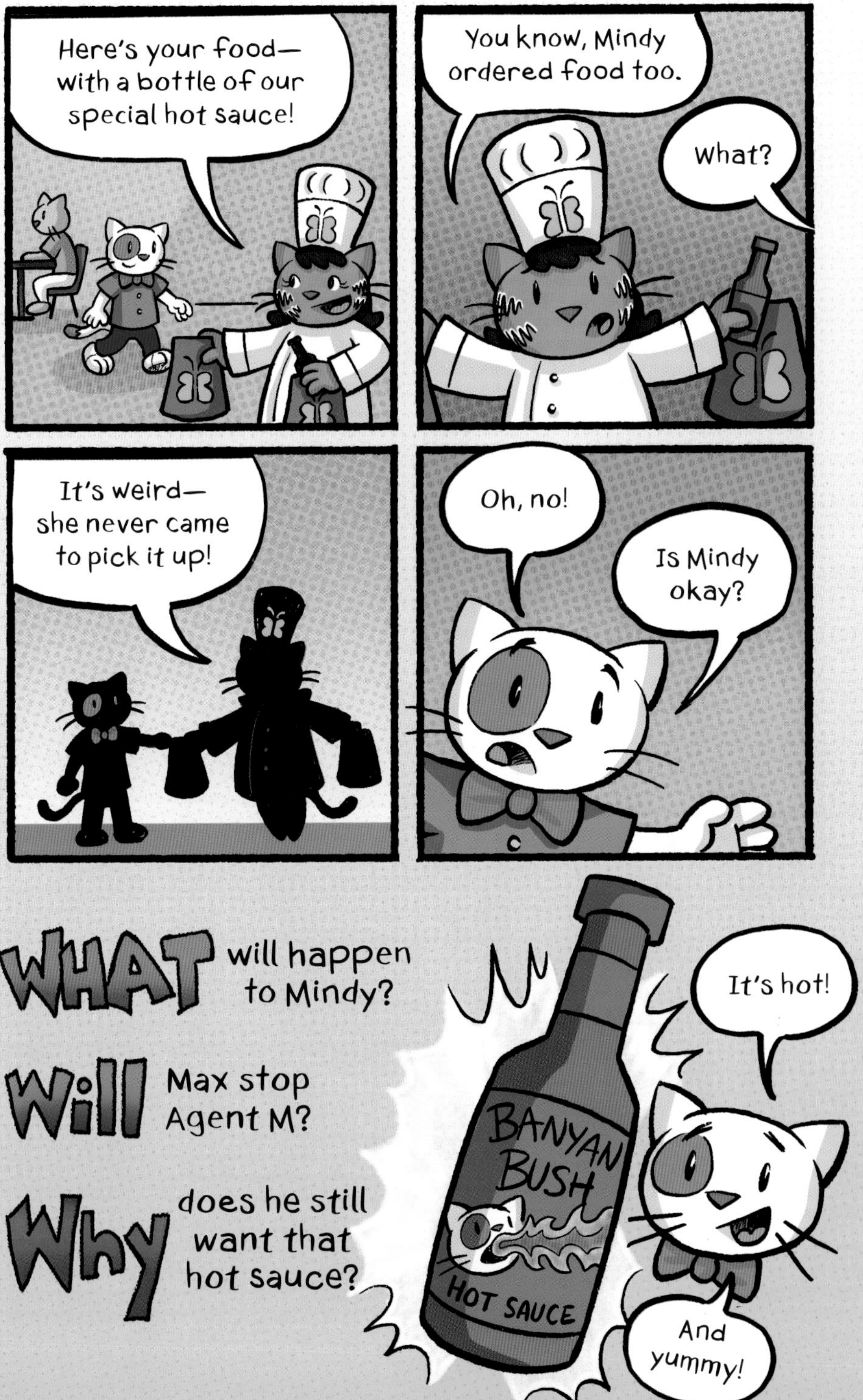
Here's your food—with a bottle of our special hot sauce!
You know, Mindy ordered food too.
What?
It's weird—she never came to pick it up!
Oh, no!
Is Mindy okay?
WHAT will happen to Mindy?
Will Max stop Agent M?
Why does he still want that hot sauce?
BANYAN BUSH HOT SAUCE
It's hot!
And yummy!

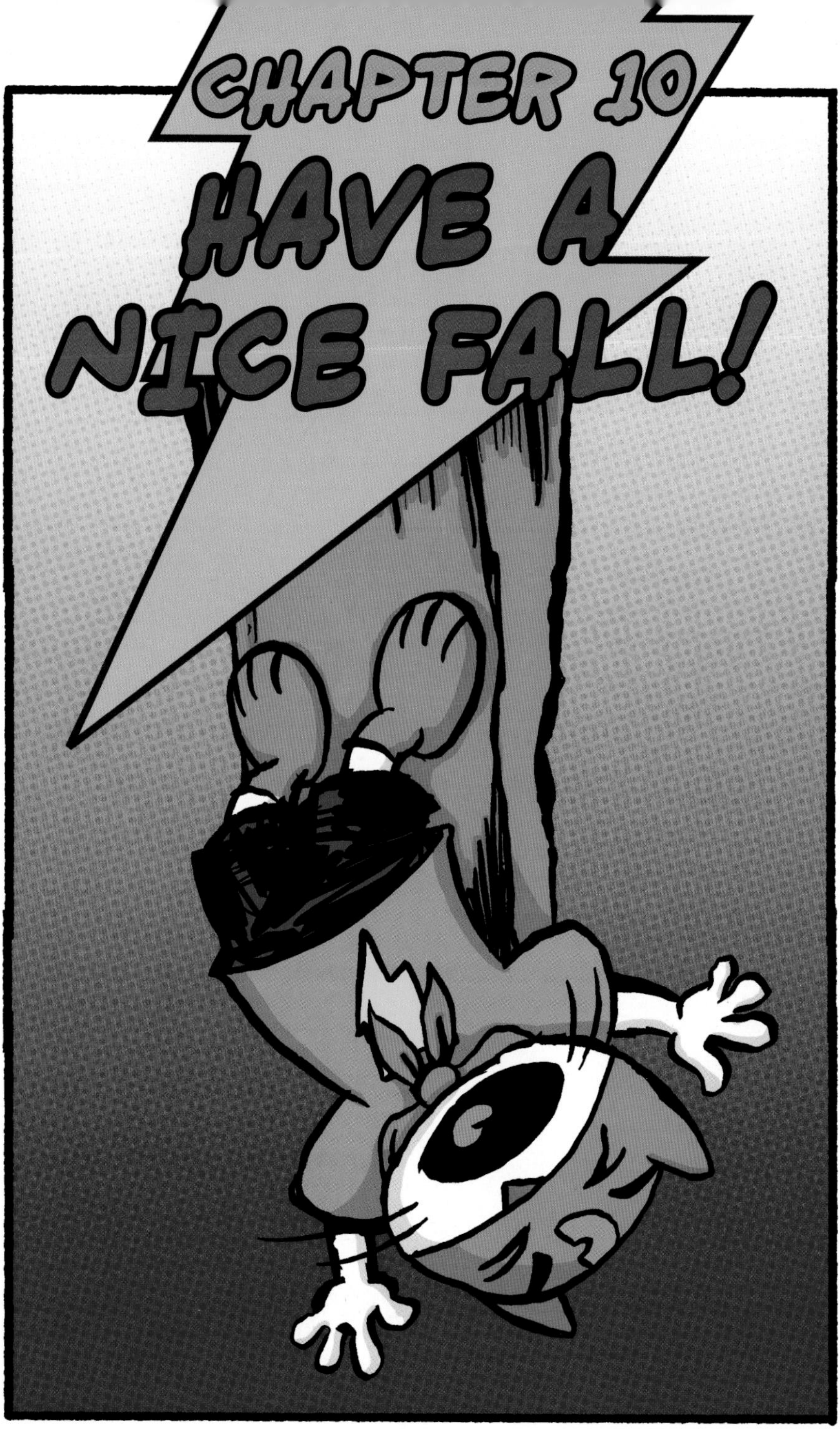
CHAPTER 10
HAVE A NICE FALL!

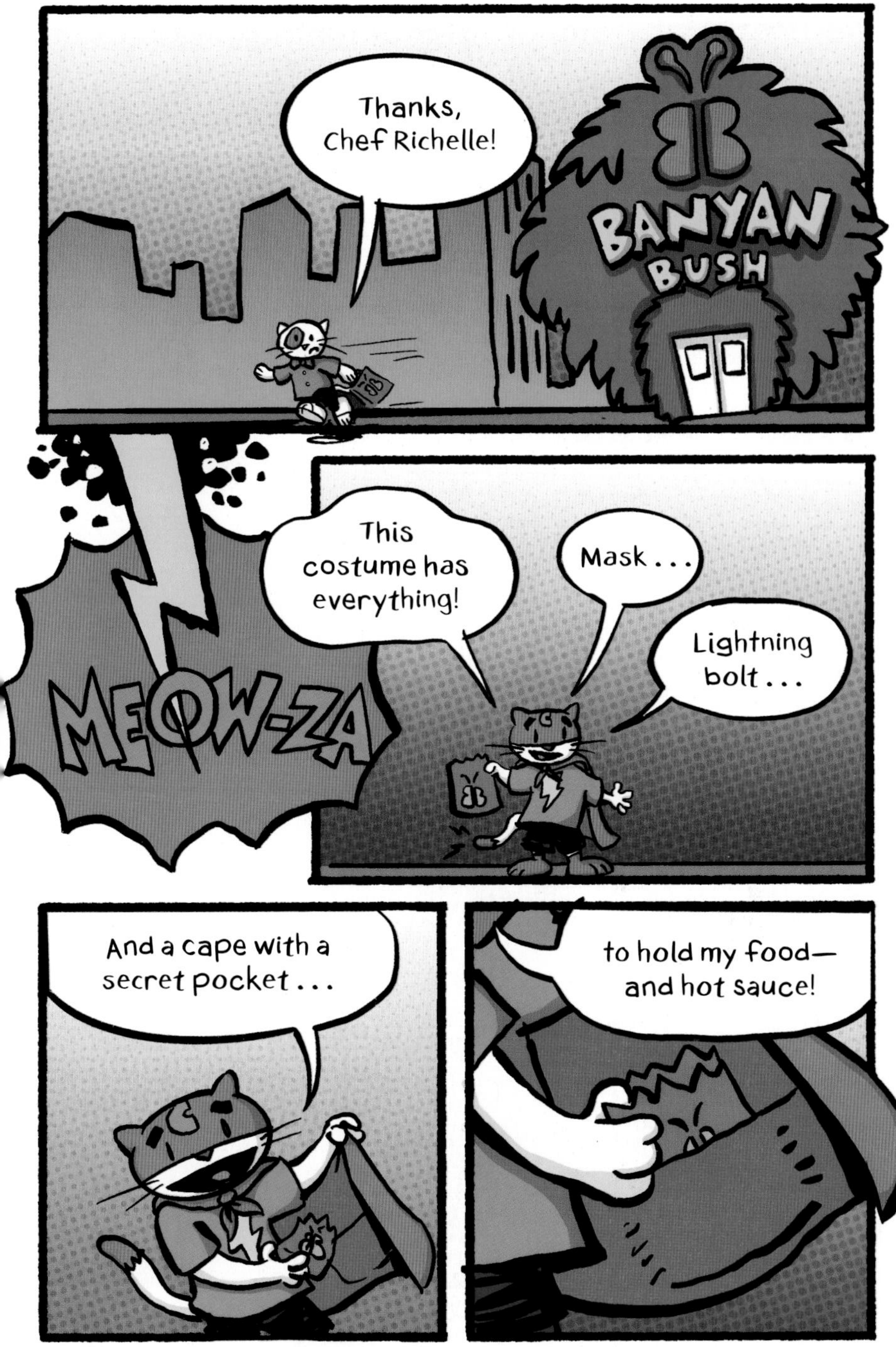
Thanks, Chef Richelle!
BANYAN BUSH
MEOW-ZA
This costume has everything!
Mask . . .
Lightning bolt . . .
And a cape with a secret pocket . . .
to hold my food— and hot sauce!

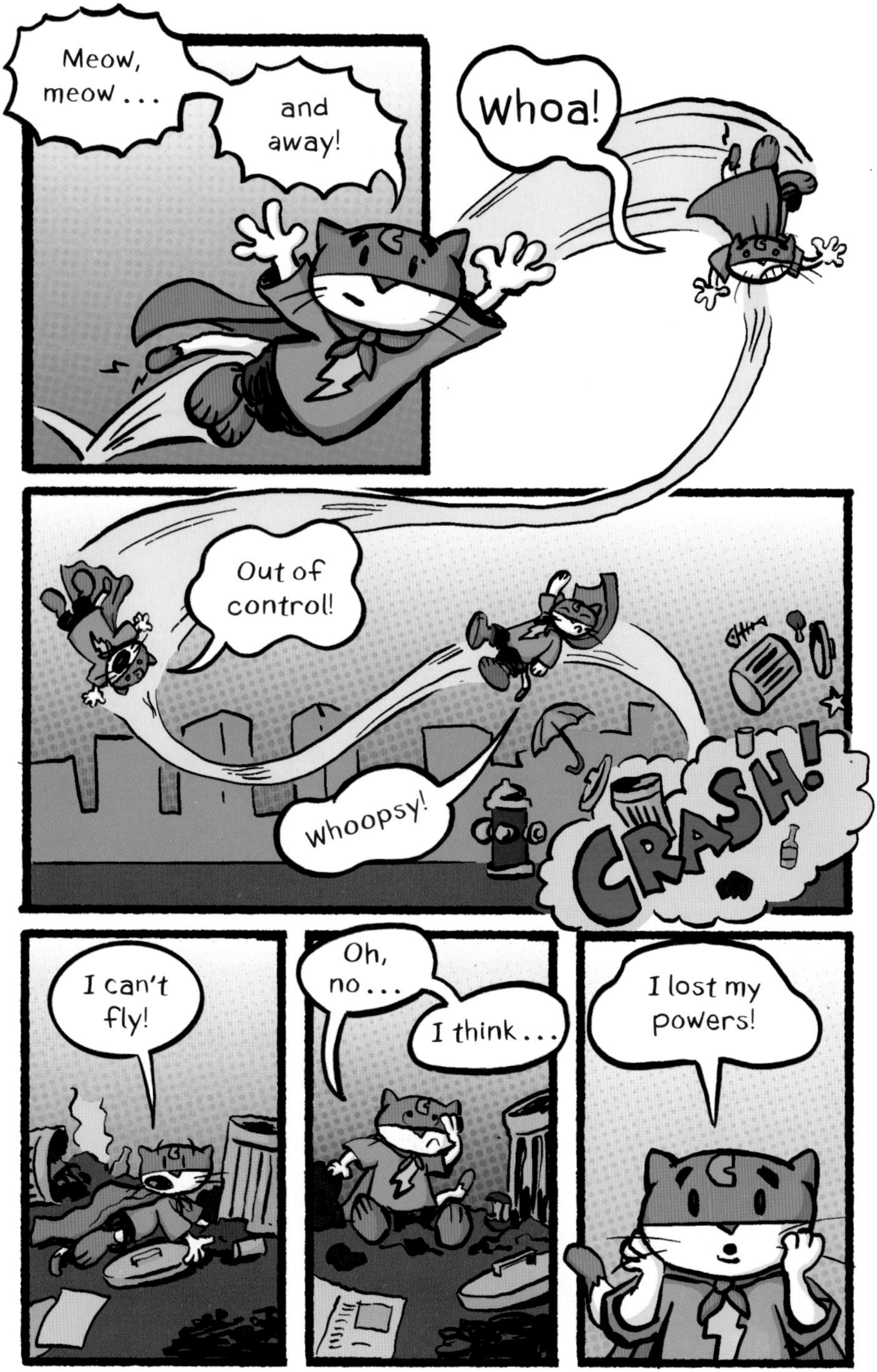
Meow, meow . . .
and away!
Whoa!
Out of control!
Whoopsy!
CRASH!
I can't fly!
Oh, no . . .
I think . . .
I lost my powers!

Meanwhile...

PRESENTING...
THE GREAT REG-INI!

1013

Wait... what are you doing?

I'm performing a magic show, silly!

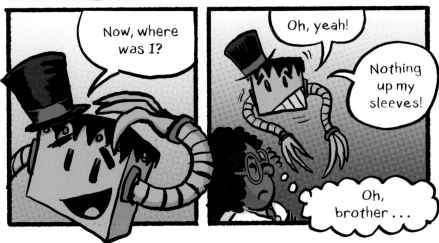

Now, where was I?

Oh, yeah!

Nothing up my sleeves!

Oh, brother...

171

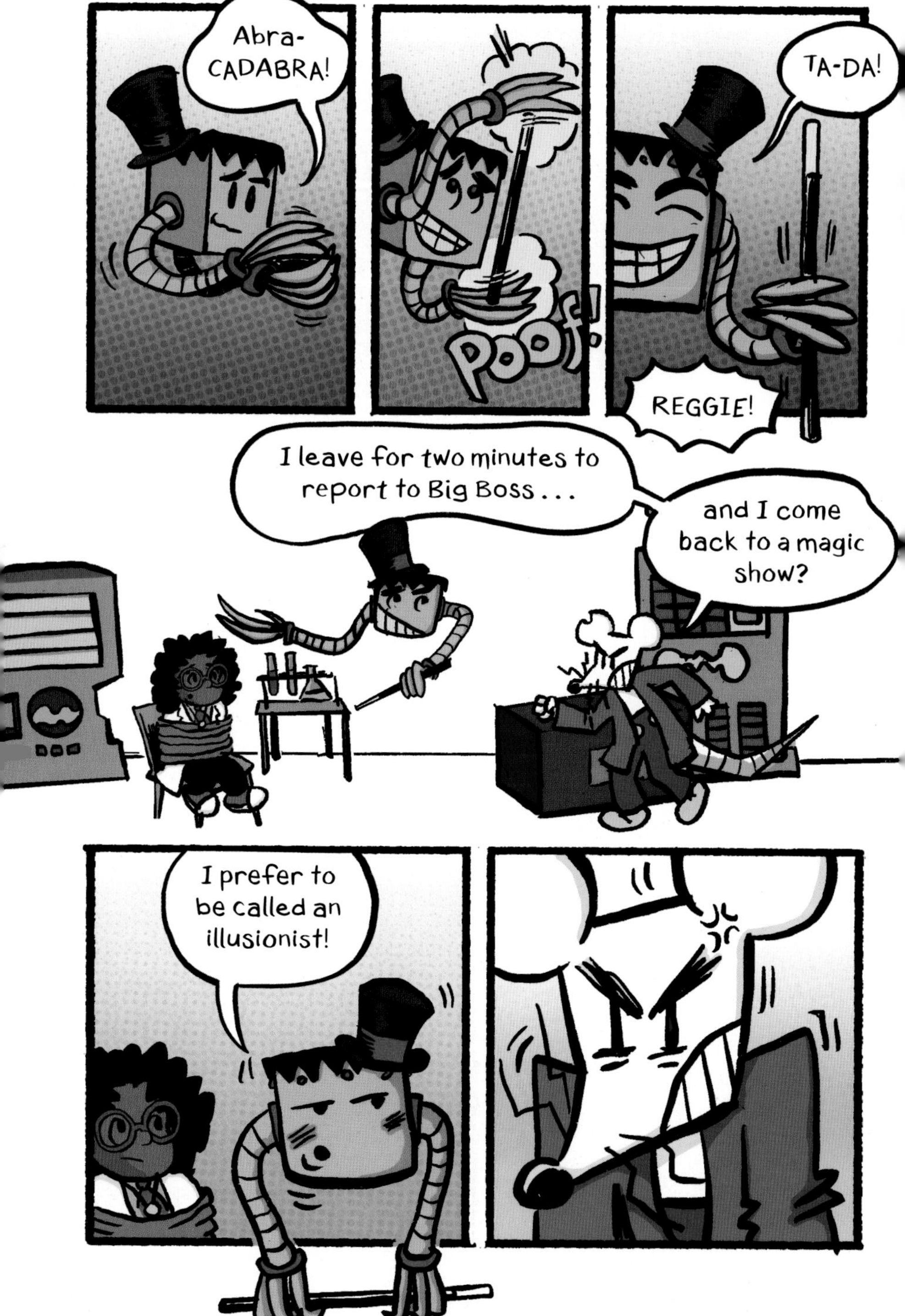
Abra-CADABRA!
POOF!
TA-DA!
REGGIE!
I leave for two minutes to report to Big Boss . . .
and I come back to a magic show?
I prefer to be called an illusionist!

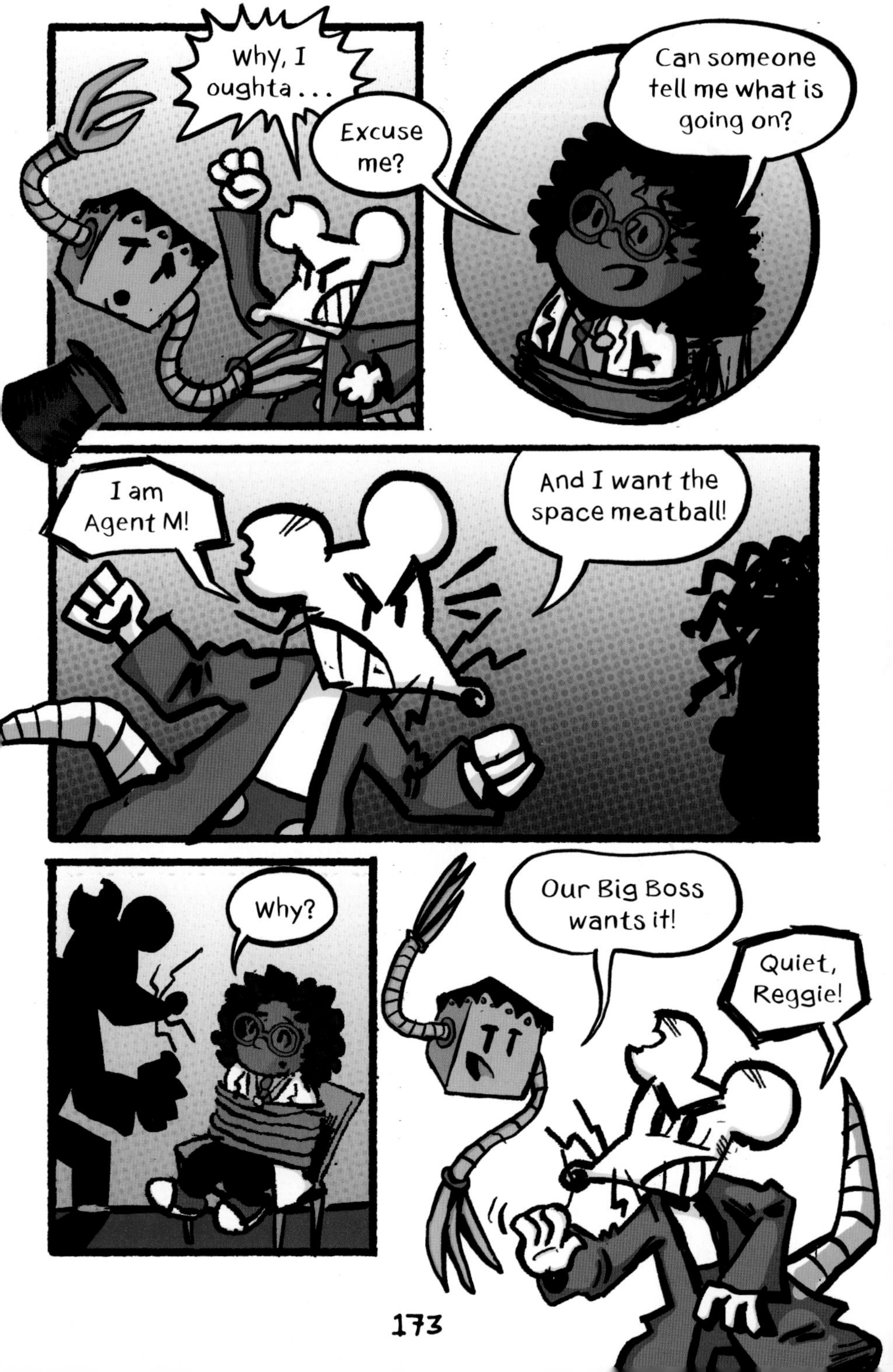
Why, I oughta . . .
Excuse me?
Can someone tell me what is going on?
I am Agent M!
And I want the space meatball!
Why?
Our Big Boss wants it!
Quiet, Reggie!

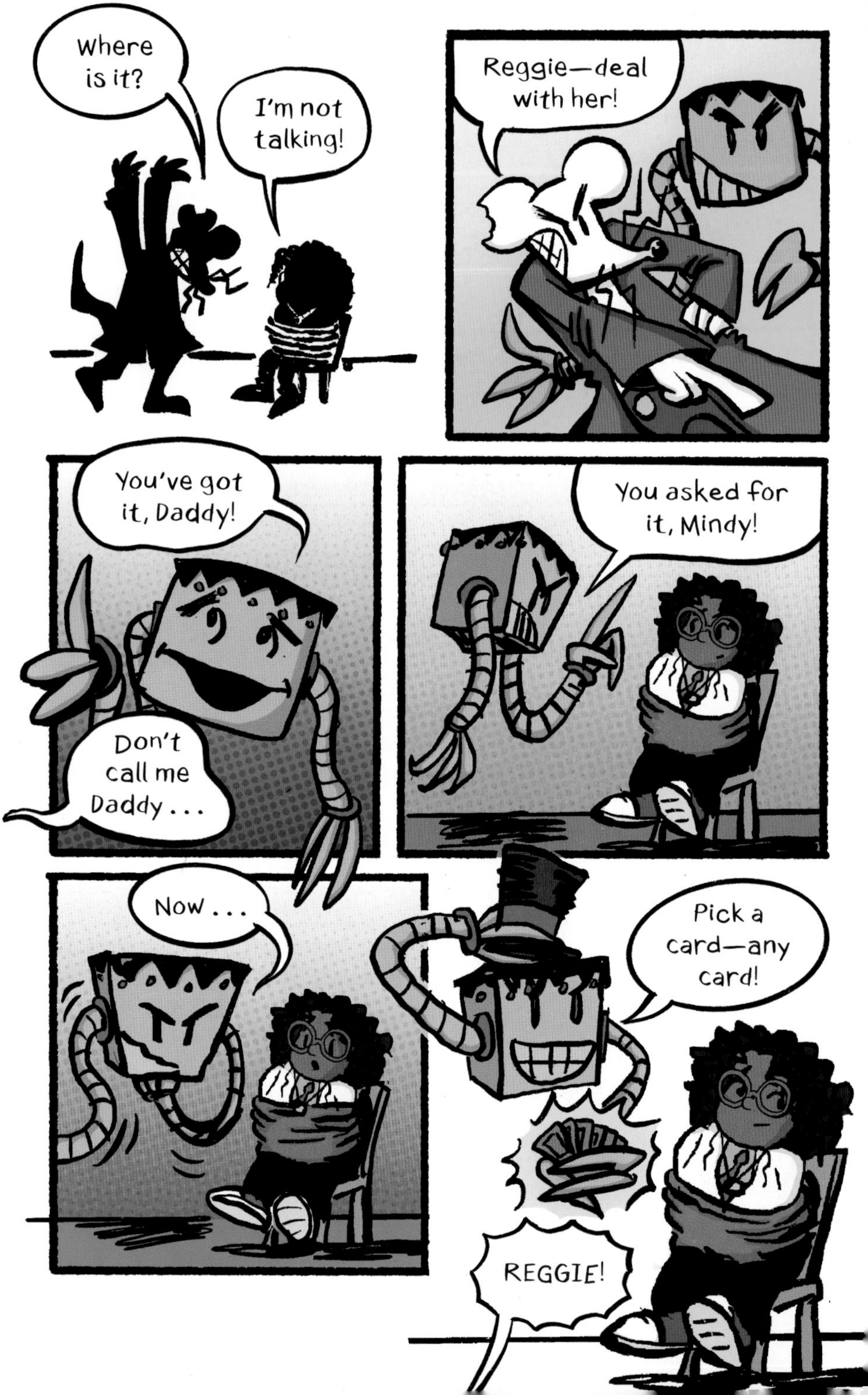
Where is it?
I'm not talking!
Reggie—deal with her!
You've got it, Daddy!
Don't call me Daddy . . .
You asked for it, Mindy!
Now . . .
Pick a card—any card!
REGGIE!

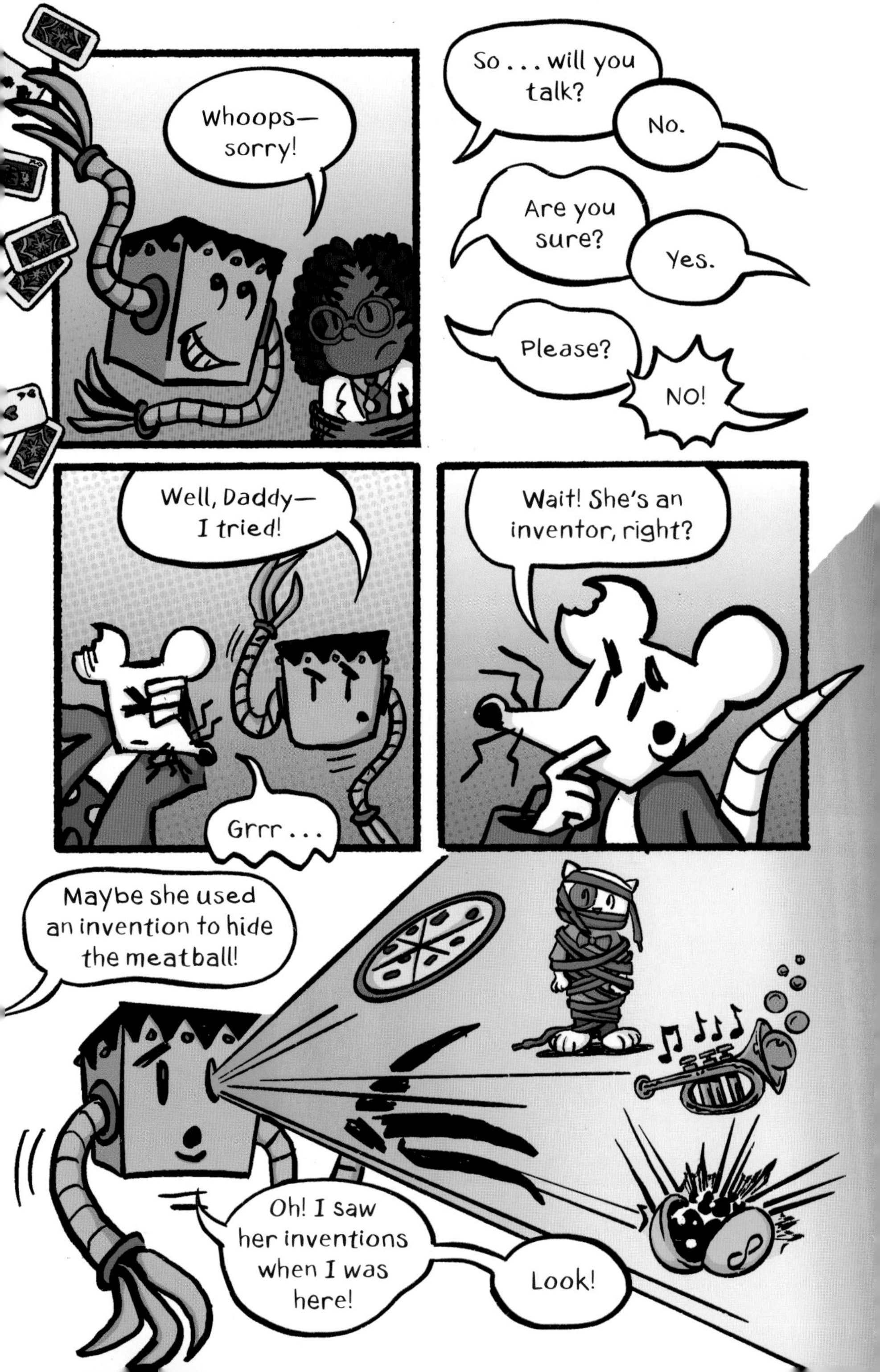
Whoops—
sorry!
So . . . will you talk?
No.
Are you sure?
Yes.
Please?
NO!
Well, Daddy—
I tried!
Grrr . . .
Wait! She's an inventor, right?
Maybe she used an invention to hide the meatball!
Oh! I saw her inventions when I was here!
Look!

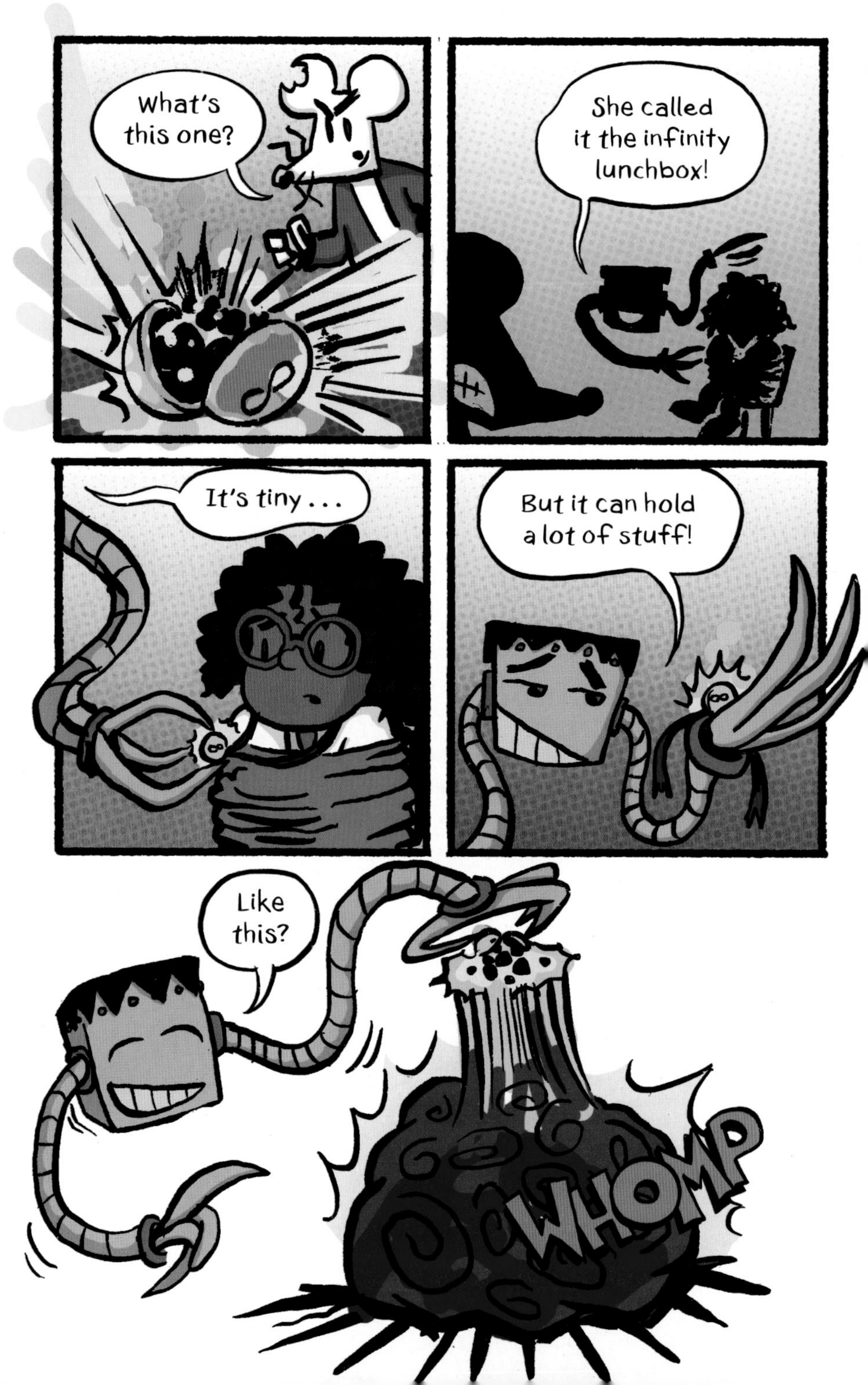
What's this one?
She called it the infinity lunchbox!
It's tiny . . .
But it can hold a lot of stuff!
Like this?
WHOMP

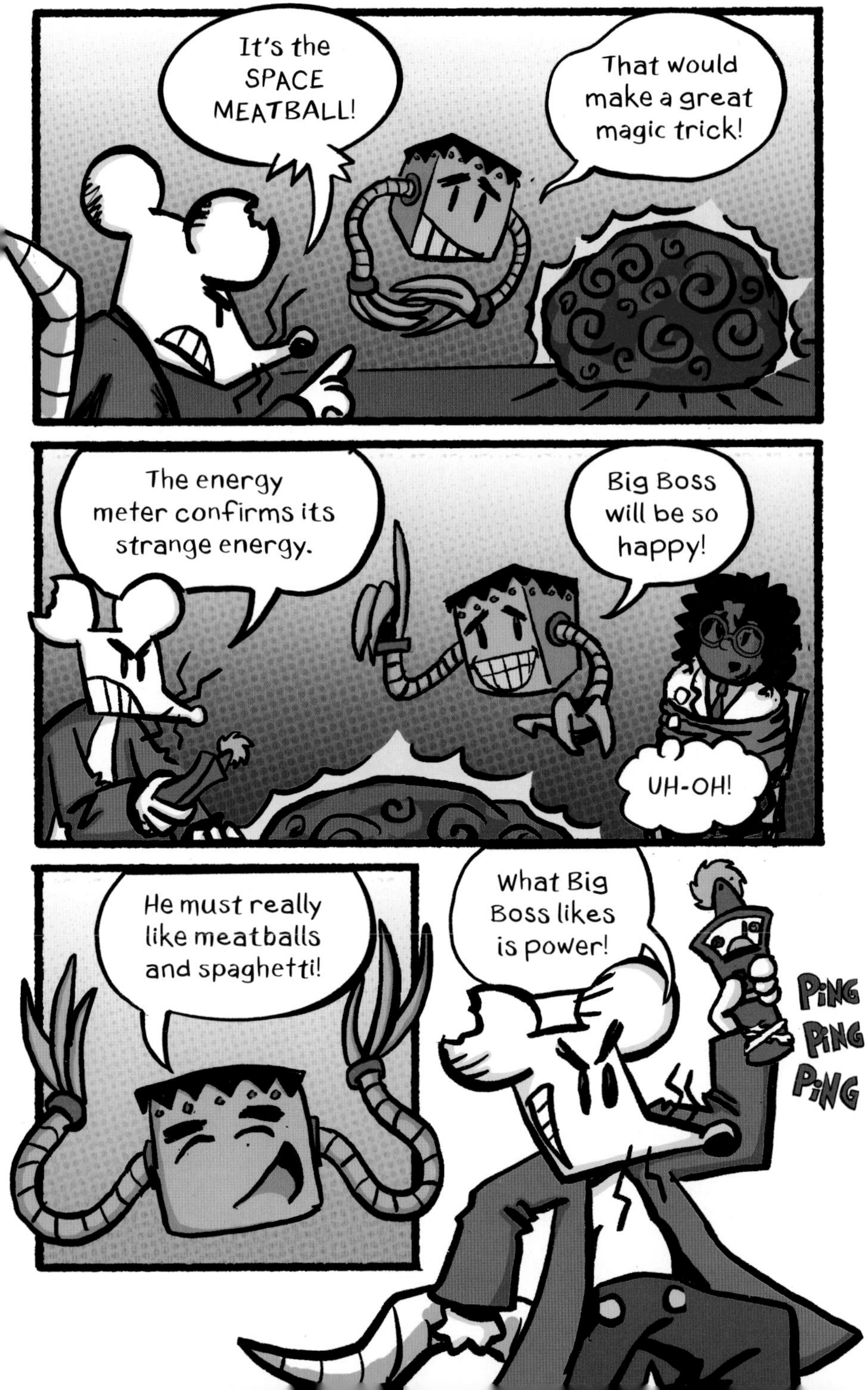
It's the SPACE MEATBALL!
That would make a great magic trick!
The energy meter confirms its strange energy.
Big Boss will be so happy!
UH-OH!
He must really like meatballs and spaghetti!
What Big Boss likes is power!
PiNG PiNG PiNG

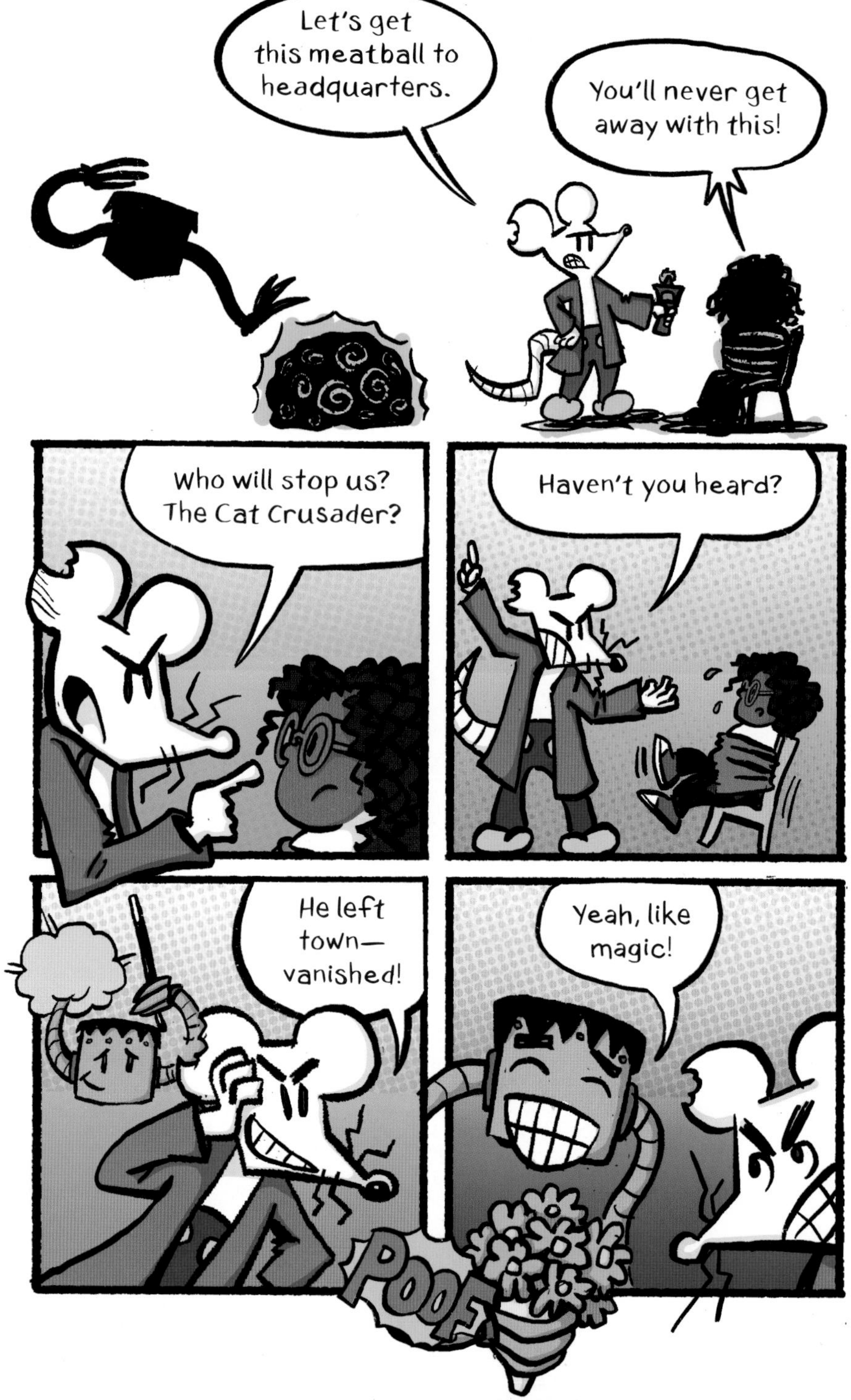
Let's get this meatball to headquarters.
You'll never get away with this!
Who will stop us? The Cat Crusader?
Haven't you heard?
He left town—vanished!
Yeah, like magic!
POOF

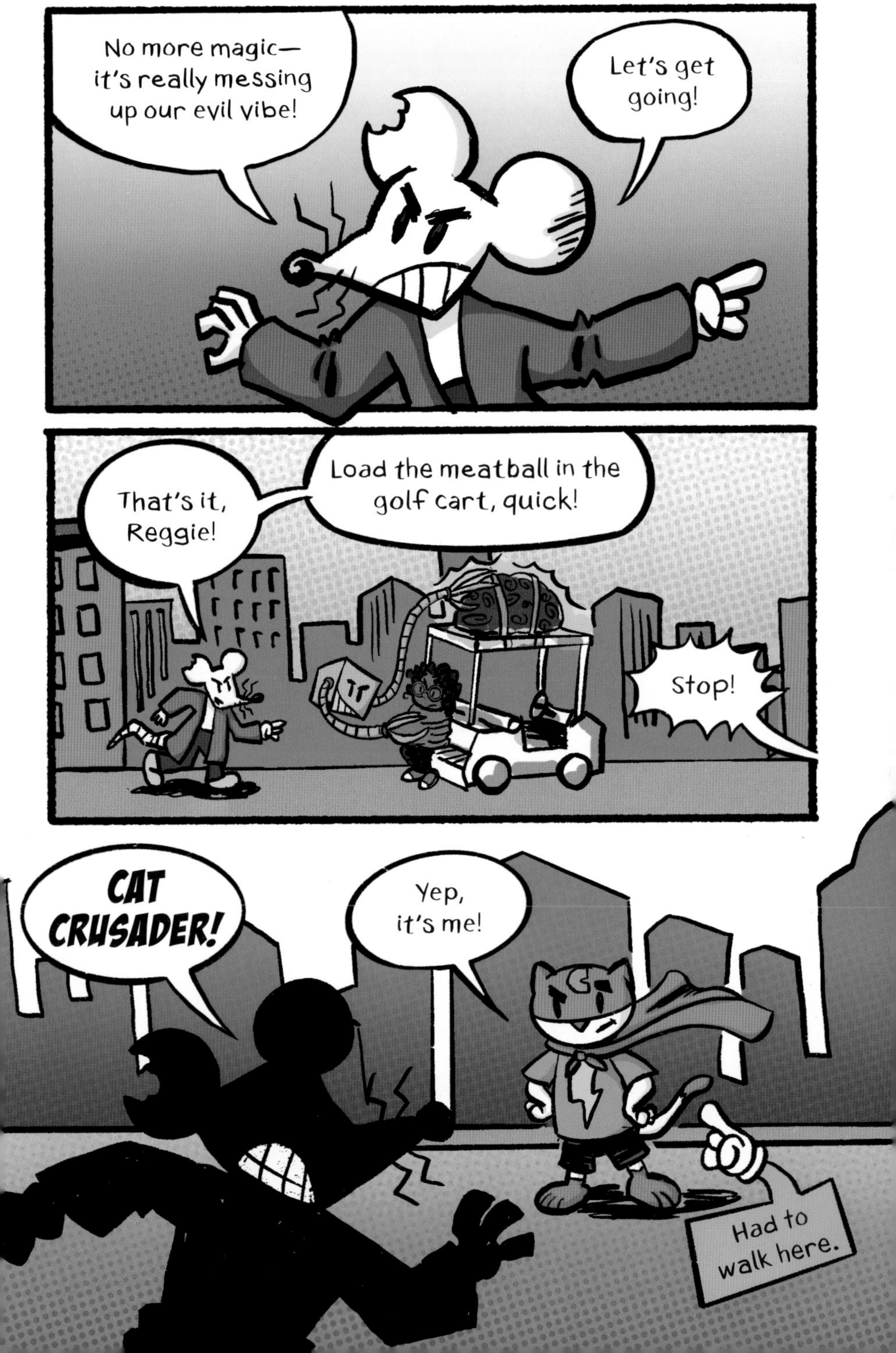
No more magic—it's really messing up our evil vibe!
Let's get going!
That's it, Reggie!
Load the meatball in the golf cart, quick!
Stop!
CAT CRUSADER!
Yep, it's me!
Had to walk here.

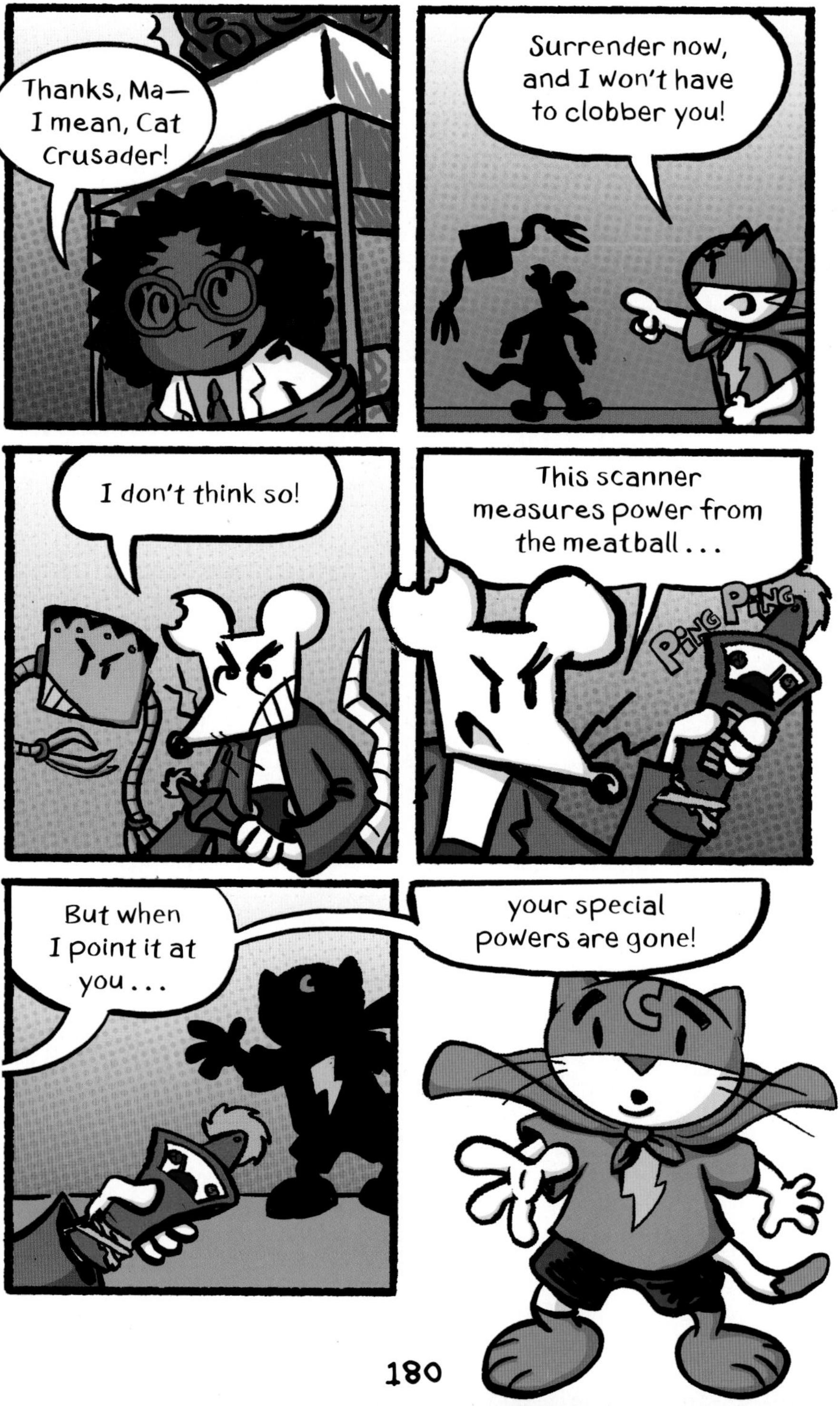
Thanks, Ma—
I mean, Cat
Crusader!
Surrender now,
and I won't have
to clobber you!
I don't think so!
This scanner
measures power from
the meatball . . .
PING PING
But when
I point it at
you . . .
your special
powers are gone!

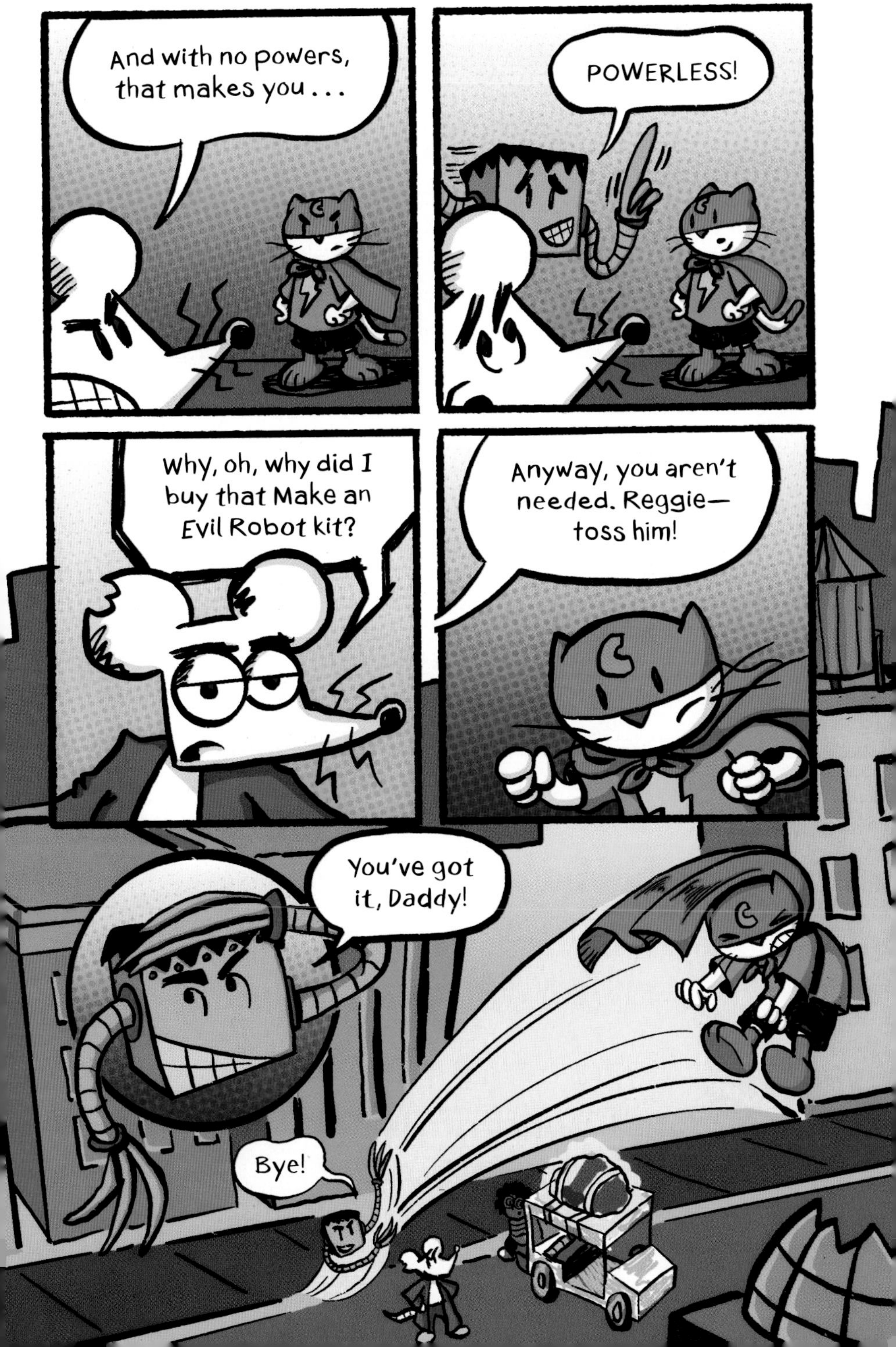

And with no powers, that makes you . . .
POWERLESS!
Why, oh, why did I buy that Make an Evil Robot kit?
Anyway, you aren't needed. Reggie—toss him!
You've got it, Daddy!
Bye!

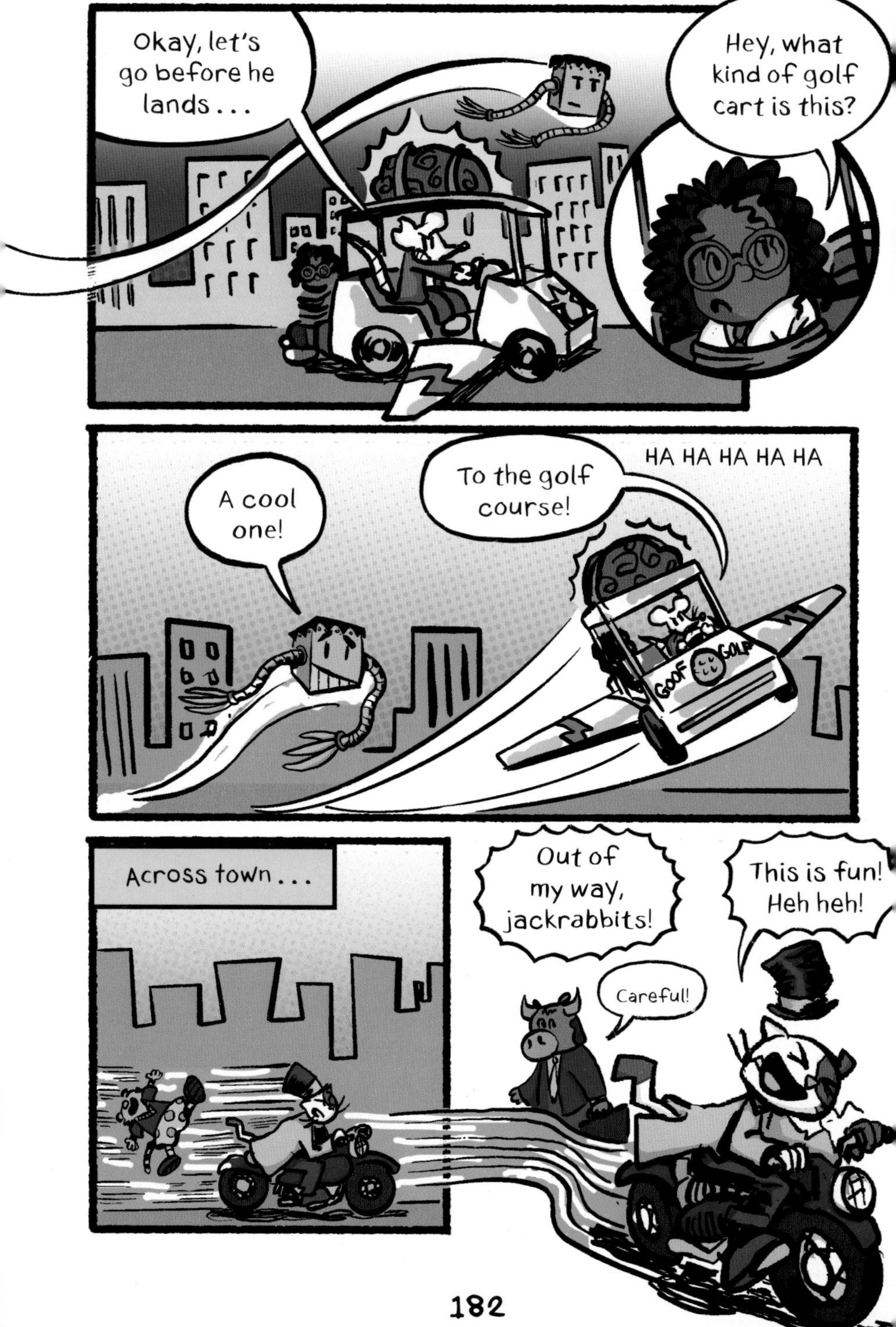
Okay, let's go before he lands . . .
Hey, what kind of golf cart is this?
A cool one!
To the golf course!
HA HA HA HA HA
GOOF GOLF
Across town . . .
Out of my way, jackrabbits!
This is fun! Heh heh!
Careful!

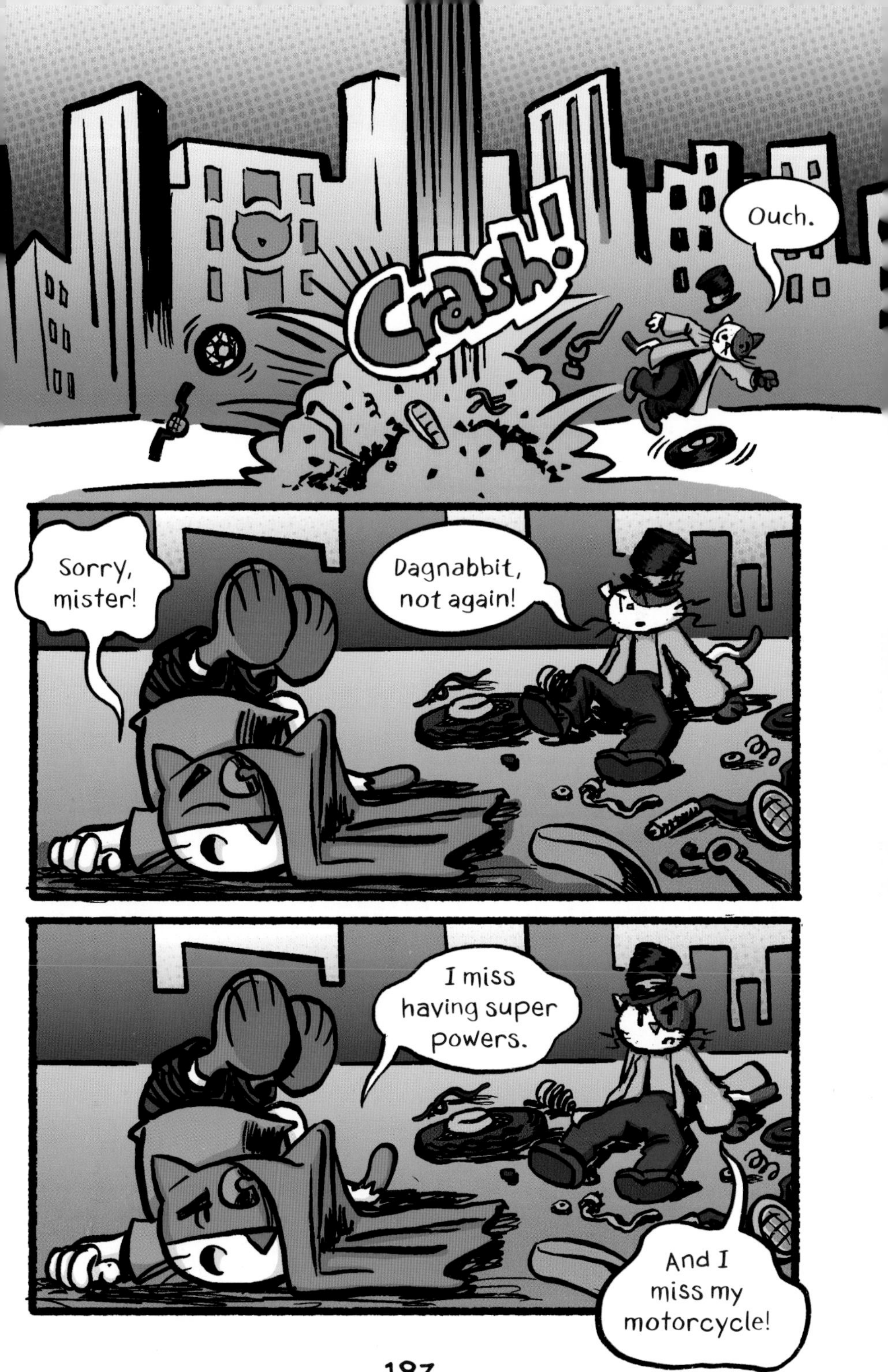
Crash!
Ouch.
Sorry, mister!
Dagnabbit, not again!
I miss having super powers.
And I miss my motorcycle!

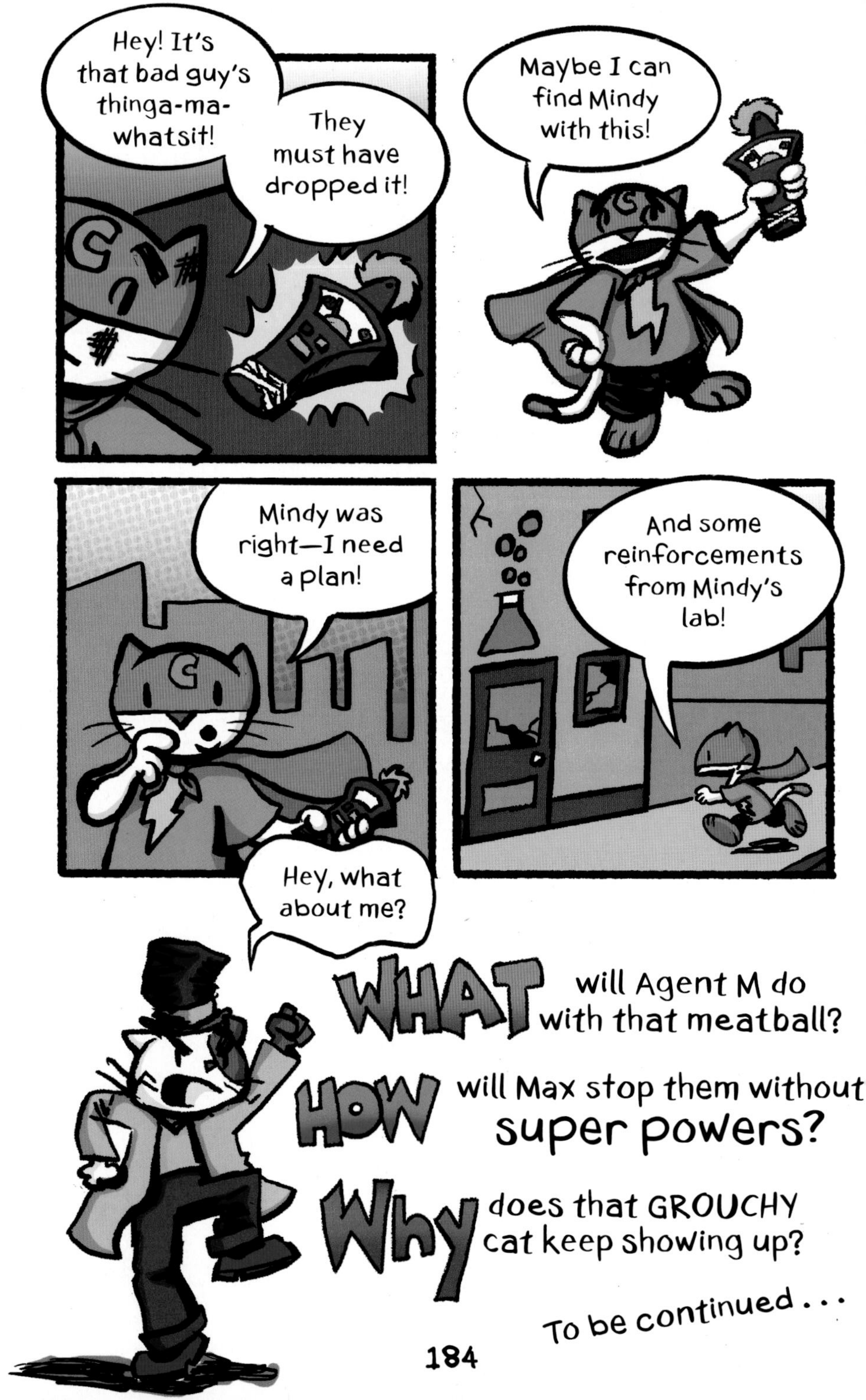
Hey! It's that bad guy's thinga-ma-whatsit!
They must have dropped it!
Maybe I can find Mindy with this!
Mindy was right—I need a plan!
And some reinforcements from Mindy's lab!
Hey, what about me?
WHAT will Agent M do with that meatball?
HOW will Max stop them without super powers?
Why does that GROUCHY cat keep showing up?
To be continued . . .

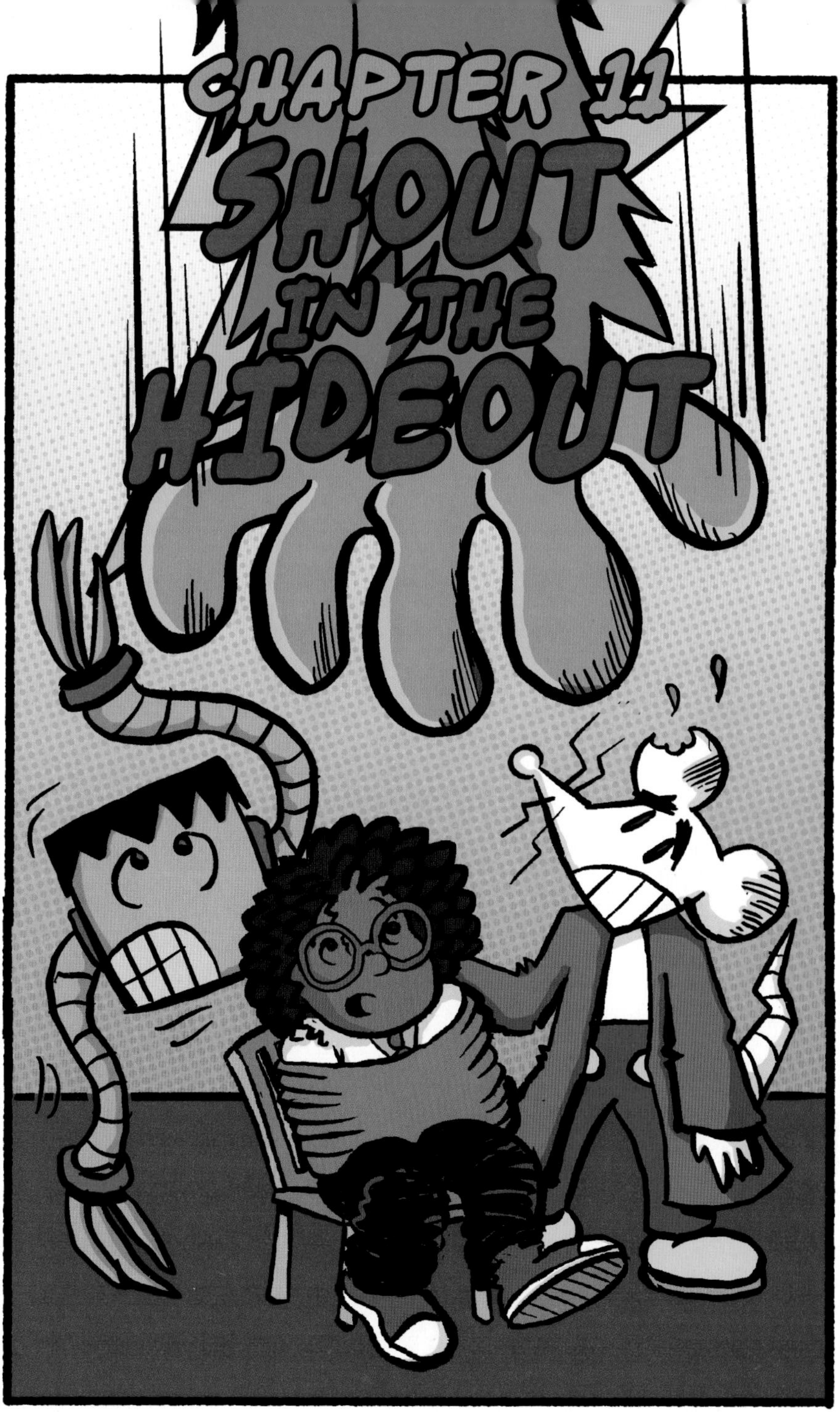
CHAPTER 11
SHOUT IN THE HIDEOUT

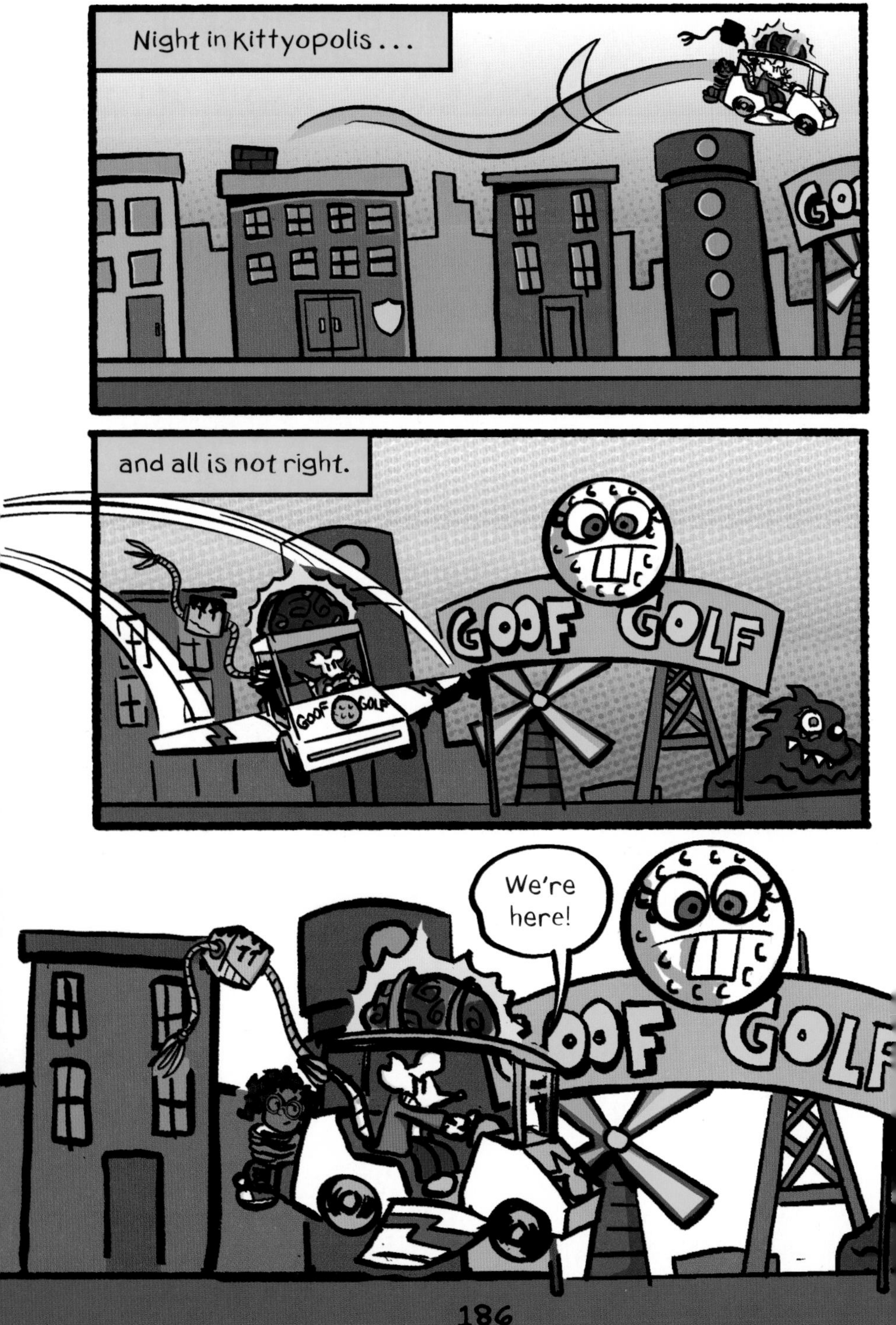
Night in Kittyopolis . . .
and all is not right.
GOOF GOLF
GOOF GOLF
We're here!
GOLF

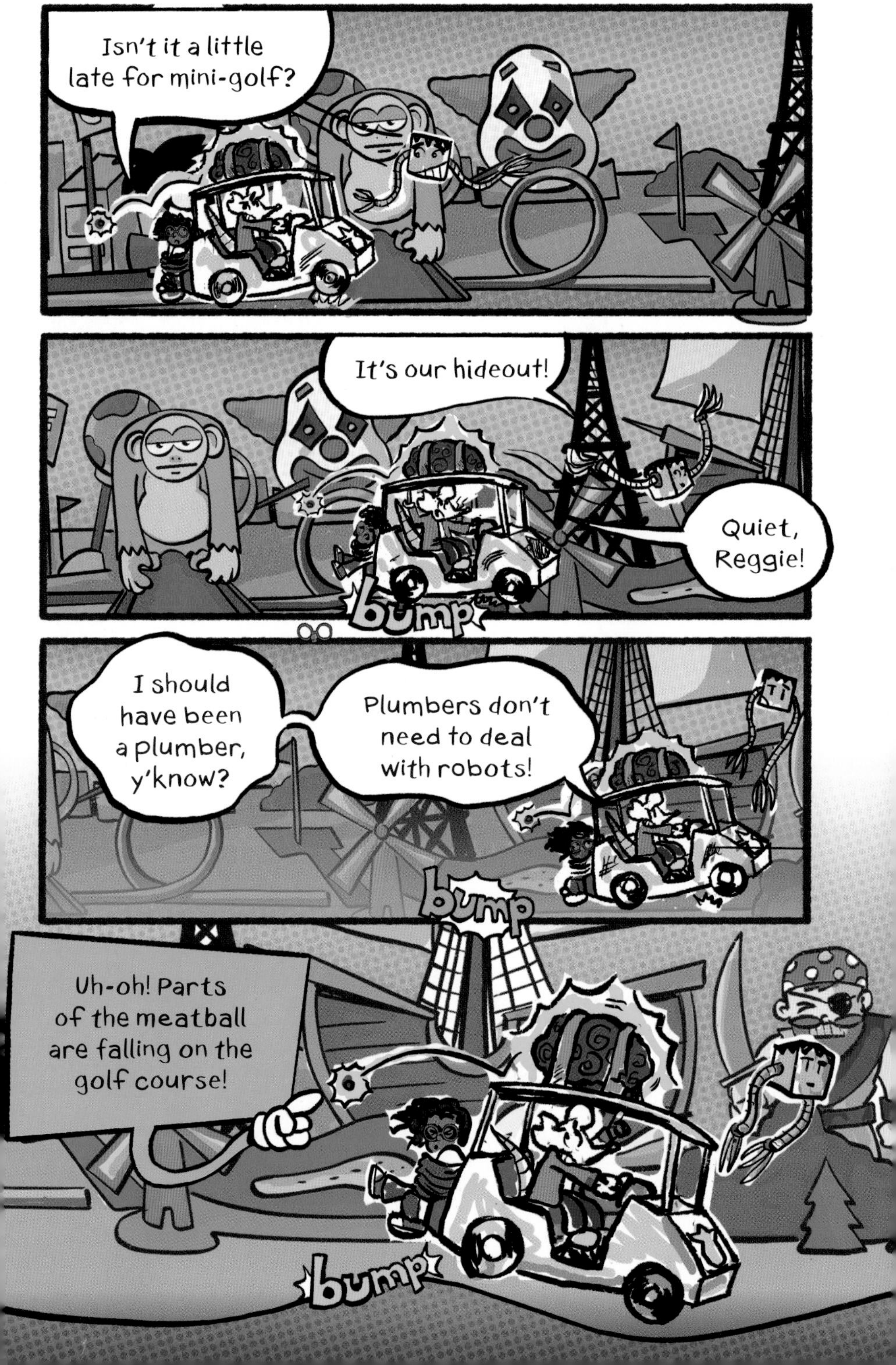
Isn't it a little late for mini-golf?
It's our hideout!
Quiet, Reggie!
bump
I should have been a plumber, y'know?
Plumbers don't need to deal with robots!
bump
Uh-oh! Parts of the meatball are falling on the golf course!
bump

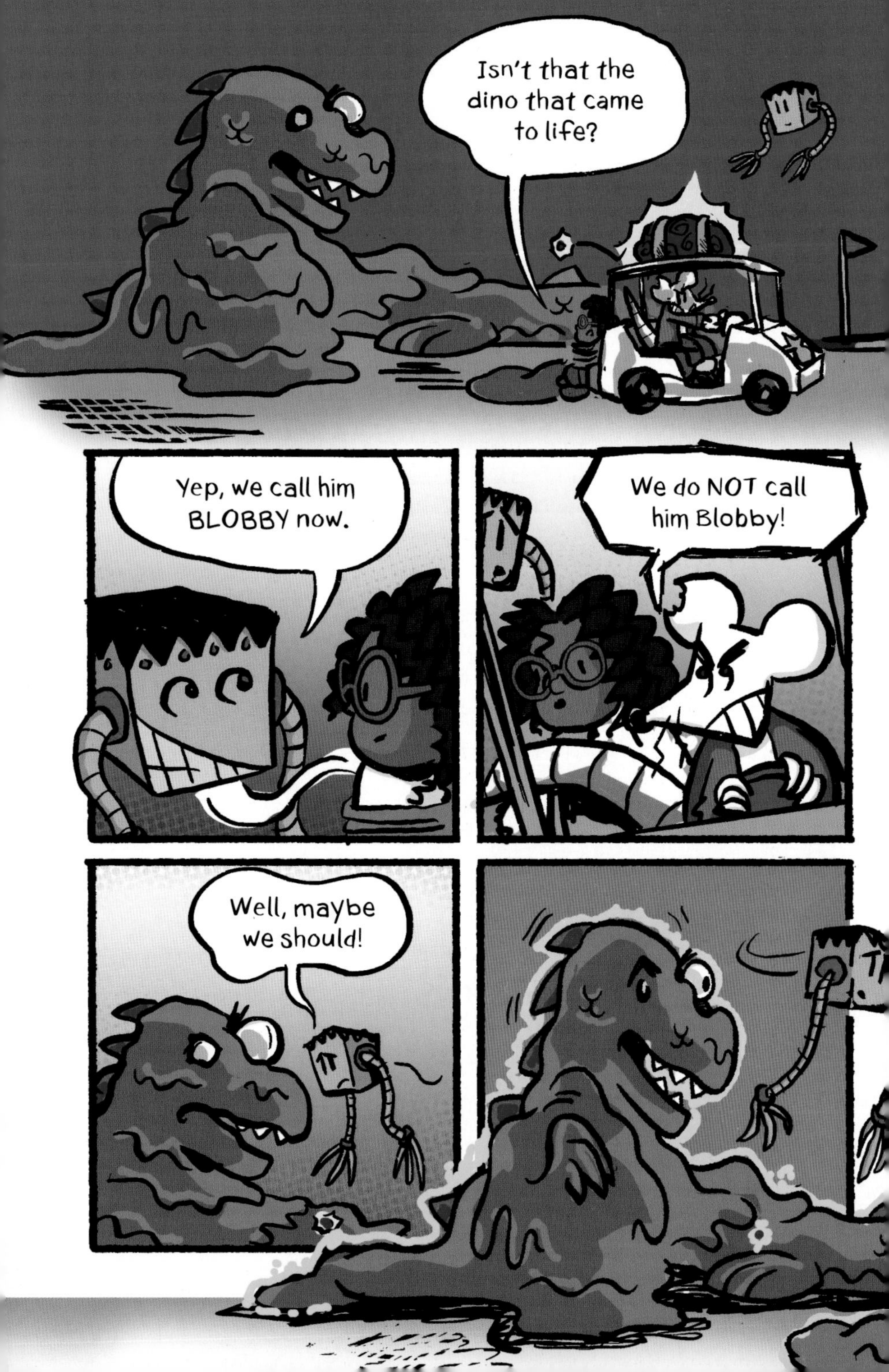
Isn't that the dino that came to life?
Yep, we call him BLOBBY now.
We do NOT call him Blobby!
Well, maybe we should!

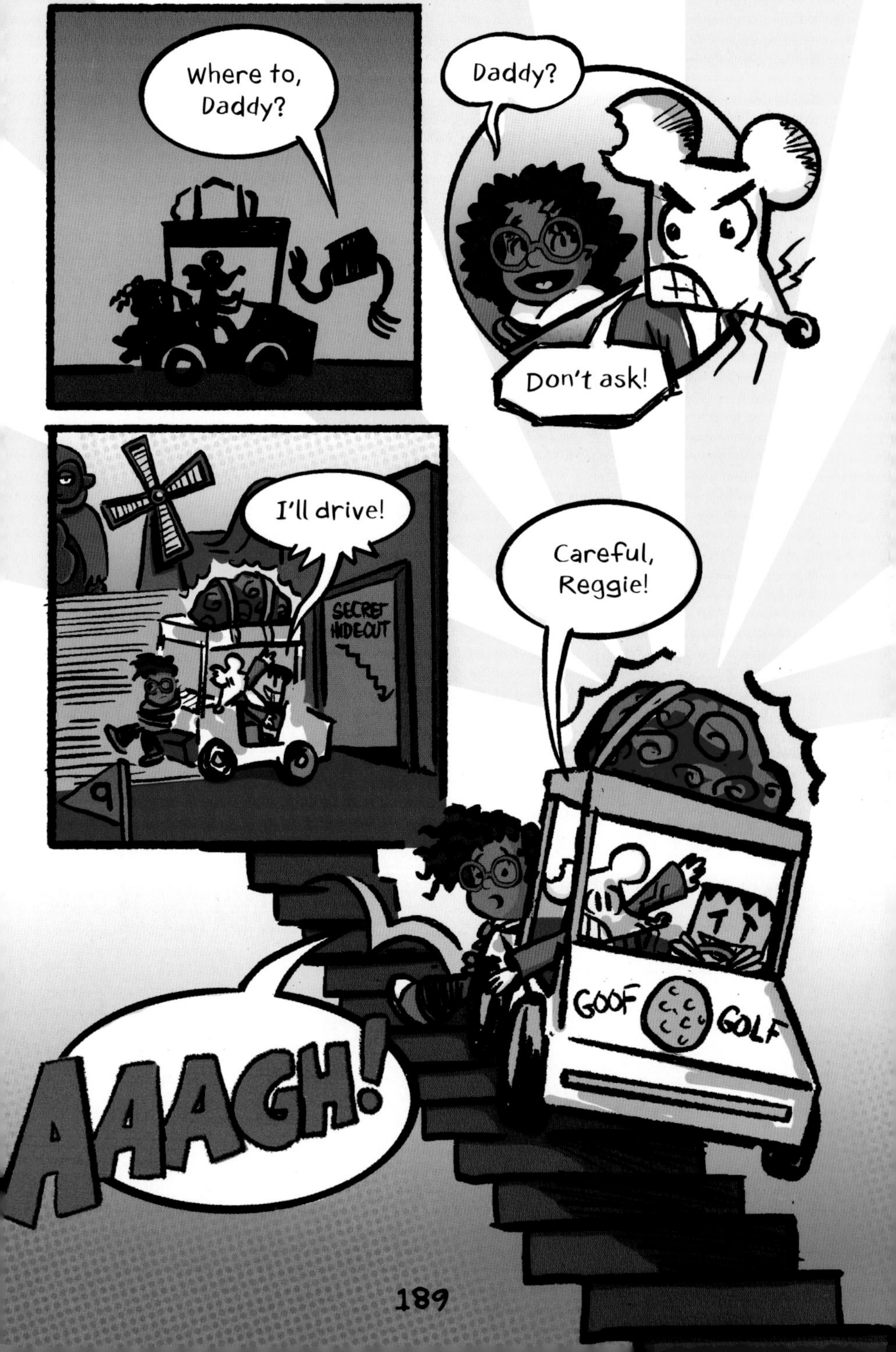
Where to, Daddy?
Daddy?
Don't ask!
I'll drive!
SECRET HIDEOUT
Careful, Reggie!
GOOF GOLF
AAAGH!

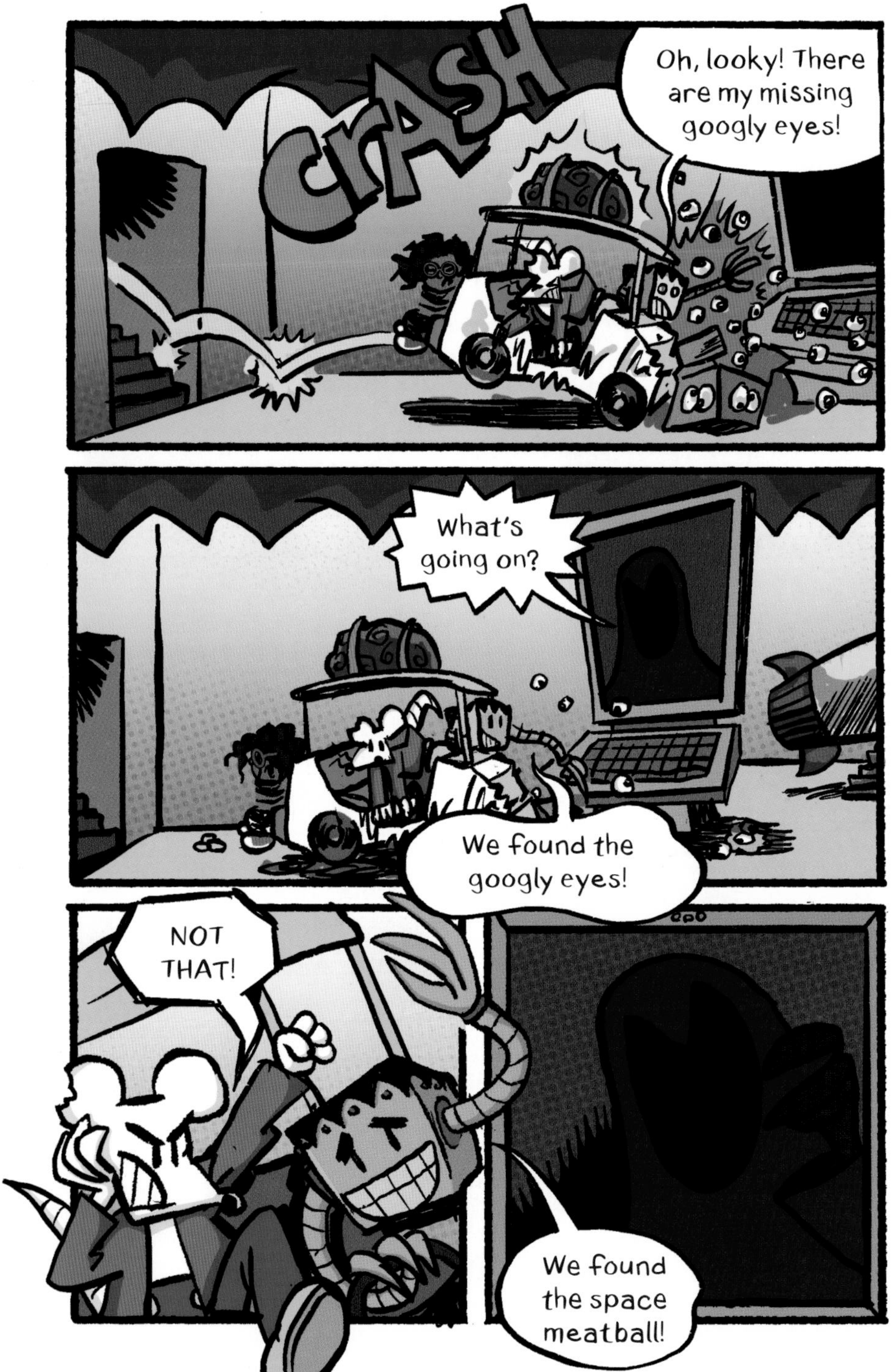
CRASH
Oh, looky! There are my missing googly eyes!
What's going on?
We found the googly eyes!
NOT THAT!
We found the space meatball!

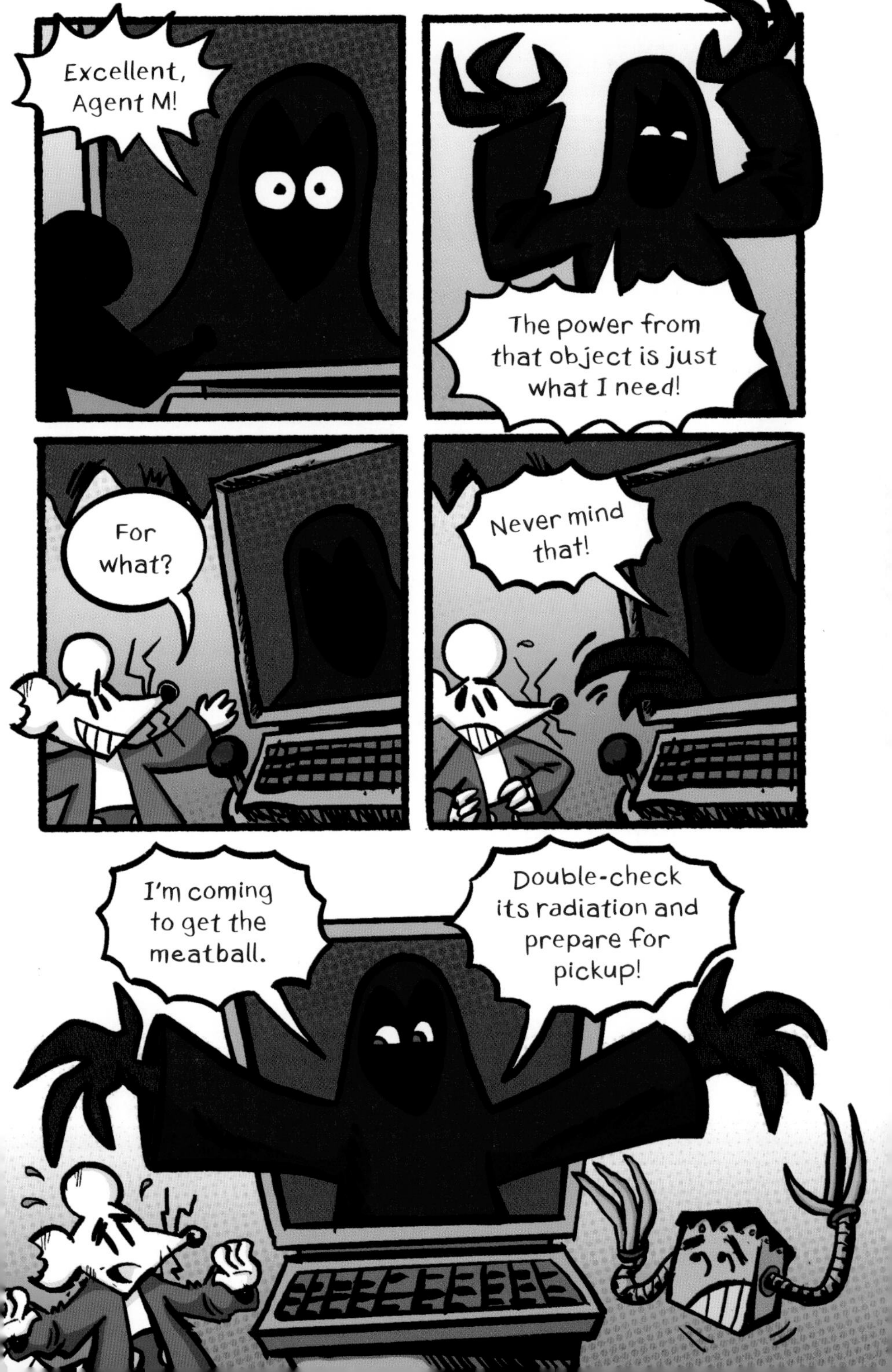
Excellent, Agent M!
The power from that object is just what I need!
For what?
Never mind that!
I'm coming to get the meatball.
Double-check its radiation and prepare for pickup!

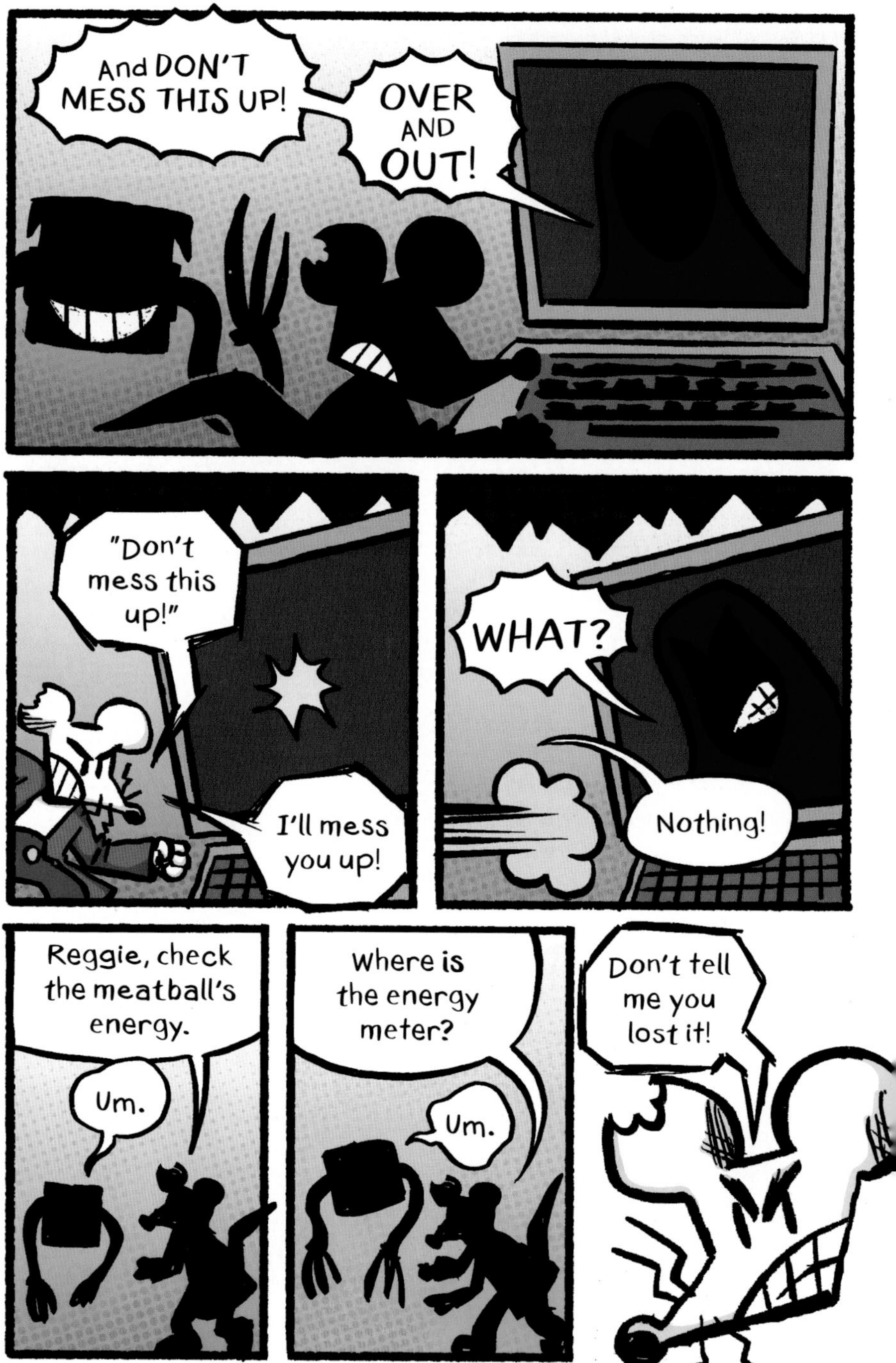
And DON'T MESS THIS UP!
OVER AND OUT!
"Don't mess this up!"
I'll mess you up!
WHAT?
Nothing!
Reggie, check the meatball's energy.
Um.
Where is the energy meter?
Um.
Don't tell me you lost it!

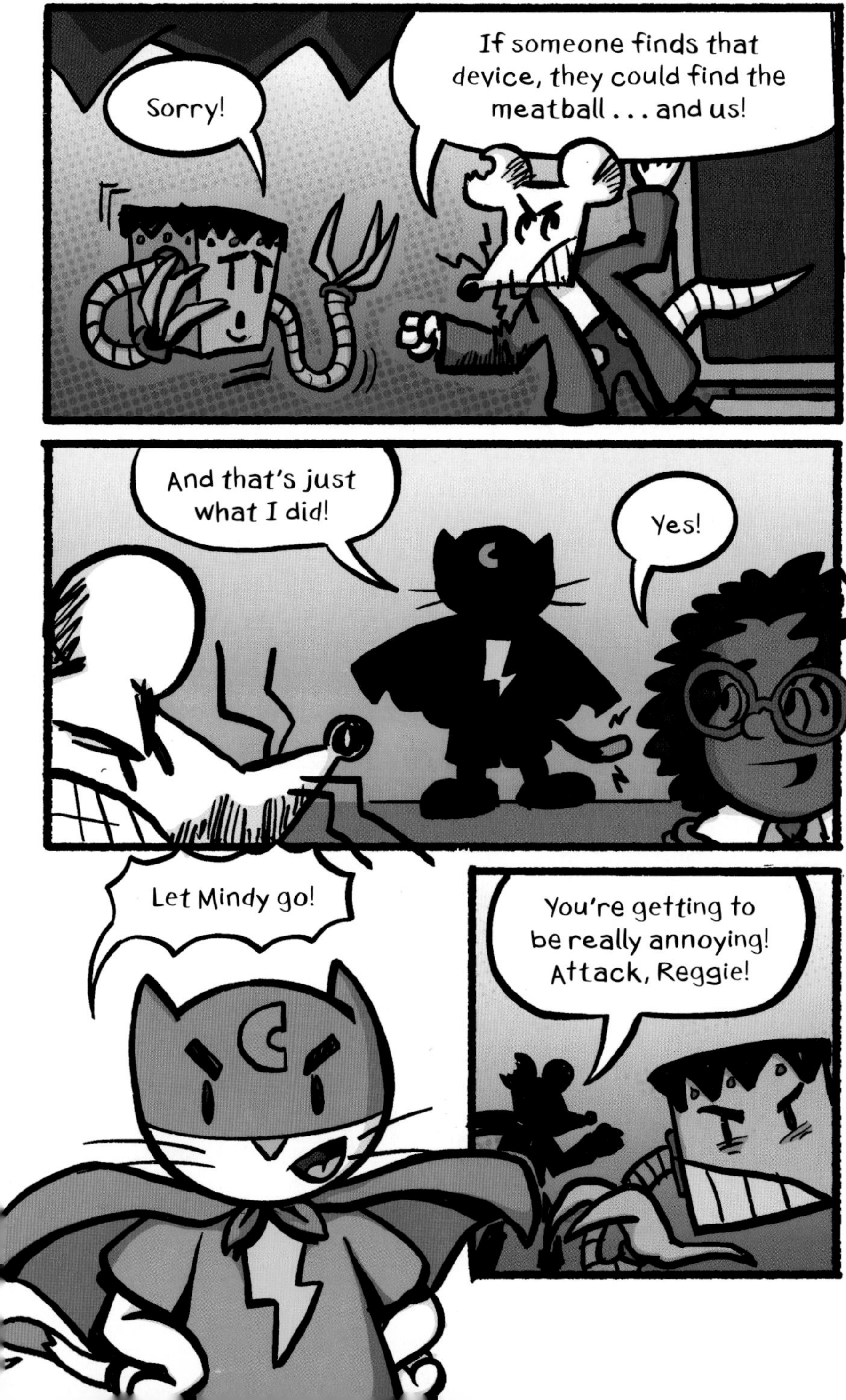
Sorry!
If someone finds that device, they could find the meatball . . . and us!
And that's just what I did!
Yes!
Let Mindy go!
You're getting to be really annoying! Attack, Reggie!

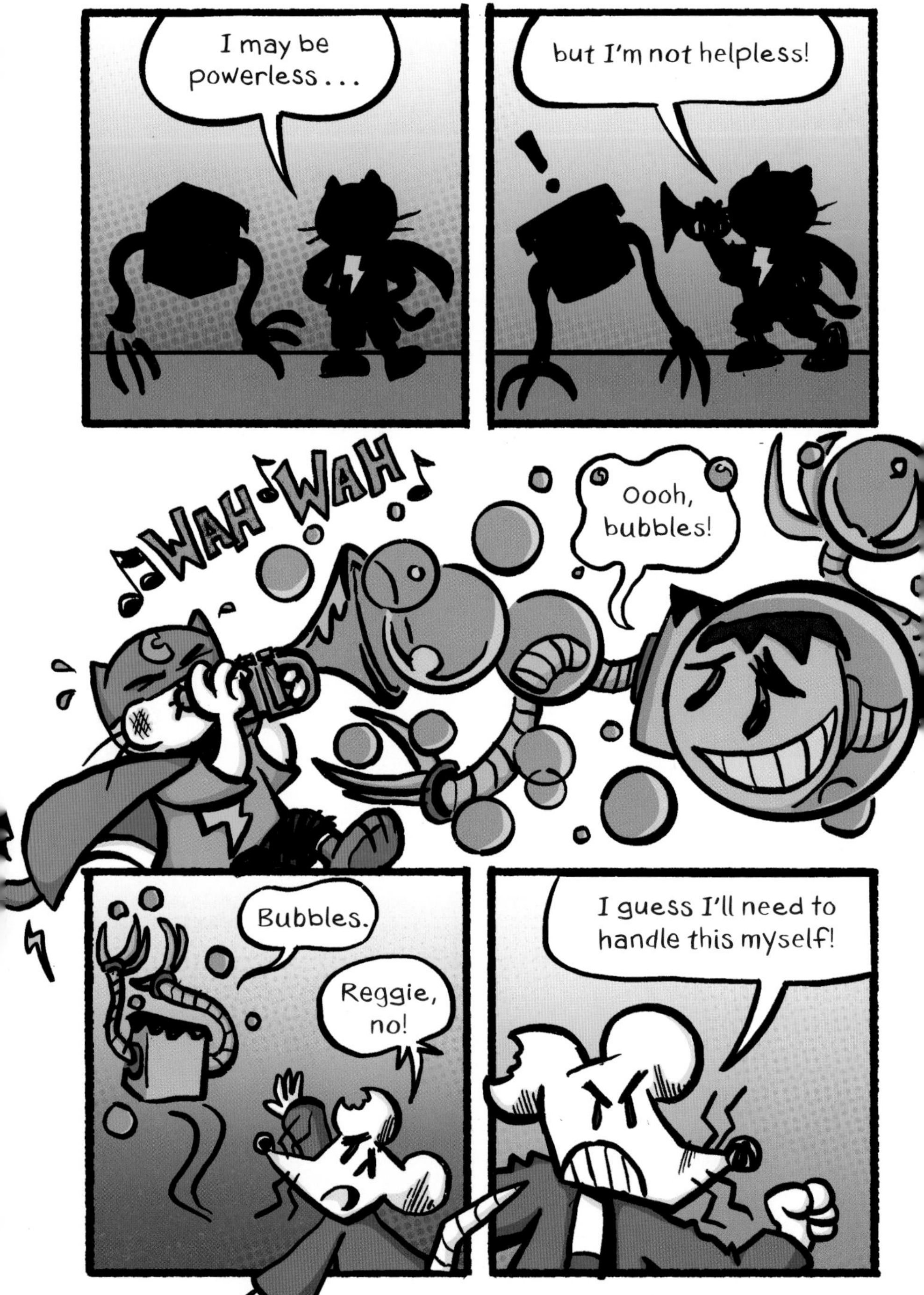
I may be powerless . . .
but I'm not helpless!
!
WAH WAH
Oooh, bubbles!
Bubbles.
Reggie, no!
I guess I'll need to handle this myself!

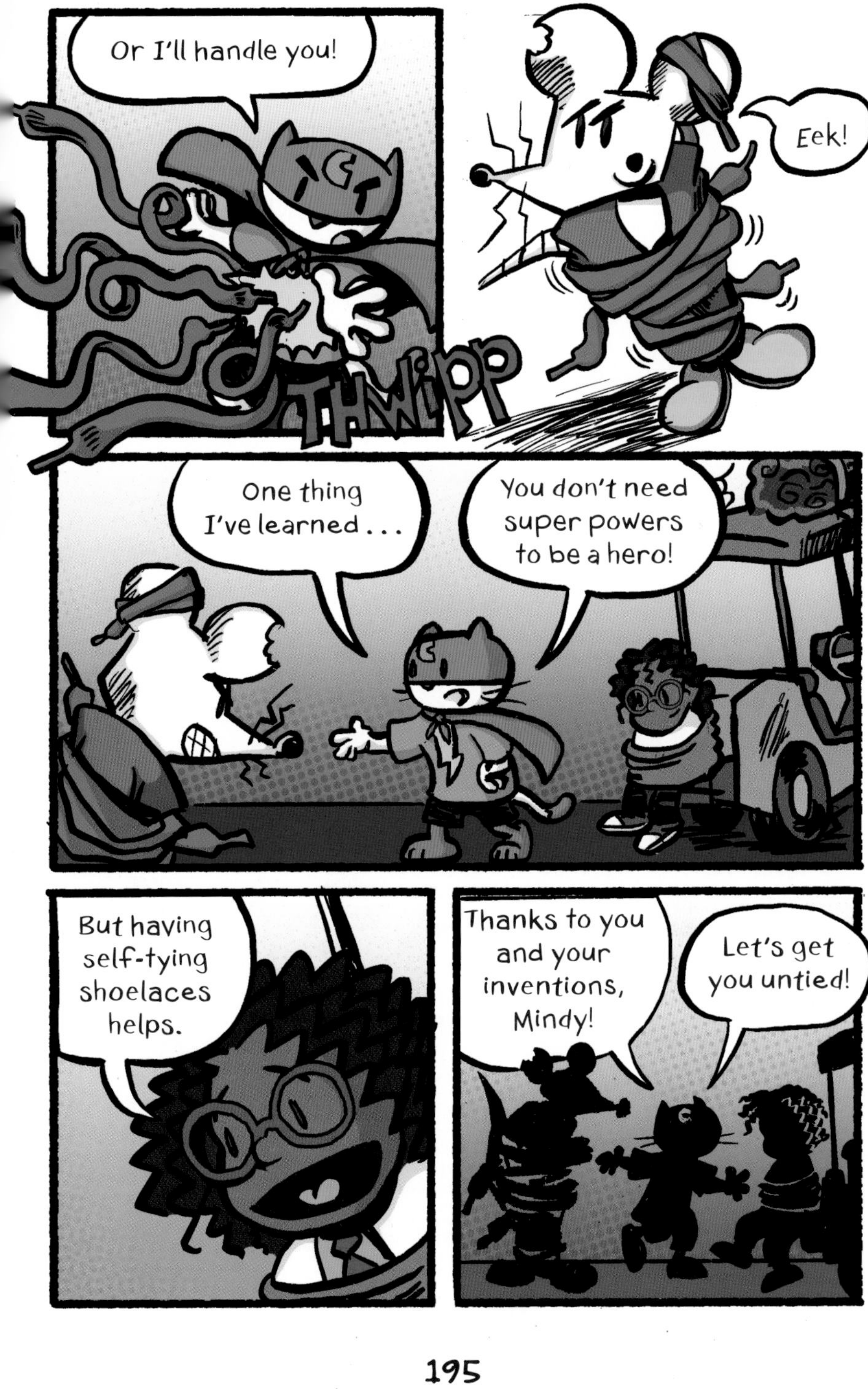
Or I'll handle you!
THWIPP
Eek!
One thing I've learned . . .
You don't need super powers to be a hero!
But having self-tying shoelaces helps.
Thanks to you and your inventions, Mindy!
Let's get you untied!

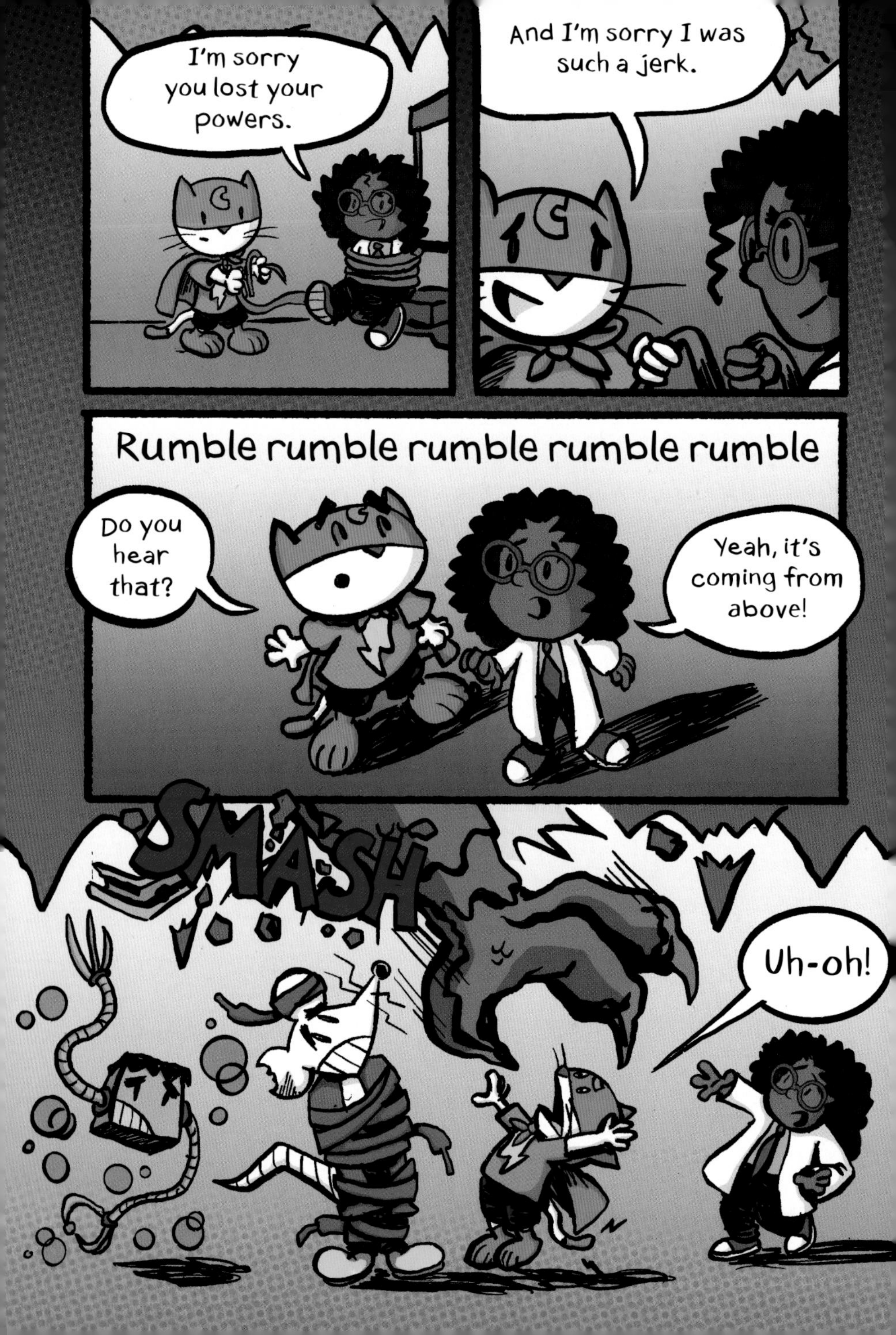
I'm sorry you lost your powers.
And I'm sorry I was such a jerk.
Rumble rumble rumble rumble rumble
Do you hear that?
Yeah, it's coming from above!
SMASH
Uh-oh!

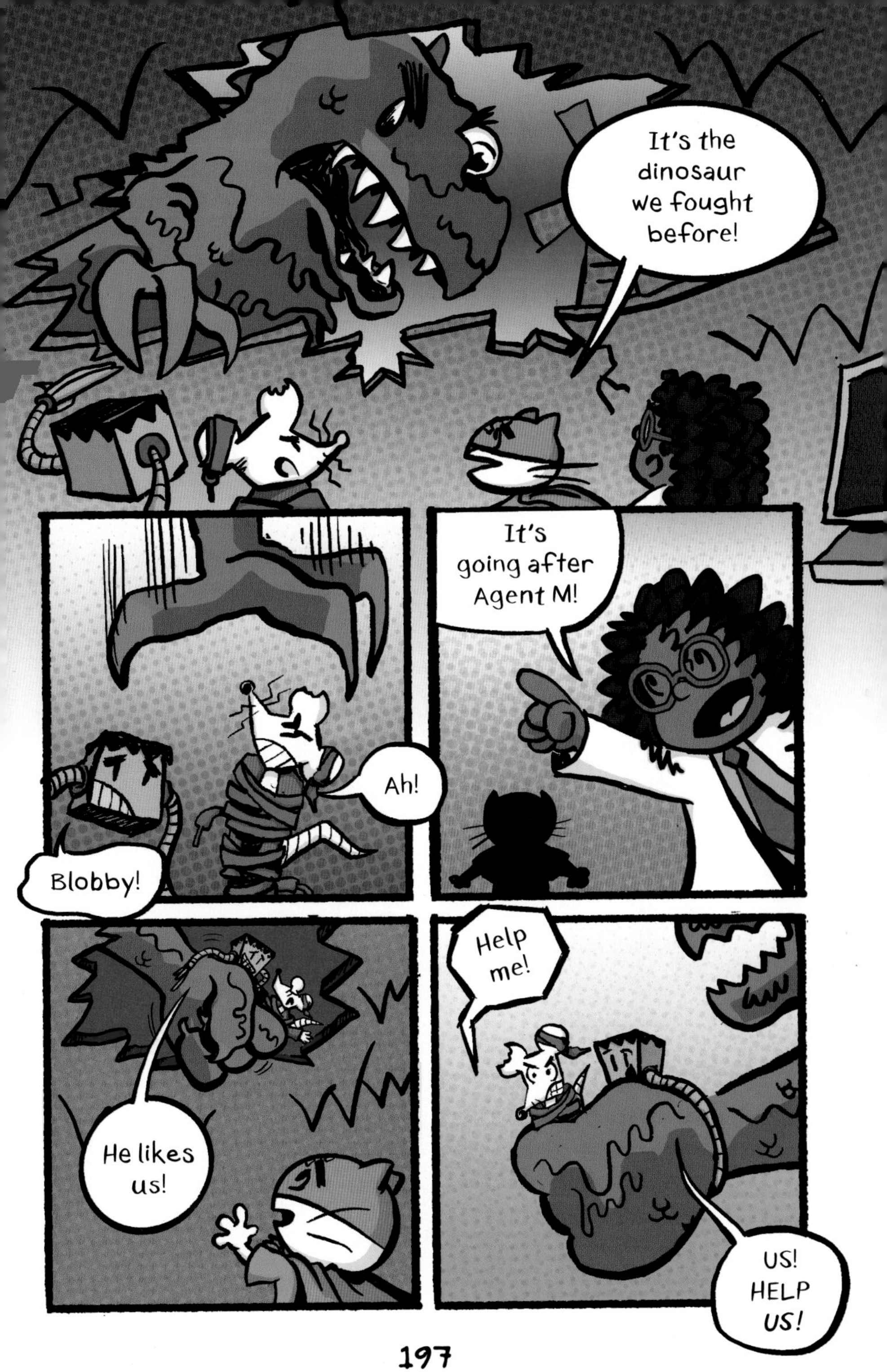
It's the dinosaur we fought before!
It's going after Agent M!
Ah!
Blobby!
Help me!
He likes us!
US! HELP US!

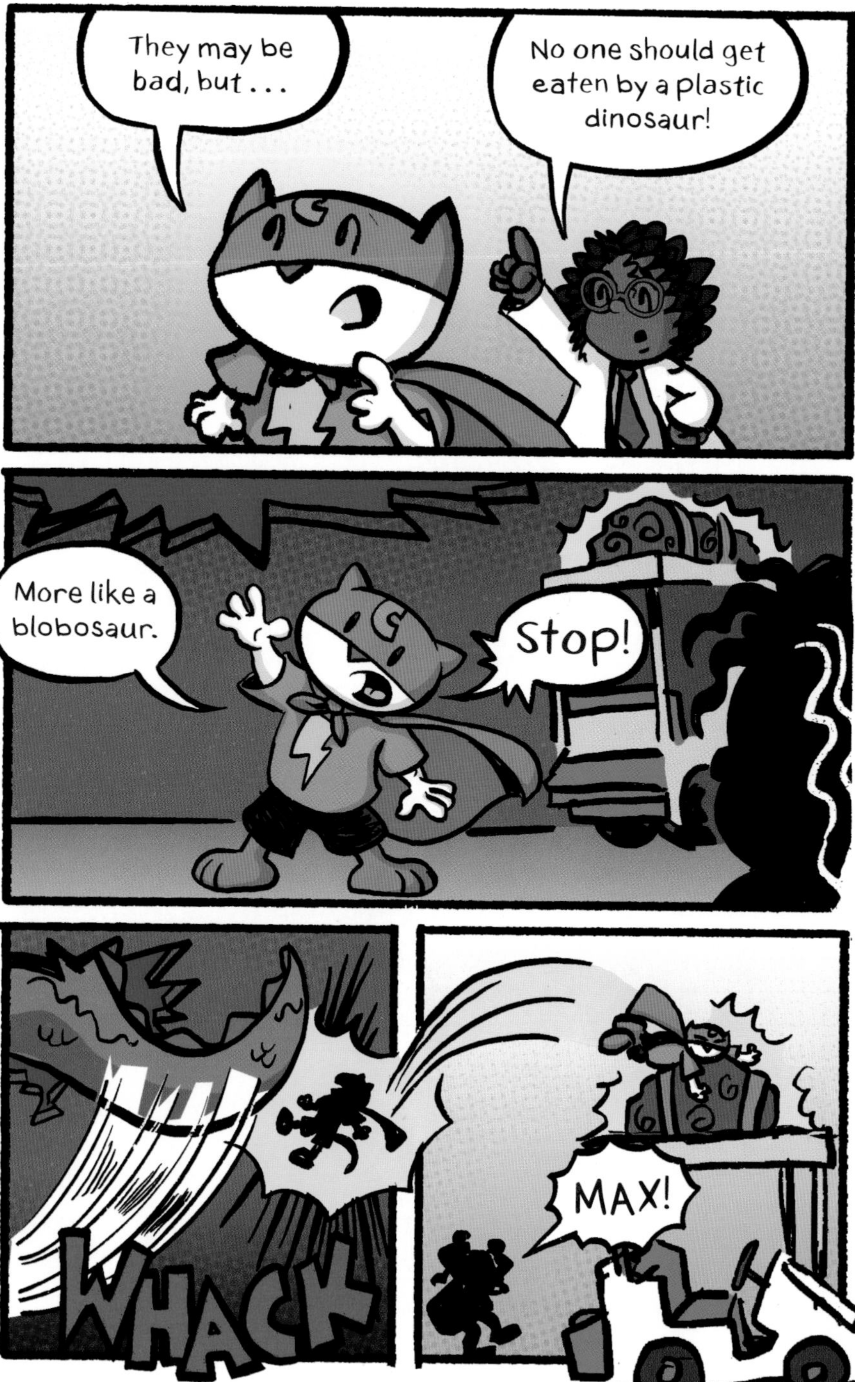
They may be bad, but . . .
No one should get eaten by a plastic dinosaur!
More like a blobosaur.
Stop!
WHACK
MAX!

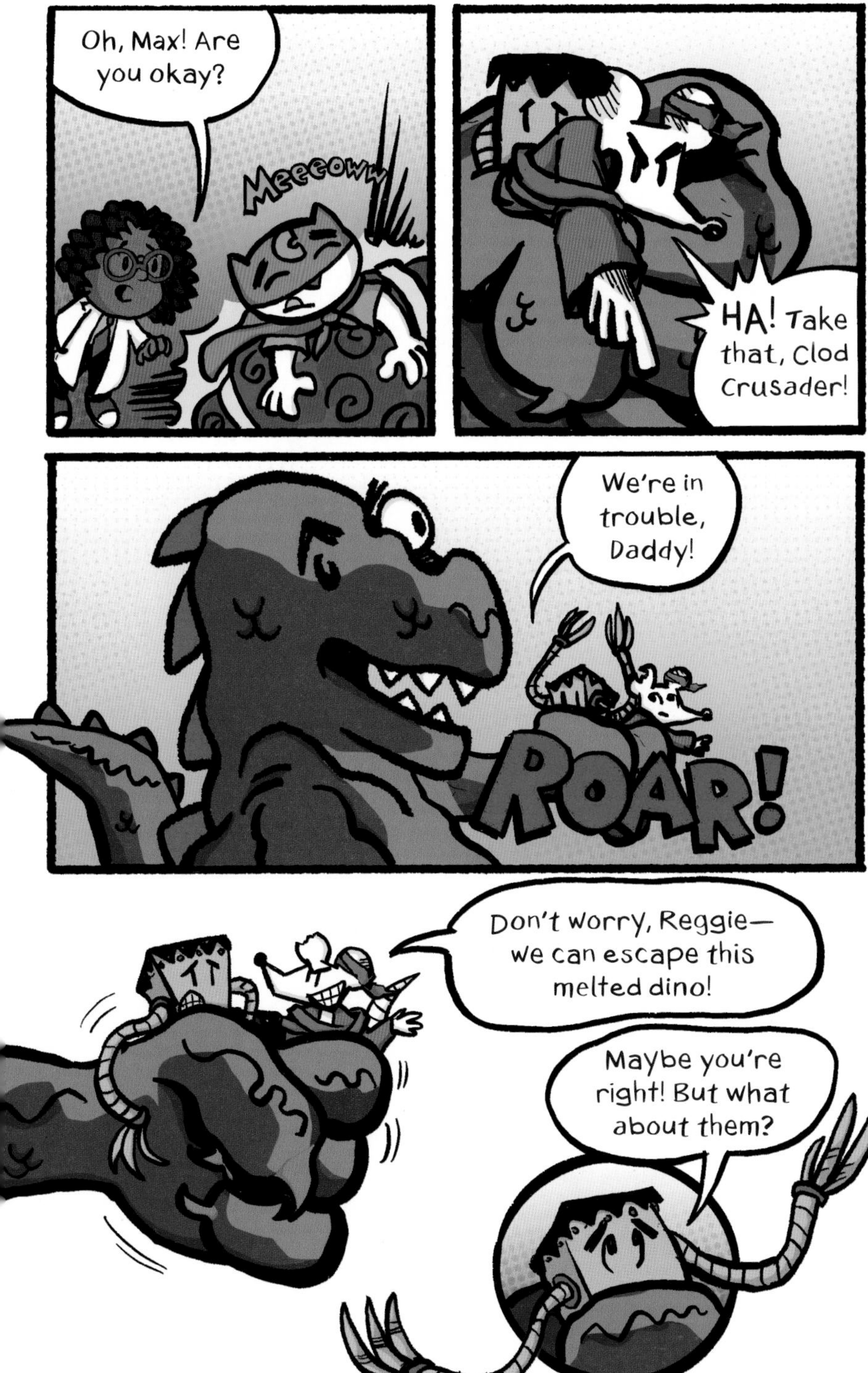

Oh, Max! Are you okay?
Meeeoww
HA! Take that, Clod Crusader!
We're in trouble, Daddy!
ROAR!
Don't worry, Reggie—we can escape this melted dino!
Maybe you're right! But what about them?

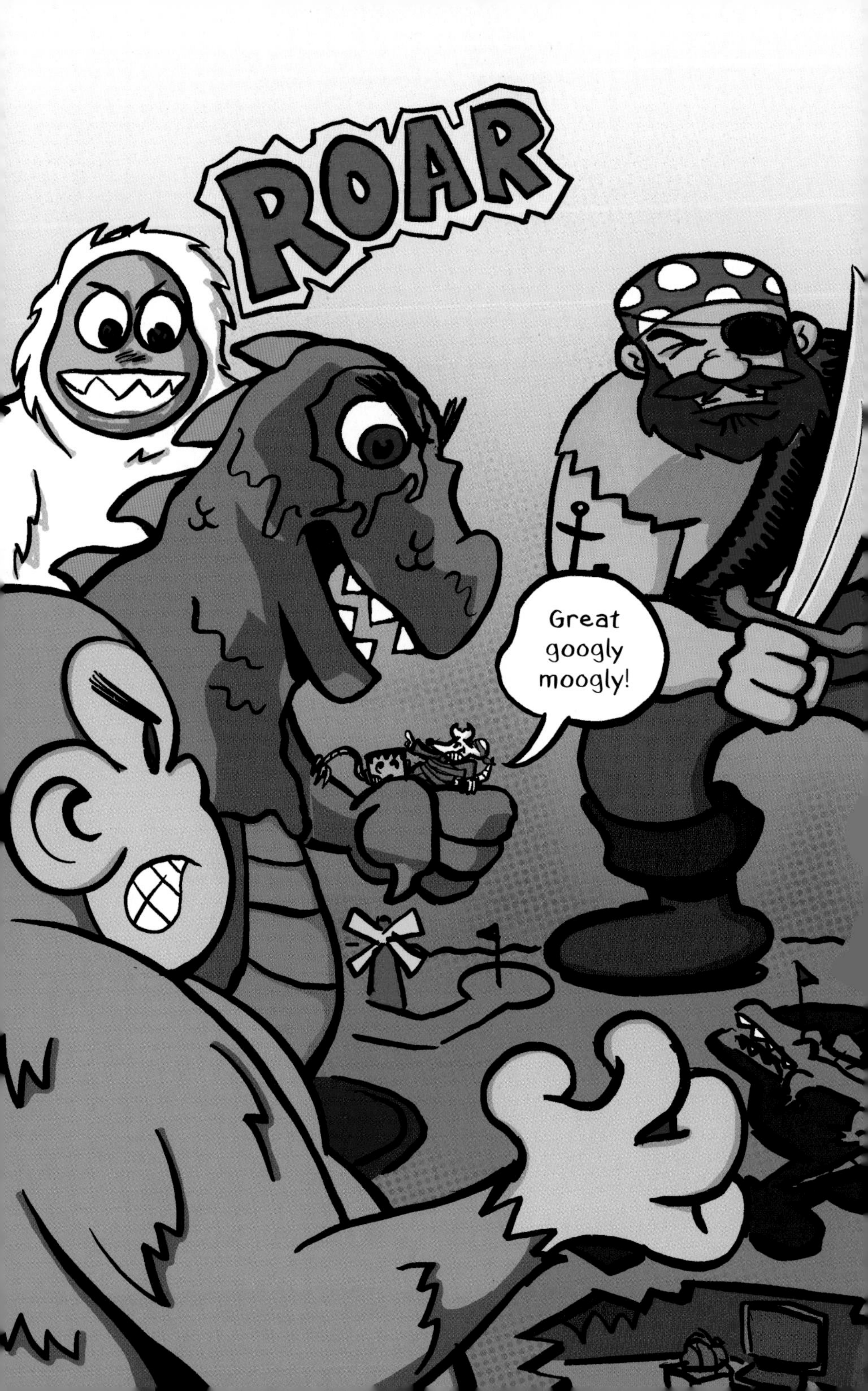
ROAR
Great googly moogly!

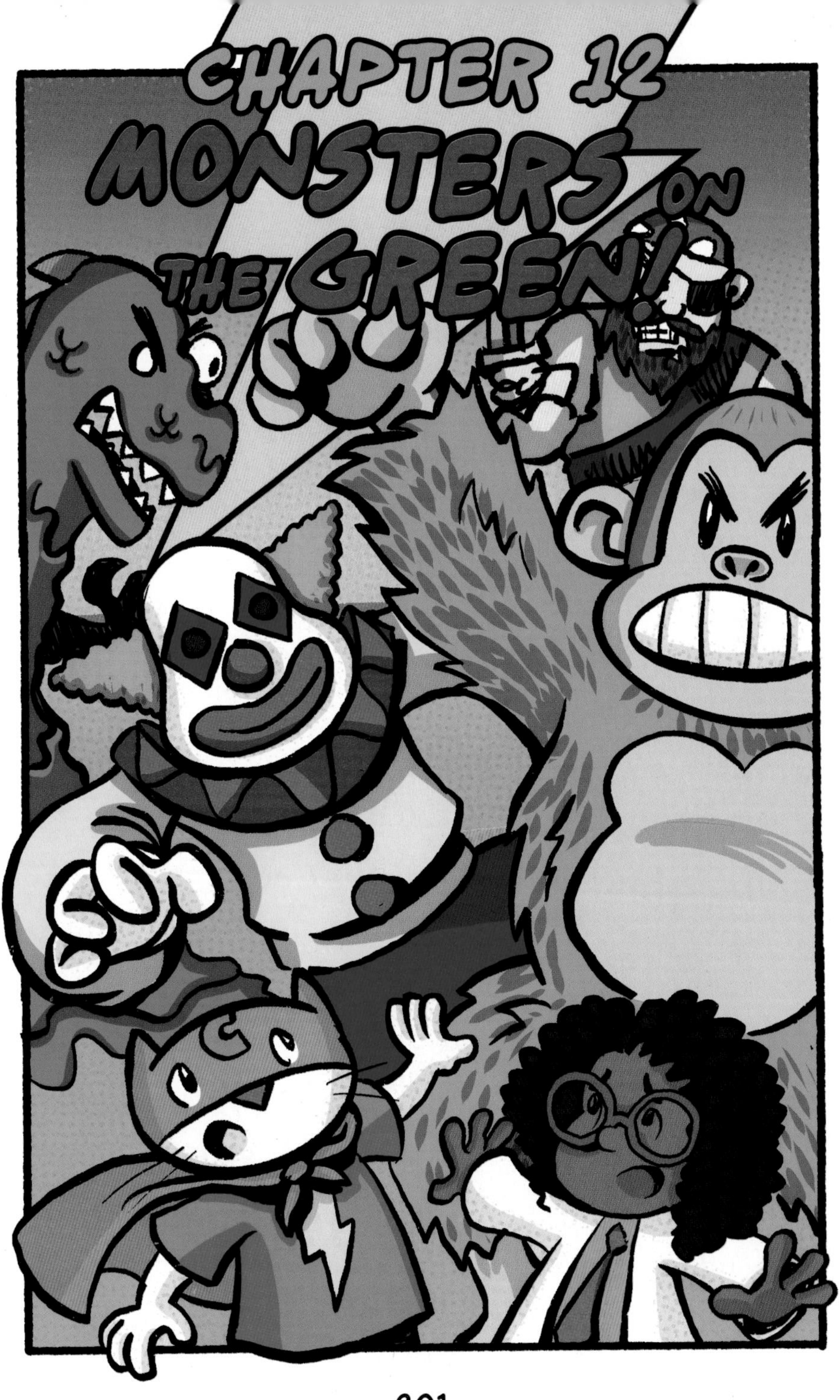
CHAPTER 12
MONSTERS ON THE GREEN!

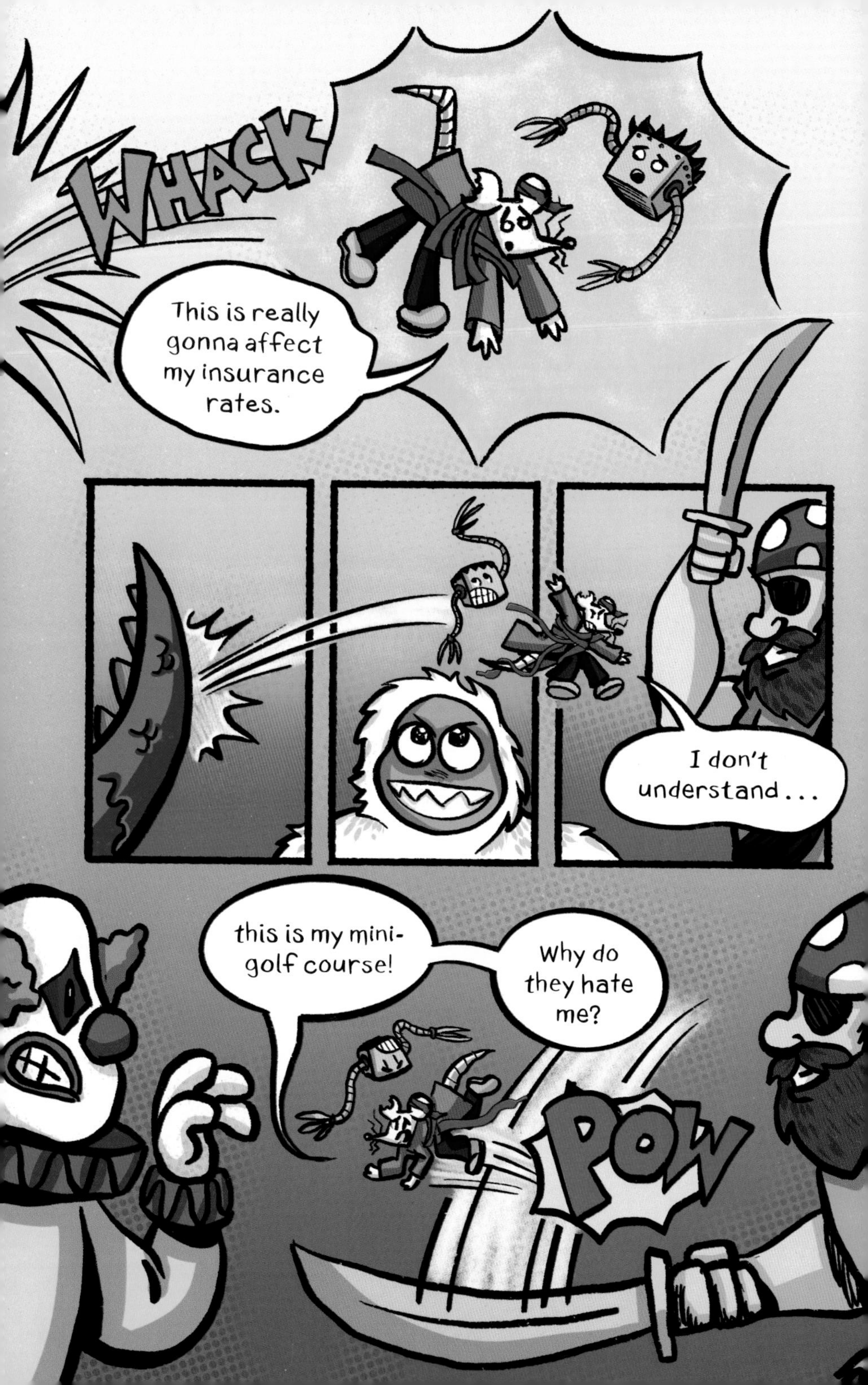
WHACK
This is really gonna affect my insurance rates.
I don't understand . . .
this is my mini-golf course!
Why do they hate me?
POW

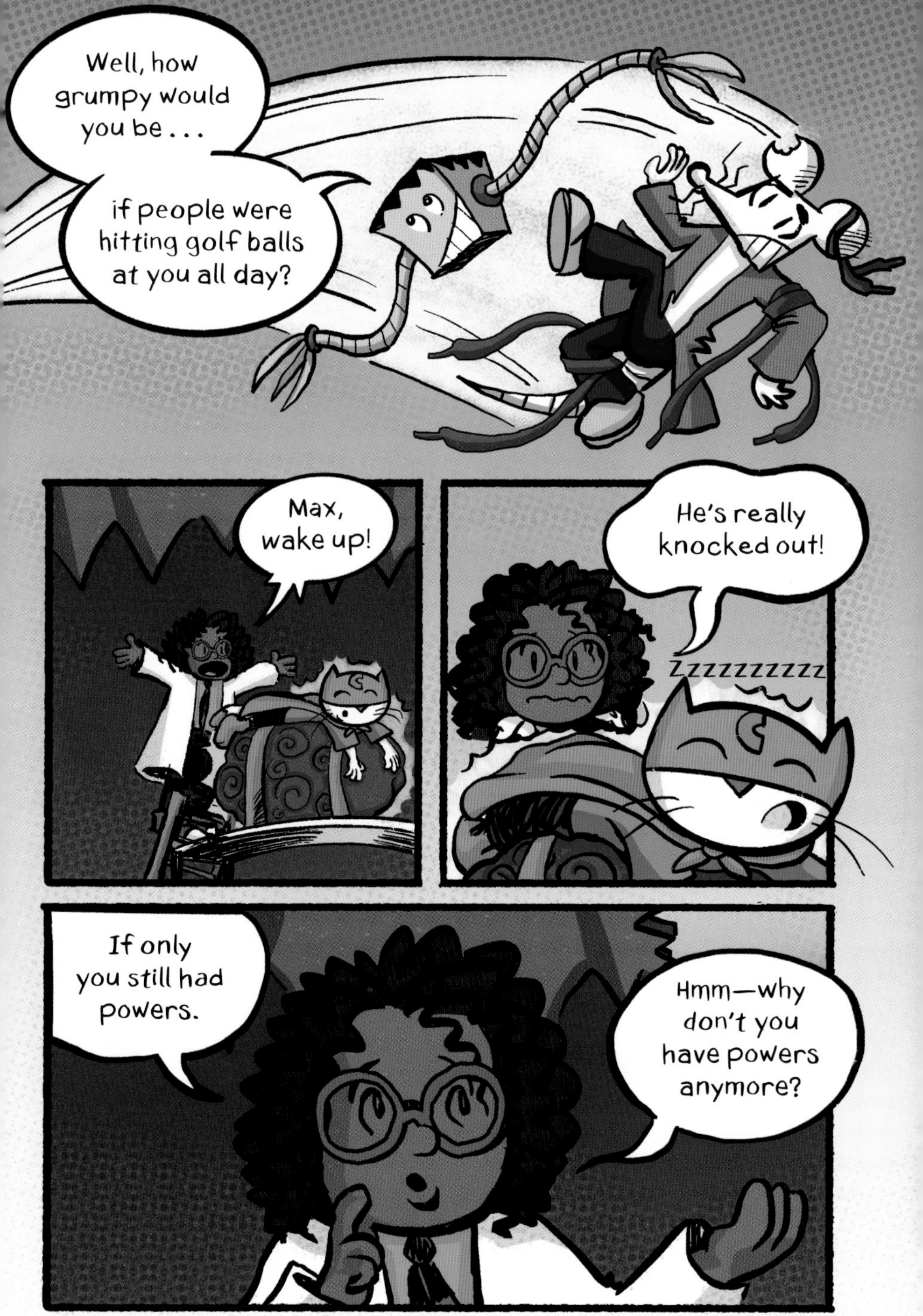
Well, how grumpy would you be . . .
if people were hitting golf balls at you all day?
Max, wake up!
He's really knocked out!
Zzzzzzzzzz
If only you still had powers.
Hmm—why don't you have powers anymore?

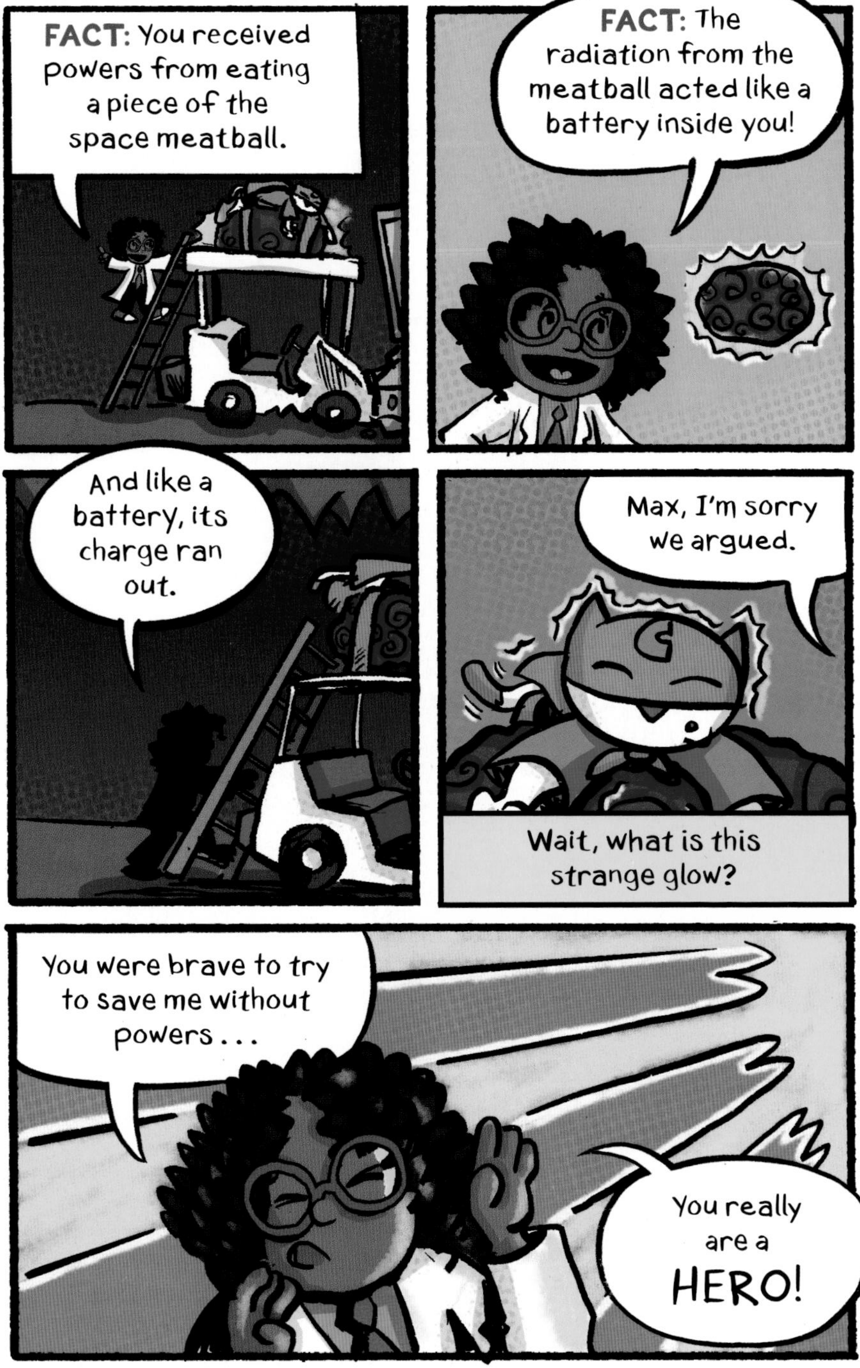
FACT: You received powers from eating a piece of the space meatball.
FACT: The radiation from the meatball acted like a battery inside you!
And like a battery, its charge ran out.
Max, I'm sorry we argued.
Wait, what is this strange glow?
You were brave to try to save me without powers . . .
You really are a HERO!

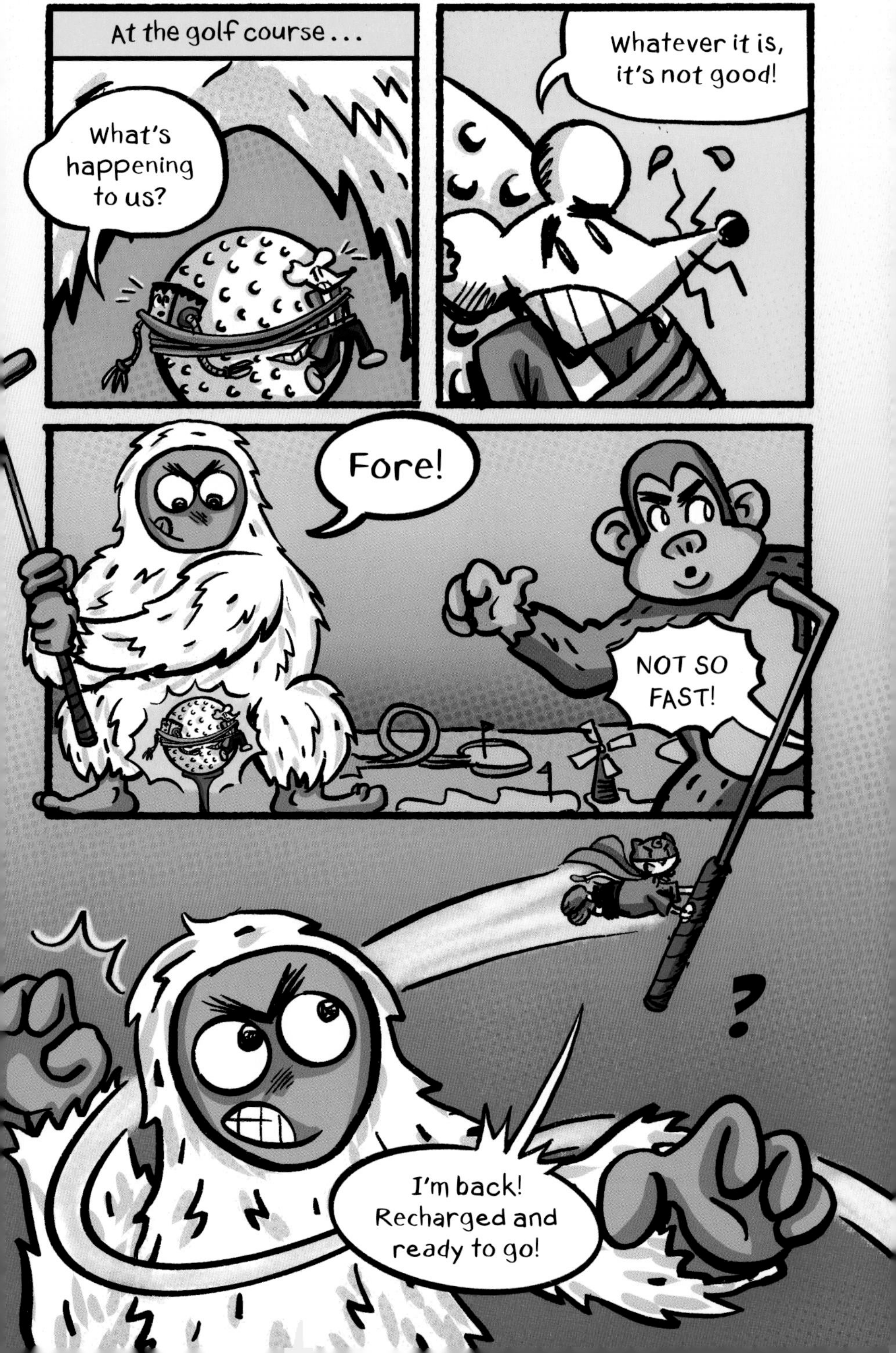
At the golf course . . .
What's happening to us?
Whatever it is, it's not good!
Fore!
NOT SO FAST!
I'm back! Recharged and ready to go!

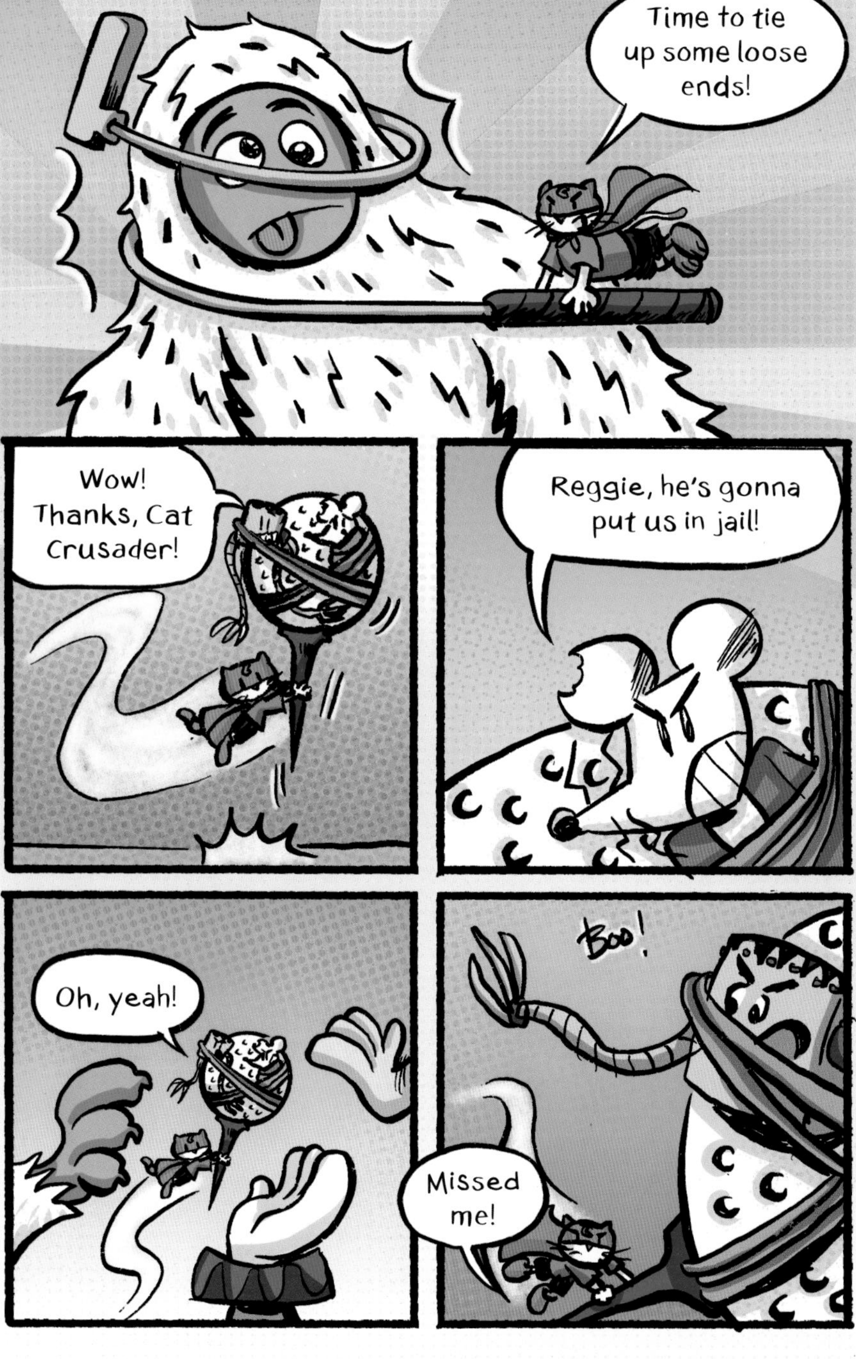
Time to tie up some loose ends!
Wow! Thanks, Cat Crusader!
Reggie, he's gonna put us in jail!
Oh, yeah!
BOO!
Missed me!

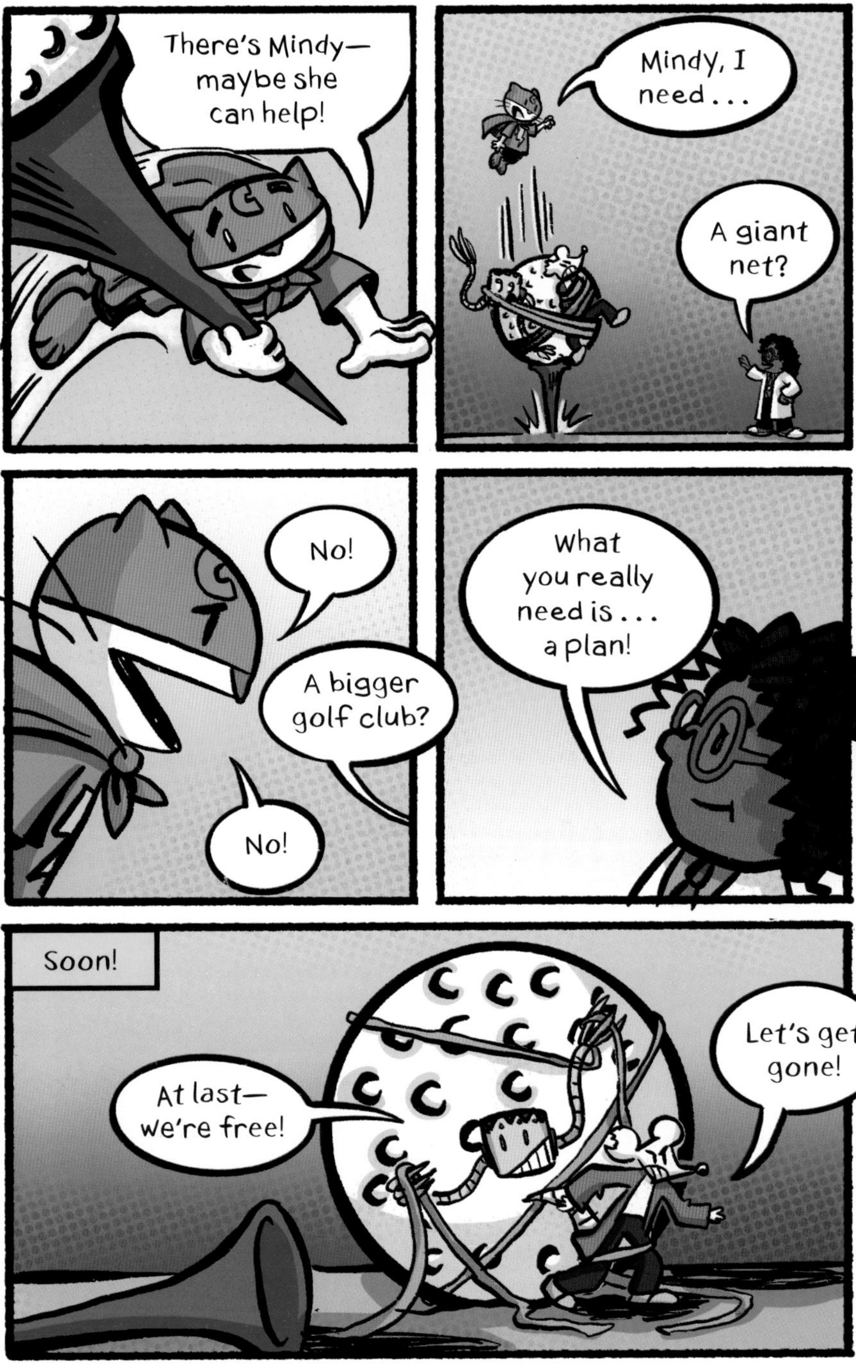
There's Mindy—maybe she can help!
Mindy, I need . . .
A giant net?
No!
A bigger golf club?
No!
What you really need is . . . a plan!
Soon!
At last—we're free!
Let's get gone!

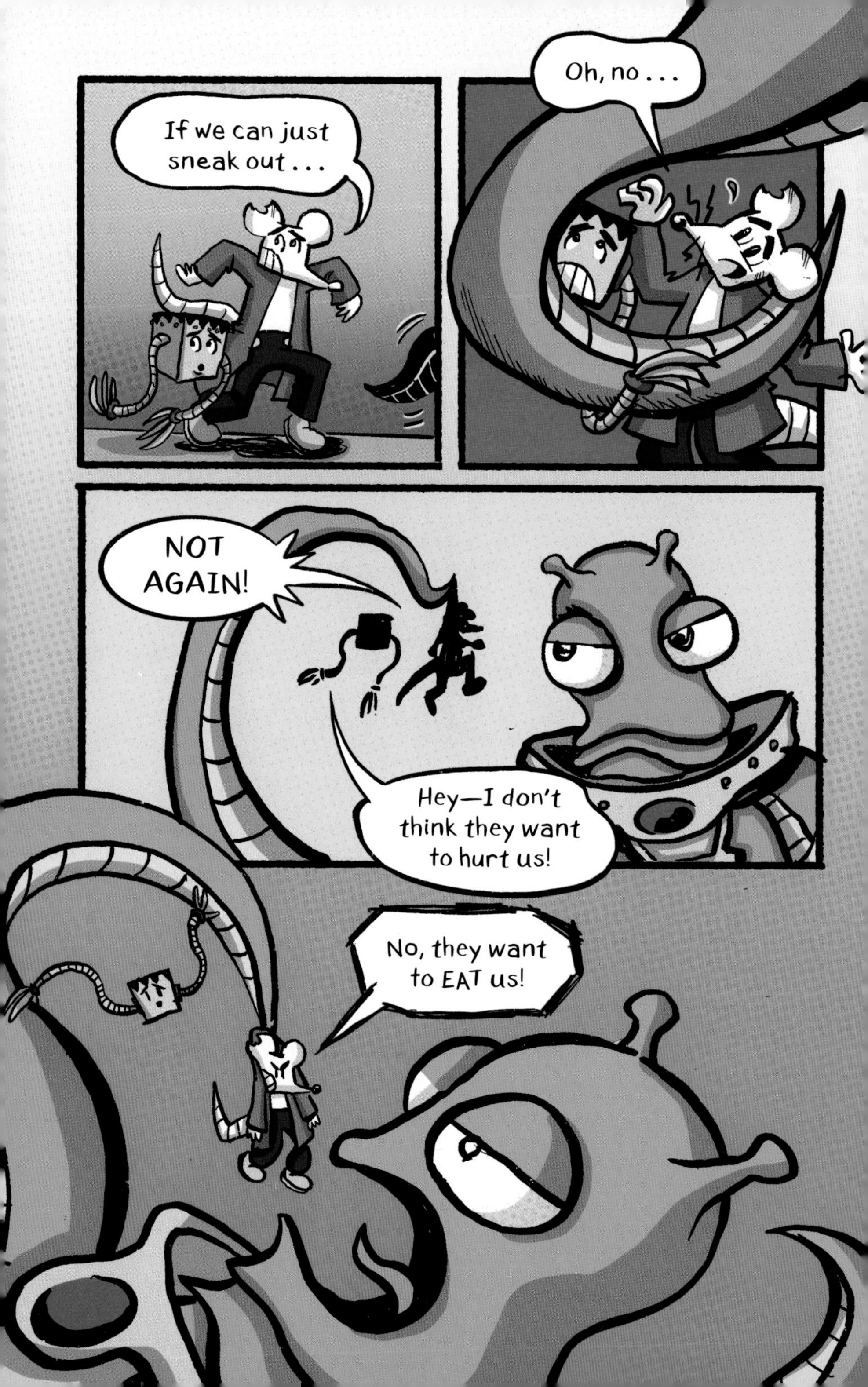
If we can just sneak out . . .
Oh, no . . .
NOT AGAIN!
Hey—I don't think they want to hurt us!
No, they want to EAT us!

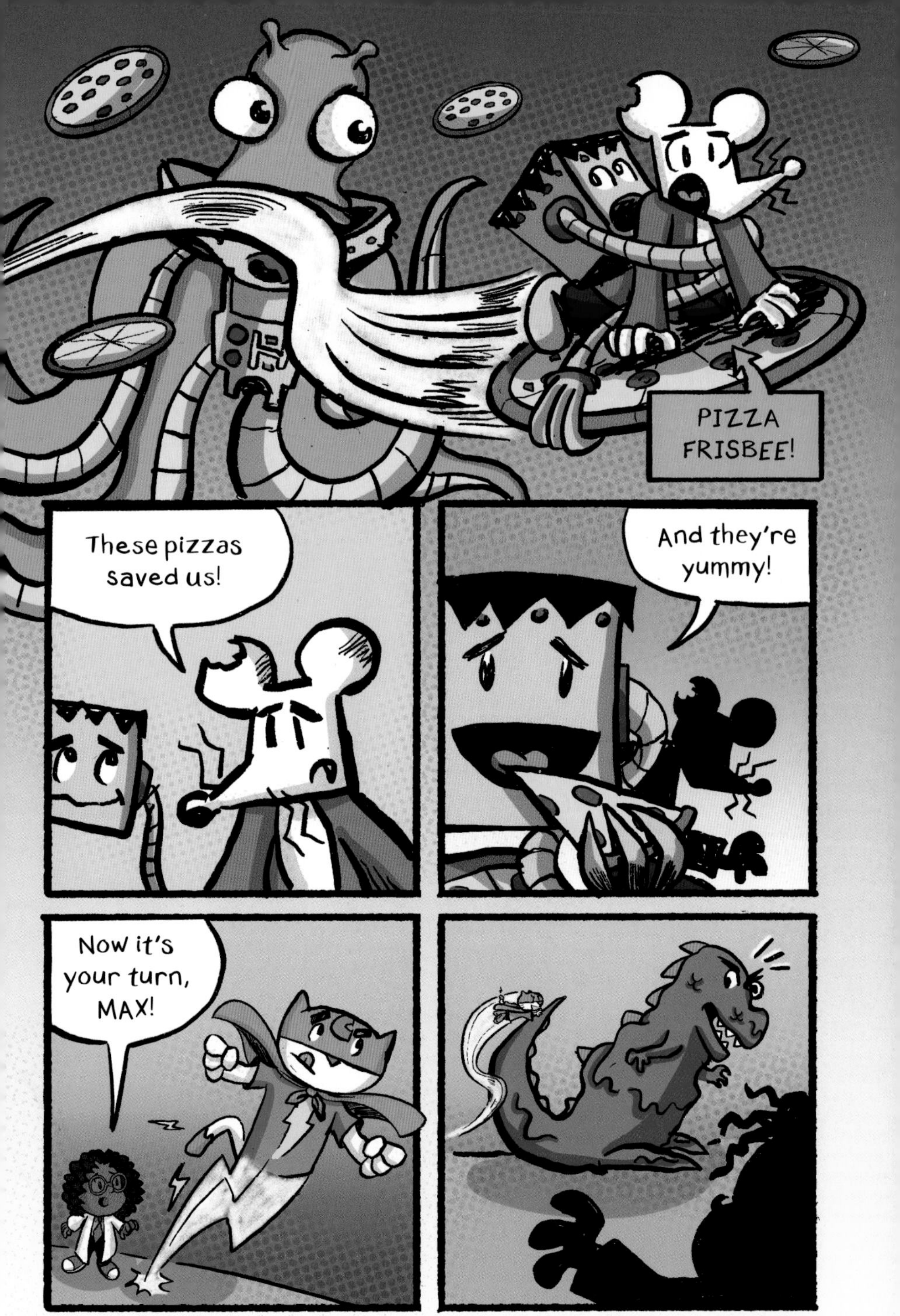
PIZZA FRISBEE!
These pizzas saved us!
And they're yummy!
Now it's your turn, MAX!

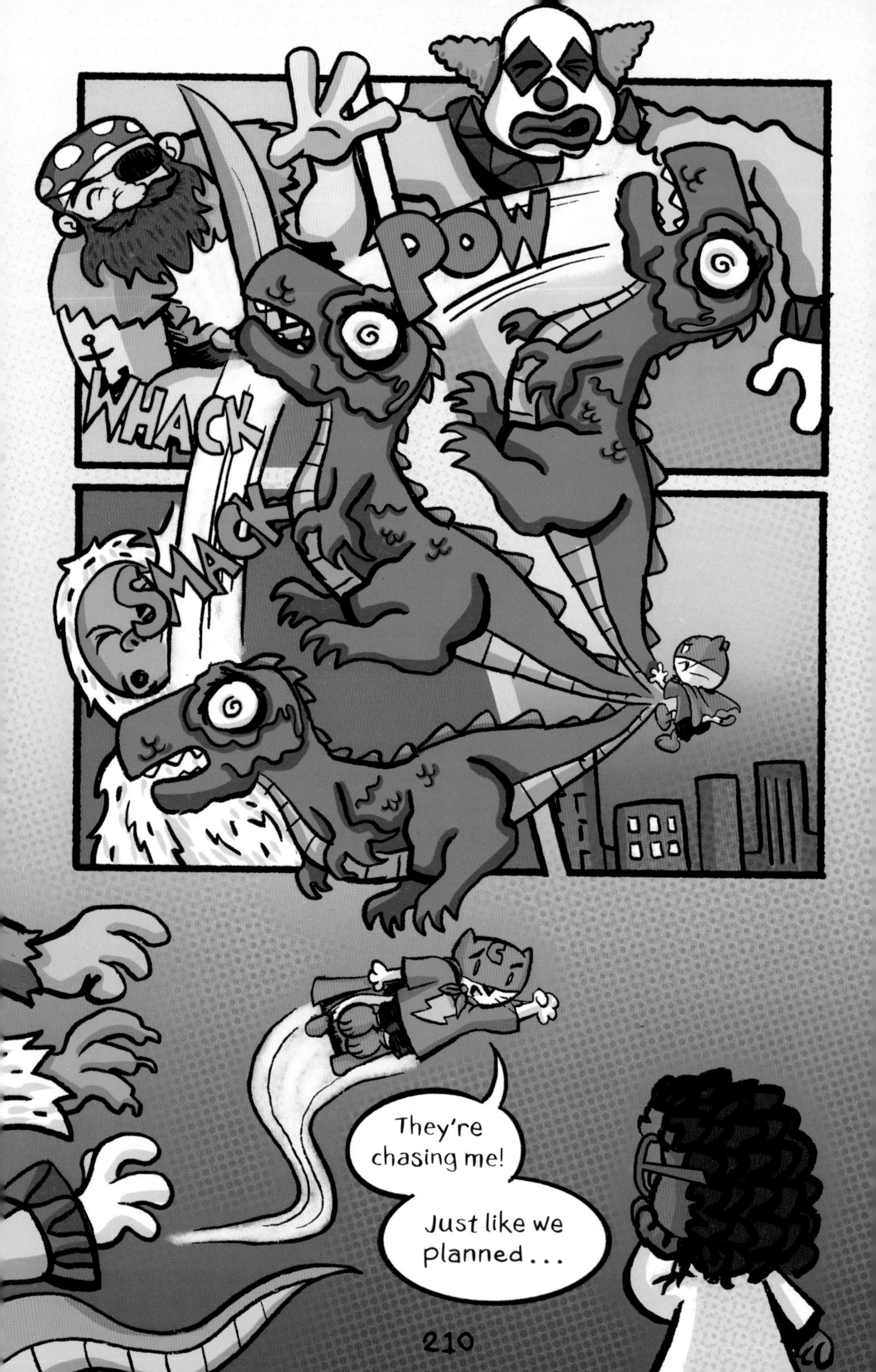
POW
WHACK
SMACK
They're chasing me!
Just like we planned . . .

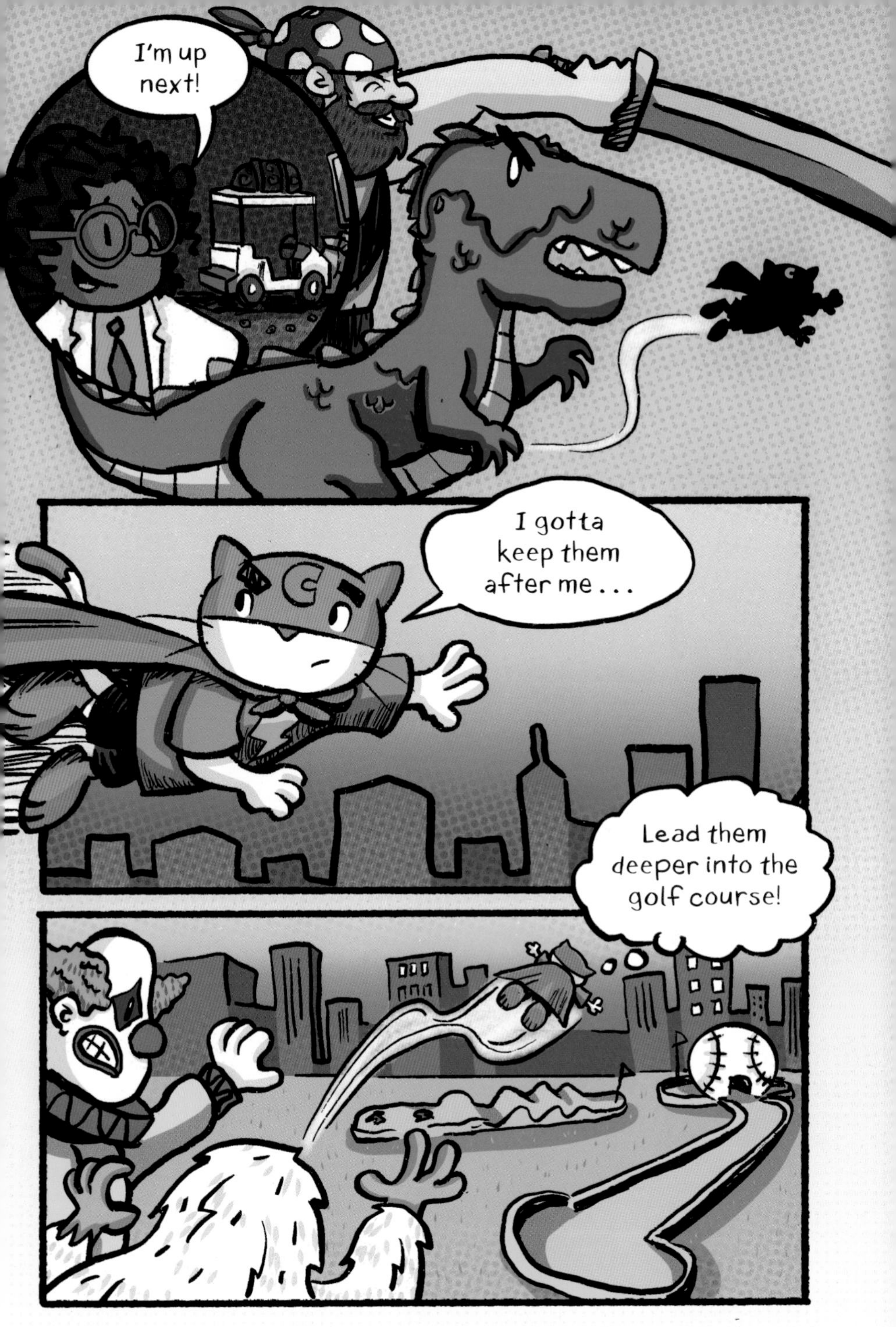
I'm up next!
I gotta keep them after me . . .
Lead them deeper into the golf course!

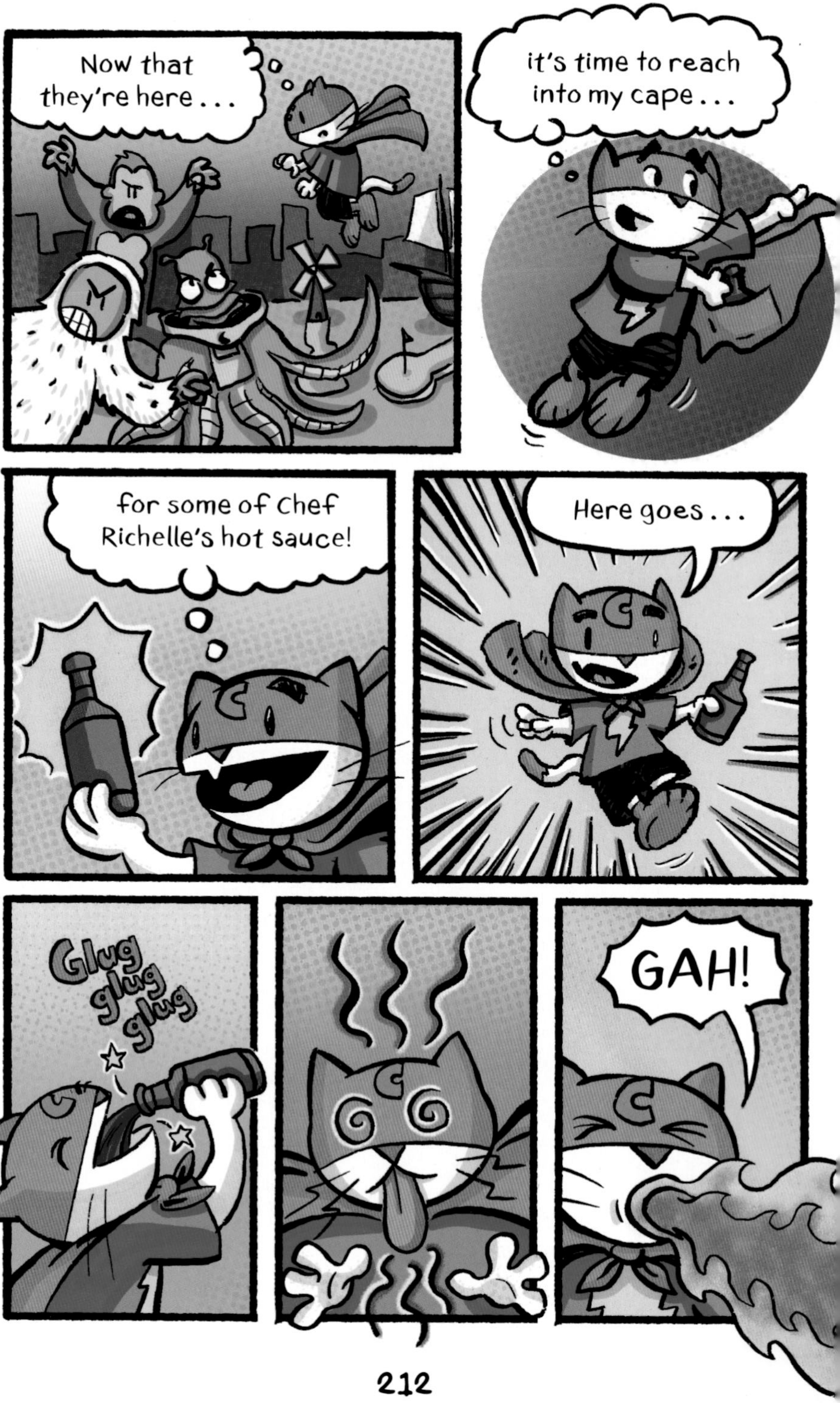
Now that they're here . . .
it's time to reach into my cape . . .
for some of Chef Richelle's hot sauce!
Here goes . . .
Glug glug glug
GAH!

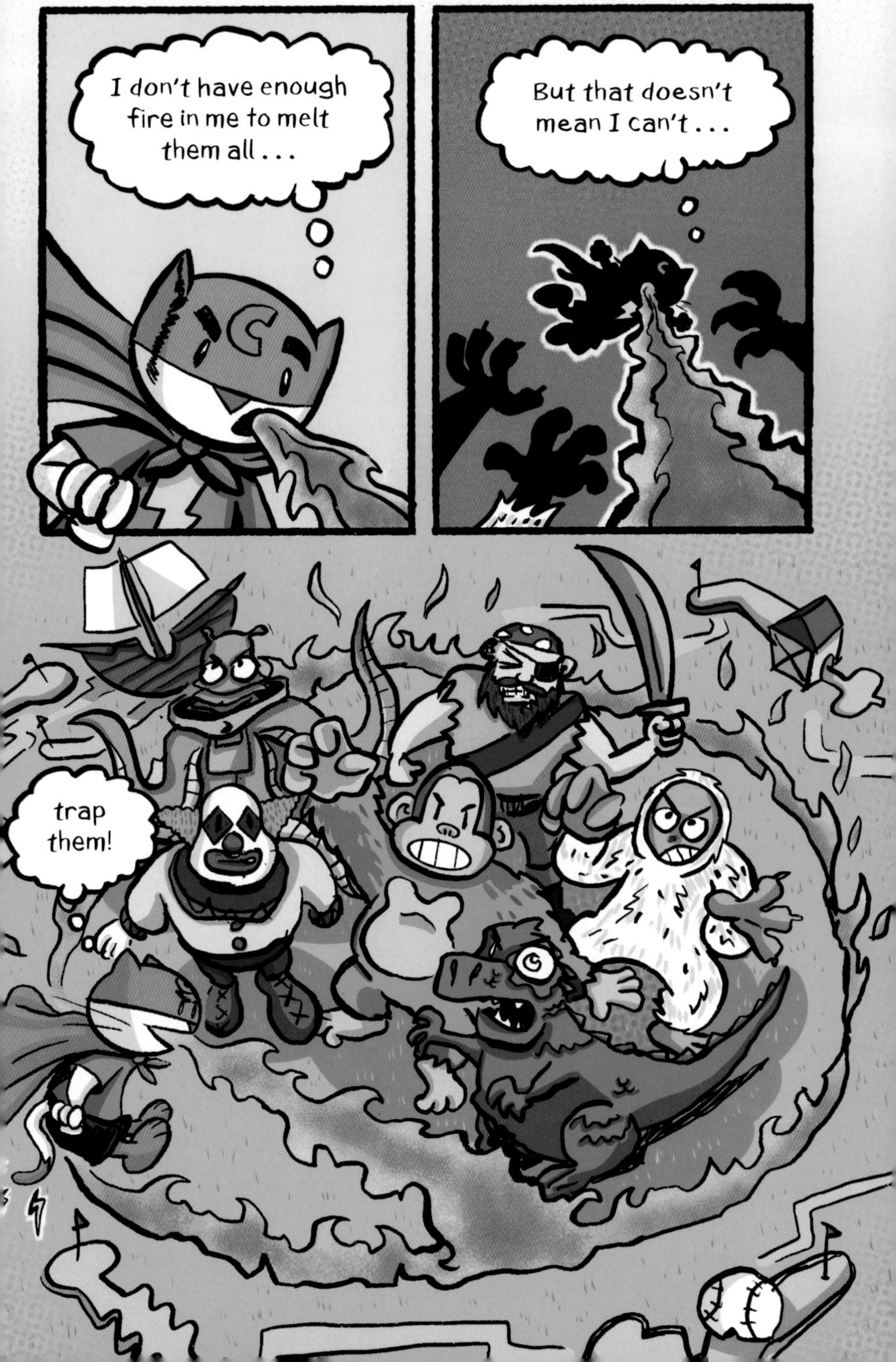
I don't have enough fire in me to melt them all . . .
But that doesn't mean I can't . . .
trap them!

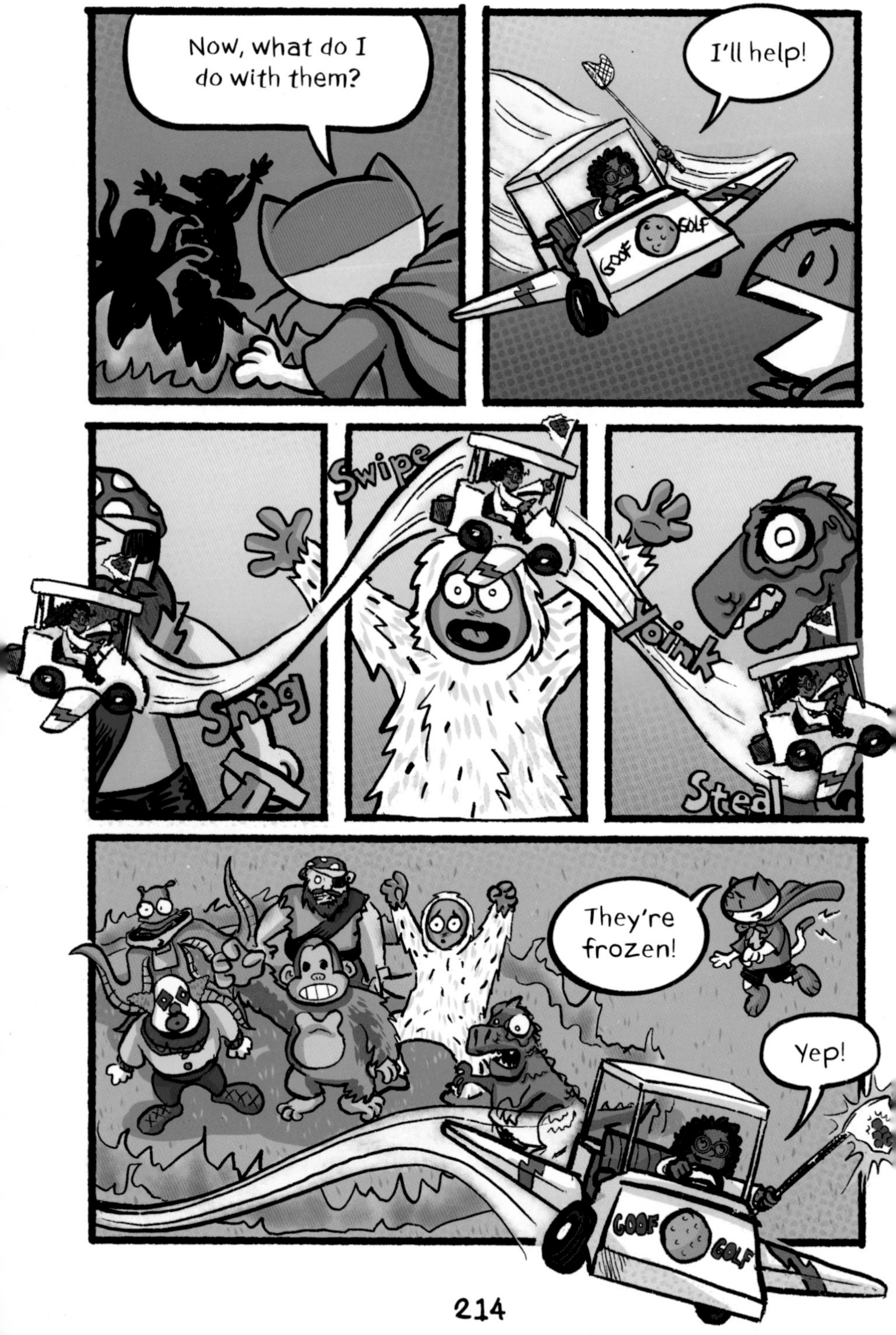
Now, what do I do with them?
I'll help!
GOOF GOLF
Swipe
Yoink
Snag
Steal
They're frozen!
Yep!
GOOF GOLF

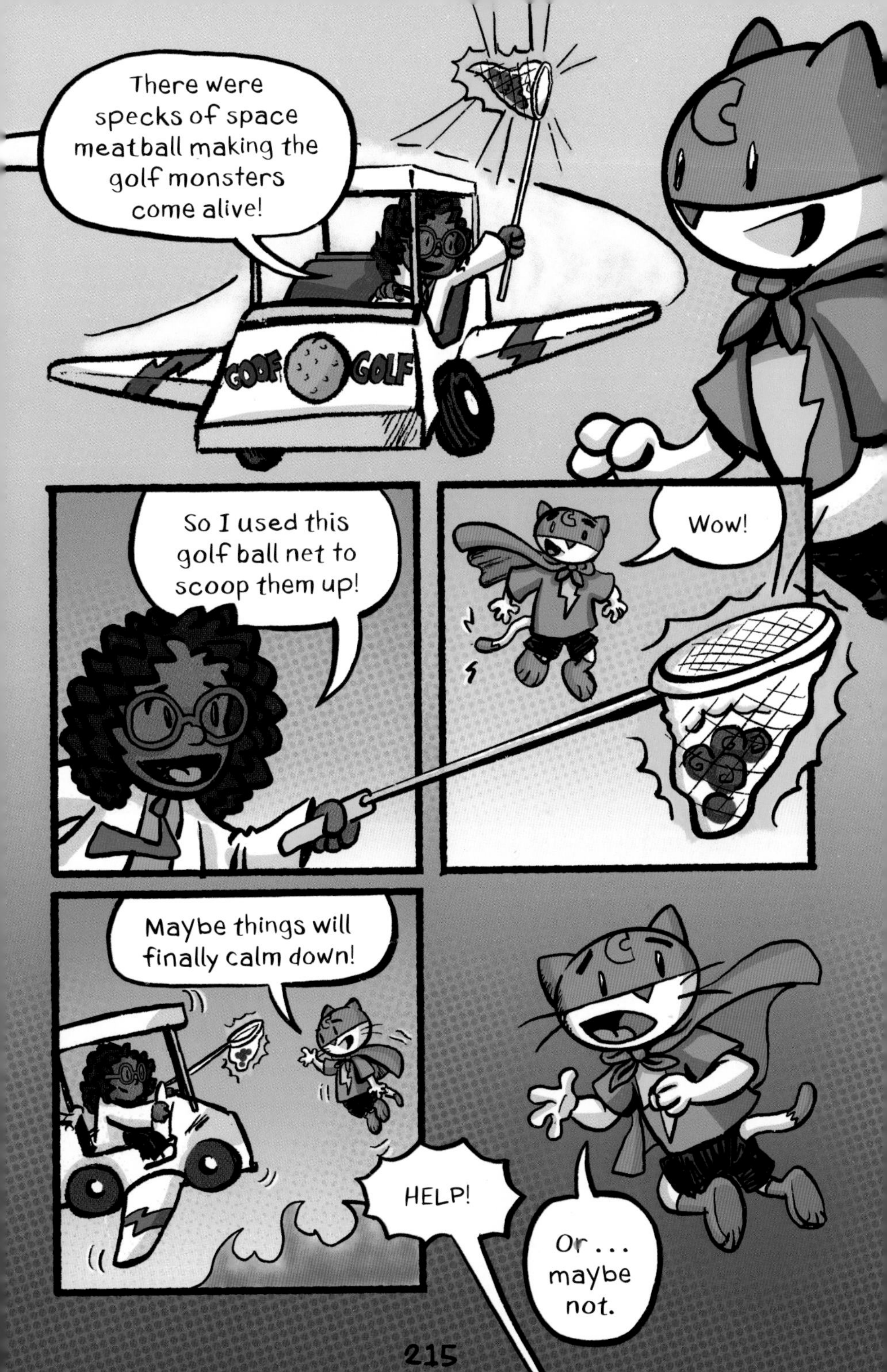
There were specks of space meatball making the golf monsters come alive!
GOOF GOLF
So I used this golf ball net to scoop them up!
Wow!
Maybe things will finally calm down!
HELP!
Or . . . maybe not.

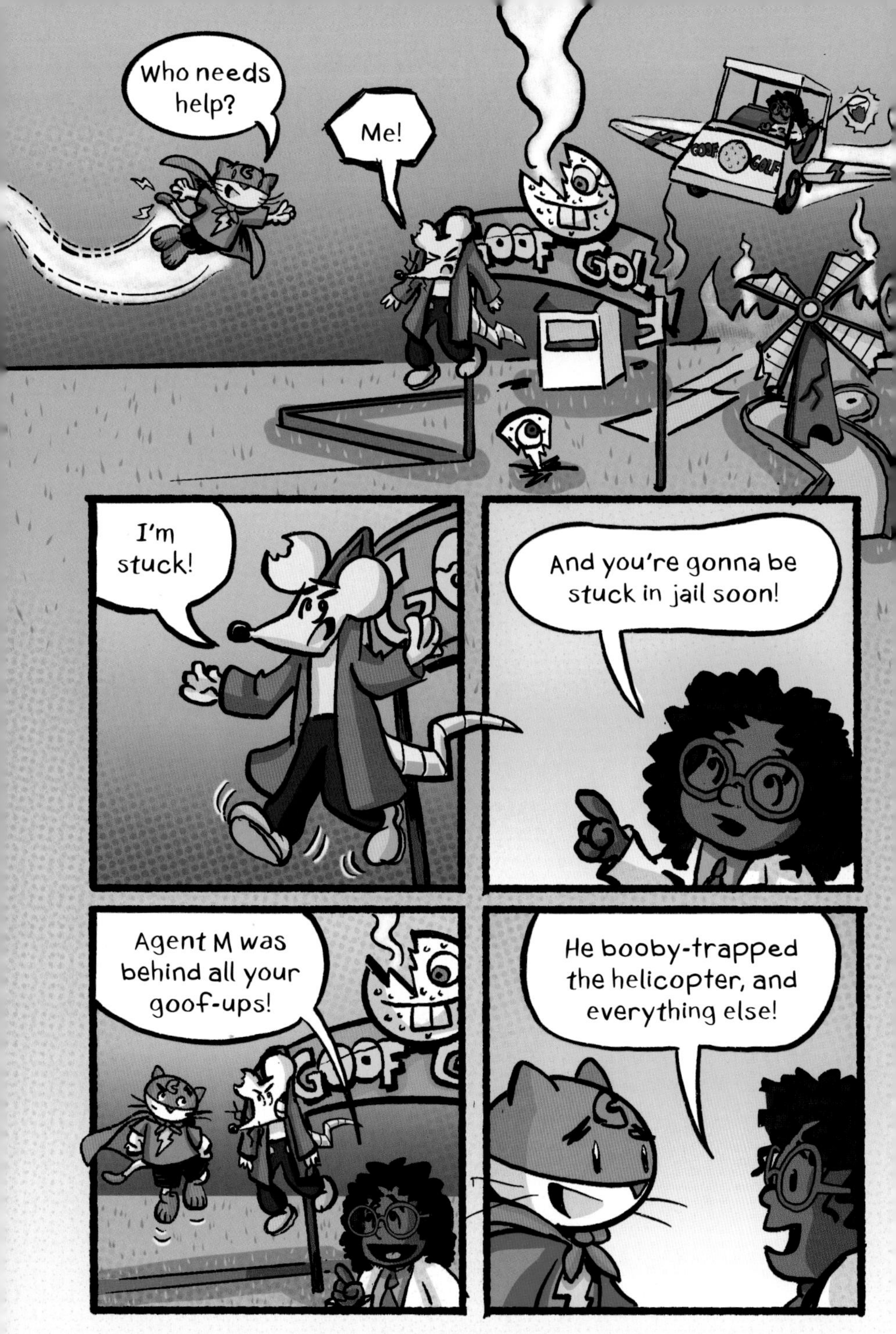
Who needs help?
Me!
GOOF GOLF
I'm stuck!
And you're gonna be stuck in jail soon!
Agent M was behind all your goof-ups!
He booby-trapped the helicopter, and everything else!

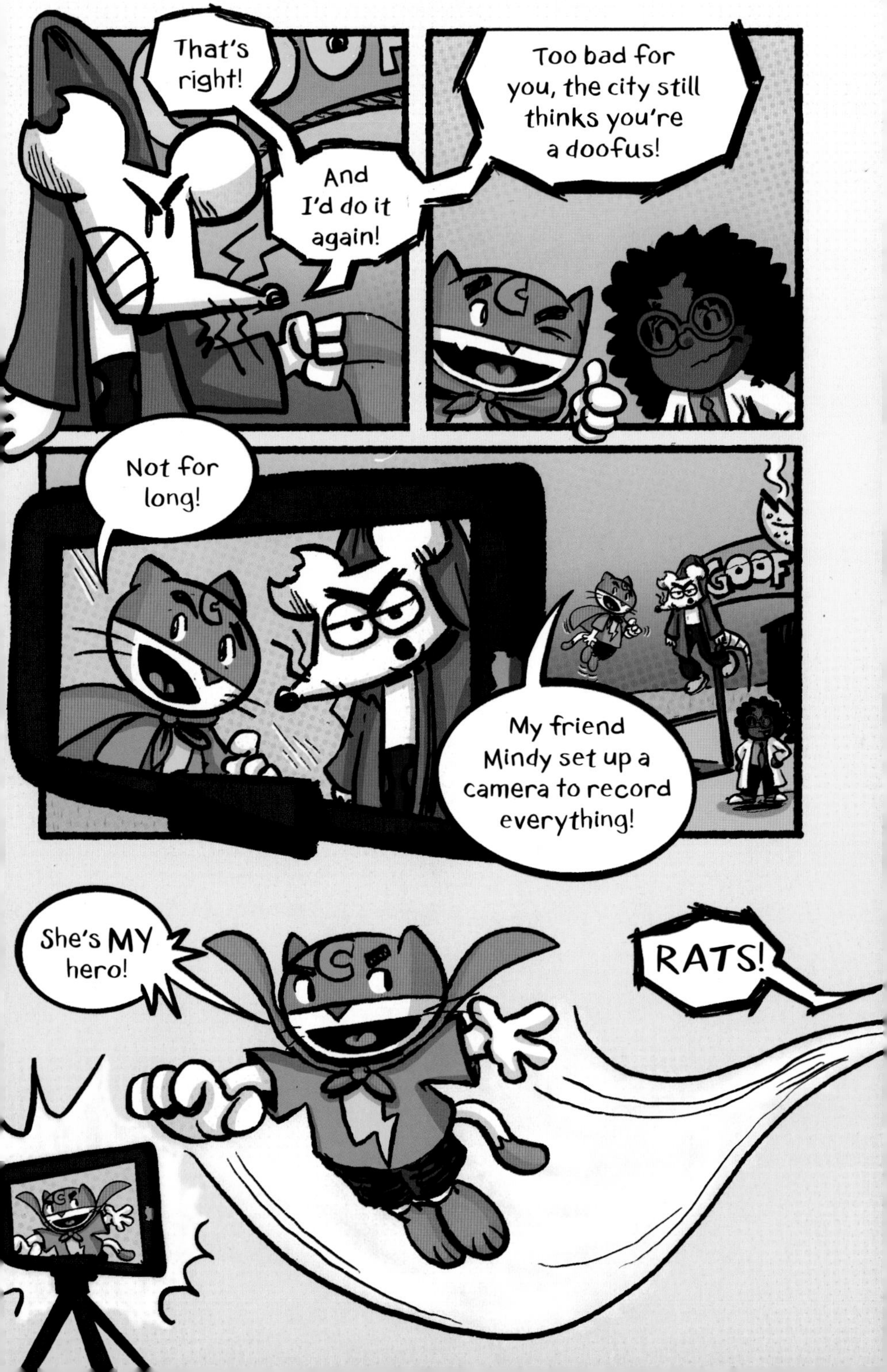
That's right!
And I'd do it again!
Too bad for you, the city still thinks you're a doofus!
GOOF
Not for long!
My friend Mindy set up a camera to record everything!
She's MY hero!
RATS!

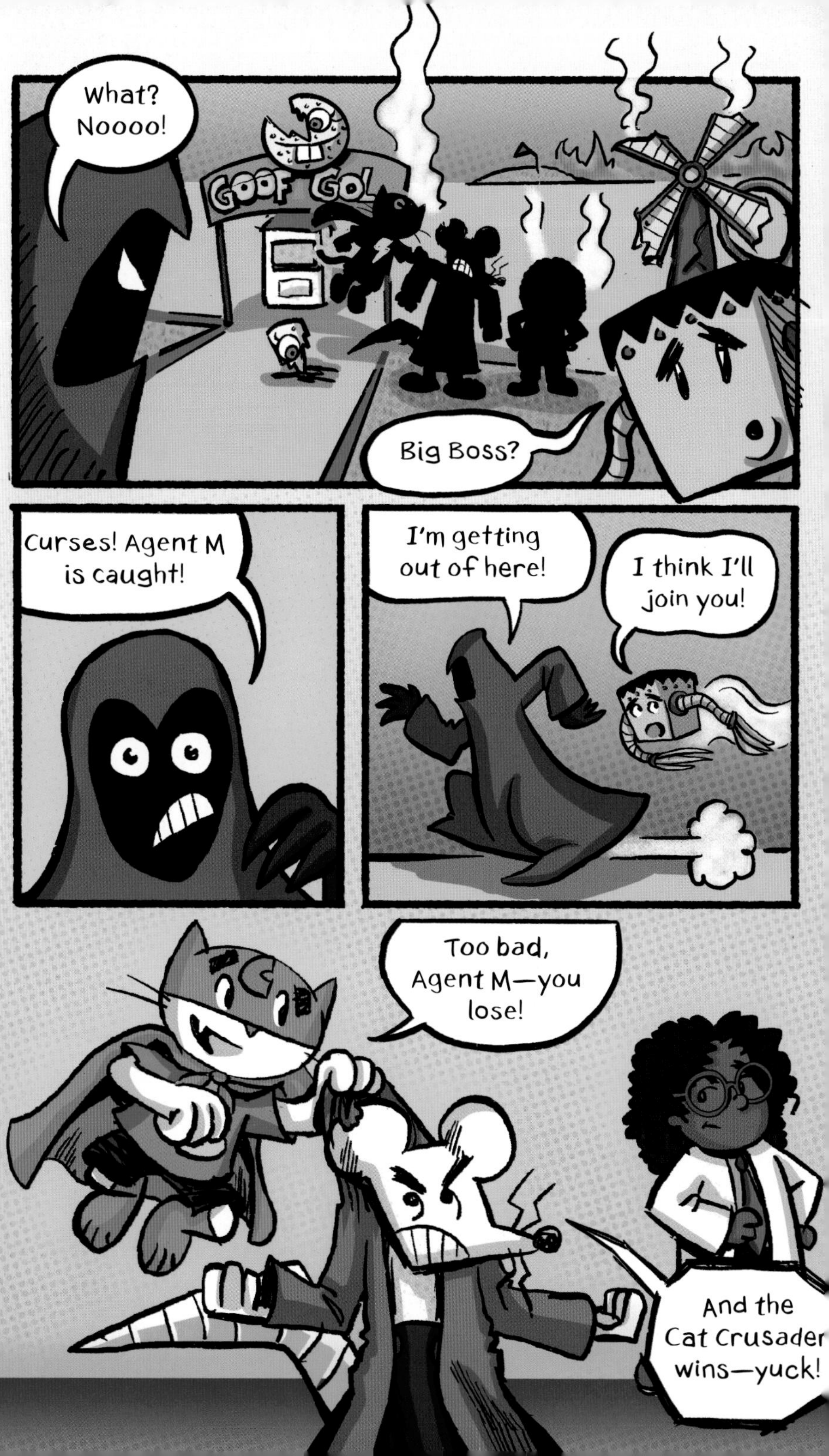
What? Noooo!
Big Boss?
Curses! Agent M is caught!
I'm getting out of here!
I think I'll join you!
Too bad, Agent M—you lose!
And the Cat Crusader wins—yuck!

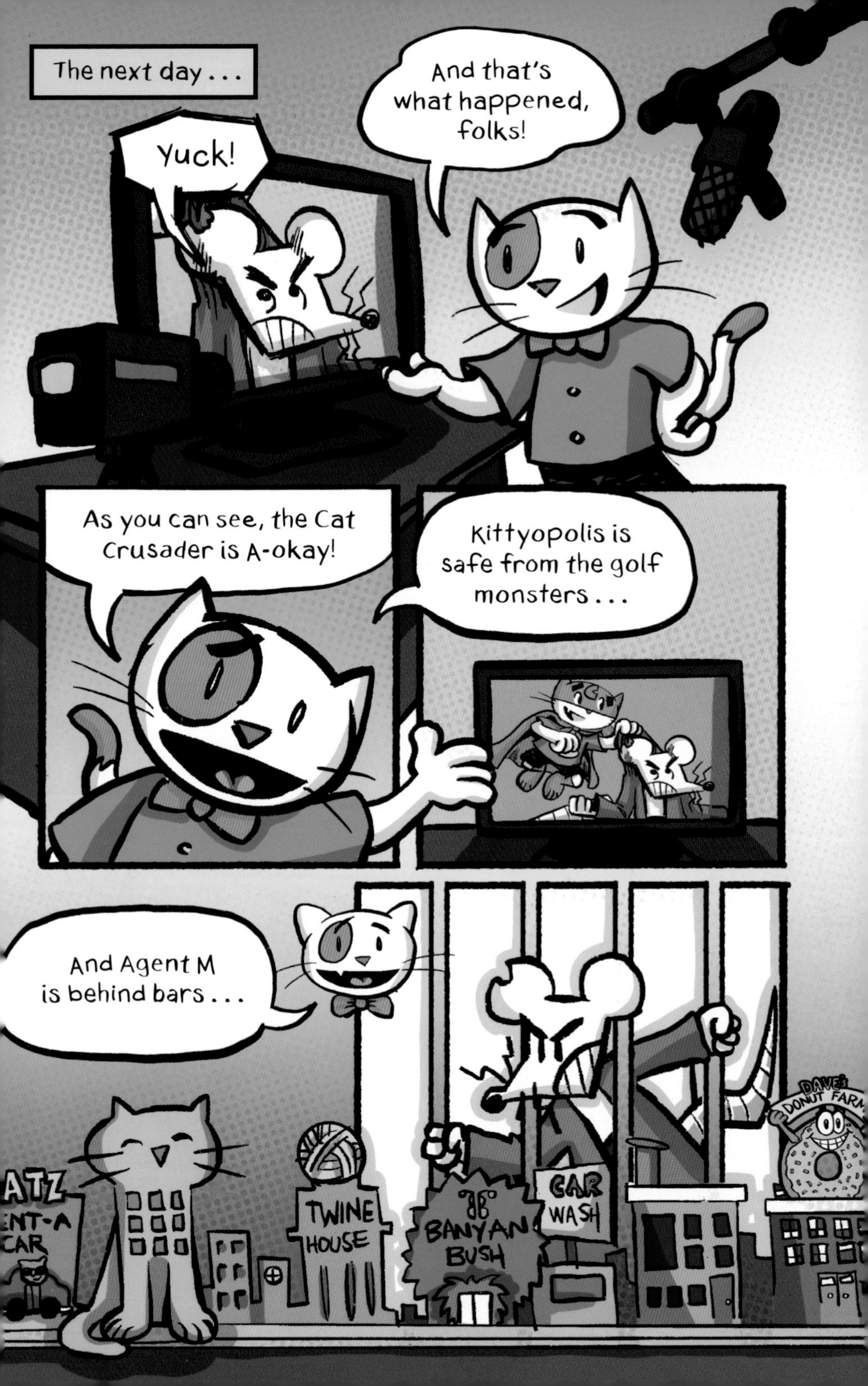
The next day . . .
Yuck!
And that's what happened, folks!
As you can see, the Cat Crusader is A-okay!
Kittyopolis is safe from the golf monsters . . .
And Agent M is behind bars . . .
ATZ
ENT-A
CAR
TWINE HOUSE
BANYAN BUSH
CAR WASH
DAVE'S DONUT FARM

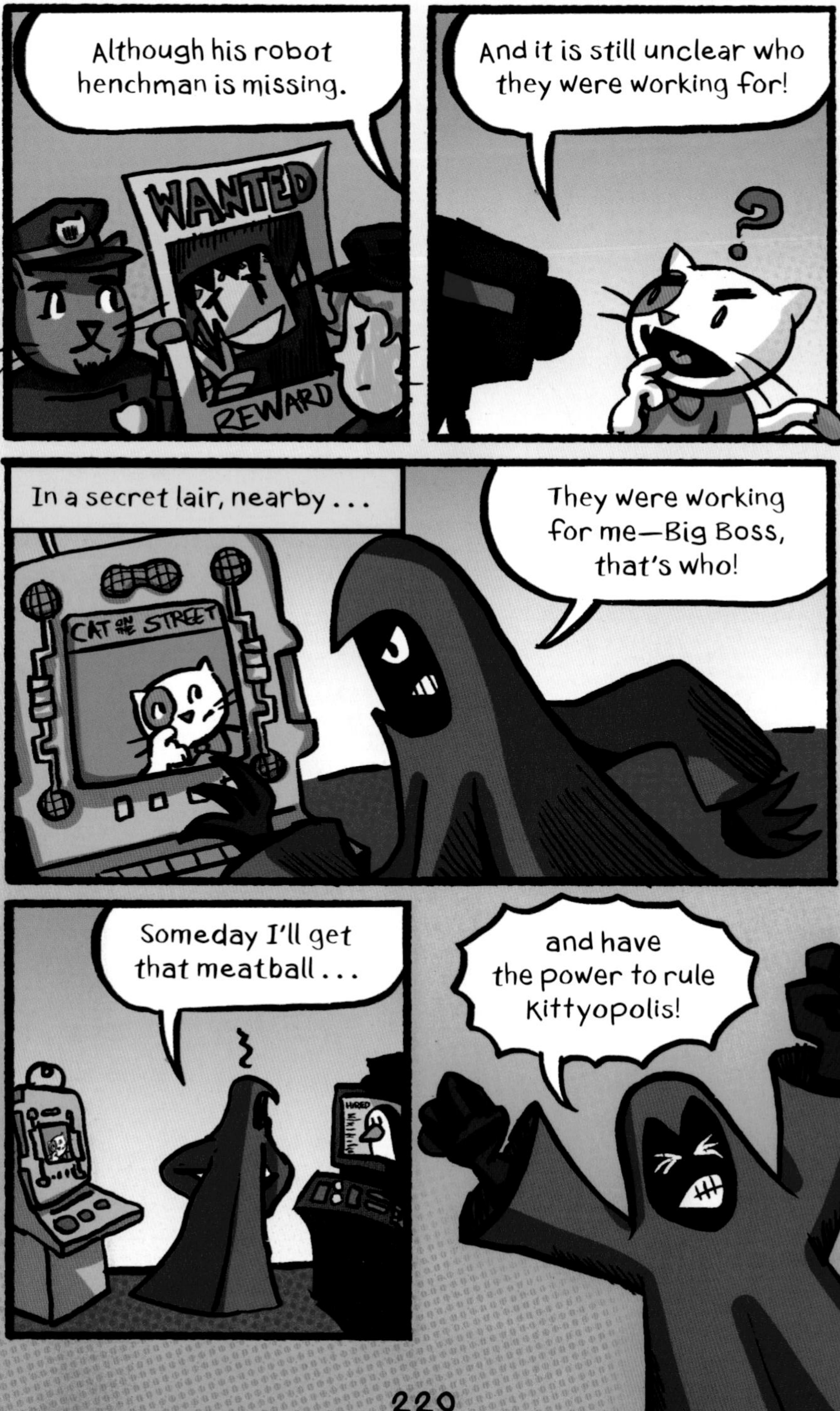
Although his robot henchman is missing.
WANTED
REWARD
And it is still unclear who they were working for!
In a secret lair, nearby . . .
CAT ON THE STREET
They were working for me—Big Boss, that's who!
Someday I'll get that meatball . . .
and have the power to rule Kittyopolis!

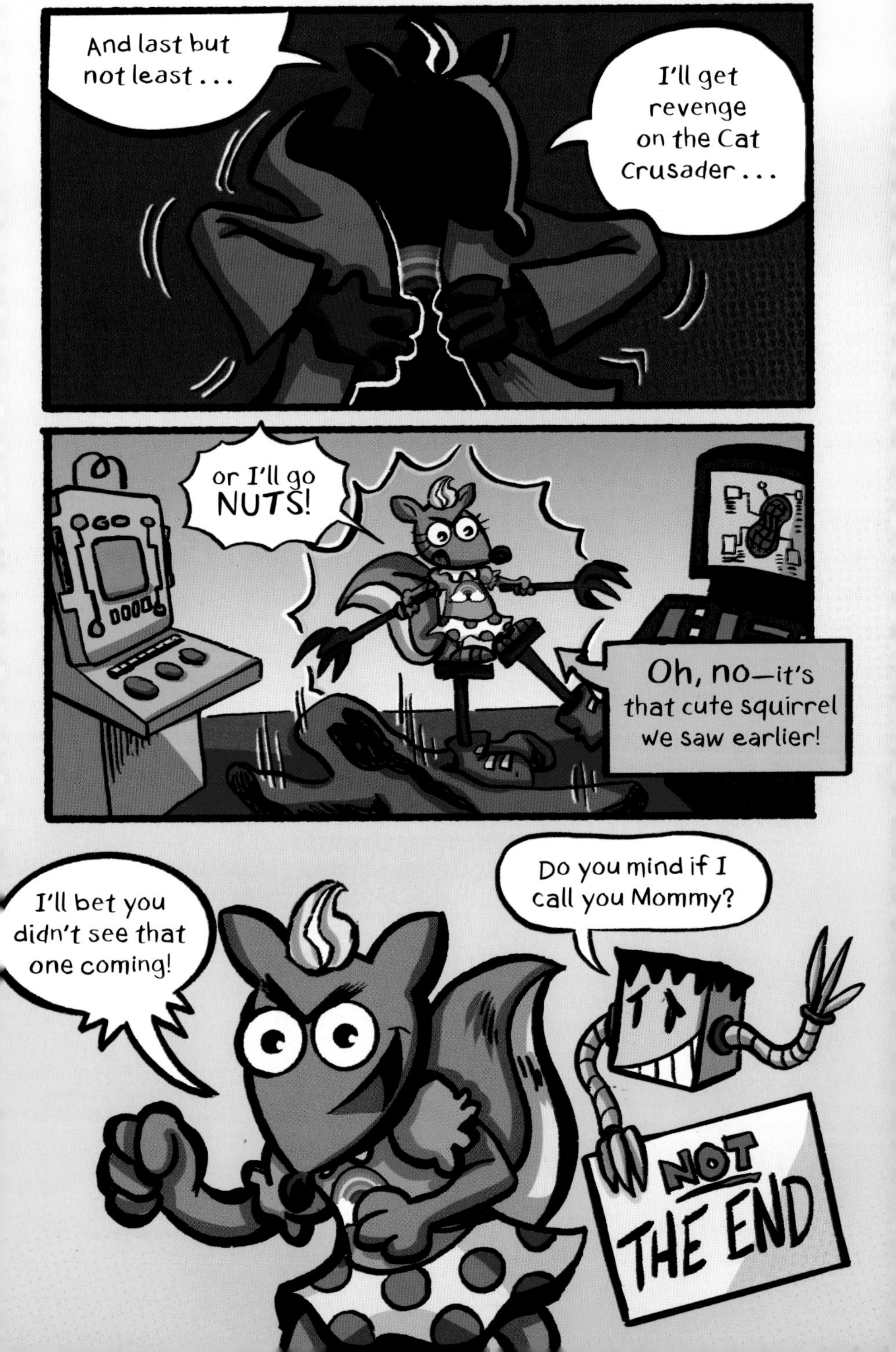
And last but not least . . .
I'll get revenge on the Cat Crusader . . .
or I'll go NUTS!
Oh, no—it's that cute squirrel we saw earlier!
I'll bet you didn't see that one coming!
Do you mind if I call you Mommy?
NOT THE END

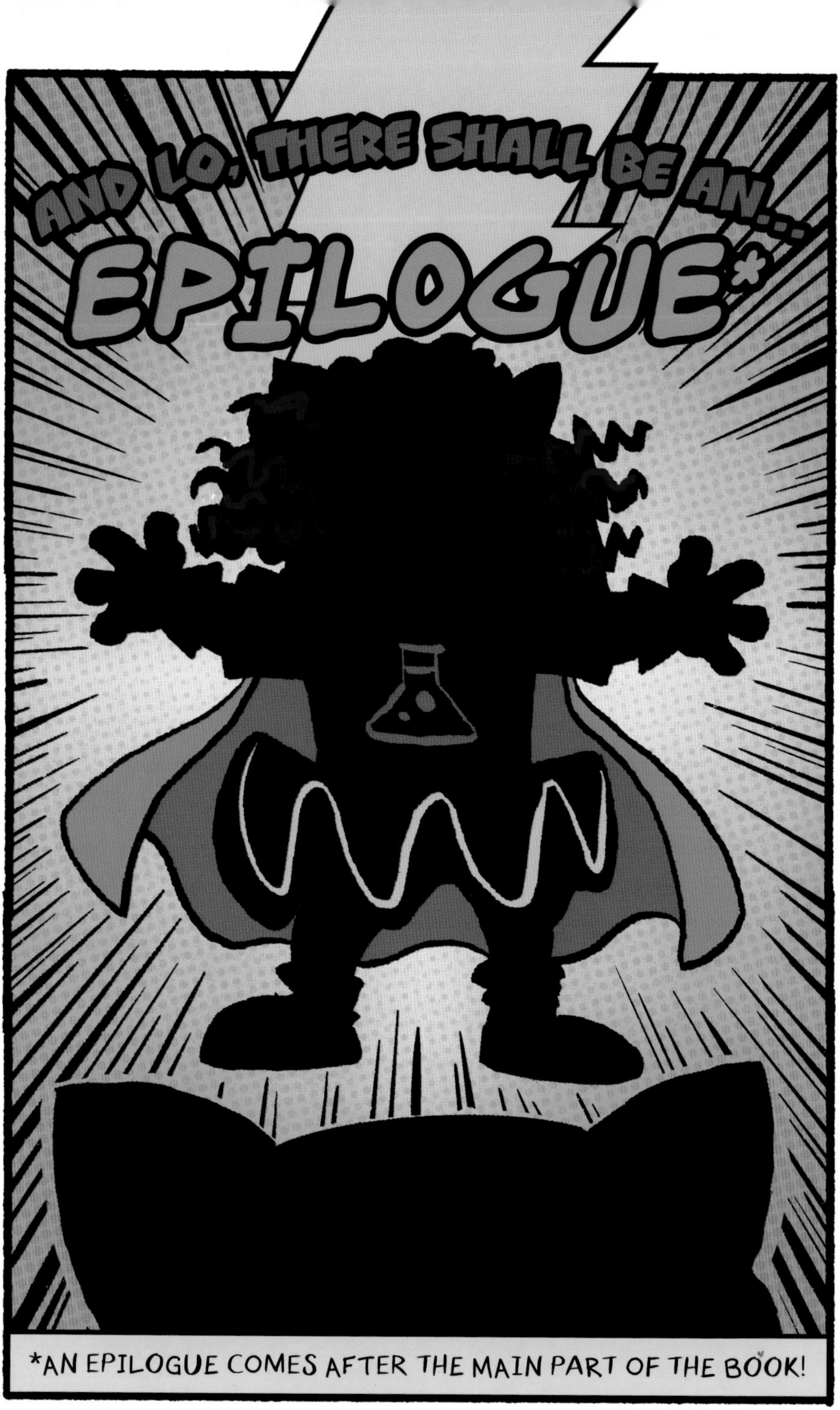
AND LO, THERE SHALL BE AN...
EPILOGUE*
*AN EPILOGUE COMES AFTER THE MAIN PART OF THE BOOK!

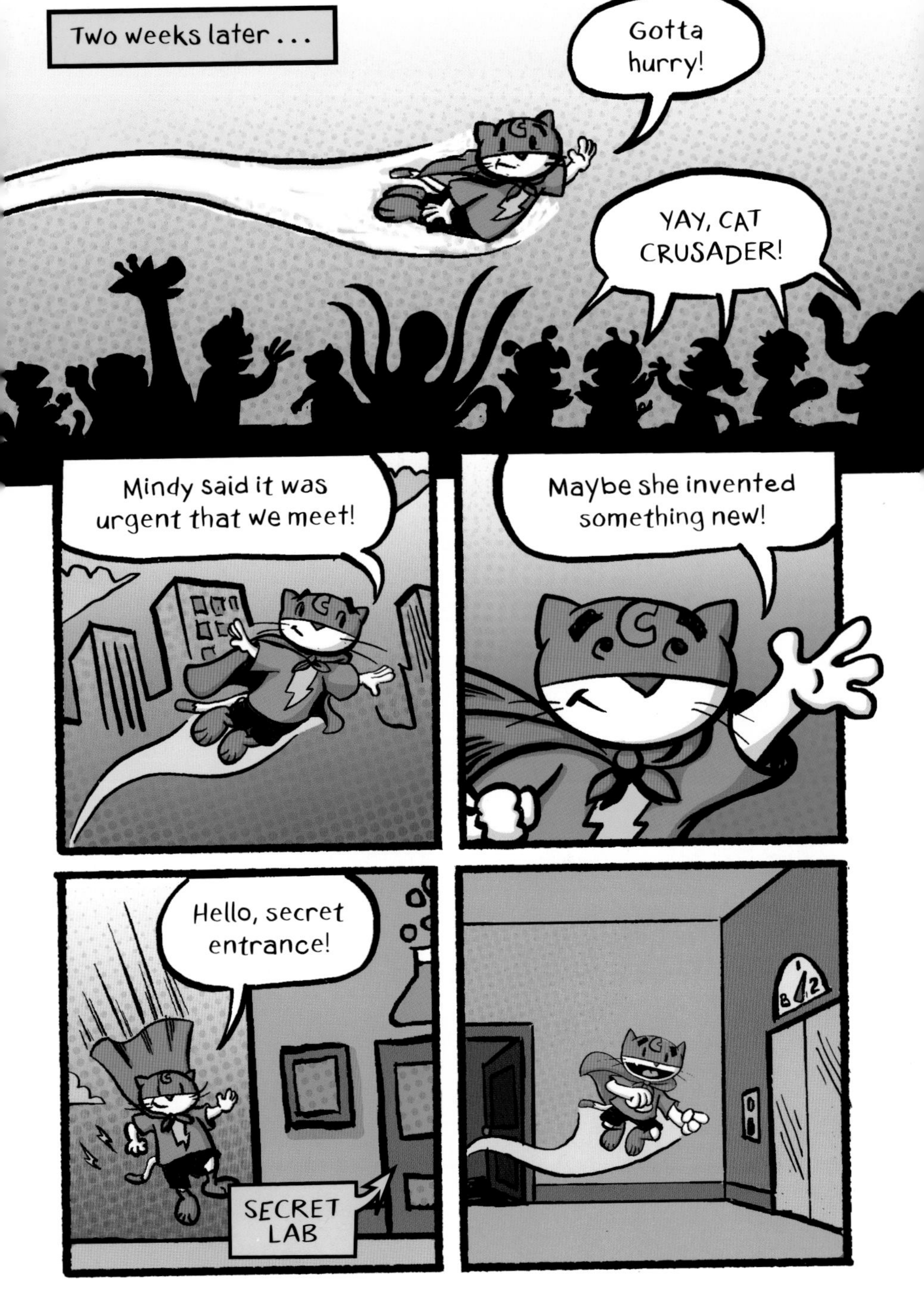
Two weeks later . . .
Gotta hurry!
YAY, CAT CRUSADER!
Mindy said it was urgent that we meet!
Maybe she invented something new!
Hello, secret entrance!
SECRET LAB
B 1 2

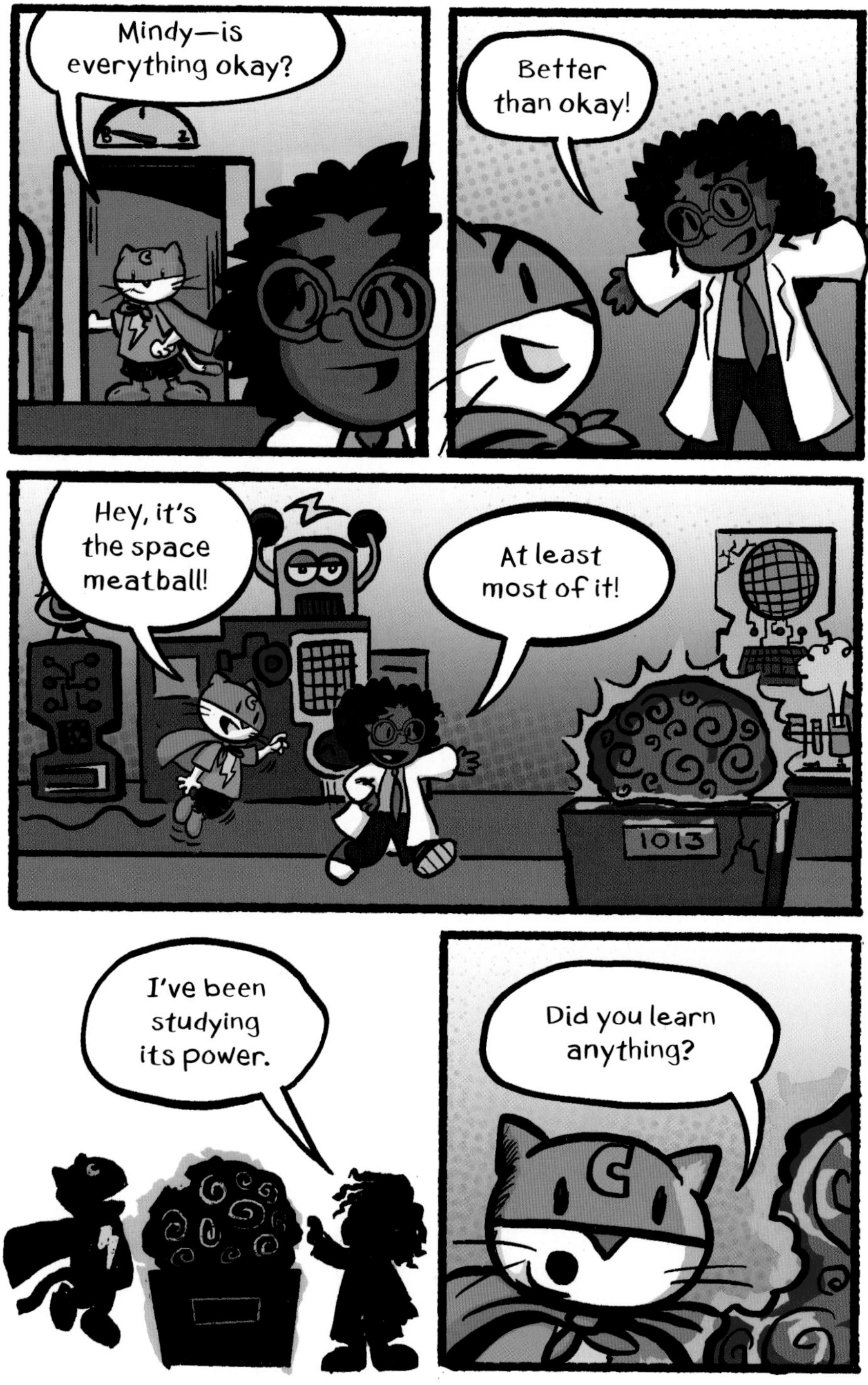
Mindy—is everything okay?
Better than okay!
Hey, it's the space meatball!
At least most of it!
1013
I've been studying its power.
Did you learn anything?

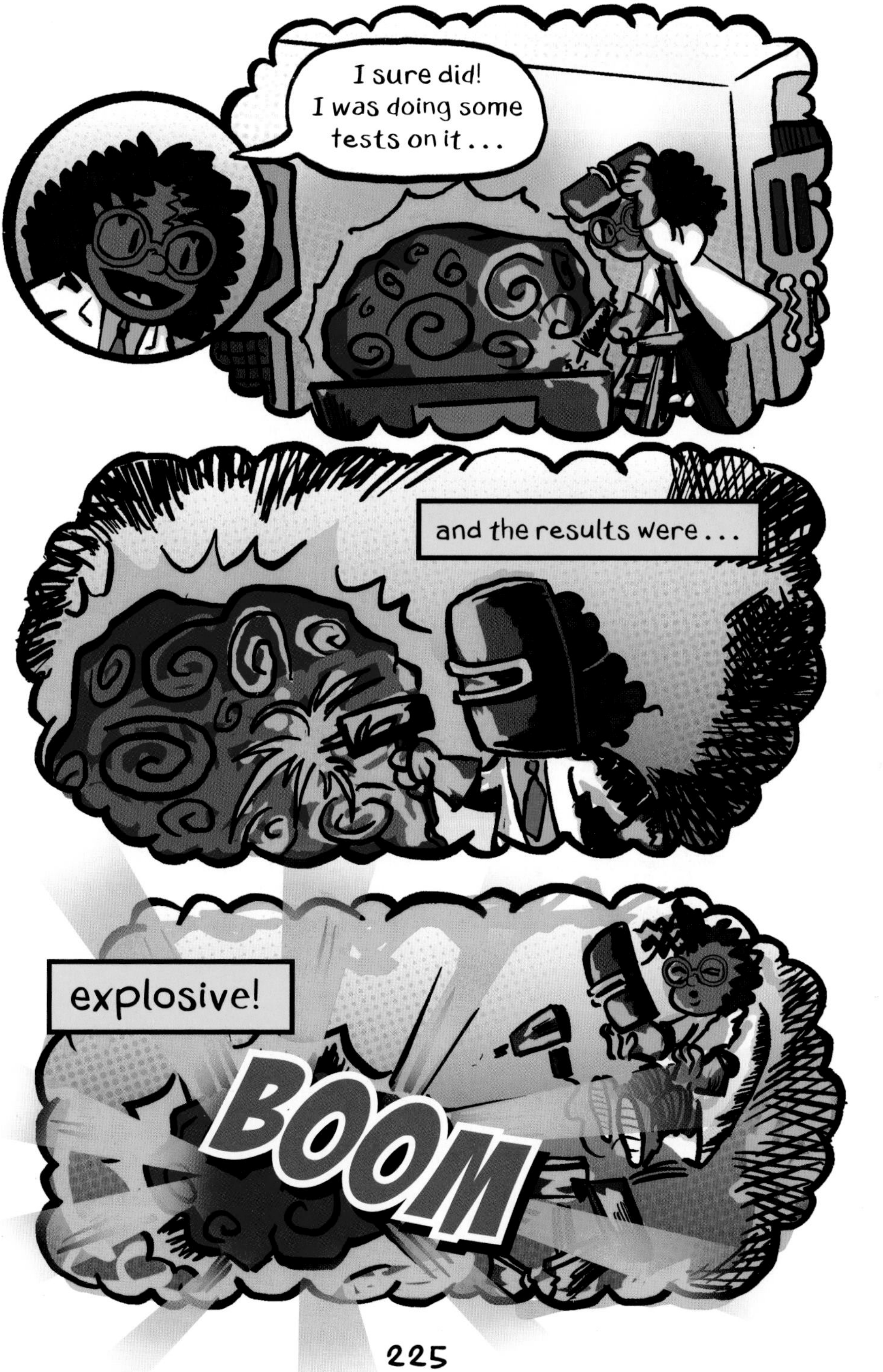
I sure did!
I was doing some
tests on it . . .
and the results were . . .
explosive!
BOOM

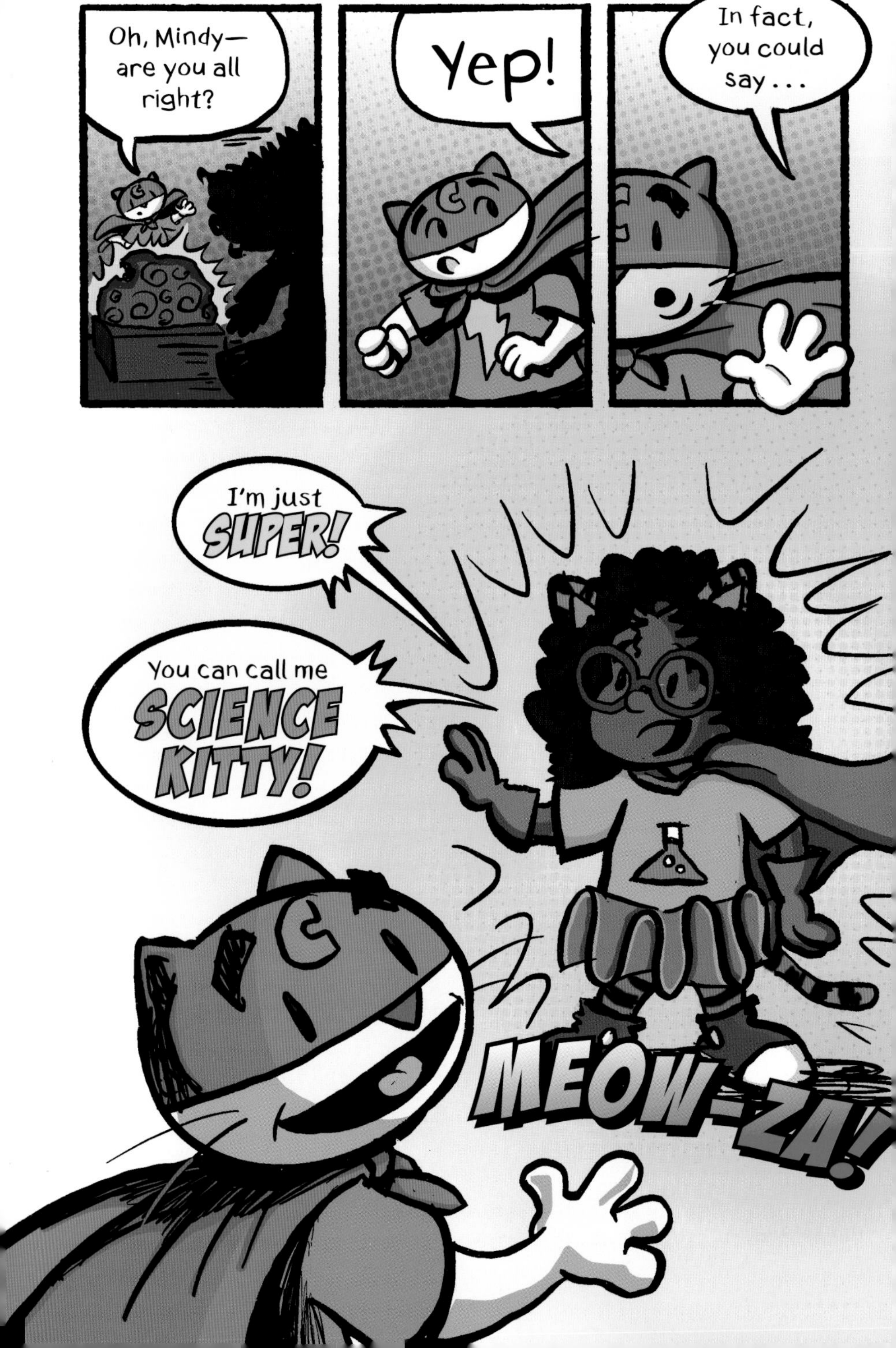
Oh, Mindy—are you all right?
Yep!
In fact, you could say . . .
I'm just SUPER!
You can call me SCIENCE KITTY!
MEOW-ZA!

DO YOU LIKE DONUTS?
DO YOU CRAVE DANGER?

Duh!

I'm not sure I...

THEN THE NEXT MAX MEOW ADVENTURE IS PURR-FECT FOR YOU!

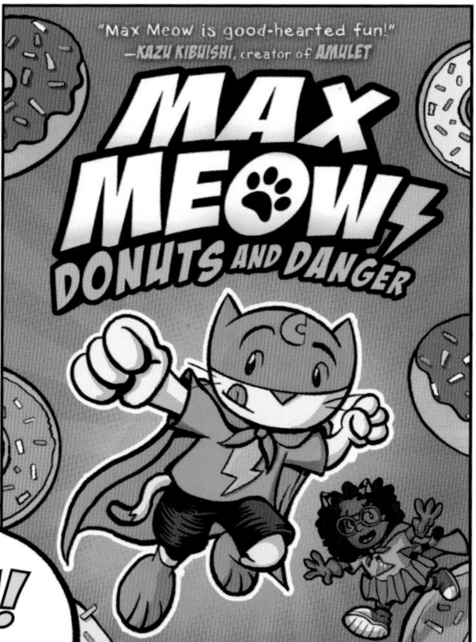

"Max Meow is good-hearted fun!"
—KAZU KIBUISHI, creator of AMULET
MAX MEOW
DONUTS AND DANGER
JOHN GALLAGHER

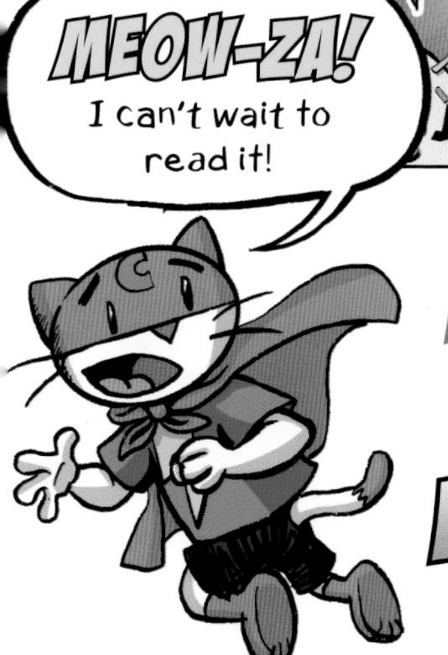

MEOW-ZA!
I can't wait to read it!

CAN MAX AND MINDY STOP THEIR EVIL LOOK-ALIKES FROM SNATCHING THE WORLD'S DONUT SUPPLY?

AVAILABLE NOW!

MAX MEOW CAT CRUSADER

Learn to draw the Cat Crusader!

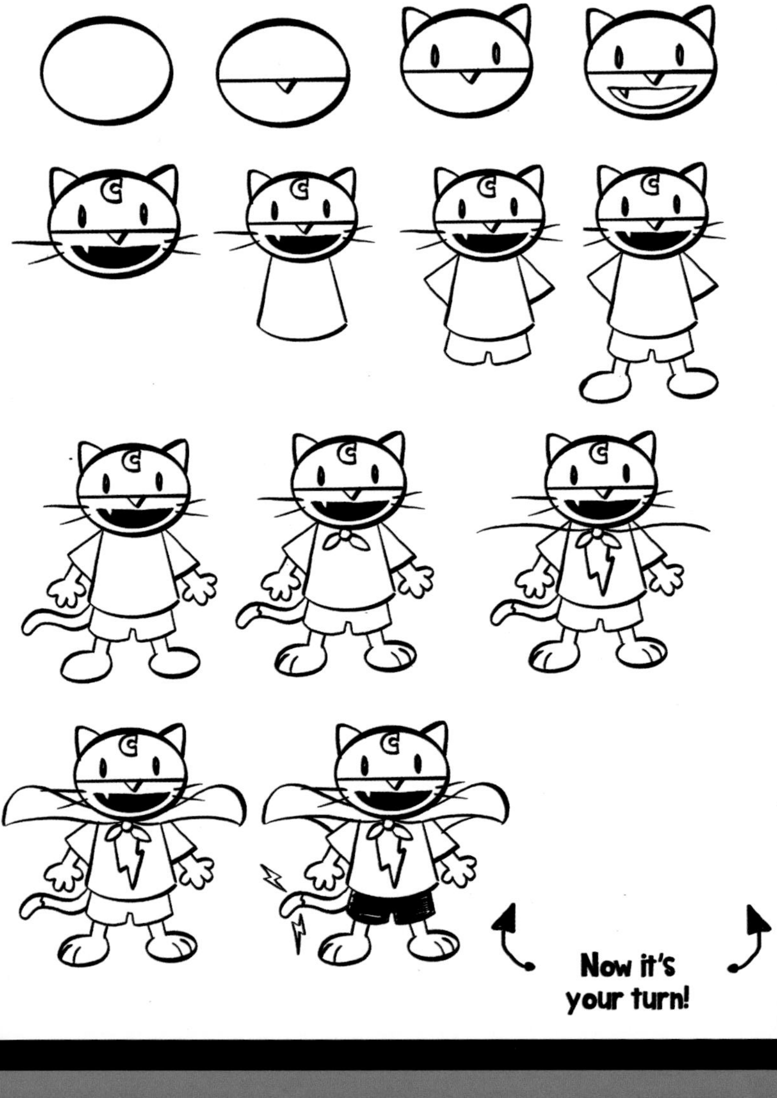

Now it's your turn!

JOHN GALLAGHER has loved comics since he was five. He learned to read through comics and went on to read every book in his elementary school library. When he told his mom there was nothing left to read, she said, "Just because a book's over doesn't mean the *stories* end. Why don't *you* tell me what happens next?" And so John began creating comics to continue his favorite stories. John never stopped drawing comics. He's now the art director of the National Wildlife Federation's *Ranger Rick* magazine and the cofounder of Kids Love Comics, an organization that uses comics and graphic novels to promote literacy. He also leads workshops teaching kids how to create their own comics. John lives in Virginia with his wife and their three kids. Visit him at MaxMeow.com and on social media.

@JohnBGallagher @MaxMeowCatCrusader

@johngallagher_cartoonist

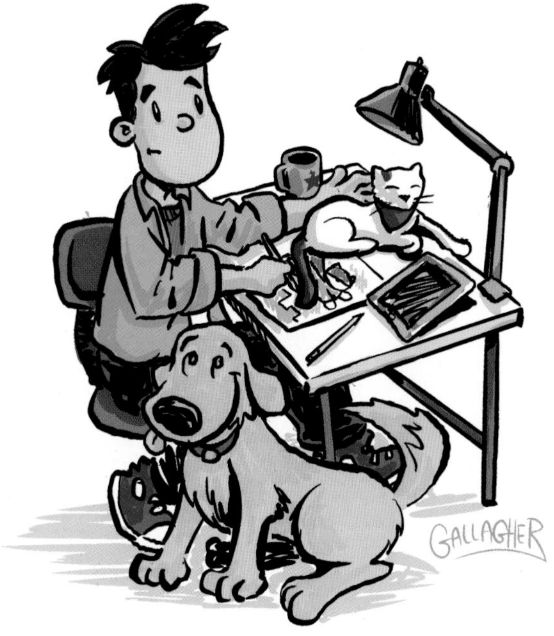
GALLAGHER

ACKNOWLEDGMENTS

STORY ASSISTANT
William Reese Gallagher

ART ASSISTANT
Chayton Koehler

COLOR AND FLATTING ASSISTANTS
Allyson LaMont
Raen Ngu

SPECIAL THANKS

My parents, Jane and Joe Gallagher; my agent, Judith Hansen;
my editor, Shana Corey; my art director, April Ward; Max's
sensitivity readers, Shasta Clinch and Saraciea Fennell; as
well as Judd Winick, Kazu Kibuishi, Mike Maihack, J. Robert
Deans, Jimmy Gownley, Harold Buchholz, Jamar Nicholas,
Mark and Chris Mariano, Rich Faber, Joe Murray, Marc and
Shelly Nathan, Kathy Irwin-Lentz, Dave Housley, Cindy and
Freya Olson, the Bartley Family, Pinecrest School, Oak View
Elementary Comic Class students, and the *Ranger Rick*
magazine team.
    And thanks to the teachers and librarians who spark the
flames of reading and creativity, and the readers for whom
this book was made.